I0671587

The Highest Stakes

A Jack Murphy Thriller

Rick Reed

KENSINGTON PUBLISHING CORP.

www.kensingtonbooks.com

LYRICAL UNDERGROUND BOOKS are published by

Kensington Publishing Corp.
119 West 40th Street
New York, NY 10018

All Kensington titles, imprints, and distributed lines are available at special quantity discounts for bulk purchases for sales promotions, premiums, fundraising, educational, or institutional use. Special book excerpts or customized printings can also be created to fit specific needs. For details, write or phone the office of the Kensington sales manager: Kensington Publishing Corp., 119 West 40th Street, New York, NY 10018, attn: Sales Department; phone 1-800-221-2647.

PUBLISHER'S NOTE
This book is a work of fiction. Names, characters, businesses, organizations, places, events, and incidents either are the product of the author's imagination or are used fictitiously. Any resemblance to actual persons, living or dead, events, or locales is entirely coincidental.

LYRICAL PRESS, LYRICAL UNDERGROUND, and the Lyrical Underground logo are Reg. U.S. Pat, & TM Office.

First Lyrical Underground edition: October 2016

ISBN-13: 978-1-60183-640-3
ISBN-10: 1-60183-640-6

First trade paperback edition: October 2016

ISBN-13: 978-1-60183-641-0
ISBN-10: 1-60183-641-4

This book is dedicated to

MR. ROBERT GROTIUS,

who passed away October 17, 2003, at the age of 79.

*Mr. G was my English and Sociology teacher at Rex Mundi H.S.
(where I served a four-year sentence).
He was the reason I became a writer.*

God keep you, Mr. G.

Chapter One

Chicago's financial district

The late July downpour in Chicago's financial district didn't stop the workforce from hurrying about their daily tasks. The sudden storm had blown in from Lake Michigan, and umbrellas blossomed like spring flowers. Women who came to work unprepared held scarves over their heads, the men pulled up coat collars, and like an army of worker ants they streamed along the sidewalks, impervious to the rain, to each other—and to Mr. Smith sitting inside the shiny black Hummer.

Smith was of average height, weight, and build with mousy brown hair that was cut not too long and not too short. He wore a dark suit like so many others. Only the lifeless gray eyes were remarkable. Behind heavily tinted windows, he watched through the intermittent movement of the wiper blades.

The Hummer was parked facing north at LaSalle and Quincy Streets in front of the Potbelly Sandwich Shop. The Willis Tower loomed in the west, the Chicago River two blocks farther on, and behind him at Lake Street the steel and wood El tracks rose above the streets. Directly in front of him was the beating heart of the financial district. The Chicago Board of Trade sat at the southernmost end of LaSalle, and the old Continental Bank building with its grand columns cattycorner. The Federal Reserve of Chicago was directly across from that. Together they formed a financial tricorner hat of sorts.

A block in front of the Hummer, a deli truck was parked on the corner with a man in a white apron and white butcher hat hawking his goods. A block distant from the deli truck on the front sidewalk of the Federal Reserve was the old-fashioned telephone booth he had under surveillance. In the last hour he had seen dozens of people duck into the booth for less than a minute while they put something in a briefcase or a purse or pulled coats over their heads before venturing out again. He felt the rumble of the subway beneath the street, while above, throngs of people crowded and pushed along the wide sidewalks. The average person made it through each day by pure luck and not by any skill or alertness. Those hapless souls had no inkling of what was to come.

He was told his real target would be in that particular phone booth at precisely noon. At twelve on the dot, a middle-aged man dressed in a smart suit came out of the Federal Reserve building, pulled the collar of his jacket up, and held a newspaper over his head as he walked directly for the telephone booth. He pushed at the bifold doors, rolled the newspaper up and put it under his arm, and then entered the glass and aluminum rectangle.

Smith started the Humvee and put it in drive. He punched a number into a prepaid cell phone and hit the send button. The shock wave from the blast rocked the Humvee. He watched as bodies were thrown about like rag dolls, some landing on the sidewalk, some hurled into the street and run over by panicked drivers. Pieces of those closest to the blast stuck to the hood and windshield of his car almost two blocks distant from the explosion. When the smoke cleared, he could see the a crater in the concrete where the phone booth had stood.

Those lucky enough to live ran in every direction. Others crawled or rolled around, their clothing aflame, their flesh melted by the heat. Some would die later, internal organs damaged from the blast.

A woman staggered out of the smoke and stumbled against his window. The left half of her face was gone. She clawed at the door and collapsed, leaving a smear down the window.

He allowed himself a smile before the next explosion came from below the street in the subway. Iron grates and manhole covers blew into the air all down the block and flipped end over end like coins before thudding to the ground. Another timed explosion came from behind him, herding the crowd south along LaSalle toward the El tracks, where a special surprise waited them. Like any fireworks display there was always a finale.

It was beautiful.

Washington, D.C.

Three blocks north of the National Cathedral in the nation's capital, Smith waited for Pamela to come home. He'd driven straight through, his route taking him south from Chicago and east through Indianapolis and then Columbus, Ohio, and on into Washington. It was dark when he'd arrived. He left the lights off, poured some Scotch, and wandered through the condo. He could smell her scent in every room.

He'd met Pamela in D.C. a year ago while he was in between assignments. She tended bar at a downtown nightclub named Madam's Organ. They talked, and she told him she was a political science major at George Washington University with dreams of working in the government, maybe for a congressman. He'd introduced himself as Alex Stanhope, a day trader. The Stanhope cover was clean, with a Virginia driver's license, a condo, credit cards, and even some debt, and his employers were unaware it existed. Like many of his peers, he had squirreled away several sets of clean IDs, with passports and cash. In between jobs he needed to disappear. Needed privacy. Needed anonymity. He had found what he needed in D.C., hiding in plain sight, so to speak.

His mentor had a saying, "Never shit in your own milk." So when he awoke beside Pamela the next morning he was surprised. Not by the fact he'd slept with a beautiful woman, but that he had invited her back to his condo and let her stay the night. Instinct told him to kill her. But he hadn't.

He found he enjoyed her company, so he had violated another of his rules and let her live with him as part of his cover. She went to school days, worked the club at night, and he stayed with her as often as possible. She never questioned his prolonged absences, or his need for angry sex immediately upon his return. His cover job explained his frequent absences and narcissistic lifestyle. Lying about who he was and what he did was like taking a breath, involuntary yet necessary.

In Columbus, Ohio, he was Daniel Whitcomb, who ran a successful consulting business. In Seattle, he was Professor Douglas Levin, on sabbatical from Shoreline College, where he taught criminal justice. There were many others, and in each location someone to complete his cover. But his employers, down to the smallest detail, had manufactured these identities. Had assigned the women who acted as his girlfriend, sister, wife, et cetera. Only in D.C. was he Alex Stanhope.

He was taking a risk with Pamela, but keeping his employers in the dark was extremely satisfying. The killings in Chicago were also satisfying. He had been held in check far too long. Like a bull in a pen, he longed to be released, to run rampant, to charge everything and create fear.

And then 9/11 came along. If he believed in God he would have thanked Him because the rules had relaxed in the aftermath, and the bean counters' coffers were filling. Then someone had the bright idea of creating even more federal agencies in the name of combating terrorism, and to coordinate investigations among the already burgeoning system. As a result the funding had slowed to a trickle, information was even more jealously guarded, and no one had benefited.

Finally the Agency had turned him loose. The "terrorist attack" on Chicago would ensure their coffers were filled to overflowing. He was like Hercules unchained, doing what he was born to do. But he was no fool. He'd been at this too long to believe they would let him continue for long before chaining him again. He was lifting the heavy loads while the pussies in the Agency were wringing their hands and crying like old women. Or more likely, planning damage control, eliminating any thread of connection between themselves and the Chicago incident, and he was one of those threads. Time to move again.

The condo was dark. He looked at the luminous face of his watch, then silenced the ticking of the wall clock. Sitting on the sofa, he closed his eyes, and let his senses take over. Pamela would be walking in the door at exactly one a.m. He would have to kill her and leave Alex Stanhope behind. Such a waste.

He heard the hum of the elevator and the soft clattering as its doors opened. Too early. Soft footfalls came down the hall. Two sets. Not the high heels Pamela wore. The steps paused. The light coming from beneath the door went out as a key slipped in the door's lock.

He knelt beside the sofa and retrieved the handgun from underneath, thumbed the safety to the "fire" position, then hurried into the bathroom. He stood in the dark with his back against the wall and used the medicine cabinet mirror to watch the front door.

The snick of the lock turning was barely audible. Soft-soled shoes, more than one set, moved into the condo. In the mirror he saw two black shapes. One tall, one short, a faint green glow floating around their faces. Night vision.

Night-vision technology is designed to magnify ambient light, so when Smith flipped the light switches on, the intruders were as blinded as if staring into the sun. Gloved hands scrabbled for goggles, but before they could pull them off, Smith shot the closest one in the throat just under the chin and the other in the mouth. Both targets were down, unmoving.

He stood between them and examined the bodies. Both wore dark clothing, balaclavas over their heads with night-vision goggles covering their eyes and 9mm Glocks fitted with silencers in their hands. Their equipment and weapons were all the explanation he needed for why they had come. Cleaners.

They were from the Agency, or maybe hired guns. In either case, their purpose was to eliminate him and erase any evidence he had ever existed. Good equipment, sloppy execution. He was insulted the Agency hadn't sent a better team, and a little angry they thought he would be that easy to dispose of.

The short one seemed familiar. He knelt beside the slender athletic body and removed the goggles and lifted the balaclava. He felt emotions he hadn't felt since he was a child. Embarrassment. Shock. Disbelief.

It was Pamela. His Pamela.

He looked out the window for signs of a backup team. Traffic was light. No parked cars. No one on the street. But he knew at least two more were waiting. Any minute they would know the first team had failed and they would come for him. This time they would come better armed, and they would come hard.

He went to the massive wooden entertainment center, lifted the plasma television out, and tossed it to the side. In the back of the cabinet was a wall safe. He worked the combination and opened an inch-thick steel door, revealing another silenced pistol, several passports, other identification and credit cards, and stacks of twenty- and hundred-dollar bills.

He stacked everything in a briefcase and stuffed his wallet with the Alex Stanhope identification in the dead man's back pocket. If Pamela worked for the same people he did, she had already reported his Stanhope cover. She may have also found this hidey-hole and reported all his aliases to the Agency. It was what he would have done.

She also would have recorded the serial numbers on the money, but he would have to chance it for now. The last item he removed from the safe was a small canister resembling a can of shaving cream. It was an incendiary device that could be detonated remotely. The condo would burn and eliminate most of the evidence. With any luck they would find Alex Stanhope's wallet beneath the burned body of the male agent. It would only confuse things for an hour, maybe less, but he needed the diversion.

On his way out of the condo he stopped and stood over Pamela. He looked down into her face. He knew now why he had liked her better than the other women he'd been with. She was like him.

He went to the open door and turned the condo's lights off. He peeked into the dark hallway. Nothing moved. He thought about using the night-vision goggles, but it hadn't worked out well for the two inside. He stepped into the hallway. Left, it was twenty feet to the stairs. Right, it was fifteen to the elevator. No professional would be waiting in the elevator. He turned toward the stairs.

He reached for the handle of the stairway door and saw it turning. He yanked the door open and shot the startled man in the throat. As that one lay gagging on his own blood, another man looked up the stairwell and was dispatched with a double tap to the face. He shot them both once more in the head and descended the stairs.

He pushed the button on the remote and heard a muffled explosion above. He stepped out the service door and into the alleyway. Once outside he scanned for other watchers. The street was empty except for an intoxicated couple getting into a D.C. cab. He walked to the cab's open door and shot the couple multiple times and then shot the cabbie.

He pushed the woman's leg inside and shut the passenger door. He then put the driver's body inside the trunk and drove away. Just another late night in D.C.

Chapter Two

Three weeks later, Evansville, Indiana

August was a bad month for Detective Jack Murphy, starting with some ex-military guys turned hit men and ending in a shoot-out where Jack thought he would be killed. Several people were killed, some good, some bad. In fact, the county prosecutor had died. Then the chief deputy prosecutor, second in command, had "flown the coop," without a word to anyone, not even to Jack's ex-wife, Katie, to whom he was engaged. Good riddance to the prick.

September was shaping up to be more of the same. The new prosecutor and new chief deputy prosecutor were pricks just like the old ones. But the worst thing of all was that he and Katie had almost gotten back together through all of this, but he'd blown it. It was a long story.

Katie wasn't taking his calls, hadn't taken his calls for several weeks, and even her sister, Moira, who had orchestrated them getting back together, was mad at him. "Sexist pig" was his new name, and that was the kind version.

Just when he thought it couldn't get any worse he'd gotten a call from the prosecutor's office asking that he come to a meeting to discuss an arrest he had made last night. Jack was expecting some repercussions for breaking the sick bastard's jaw, but it felt like the right thing to do at the time, and he'd do it again given the same circumstances.

It was early enough that Jack hadn't any trouble finding a parking place in one of the city council spots behind the Civic Center. He even walked through the unmanned security station that led to the judge's chambers and the prosecutor's office. He wondered why it wasn't manned by security as soon as the Civic Center was opened for the day. But he didn't make those decisions. Civilians with political aspirations and the right connections made them.

Jack entered the prosecutor's offices unchallenged. The second set of doors that were normally locked was cracked open. He walked down the hall to where he remembered the conference rooms were located.

Moira Connelly's office was just ahead on the left. He could tell she was in because he could hear music coming through the thin wall. Maybe she could tell him what this was about. He knocked on her door. The music stopped and a voice said, "Come in."

He pushed the door open and found Moira doing Pilates in front of her desk. She was wearing a blue two-piece power suit with a red silk blouse. She straightened up and tucked the blouse in where it had come loose.

"Just getting warmed up before the meeting," she said, a little out of breath.

"I always wondered what attorneys did before court," Jack said with a grin.

Moira was Katie's younger sister, and where Katie was short, like their mother, Moira was tall, like their father. Both women were beautiful, but a striking feature they shared was their bright red hair—thick, wavy, and long. Moira pushed her hair back into place and picked up a file from the top of her desk. She was settling in nicely to her job as deputy prosecutor.

She squeezed past him and out of the door. "Let's get this party started," she said and led the way down the hall.

Outside the conference room, she hesitated, her hand on the doorknob. Jack could hear men's laughter coming from inside the room. She looked at Jack and said, "The new prosecutor went to law school with the defense attorney, Joe Miller. He might call him Boom Boom. That's Miller's nickname. Try to keep your temper."

Miller wasn't exactly a big gun as far as defense attorneys go. But he was ruthless and not above cheating, stealing, and lying to get his client off the hook. "What am I going to get mad about?" Jack asked, but Moira was already pushing the door open.

The new prosecutor's name was Mike Higgins. He preferred being called Mr. Prosecutor. He was appointed to his position a few months ago after the last guy ate his gun. Higgins was a little guy with a giant ego, but so far Jack had no reason to dislike the man. All that was about to change.

The prosecutor was slumped behind the big conference table in a leather-covered office chair, feet on top of the table, and pretending to be reeling in a fish. By the looks of his mimicry, he was catching a "big" one. Higgins was new to Evansville, and even newer to holding a lofty office such as prosecutor of the third largest city in Indiana. He had come from Boston, where he had worked in the prosecutor's office as one of the grunts. No one knew how he got this job.

Higgins's voice was deep, and his laugh was infectious. That was deceptive because he could be laughing and smiling and that's when you knew you were in his gun sights. His Boston accent was thick, and he had already earned a reputation for taking no prisoners. He was five-foot-five at best, and his prematurely graying hair didn't match his boyish looks. All in all, Mike Higgins was a conundrum, but to Jack he was just another attorney that he was going to have to deal with sooner or later.

Higgins sat up when he noticed Jack and Moira and motioned them to come in. "This is Joe Miller," he said, introducing the man who was standing in one corner of the conference room still holding his hands apart as if measuring something. "We were just reminiscing about a fishing trip to the Keys when we got out of law school."

"I assume the fish got away," Jack said to Higgins, with as little sarcasm in his voice as he could manage.

The two attorneys shared a look. "I told you he was a pistol, didn't I?" Higgins said.

"I think the word you used, Mike, was 'smart-ass,'" Miller said.

Miller was the exact opposite of his colleague in appearance. He was tall and heavyset with dark curly hair that swept back from his forehead and grew long and thick in the back in a mullet. His face was wide with jowls that shook when he talked. He reminded Jack of a basset hound—minus the dog drool.

"Have a seat, Murphy," Higgins said.

Not Jack. Not Detective Murphy. This was going to be bad. Jack sat and Moira took a seat beside him.

The defense attorney, Miller, sat across from Jack. The prosecutor broke from tradition and was sitting beside the defense attorney. Any closer and they could hold hands, but Miller was all business now.

"We have a problem with the arrest you made last night," Higgins said.

Moira looked down at the table with a neutral expression. Jack could feel his blood pressure rising.

"By 'we' do you mean the royal 'We'?" Jack asked. "And are you referring to my arrest of a serial rapist last night? The one who's put four of his victims in the hospital? The same one who's been in the newspaper frightening the public for over a week?"

"That attitude is exactly why we're here," Higgins blurted out.

Miller put a hand on the prosecutor's arm and said, "A picture's worth a thousand words." He produced several color photos from the manila folder and slid them across the table.

Jack glanced at several 5x7 color photos of a black male whose face was misshapen and whose eyes were swollen shut. Jack thought he looked like a praying mantis but kept that to himself. He knew the guy's jaw was broken because his fist still hurt. He pushed the pictures back to Miller.

"Nate Cartwright," Jack said. "I arrested him last night. So?"

Miller said, "This will never make it to court, my friend."

Higgins sat stone-faced, arms crossed, saying nothing in Jack's defense. Murphy knew what was going on here. The defense was brokering some kind of deal with the prosecutor.

Miller smiled and said, "My client is only guilty of having bad taste in women. He spurned her, and she attacked him in a jealous rage. He was defending himself and was actually glad the police arrived. And then you beat him while he was handcuffed because you, Detective Murphy, are a racist."

Jack looked to the prosecutor to say something, but Higgins folded his hands on top of the table and remained silent.

Jack asked, "So how does your client explain the victim's vaginal and anal tearing? How does he explain that he was completely naked and her pants and blouse were torn?"

Miller made a dismissive motion with one hand. "She did that to herself. My client was fighting for his life. His penis might have penetrated her vagina while he was trying to get away from her."

"Are you really going to court with that bullshit?"

Higgins looked at Jack but addressed "Boom Boom," his school chum. "Joe, if I drop your client's charges to sexual battery, will you dismiss the federal charges you filed against Detective Murphy?"

"What charges?" Jack demanded.

Miller sat back in his seat and let Higgins explain. "Here's the situation as I see it." He leaned toward Jack, hands folded as if in prayer. "Your arrest of Mr. Cartwright wasn't within police department guidelines. Even though Mr. Miller may be stretching things a bit far to suggest you beat Mr. Cartwright while he was hand-cuffed, we can't ignore the fact that his jaw is broken and there are other injuries to his face that you admittedly caused. You stated so in your arrest affidavit. Your report simply says Mr. Cartwright resisted arrest. So it would leave a reasonable person to assume you would show some injuries too, and you look fine to me."

Jack said nothing, waiting to hear what charges the defense had dreamed up.

The prosecutor continued. "Mr. Miller, acting on behalf of his client, who was too injured to speak to the FBI, filed a criminal complaint against you. He also filed a civil suit against you, the Evansville Police Department, the Vanderburgh County Jail, and my office. There will probably be an investigation by the Department of Justice Special Litigation Unit."

"So that's the real problem. This asshole is threatening to sue you." Jack cocked his head to the side. "So I'm going to be arrested for getting a serial rapist off the street? A guy, who, by the way, I caught in the act. He goes free or I get charged."

Higgins sat back in his chair and wouldn't make eye contact with Jack.

Jack was past his anger and was becoming calm. It was the calm before the storm. He said, "The only reason I didn't file 'battery on a policeman' charges on your client, Mr. Miller, was because he was already being charged with rape, aggravated assault, and sodomy." Jack put his hands, palm down on top of the table. "Your client came at me in a rage because I was interrupting his fun. I tried to stop him but he flung his face into my fist several times. I defended myself, and I have proof," Jack said straight-faced and pointed out the bruised knuckles on his left hand as evidence. "Maybe I should go to the ER and get checked out."

Miller let out a deep sigh and said, "I guess we're done here. See you in federal court, Detective Murphy." He turned in the doorway and said, "I suggest you get yourself a good attorney, my friend."

"Jack, wait." Moira said catching up with him in the hallway. "I'm sorry, Jack. You know this wasn't my call. Right?"

Jack was too angry to talk.

"I'll talk to Mike. Maybe I can make him see reason."

"Whatever," Jack said.

"You didn't do yourself any good in the meeting just now. Not every problem's a nail, you know."

"What does everyone expect me to do? If I use any force at all, the public crucifies me. If I don't stop the criminal, I'm crucified. I'm starting to get a Jesus complex."

"My boss can be a real jerk sometimes, but he really isn't a bad guy. I think he's afraid of any bad publicity."

Jack could see her point. Mike Higgins was still learning the ropes with the prosecutor's position, the city, and politics. The publicity of a lawsuit like this would be a death sentence for his career. He was new to the Midwest. To Evansville in particular. Jack would give him the benefit of the doubt. Unless, that is, Higgins was stupid enough to surrender and let a serial rapist have a free pass.

Moira said, "Maybe I'll point out to him that he needs to recuse himself from the case since he's best friends with the defense attorney."

"You're learning to play the game," Jack said, and she smiled, taking his remark as a compliment. "That's scary," he added and she stopped smiling.

"I get it. You're mad. But don't take it out on me," Moira said.

"I'm not taking it out on you," he protested, but she gave him the look. "Okay, maybe I was taking it out on you a little, but I'm not angry." He knew he couldn't affect the prosecutor's decision, so he decided to do what any good cop would do. He'd take his partner to eat copious amounts of donuts and violate some citizen's rights while he was at it.

Her smile was back. "How's Cinderella?" she asked.

"Cinderella's fine. Plenty of shoes and furniture to eat. I'm waiting for her to go potty so I can look for a pair of cufflinks."

Cinderella was Jack's dog. She was sort of a mix between a large poodle and an alien. Jack had inherited her—sissy name and all—when her owner was murdered and she'd been left injured and home-less. Then a redneck police chief in Illinois had wanted to shoot her and Jack couldn't allow that. Jack had made some excuse about the dog being evidence in a murder investigation and taken her to Evansville, first to his veterinarian friend, and then to his cabin. He hadn't wanted a dog. Being an animal owner didn't mix well with his job because of his uncertain hours.

Like the famous circus owner, P. T. Barnum, said, "A sucker is born every minute." Jack knew he was that sucker. Cinderella was strong-willed, shedded constantly, chewed anything left on the floor, and sometimes left steaming presents in the shoes in his closet. She wouldn't respond to any other name, a whistle, or even Jack's "doggy-voice-of-doom."

"Cinderella loves you, Jack," Moira said.

"She didn't bite me this morning," He knew that way down deep inside, she really hated him. It had become his mission in life to make her love him. What's not to love?

Jack needed something stronger but he'd settle for coffee. As usual the coffeepot in the detectives' office was empty. He made an extra dark brew, found his mug, and filled it with the sinister black liquid. The oversize coffee mug was a gift from his partner, Liddell Blanchard. JACKENSTEIN was embossed on the side—a reference to the long scar that ran from just under Jack's left ear, down his neck and across his chest ending at his right nipple. The injury had ne-cessitated stitches and staples and a month of physical therapy and was a gift from Bobby Solazzo's bowie knife. Jack, believing it was better to give than to receive, had given Bobby a gift that all the king's horses and all the king's men wouldn't have been able to put back together.

Jack sat, sipped his coffee, and stared at a family photo on his desktop taken when he was a teenager. His mom and brother were smiling gaily. His dad was scowling. Jack was looking away with a bored expression. That snapshot told the history of the Murphy family pretty well. Since his father's death, his mother had harped on him and his brother to settle down and bring some little Murphys into the family. She was like a tiny dog with a big bone, whittling them down with her sharp wit and even sharper remarks.

Another photo on the desk showed his father, Jake Murphy, in police uniform complete with eight-point cap, oak billy stick, and a wide leather gun belt that was canted from the weight of the big .357 he carried. Murphys had been cops in Evansville since Great Grandpa Murphy came in through Ellis Island.

An unpleasant thought struck Jack. He might be the last generation of Murphy cops. He was divorced and childless, and his older brother, Kevin, would never have time for kids. Not that Kevin was gay. He was as heterosexual as Bill Clinton on meth. Kevin was an oceanographer. His job was to study boring stuff like why sand deposited on beaches. Jack was interested in studying other things deposited on beaches: blondes, brunettes, redheads. He was an observer by profession. Anyway, Kevin was more than dedicated to his work. It was his life. Kevin and Jack were alike in that way, but different in almost every other.

When they were growing up, Kevin was the good son, the popular one, the athletic one, the one who brought home perfect report cards. Jack came home with clothes that were bloody from fistfights or was suspended from school. Kindergarten was a tough place.

In grade school and high school, Kevin still came home with perfect grades but he wasn't as outgoing anymore. He shied away from sports and stayed in his room studying, planning a career. Jack still came home with blood on his clothes, but it was someone else's blood.

Jack's desk phone rang and he answered.

"Jack. It's your mother," his mother said as if he wouldn't remember her.

Murphy's Law says: "If you think about your mother, she will call."

"I was just getting ready to call you," Jack lied. Lately she called once a week, sometimes more, to complain about Kevin's needing to find a good woman. She seemed to think finding this "good woman" was Jack's job. Trying to be a good son, Jack knew he should talk to Kevin and pass on their mom's fear that Kevin would be happy with his life minus a woman. So he had called his brother and said, "Hey, Bro, mom says you should find a good woman and settle down." Kevin had laughed, Jack had laughed, and the topic was closed as far as Jack was concerned because he wasn't his brother's pimp.

"Are you listening, Jack?" his mother said, dragging him back into the conversation. He wondered if he could find a "nagging filter" for his iPhone. Maybe there's an app for that?

"Kevin's a grown man, Mom," Jack said. "He's successful. He's happy. He doesn't need advice from me."

"Jack. Help your brother. God knows he would help you. That's what families do, Jack. They take care of each other."

"I know, Mom. I'll call him as soon as we hang up. I promise, Mom." He knew he would go to hell for lying to his mother, but sometimes it was the only way to get her off the phone. The last thing he needed was Kevin setting him up on a date. He shuddered at the thought of some feminine academic hauling him to stuffy conventions. Look what that type of atmosphere had done to Einstein's hair.

"And how is my little Katie?" she asked.

Jack cringed at the mention of his ex-wife because that was followed by his mom extolling Katie's virtues and saying how much his dad had loved her, and how could Jack have let her get away and so on and so forth.

"You're just like your father, God rest his soul. He never spent enough time with his family," she said. And then came the final dig, "Katie calls me all the time, Jack. More than my own sons."

Point taken. He knew he should call his mom more than he did. Life always seemed to get in the way. Her last remark was also meant to prompt him to ask what she and Katie talked about. He didn't dare open that can of worms. She had always hoped Jack and Katie could get back together. He hadn't told her that had almost happened a while back. This was before he and an attractive state trooper had almost been killed by two psycho mercenaries, and Katie had caught Jack in the trooper's hospital room. It wasn't his fault if Katie had walked in and saw him being tongue raped by a woman who was grateful Jack had saved her life.

"Mom, I'm busy on an important case. This isn't a good time."

"It's never a good time. That's what your father always said.

Aren't there other detectives? You worry me. You always worried Katie. She'd die if she knew I told you this, but she calls me worrying about you being hurt. She's a saint, that one."

"I'm working on a serial rapist case, Mom. I have to get back to work."

"You call your brother like you promised your mother. You should never break a promise to your mother, Jack."

"I'll call Kevin. I will, Mom. Oh. Here comes the captain. Gotta go," he lied and gently placed the phone in the cradle.

A detective stuck his head in Jack's office. "Bank robbery. National City downtown."

The detectives' office had become a beehive of activity in the short time he was on the phone. He shoved his portable in his back pocket and hurried from the office. Liddell met him in the hallway.

"Banks don't open for another half hour," Liddell commented, as he and Jack got in Liddell's Crown Vic and sped away from headquarters.

"These might be the 'takeover' robbers," Jack said. The detectives' office had received a memo from the local FBI telling them about a team of bank robbers who were forcing their way into banks before the bank opened. They would catch an employee going inside and put a gun to his or her head. The FBI said they working their way across the country. The last Jack had heard, they were in Florida.

Most bank robbers were numbnuts. They would go in during business hours when the lobby was full, make a ruckus, and end up with the bait money—a package of bills loaded with an explosive dye pack, and all the serial numbers had been recorded so ithey could be traced. The dye was red and most of these idiots were literally caught red-handed.

This team, if the FBI was correct, had already robbed more than a dozen banks and netted close to half a million. They didn't stay in the bank long enough to worry about the bait money. Even if the dye pack went off, they were gone before the police got to the scene. The FBI had only been able to track them by the red-dyed money they had passed, but the robbers didn't stay in one place long enough to be caught. They were heavily armed and wore body armor like SWAT teams.

Jack's Kevlar vest was at home in the top of a closet. It was too tight and hot, and it made him itch. He wished he had it now. He looked over at Liddell and remarked, "You're wearing body armor."

Liddell chortled. "You?"

"Body armor's for pussies and old women," Jack answered.

"Well, here's to old ladies," Liddell said, and stomped the gas pedal.

Chapter Three

As they were arriving they saw several official vehicles leaving the bank's perimeter. One police car remained in front. A uniformed sergeant was in it. Liddell pulled up to the car and windows were powered down.

"False alarm," the sergeant said. "The manager accidentally set it off." He looked pissed off. "I spilled hot coffee all over my crotch. Shit!"

Liddell grinned and said, "You should sue McDonald's. Everyone else does."

The officer said, "Blasphemy. This is Donut Bank coffee. I drink the big boy stuff."

Donut Bank Bakery was Copland. No self-respecting police officer would drink a brew from anywhere else.

Liddell said to Jack, "Speaking of which . . ."

Five minutes later they were standing at the counter of the Donut Bank on St. Joseph Avenue. A girl of about sixteen beamed a smile at Jack. She held a tray with two plates and two ceramic mugs. One plate held a chocolate long john with a thick strip of sweetened bacon lying across the icing. The other was heaped like a pyramid of pastries. "One Millionaire Bacon long john for you, Detective Murphy. And a diabetic coma platter for you, Detective Blanchard."

"Make that two more glazed donuts for my partner, Cindy," Jack said. Liddell nudged him and Jack said, "Better make that three more, Cindy. My partner here is eating for eight."

He started to get out his wallet and Cindy said, "The owner says your food is always on the house." She filled a wax paper sack with glazed donuts. "Better have some for the road, Detective Blanchard."

"Call me Liddell. Detective Blanchard makes me sound old."

Jack handed the girl a twenty and said, "For the tip jar, Cindy," which earned him another huge smile.

Jack's portable cued and the dispatcher said, "All cars. Bank alarm at First Union Bank on Red Bank Road. All cars. Bank robbery in progress. Alarm confirmed." She repeated the dispatch, and a dozen cars responded they were headed to the robbery.

For the second time in less than an hour they were running for their car. Jack keyed the radio. "Two David 5-2 and Two David 5-3 responding," he said and climbed in the passenger side. Liddell peeled out of the parking lot and tweaked the siren to get around a car that wouldn't budge. He jumped the curb and rode with the right-side wheels on the sidewalk to make the right turn. "Sorry" he said, seeing he had startled the other driver, and then stomped on the gas, heading west, engine screaming. Traffic was light for this time of morning, as people were already at work or sleeping after a late shift. They sped down Highway 62, no emergency equipment operating. Only in the movies do the police run with lights and sirens all the way up to the crime scene and then get into a gunfight.

They neared the intersection at Red Bank Road. Jack held on to the strap above his window and swiveled his head, searching for backup. "Looks like we're on our own, Bigfoot."

"Three civilian cars in the bank lot. Look at that one there," Liddell said, and Jack saw the vehicle Bigfoot was talking about. It was a primer-red Pontiac GTO muscle car. It was backed in right in front of the bank's doors. A figure in all black clothing sat in the driver's seat.

"That's got to be them," Jack said. Liddell skidded sideways into the lot, as three black-clad figures ran out of the bank toward the GTO. They were dressed in SWAT gear with balaclavas covering their heads and all were armed. One was a giant, maybe bigger than Liddell, and carrying a large duffel bag in one hand and a stubby assault rifle in the other. The other two were slightly built and armed with handguns; web belts loaded with ordnance crisscrossed their chests. It gave them the appearance of Mexican bandits in a Western movie. Several black spherical objects hung from one of the web belts. The objects looked like flash bang grenades to Jack.

"Arms inside the vehicle at all times, children," Liddell muttered, aimed the car for the passenger door of the GTO, and floored it.

The GTO driver's head swiveled in their direction. The three running figures slowed and raised their weapons toward the kamikaze detectives' car. Jack saw muzzle flashes exploding from the barrels of the robbers' weapons, and bullets stitched lines up the Crown Vic's hood. Then Liddell slammed their car into the GTO's passenger side.

The Crown Vic's air bags deployed and Jack was hit in the chest and face. The inside of the car was suddenly filled with dusty white powder. Jack pushed the air bag out of his face and asked Liddell. "You okay, Bigfoot?"

Liddell grunted. "You?"

Jack tested his arms and legs. He was okay, but there were still three perps out there and they were armed. Jack and Liddell popped their seatbelts and bailed out, guns in hands, eyes and ears searching for targets.

The GTO lay over on the driver's side, Jack and Liddell moved up to the undercarriage for cover. Jack peeked down inside the GTO and said, "The driver's not moving."

Jack heard a groan and sensed movement on the other side of the car. He peeked around the bumper and dropped to his stomach, gun thrust in front. He saw the big guy lying on his back only a few feet away, but still moving. He couldn't see the other two, but he kept his gun pointed at the big one.

"I got one straight ahead. Ten feet. The big one with the rifle," Jack yelled to Liddell. To the robber he said, "Don't move. Just lie there."

Liddell peeked around the other side of the overturned car. "I got nothing," he said. "Where the hell is our backup?"

The big guy quit moaning and began to get up, first to his knees, then to his feet. He still held the stubby assault rifle. Jack could see two banana clips taped together and fed into the gun.

Jack aimed center mass at the big one and yelled, "Police. Drop the gun! Drop the gun!" He automatically scanned the field of fire, looking behind the robber and to the sides. There was nothing but the brick side of the bank building. No sign of the other two.

The giant looked at the rifle in his hand and seemed surprised it was still there. His head came up and his eyes fixed on the smashed-up getaway car. His head swiveled right, then left. Jack could hear a guttural sound like a growl coming from him.

"Do you see the other two?" Jack asked, Liddell.

"Nada," Liddell said.

The robber's head swiveled back toward Jack and even with the balaclava hiding most of his features, Jack could see a look of calm settle in his eyes. The growling stopped and the rifle barrel began to climb toward Jack and Liddell.

"Oh, shit!" Jack fired twice. Both shots struck the gunman in the chest. Jack could see their impact. But the giant just shook them off and the rifle spat death in Jack's direction. Jack dropped to the ground as the robber sprayed the car from left to right. If the driver wasn't dead before, he probably was now.

The firing stopped. Jack rolled out in the clear and saw the gunman ejecting the empty banana clip. Jack aimed and shot him in the face. The head snapped back and he slumped to the ground.

"This one's down," Jack said and rolled back behind the GTO.

Liddell had ducked for cover when bullets tore through the car's roof. His eyes were fixed on the ground and for a moment Jack thought a stray bullet had hit him. Liddell pointed down. Jack looked. A black boot attached to a leg stuck out from under the car. The GTO must have rolled onto one of the robbers.

"One to go," Jack said and looked around.

Liddell said, "Jack. Left side of the bank."

Jack caught a glimpse of a black-clad figure disappearing between the bank and several large Dumpsters.

"Cover me," Liddell said, but Jack stopped him.

"You haven't shot anyone yet. Call it in. I've got this one." Jack sprinted after the remaining robber. No use in both of them being suspended. He ran to the front of the bank and glued his back to the wall. Carefully he began to peek around the side just as something green came rolling toward him. He dropped to the ground, squeezed his eyes shut, and was able to throw his arms over his head before the ground rocked beneath him. The explosion was so close his hands were burned from the heat. His ears weren't just ringing. They were playing show tunes on dog whistles.

He lifted his head and looked at his arms. No cuts. No shrapnel.

No blood. It was a concussion grenade. What police call a flash bang. First there is a burst of white light and then a blast of heat, The purpose was to disorient wrongdoers until police could subdue them. It was working. He was disoriented, a little nauseous, and he knew he needed a bigger gun.

He gritted his teeth and tried to stand, but he was unsteady. He tried to focus his eyes, and some of his vision returned but he couldn't hear. The side of his face felt sunburned. He touched it, and his hand came away sticky with blood. He traced the blood to his ear. The explosion must have ruptured his eardrum.

He thought he heard sirens but they were far away. He gripped his .45 in both hands and ran into the alleyway. The robber was ten feet in front of him, standing by a Dumpster. A duffel bag was clenched in one hand and a semiautomatic handgun in the other. The eyes inside the balaclava grew wide, the mouth opened and closed, and then the lips clamped together in steely determination.

Jack said, "Don't be stupid." Or at least that's what he thought he said, but that's when the duffel bag exploded. A cloud of stinging red smoke and gas enveloped the robber. The bag hit the ground. Jack heard coughing and retching. When the smoke cleared he could see the suspect's gun coming up.

Jack fired twice. Once again the bullets impacted close together on the robber's chest. This one wasn't as big as the last. This one went down like a dishrag and lay still.

Jack waited for the cloud of tear gas to dissipate before he stepped forward. The robber's ballistic vest had stopped his bullets. This one would live. He kicked their gun away, rolled the perp over, and slapped on a pair of handcuffs. Then he felt for a pulse. It was strong. He rolled the robber over roughly and said, "Wakey, wakey, asshole."

The eyes behind the mask popped open and the mouth gulped air.

Jack said, "You've just had the wind knocked out of you. Slow down. Take shallow breaths. You'll live . . . if I don't kill you first. So don't move." Jack reached down and pulled the ski mask off.

"What the . . . ?"

It was a girl, barely a teenager. "You shot me!" she said, and spat in his face.

* * *

Jack and Liddell sat on cots in the back of an ambulance while a paramedic checked them out. The getaway driver looked dead but had somehow survived the crash and the car being shot up by his partner and was on his way to the hospital. He looked about 40 or 50 years old. The giant was young, a little older than the girl maybe, but he would never get any older. The one crushed to death like the Wicked Witch of the West turned out to be a woman in her forties. The grenade-tossing girl was in another ambulance, handcuffed to both sides of the gurney and screaming obscenities while paramedics attended to her. None of them had any identification. The GTO's VIN plate had been removed, and any other identifying numbers had been destroyed. The license plate was stolen from Florida. It would be impossible to trace.

"You think there's a family resemblance?" Liddell asked Jack.

Jack heard Liddell, but his ears were ringing and hurting like a bitch.

"We'll be on Oprah now," Liddell said.

"Jerry Springer more likely," Jack said much too loudly.

The news media was closing in like a pack of wolves. A Channel 6 helicopter hovered overhead to bring the bloodshed directly into the audience's homes. All that was missing was the street vendors and clowns. And speaking of clowns, Liddell pointed at the yellow crime scene tape where the arrival of a shiny black SUV was causing quite a stir.

"Don't look now but I think the eagle has landed," Liddell said.

Deputy Chief of Police Richard Dick, otherwise known as Double Dick, eased himself out of the back of the SUV, brushing at imaginary lint. The SUV was a brand-new Cadillac Escalade that had been seized during a drug bust and claimed by Double Dick for his permanent police vehicle. His driver, Captain Dewey Duncan, held the door open and stood at attention.

Double Dick hadn't been nicknamed so because he had two first names. Rather, because of his reputation for handing out overly harsh punishments for the slightest perceived wrongs. And he didn't stop there. He dicked the same officers over and over again. Hence the name, Double Dick.

Captain Duncan shut the back door of the SUV and stood at parade rest as Double Dick made his way to a spot just inside the crime scene tape. He turned and stood tall, watching the media and curious rubberneckers jostle each other for positions. He was in his dress blue uniform with silver piping on the cuffs, shiny black Corfam dress shoes, and a chest full of ribbons he had undoubtedly bestowed upon himself. Carefully positioned on his precisely cut head of hair was a pimped-out police commander's hat. Dick was blond-haired, blue-eyed, tall and lean, and every bit the Aryan poster child. He cleared his throat and spread his arms out like a maestro calling for quiet.

Liddell pointed to the Escalade and said, "There stands a police captain whose only purpose in life is to be a chauffeur for the commandant." He nudged Jack. "Did I ever tell you that when Double Dick had his hemorrhoids removed he promoted them to captain and made them his driver?"

Jack forced a chuckle even though he'd heard this line a hundred times. He would have felt a little sorry for the captain, but the man had never worked outside of an office in his life. He was a born gentleman's gentleman. Why he had become a policeman was anyone's guess.

A paramedic stepped in the back of the ambulance. "Let me take a look," he said loud enough for Jack to hear. The medic lifted the blood-soaked gauze pad from Jack's right ear.

"It's stopped bleeding," he said. Jack didn't know if that was good or bad until the paramedic covered Jack's left ear and spoke in a normal voice. Jack could hear a little with his right ear.

The medic put a fresh gauze pad against Jack's ear and told him to hold it there. "I hate to tell you this, Jack, but you might have a problem with the left one too. We need to go to the ER and have Doc check you out."

Jack said, "Did you say you want to give me some Scotch and the doc will take the check?"

The paramedic chuckled. "Yeah. Ask him about it when you get there. It's Doctor Findlay today."

Jack knew Dr. Findlay. If Jack wanted some Scotch all he had to do was wring Findlay out. He drank like a fish. On second thought, even a fish didn't drink like that. But he was a good doctor and knew his shit. Jack would take Findlay drunk over most of the new doctors sober.

Liddell cleared his throat and said, "I guess I don't count. I'm not here. I'm like a cheap date. Just use me and kick me to the curb."

The paramedic laughed. "I've got something for you," he said, and stuck a Bugs Bunny Band-Aid over the small cut on Liddell's forehead. "You were a bwave boy," he said in a baby voice. "If you're good on the trip to the ER I'll get you a sucker."

"I've got your sucker," Liddell said grabbing at his own crotch.

Sergeant Wolf said from the door to the ambulance, "I hope you're not injured there. I'm not going to write that up in my report."

"I was just . . ." Liddell said, but Sergeant Wolf waved the comment away.

"Will these two guys live?" Wolf asked the medic.

The medic said, "Jack might have a ruptured eardrum. This other clown might have a brain injury."

"Hey," Liddell protested, "I resemble that remark."

"I'm supposed to take your gun, Jack," Wolf said. "I'll have a patrol officer follow the ambulance to the hospital and I'll meet you there. You know the drill."

Jack knew it all too well. Sergeant Wolf would take his gun per the SOP regarding police-involved shootings. Then Jack would be taken to the hospital where an officer would babysit him until he gave a blood and urine sample. He would be taken home by another officer minus his duty weapon. He would be on administrative suspension—with pay—until a shooting board convened to decide if Jack's use of force was justified or if he was in deep doo-doo.

Jack was about to hand his gun over when Wolf stiffened and said in an exaggerated voice, "So, Detective Murphy, you identified yourself as a policeman and gave the deceased an order to drop his weapon?"

Jack saw that Double Dick had snuck up on them and was standing off to the side listening. Sergeant Wolf held his hands to his mouth like a megaphone and repeated the question even louder.

"I did," Jack yelled, unnecessarily. "He was bringing the rifle up. I had no choice. If I'd have hesitated I'd be the one on the way to the morgue."

Liddell hurriedly added, "I can back up everything he said. Do you need to take my weapon, too? Or can we all go to a bar and drink and then get into some more action like on *CSI*? Those guys are the real thing."

Sergeant Wolf said, "Keep your weapon for now." To the ambulance driver he said, "Hurry up and take these two to the hospital."

"Hold up," Deputy Chief Richard Dick said.

The sergeant turned to him and said, "Detective Blanchard was just kidding about going to a bar. He's just venting his frustration. I'm almost through here and I need to get them to the ER to get blood drawn. "

Deputy Chief Dick focused on Jack. "I expect a full report on my desk in the next hour, Detective Murphy."

"I'm fine, sir. Thanks for asking," Jack said loudly as if he hadn't heard the comment. He reached out to shake hands with Double Dick.

Double Dick stepped back as if he had been assaulted. "Detective Murphy . . . I . . ." Double Dick said, but Jack talked over him, pointing at his ears and yelling, "I can't hear you, sir. I'm just grateful you came to see how we are. It means a lot to me."

"Jack was very close to an explosion, sir," Sergeant Wolf explained. "The medic says he might have ruptured eardrums."

Jack watched Dick fight a smile. *The son of a bitch is enjoying this.*

Dick puffed up and picked at an imaginary loose thread on his highly decorated sleeve. He looked at Liddell and said, "And you, Detective Blanchard, deliberately wrecked a brand-new vehicle." To Sergeant Wolf he said, "You will take Murphy's weapon according to police department policy." He pointed to Liddell and said, "His too if he fired his weapon. Or even if he hasn't."

Liddell said, "I didn't shoot anyone."

Dick looked at Sergeant Wolf as if Liddell hadn't spoken. "And then you will personally go to the hospital and have blood and urine drawn from both detectives. I want alcohol and drug screening done immediately, and I want a report within the next hour. Do I make myself clear, Sergeant?"

"I don't think they can draw urine from us, Deputy Chief . . . sir. I think we just pee in a cup. No needles involved," Liddell said.

Dick ignored the remark and said, "Sergeant. Do it now."

Sergeant Wolf looked at Jack and held his hand out. Jack pulled his .45 out of its holster, popped the clip, stripped the live round from the barrel, and handed everything over. Liddell followed suit.

Dick looked at Jack and said, "I assure you, Murphy, there will be a full investigation."

Jack cupped his hand to an ear, and said, "Did you say there was some misinformation, sir?"

Before the Deputy Chief could respond Liddell said, "Too bad you didn't have our reports before you talked to the media, sir."

Dick stepped back like he'd been slapped in the face as Sergeant Wolf closed the back doors and slapped the back of the ambulance. It made a hasty exit, lights and siren all the way.

Chapter Four

At the hospital Sergeant Wolf oversaw the drawing of blood from Jack and Liddell, as ordered by Double Dick. Their test results showed they were clear of any alcohol or drugs in their systems. Liddell got a few stitches, but Doctor Findlay was nice and hid them in the hairline. Then Dr. Findlay faced Jack and moved his mouth like he was talking but there was no sound. Jack panicked, thinking he really had gone deaf, until the doctor grinned and said, "Just kidding. Who'd you shoot this time, Jack?" *Everyone's a comedian.*

Since Double Dick wasn't having them arrested, Liddell went home to his loving wife, and Jack to his loving Glenmorangie thirty-year-old single-malt Scotch. He'd had a brief fling with a Macallan fifty-year-old Scotch a few years ago, but it didn't last because of their age difference, and he couldn't afford her. He'd stopped comparing the two because after the first sip it all tasted the same. He got home to find that Cinderella had ignored her new "doggy door" and taken a dump in a pair of his shoes. He loved that dog.

The media assault went into full swing, and for two days Castle Murphy was under siege by raiding hordes of news-Mongols. Jack didn't hate the media. That was too weak of a word. On his scale of dislike, reporters fell in somewhere between attorneys and catching syphilis. Or vice versa.

The reporters walked in along the public riverbank. Some came in boats. Some took pictures of his cabin and yelled "Jack, come out." It reminded him of the old Charlton Heston movie, *The Omega Man,* where the vampire-like creatures came out at night and yelled for Heston to come out of his barricaded house so they could kill him. He could take them down with a shot to the head, just like he'd seen on that TV series *The Walking Dead*. But the noise would only attract more of them.

His answering machine was full of the same old same old from the media. "Jack, did you know she was only fourteen years old when you shot her?" "Detective Murphy, what does it feel like to shoot a child?" But his favorite question was "Couldn't you have used pepper spray?" *Pepper spray against grenades and hand-guns? Maybe the media would shut up if I had shot the grenade out of her hand, or overpowered her with love and understanding.* He'd even gotten a call from a producer for *48 Hours*. They wanted to do a re-creation of the shooting. If they showed up at his cabin he'd be happy to accommodate. There was no doubt in his mind who had given the media his unlisted landline phone number. It was a Dick thing to do.

By the third morning, all the reporters were gone. At first Jack thought maybe the Rapture had come, but there were no piles of clothing, notebooks, and microphones lying on the ground outside his cabin. He decided that some local politician had done something stupid. Or maybe more pictures of Anthony Weiner had surfaced. No pun intended.

The shooting board would make their determination this morning, and Jack would either be cleared as a justified shooting, or arrested. He decided not to attend the hearing as Double Dick had ordered him.

Jack showered, shaved, and dressed in a Hawaiian print shirt, white cargo shorts, and flip-flops. He looked at himself in the mirror. His dad had once told him, "The job demands a lot from you, Jack. The important thing is that you can look yourself in the eye every morning." He could.

He went to the kitchen and found the remnants of a box of Rice Krispies and a loaf of whole-wheat bread. The bread was moldy and the Rice Krispies didn't look much better. He tossed the bread in the trash and rummaged through more cabinets. He found three cans of Alpo and three cans of Guinness. No milk. He put a pot of coffee on and found a semi-clean mug.

"What the hell," he said and poured some Rice Krispies in the mug, popped the top of a Guinness, and poured it over the cereal. It wasn't half bad. Beer-eal. The breakfast of drinking champions. He carried the beer-eal and two cans of Guinness out to the porch, sat down in his rocker, ate his breakfast, and pondered what his last day off would bring. He wasn't suspended; he was just on administrative leave. That was a nice way of saying that if the shooting board thought he had screwed up, they would crucify him and say, "The public is safe from the menace known as Jack Murphy, child shooter, monster." Or he might be going back to work tomorrow. He hoped they wouldn't make him see a shrink before he came back to work this time. If you want to meet someone truly insane, talk to a shrink.

The shooting board had convened an hour ago, and he smiled remembering Double Dick calling to order him to appear. Jack had yelled into the receiver, "I'm on the no-call list, asshole!" and hung up. Dick tried to call back several times, but Jack unplugged the landline and turned off his cell phone. He'd turn it back on later. Liddell was at the shooting board hearing and Jack needed to talk to him afterwards. On the other hand, Double Dick could go stuff himself. Twice.

He ate the last of the beer-eal and stared at nothing. Then he noticed the newspaper was on the porch. He put the mug down, picked up the paper, and unfolded it to the front page. The headline was a variation of the one on the last two days' papers. "TWO KILLED—GIRL SHOT DURING DARING BANK ROBBERY ATTEMPT."

Attempt? One guy was spraying .223 bullets around and the "girl" tried to blow me up.

Below that was a photo of the scene with Double Dick at the ambulance. Jack had an angry look on his face, and Double Dick was obviously chastising him. In a side photo were two bodies covered in white sheets laid out near the overturned GTO. The bottom section showed a photo of Jack sitting on his porch, with a beer in his hand, smiling. He remembered that one being taken yesterday by one of the newspeople down by his dock. Maybe he shouldn't have toasted the guy with the Guinness.

He flipped to the second section, where the story was continued with the headline, "FAMILY TIES: Robbery of West Side Bank (cont. from p.1)." Under the headline was a spread of postage-stamp-sized individual photos. The news media had probably obtained these from previous arrests elsewhere.

Below the tiny photos were larger ones showing the family together, a Christmas tree in the background, presents in partial states of unwrapping, faces beaming and hamming for the camera. Jack's mind didn't see a Christmas photo. In his mind he wondered who was taking the photo and if that person was a part of the ring of robbers. There were two other pictures of family gatherings, but none showed them wearing the SWAT gear and heavily armed. The last picture was of the "girl" robber alone. She was sitting on a steel bunk in her jail cell with a piteous look on her face. She had pulled her orange top up under her breasts to show two blue/black splotches in the middle of her chest. Impact by a .45 hollow-point slug will do that. Jack thought it was an impressive spread. The bruises almost overlapped each other.

He and Liddell had talked a few times and Liddell said the robbers were a family of four—two now—from Arkansas. Daddy Robber had been the getaway driver. There were no air bags in the GTO, so Daddy was banged up pretty good with a punctured lung and maybe some brain damage but would live. The Big Brother Robber was the giant Jack had killed. He was named "Hoss"—his real name—and he was twenty years old. Hoss had spent much of his life in and out of boys' school and prison. He was armed with an AK-47 rifle that was illegally modified to fire fully automatic.

According to Liddell's investigation, Mommy Robber had been a stay-at-home mom until her baby girl turned thirteen. Then the life of crime had become a family affair. Surprisingly, Mommy had little on her record except minor drug charges and a DUI in Arkansas.

The Girl Robber, the baby of the family, had celebrated becoming a teenager by shooting a bank security guard in a Nebraska holdup. Liddell had tied her to seven other bank robberies so far. But now her career was over. She had three broken ribs from the impact of the .45 rounds, but body armor had saved her life. She was in an isolation cell at the jail because of her age and because she had bitten one of the matrons.

Barely fourteen years old and she was looking at a life sentence. When she was finally released she would probably run for public office.

He pitched the empty beer can over the rail and popped the top on the last of the Mohicans. He gazed across the river where several bikini-clad young women were wading the shallows out to a sandbar. They carried beach towels and two of them pulled a red-and-white cooler. Maybe they needed some help? He went back inside and came back out with binoculars. He sat in the rocker again in time to see the sun worshipers frolic in the water to cool off and then roll back onto the sandbar like a wave of tropical oils and sun-tanned flesh. They took their sunning seriously. So did he.

One pulled on a fluorescent pink top that barely covered her . . . top part. He focused the binoculars and read the words, "If you think this is pink . . ." An arrow pointed down at the panties.

His work cell phone rang from inside the house. He didn't want to talk to anyone, but thinking it might be Liddell, he went in and looked at the screen.

"I gave at the office," Jack said into the phone.

"Well, I happen to know you're not in your office so you can give again, you cheapskate asshole," Killian said.

Jack laughed and asked, "Wha's'up, bru'tha'?" George Killian was one of Jack's fishing—and drinking—buddies. Killian was also a special agent with the ATF—Alcohol, Tobacco and Firearms. He was a fit, good-looking black man with intense dedication to his work.

Killian asked, "Did you read today's paper yet?" Jack didn't answer. "I'll take that as a hell no. I just wanted to check on you. See if you're okay. Well, we know you're not okay because you're the incredible Jack Murphy, but how the hell are you holding up, bru'tha?"

"I don't have to hold it up," Jack said.

"Screw you, Jack," Killian said.

"In your dreams maybe. So how's the ATF treating you? How's that new boss of yours? What'is name?"

"His name is Misino. He's Italian. Don't mess around with a paisano. You go fishing with 'em, you might end up sleeping with the fishes."

They both chuckled. Jack was glad Killian had called. He needed some cheering up.

"I don't need anything," Jack lied, although he was out of everything, including most of his clean clothes. "Just hearing your voice makes me glad I'm not working."

"Well, if Double Dick gets his way you will be looking for a job. I'll put in a good word with my boss. Italians and Irish get along nowadays, don't they?"

Jack heard the sound of tires crunching on gravel. "Someone is coming. Let me call you back in a few minutes. Is that okay?"

Killian said, "Hey, you don't need to. Just checking on you. Go take care of business. And Jack . . . Don't shoot anyone."

"Bite me," Jack said, and disconnected.

Better not be a goddamn reporter. He went back to the porch and sat in his rocker.

Jack's cabin faced due south, overlooking the Ohio River, with a gravel drive on each side and a gravel parking area behind. A set of wooden steps led up on each side of his porch. He put the binoculars in his lap and waited as a bright red Crown Vic eased into view and stopped.

Cinderella pushed the screen door open with her nose, sniffed the air, then lost interest and lay down inside the door.

"Some watchdog you are," Jack said.

She bared her teeth, not even bothering to growl, and slinked away.

"And stay out of my damn closet!" Jack said.

The car window buzzed down and Liddell leaned across the seat. "I come bearing gifts, O Drunk One."

"Hardly drunk," Jack said. "I only had three Guinness left in here. I hope you brought a fresh supply."

Liddell weighed in at full-grown yeti. The car groaned and lifted several inches as he got out. He walked up the steps carrying a paper grocery sack and stood blocking Jack's view of the sandbar.

"Are those binoculars in your lap or are you just happy to see me?" Liddell asked.

"Bite me, Bigfoot. I see they've given you another car to wreck. Fire-engine red? Appropriate."

"It's a loaner from the garage," he explained. "Your hearing come back?"

"What?" Jack said exaggeratedly and cuffed a hand beside his ear.

"Pussy. When I was with Iberville Parish Sheriff's Department we trained with grenades just for fun. They would fire machine guns over our heads and drop mortar rounds on our position. If you came out alive you passed and moved on to the Blackhawk helicopter strafing runs with Hellfire missiles. It was messy but it separated the men from the boys. You wouldn't have made it past the grenades."

"Want to go buy some more beer?" Jack asked.

"I'm on duty, and it's a little early for me," Liddell said. "I usually have to be awake more than an hour. Want to go to breakfast?"

"No. Can't you see I'm busy?" Jack said.

Liddell held a hand out for the binoculars, and Jack grudgingly gave them up. Liddell focused across the river, whistled softly, and said, "I can see you're making the most of your days off."

Jack took the binoculars back and shoved Liddell out of the way with his leg. "Yeah. I was mad at you for a while for wrecking the car and getting me into this mess."

"Me? I got you in it? You're the one that ran off like a one-man SWAT team."

"Well, if you hadn't played demolition derby without warning me . . ." Jack grinned. "That was pure genius, by the way. Saved us hours of a standoff."

"Thank you," Liddell said.

"You're welcome."

"Speaking of a standoff. You're going to have to go toe-to-toe with Double Dick sometime. You should have come this morning. Double Dick almost had a stroke."

"Now that I would have come to see."

"Oh. In case you're wondering, the shooting board cleared you."

Jack opened the paper sack Liddell brought him and took out his confiscated .45 and the empty magazine.

"Captain Franklin says you can come back to work today."

Jack worked the slide, locking it back, showing an empty chamber.

"Two questions," Jack said, and laid the gun on the windowsill behind him. "Is the FBI taking the case? And . . . where are the bullets?"

"Oh yeah," Liddell said. He dug in his pocket and came out with a handful of ammo. He held the bullets out in both palms while Jack reloaded the magazine and slapped it home.

"Since there are multiple robberies in multiple states involving banks, I'd say the FBI might go out on a limb and prosecute this one. But as of today, they haven't committed. You got so much bad publicity I guess they don't want to make us look any worse."

"Since we're on the topic of the federal government, did that asshole attorney, Boom Boom, file federal charges against me for punching the rapist? Because if he did I'm gonna need a lot more Guinness and Scotch."

"I heard on the snake-vine"—he was referring to the super-visors' grapevine—"that Double Dick is champing at the bit to have you fired for that. However, since you arrested this guy, several women have come forward and identified him and filed rape charges against him. I don't think you have a worry there."

"Maybe Prosecutor Higgins will take all this into account when he finally decides to either file charges against the rapist or to go after me."

"And don't forget, Double Dick wants your ass on the bank rob-bery, too, pod'na."

Jack laughed and said, "He just wants my ass, but I'm not that easy. He's going to have to take me out and buy me dinner first."

Liddell chuckled then became a little more serious. "I've got some other news, pod'na. But it's good news . . . I think. Anyway, Katie called Marcie last night." Marcie was Liddell's wife. "Katie asked about you. How you were, if you were eating right—you know."

Without looking down, Jack slid the beer-eal mug under his chair with a foot.

"Marcie told her to call you. I hope you don't mind. You know Marcie thinks the world of you two. I told her not to meddle."

Jack felt the familiar sense of loss. He wanted to ask what else Katie had said, but he wasn't sure if he wanted to know.

"She still loves you, Jack. What the hell is wrong with you? Call Katie. Crawl if you have to," Liddell said. "At least come back to work to keep busy. You can't sit out here for the rest of your life, pod'na."

Jack motioned to the sandbar. One of the ladies had taken off her top and was rubbing oil on herself. "Wanna bet?" But he was tired of sitting around, not leaving his cabin to avoid the press, or the looks people would give him because of the news media. He'd ventured out just once to go to the restaurant he co-owned, Two Jakes, and a woman had tucked her kid behind her. Jack turned around and went home. He didn't want to run off business at Two Jakes. Although, he'd talked to Jake Brady, his partner, and busi-ness was booming. Jack was a celebrity. *Yeah. Right.*

"She'll never forgive me, Bigfoot. The timing of her showing up really sucked, and the irony is that I didn't kiss that woman. She kissed me."

"Come on, pod'na," Liddell said. "You didn't resist too hard. She was laying in a hospital bed and barely able to move and Katie saw you leaning over and . . ."

"All right. All right, I get the picture. I'm an asshole," Jack said.

"Well, at least Moira's talking to you," Liddell said.

"She hasn't called or come out since I saw her in the prosecutor's office. Maybe she hates me again. Let's change the subject. How are things with you? I mean, after wrecking the car and all that."

Liddell groaned. "Two hours at the hospital with you getting blood drawn and such. Then about six hours of accident forms, another four hours filling out the affidavits of arrest, then I got a reaming from Deputy Chief Dick, and then the lieutenant, and then the captain, and then Deputy Chief Dick again. Both times Dick threatened to charge me with causing the momma robber's death. Vehicular manslaughter he called it. But the prosecutor refused to file charges, so Dick tried to suspend me and the chief wouldn't let him." Jack and Liddell had talked several times, but he'd never gotten the full story of what Bigfoot had gone through.

"That's why we call him Double Dick," Jack said. "He 'dicks' you over more than once. You're lucky your name isn't Jack Murphy. The dicking never ends."

"Guilt by association?"

"Welcome to my world," Jack said. "So what have they got you doing today besides delivering my gun and the message from Captain Franklin?"

"I'm in Missing Persons. I've been doing the research on the bank robbers but since the Feds are unofficially, or maybe, going to be in charge of that one, the Deputy Chief ordered Captain Franklin to reassign me. Double Dick thought I could be better used somewhere that I couldn't get in a shoot-out or wreck anything."

Jack couldn't believe they had put an experienced detective like Liddell in the missing persons unit working with a waste of breath like Larry Jansen. Jansen's uniform was a rumpled gray suit, a wrinkled red tie, and a trench coat with the buttons missing. He wore the same summer and winter and never took the trench coat off. He fancied himself like Columbo, the rumpled detective in the seventies detective series on television. The difference was that Columbo never snitched to the brass—plus he always solved his cases.

"By the way, Marcie wants you to come to dinner tonight." Liddell said.

"I'm sorry I got you in trouble, Bigfoot. Listen, I appreciate the offer, but—"

"She said I should twist your arm." In a confidential tone, he said, "She's worried about you. Just between you and me, I think she's invited Katie. Neither of you is supposed to know about the other one coming. Maybe you should come. Eh?"

"I really don't need help with my personal life, Bigfoot. Tell Marcie I appreciate the offer, just not tonight."

"Marcie's not someone you want to get on the wrong side of, pod'na. She says jump, you find a cliff."

"Okay. What time?"

"Five o'clock," Liddell said and pointed at the empty beer cans. "You want me to come and get you?"

"I'll be okay, Mother."

After Liddell left, Jack thought about their conversation. Mostly about Katie. She had probably seen the news too and knew he was going through a bad time. He wasn't the type to sit around feeling sorry for himself. He wasn't going to let Double Dick or the news media get to him. He waved at the sunbathers and one of them waved back and motioned for him to join them. It wasn't even tempting. He would rather be over there with someone else. Katie looked really good in a bikini.

He picked up his empty cans, the binoculars, and his gun and went inside to change clothes. Captain Franklin said he *could* come back to work today. It wasn't an order. A cruise upriver would help clear his head—both of them. Maybe he'd spend some time at Two Jakes. Get some breakfast. Maybe go out and shoot up a convent so he could get more days off.

Two Jakes Restaurant and Marina lay along a half-mile stretch of a sandy bank of the Ohio River west of Jack's cabin. Two miles west of that was the newly built 2,700-passenger Blue Star Casino Riverboat. The New Jersey owners bought several blocks of riverfront on both sides of Riverside Drive and built nightclubs, hotels, restaurants, and a five-story parking garage. The "gambling district," as it had come to be known, drew customers from far away, but Two Jakes had an already established reputation and hadn't been hurt by the competition. If anything, it had helped Two Jakes' business by allowing visitors to get away from the crush and rush and noise.

Two Jakes was named after Jake Brady and Jack's dad, Jake Murphy. The two men had been street cops for the Evansville police force and worked the same car as partners for almost thirty years. Just before they retired, they bought thirty acres of mostly unusable, completely undeveloped, therefore undesirable, riverfront land. The lot was an uneven shape but included almost a third of a mile of land along the Ohio River. Over half of the land was swamp and the other half covered in wild growth of trees, vines, and one fishing shack with a caved-in roof that was home to water snakes. Everyone, including Jack's mother, thought they were crazy— throwing good money after bad. So the two men bought another five acres of the surrounding property to give them access to two roads. They tore down the shack, and bought a barge that they permanently anchored where the shack had been.

They had cashed in their retirement and used all of their savings, not to mention taking on a huge loan, but soon a restaurant was built on the floating barge, parking areas were cleared and graveled, and Two Jakes was born. It was an instant hit. The loan had been paid off in just a few years. A marshy inlet was dredged out into a bay, and a marina where boats could be repaired and housed was built. The addition of a second-story bar on the restaurant turned Two Jakes into a multi-million-dollar enterprise.

When Jack's father died several years ago, Jack and his brother, Kevin, had inherited half of Two Jakes and a cabin farther downriver that his grandfather had built. Kevin never had an interest in either the river cabin or the business, and so Jack bought him out. The deal had worked out for both of them. Kevin used the money to start a scientific consulting business. Jack elected to let Jake Brady, his co-owner, run things at Two Jakes. Brady proved to be a shrewd businessman and a skilled chef, too.

Two Jakes was a two-man operation, and with Jack's dad gone, Brady couldn't cook and tend bar by himself. So he hired Vinnie, a small, wiry man with a tan so deep his skin was as tough and wrinkled as leather. His face was creased with lines that belied his true age, probably somewhere between twenty-five and sixty. Thick blond hair was pulled back in a nub of ponytail. Year-round he dressed in short sleeved, tie-dyed shirts; blue jean cutoffs, and deck shoes. He fancied himself a "flower child" of the sixties. But, unlike most of the flower children, he was extremely clean, and polite. If he had a last name, Jack had never heard it. Jake Brady had hinted that Vinnie had a questionable background, but he also had a talent for mixing drinks and keeping customers happy.

Jack slipped his newly returned and loaded Glock in the waistband of his cargo shorts, pulled on a Tommy Bahama polo shirt, stepped back onto the porch, and checked on the sunbathers. Just to be sure none of them was getting too much sun. His earlier plan was to do nothing except soak in his hot tub, get seriously shitfaced, and do more of nothing. But now he'd promised Liddell that he'd come to dinner. It was a dilemma. Go to dinner at Liddell's as promised or do nothing. He leaned toward doing nothing, but, as they say, "The problem with doing nothing is you don't know when you're finished." The same could be said about drinking. In either case he needed to go to Two Jakes for more supplies. Maybe have something healthy for a late breakfast. A sausage sandwich, a Guinness, and a large slice of Jake's homemade cherry pie. That was as healthy as it gets.

He headed down the steps of his private dock to the love of his life, the *MISS FIT,* a twenty-five-foot cabin cruiser with all the bells and whistles. The short trip to Two Jakes would do him good. He could forget about investigating the bank robbery because it was basically the Feds' problem now. And he could tamp down his anger with Prosecutor Higgins and his frat buddy, Boom Boom. *Who would be proud of that as a nickname?* Jack knew he probably shouldn't have let his temper reach his fists, but the "alleged" rapist was lucky it hadn't reached his Glock.

Jack pushed these thoughts out of his mind and climbed aboard the *MISS FIT.* He stowed the top, fired up the twin inboard engines, and let them idle, savoring the deep guttural sound. Feeling the rumble of powerful engines under his feet never failed to cheer him. He'd have to mention that to the department shrink when he saw him, or her, again. He was sure Double Dick would insist that he see the department's witch doctor, and he was equally sure that the shrink would tell him that his love for the *MISS FIT* was unhealthy. A Freudian-macho-sexual thing. Maybe Jack wasn't breastfed enough as a baby, or maybe he'd been breastfed too much.

He slipped the port lines, backed out of the slip, and pointed the *MISS FIT* in the direction of Two Jakes. He pushed the throttle forward and took her out of the quay, and felt the bow lift as he opened her up.

Boner.

Chapter Five

Alcohol, Tobacco and Firearms Special Agent George Killian took the off-ramp and zigzagged lazily through mostly abandoned neighborhoods of shotgun-style houses. The houses surrounded decaying factories and warehouses and parking lots that had turned to rubble and waist-high weeds. Between the 1940s and the 1990s this area had been known as the Franklin Industrial Complex. The factories had been built to aid in the war effort, and when the war was won, they employed the returning World War II veterans. And then more houses were built and the veterans' offspring had found employment in the same factories where one or both of their parents had worked. A decent living could be had.

Time, an upturn in the economy, and the increased mobility of families had made the housing superfluous. The kids were no longer interested in working the same job for 25 or 30 years as their parents had done. They were the New-Agers. They'd never experience the inconvenience and sacrifice the war had demanded. They saw their future on the horizon, and not under their feet. They moved away for school, and sometimes didn't come home, living *their* dream and not the one their parents had envisioned for them.

Back home, the parents were also more mobile, thus able to find more lucrative employment, and soon they were no longer satisfied with the small houses. Those who could move out had done so long ago; those who couldn't had hunkered down and done whatever it took to survive. That included prostitution, selling drugs, street robberies, carjacking, burglaries, going on welfare, or any combination of these. Very few made it out except to go to prison. Killian was one of the few success stories.

He grew up in this neighborhood in a house no bigger than a

cracker box. Two brothers and two sisters, a mom, and a dad made up one of a hundred large families of poor blacks. His father worked from sunup to sundown scraping a living out for a family of seven. His father would give you the shirt off his back. He was too proud to take handouts. He had instilled in his children the deep-seated belief that right was right and wrong was wrong. The world didn't owe you anything. If you wanted something you had to work for it.

His father had taught him that being black wasn't any different from being white or Asian or Hispanic. The color of your skin wasn't who you were, and because of your color you didn't have to prove to anyone that you were just as good as them. Nor did it give you special entitlements. He had said, "Just be the best man you know how to be, the man I know you'll one day become, son, and you'll be fine. There are lots of black people and lots of white people and every other color, but there is only one you—only one Killian—and I'll always be proud of you."

Killian and his two brothers and two sisters had turned out all right. Killian had never forgotten where he came from, or the lessons his father taught, and he would make sure he passed them on to his sons. Being black didn't mean the same thing now as it did when he was a kid. He had seen true racism, up close and personal. But he had also seen people try to use their race as an excuse for bad behavior or lack of ambition. He didn't hold with that type of thinking.

He turned into the defunct warehouse/factory district and slowed to a crawl. He counted the warehouses as he passed them. At the fourth one he turned right, into an alleyway, and then another right. Behind the building he came to a set of speed bumps partially hidden by weeds. His Crown Vic bounced over them. He stopped when he came to a chain-link fence with gaps where it had rusted and been spread open by trespassers. He would have to go the rest of the way on foot.

His source said two cops were involved in a weapons deal. The source—he couldn't really be called an informant because he didn't know anyone and hadn't seen anything—didn't know who these cops were, and couldn't even describe them, but he heard the word "explosives." That got Killian's full attention.

The source had explained that he had met a hobo who had jumped off a train near Mary Street, where the tracks run under the Lloyd

Expressway. At first the source said the information he had came from that hobo. The source obviously was scared to be personally involved in any way, since cops were involved. Killian had pieced enough of the story together to merit a look-see. The guy said he was inside, actually underneath, what used to be one of the guard shacks here. He explained that he was under the shack because it was cooler and he needed a place to sleep. He had a bottle of hooch and had just finished it off when he heard someone come inside the shack. He peeked through a crack in the floor and saw legs and gun belts. Cops. He said they were talking, waiting for someone. The cops talked a little more and then left. When he heard their car—one car—leave, he climbed out of the back and got out of there. He said he had gone to St. Anthony's Shelter, where he really did meet a hobo.

For an extra twenty dollars the snitch's memory got better. He came up with the location of the abandoned warehouse and the exact guard shack where he had heard the two cops. For another ten he remembered they had said something about a delivery, but they didn't say when. He'd heard them say the word "explosives," and that was all he needed to hear to get the hell out of there.

Killian didn't know if any of this crap was real and not the product of too much alcohol, but it had to be checked out. That was his job. This is the second day in a row he'd done surveillance on the guard shack and so far it had been a waste of time. He hadn't seen a single police car. Not even one coming through on routine patrol. There was nothing left to steal, and no one seemed to care about vandals or homeless people unless they started a fire.

He had thought about taking this information—not quite what they called a lead—to his chief and doing things up right, but that would mean briefing several other agents and notifying the FBI's tactical squad. Before that, he would have to send the information to regional headquarters and get the green light, and that would take too much time. Plus there could be the problem of accidental leaks of information. That was always a risk when information involved the government in any way.

He'd considered asking his buddy Jack Murphy to help him out on this one while he had him on the phone, but Murphy was up to his gonads in this bank robbery thing. He and Jack had attended the police academy together. They remained friends over the years, even when Killian joined the ATF and was posted in Atlanta for a few years. Jack had kidded him for becoming a Fed, but it didn't stop them from fishing together when they had a chance. He didn't want to see Jack in any more hot water. The news media was already questioning Jack's methods. So Killian would have to go it alone. As Jack would say, "Better to ask forgiveness than permission." He grinned at the idea of what Murphy would really say. Probably something like "Screw a bunch of brass." Jack was good with words.

He opened the glove box and took out the pink digital camera that his wife, Barbara, kept handy for opportunities to stuff their photo scrapbooks. He brought it from home because he didn't want to raise any flags by checking one out at work. He switched it on to check the battery and a picture came up on the viewer. It was a "selfie" of him and Barbara, cheek to cheek, her laughing and him making a goofy face. He put the camera in the top pocket of his fatigue jacket and checked his handgun. Time to go.

He exited the car, quietly shut the door, and walked to the back of the warehouse. He'd scouted the area and this was by far the best place to watch from. It had been no problem getting inside. Vandals had already pried the back door open back when there was still something to steal. Homeless people still stayed here sometimes, but it was empty right now. The warehouse sat cavernous and dark with all the windows painted over. The smell of machine oil and the stench of old urine and feces permeated the air. He was swallowed by near darkness as he felt his way across the floor to the stairs that ascended to a metal catwalk. He paused and listened, then made his way to the top, where metal-framed painted-out windows ran the length of the catwalk.

Something rustled behind him. He ducked and drew his gun. A pigeon had somehow found a way inside. He holstered the gun and moved down the catwalk to the window he'd left unlocked. The window was already pushed open. He wondered if he had left it that way. Or maybe someone had been up here. He opened the window. Across the street was a wooden shack guarding the entrance to a parking lot. A six-foot-high chain-link fence had once surrounded the lot, but now all that remained were posts, sticking up like broken teeth.

Two vehicles were backed up to the guard shack. One was an Evansville Police Department marked unit. The other, a white Chevy panel van, was backed in, back doors open almost touching the open front door of the shack. He didn't see anyone around the vehicles and nothing moved on the street.

He was about twenty yards from the shack but he could hear indistinct voices drifting across the space. He lifted the little digital camera, pushed the zoom knob to its limit, and snapped some shots of the vehicles. It actually had a better zoom lens than his iPhone. He then zoomed back slightly and took a shot of the shack and warehouse. The distance shots wouldn't be great, but the FBI's lab could enhance them. If only he'd gotten there an hour earlier. Shit. Shit! He reached for his cell phone to call in the reinforcements. He shouldn't go down there by himself. But he would if he had to.

The van's back doors shut. A man, maybe Indian or Pakistani, or perhaps Middle Eastern, walked around and got in the driver's side. The van pulled onto the street. Killian put his phone on the window ledge, grabbed the digital camera, and took several shots of the man. The van drew closer. He snapped a few shots of the driver and several more as the van drove out of his field of view. He was excited now. If the pictures could be enhanced, he could run the driver through the federal databases. If that didn't work, he would request Interpol assistance. If he was lucky, he might have gotten a clear photo of the license plate.

Talking and laughter drifted from across the street. He turned back in time to see the back of a gray-haired man in a police uniform. The man was standing in the shack's doorway but from the man's posture, he wasn't the one laughing. Killian listened closely. He couldn't hear what was said, but the voices were plainly angry. He was about to get on his phone again but the gray-haired policeman turned around facing the street.

Well, I'll be damned!

He raised the camera and snapped away until the "low battery" warning blinked on the screen. Damn! He turned it off and back on, hoping to get one or two more shots. It worked. He zoomed in and was so fixated he didn't hear a man come up behind.

The van had unloaded two wooden crates, one the size of a suitcase, the other the size of a cereal box. Both bore the mark of the U.S. Army with CAUTION and EXPLOSIVE ORDNANCE stenciled on them. The larger crate sat on the floor in the empty and dilapidated room. The top had been pried off and the younger policemen, known as Moon Pie, stared anxiously at the crate as if it were a living thing. Moon Pie was short, heavily muscled, seemingly with no neck, and had a too-big head with overly exaggerated features. Describing him as ugly was like describing the sky as blue. His eyes darted from the crate to the open doorway as he stood; feet spread, one hand on the radio mike clipped to the epaulet on the shoulder of his uniform shirt.

The other policeman, Shirl, was older, with short gray hair that stood out from his pink scalp like a wire brush. He wore small, round, wire-rimmed glasses and stood almost two feet taller than Moon Pie. He was less muscular, but he was lean and hard with lips that stretched into a perpetual sneer. Shirl was the senior partner and the sneer became more pronounced when Moon Pie opened his mouth to speak.

"What are we waiting for?" Moon Pie asked. "Let's see if the camel jockey left the right stuff and then get the hell out of here. Man, if we get caught with this in our car, we are royally screwed."

Shirl knew the contents of the crate were the real deal when he pried it open with his knife. That wasn't why he was hesitant. So far they had only talked about doing the job. But his muscle-head partner was right. This . . . they'd reached the point of no return. They were police officers. They would normally arrest someone for doing the very thing they had done just now. His mind sought a way out. He could still call police dispatch. Say he saw a suspicious van leaving the building. Say he went in, found the crate and opened it. It sounded like a story—even to him. And once they drove off with this stuff . . .

If they were caught he'd go to federal prison . . . if he were lucky, that is. Cops don't do well in state prisons.

Shirl had picked the guard shack for the delivery because there was nothing moving for ten blocks in every direction. He and Moon Pie had come down hard on every vagrant or homeless person they'd found in the vicinity. They had taken all of them to jail on trumped-up charges and given them a personal warning not to return. So far no one had.

"Man, we're gonna kick ass," Moon Pie said and his hands mimed a bomb exploding. When he did this the new tattoo on his right forearm glistened like raw meat topped with Vaseline. The tattoo read "Harly Davison." Under the misspelled logo was a likeness of a chopped bike with flames roaring from the tailpipes. Unlike the atrocious spelling, the art was pretty good. Moon Pie was quite proud of the tattoo he'd done himself.

"Shut your pie trap, Moon Pie," Shirl ordered.

"You know I don't like that name," Moon Pie bristled. "Call me Skip. You should stand up for me. I'm your partner."

"Quit talking. Get to work."

"I'm just excited, Shirl. Ya' know." Moon Pie's voice shook like a ten-dollar whore seeing a Corvette rolling to the curb. "Two million dollars does that to me. Shit, partner! Two million bucks each!" Moon Pie threw his head back and literally howled in delight.

Not for the first time Shirl questioned the little muscle head's sanity. The steroids had disturbed more than his features. But Moon Pie was right about the money. Maybe Shirl's luck had changed. In the past, all he could see in his future was finishing his forty years at this glorified babysitting job, trying to keep people from killing each other, directing traffic until his whole body was numb from fatigue or cold, or both. For all of that he could retire with a piss-pot pension that would barely pay for a roof over his head. If this job went as planned, his future held the promise of wealth and power and something else he hadn't had for years. Respect.

Shirl produced a KA-BAR knife from his gun belt. Inside the crate were several small square blocks wrapped in wax paper—each about the size of a stick of butter. The word SEMTEX was printed on the wrapping, and under that, DANGER! EXPLOSIVES! He stabbed one of the blocks with the point of the knife and held it up, causing Moon Pie to run several steps away in a crouch, arms held up to shield his face.

"What the hell ya' doin', Shirl?"

Shirl knew the Semtex was safe without a detonator. It was highly flammable, but malleable like children's clay and could be cut and shaped. Back in his army days, the guys in his unit had used chunks of it to cook with. But apply a small electric charge and one stick of this stuff was like ten sticks of dynamite. BOOM!

"Where are the timers?" Shirl asked.

"Why are you asking me?" Moon Pie whined.

"Because that was your job. Didn't you get everything out of the van?" Shirl stabbed another brick and tossed it to Moon Pie. Moon

Pie fumbled the block of Semtex and it fell to the floor. The look of panic on his face was comical.

Moon Pie carefully picked the Semtex up and put it back in the crate. He hated it when Shirl treated him like a fool. He hated it even more when he called him Moon Pie. His real name was Skip Walker. He was a bodybuilder and had competed all over the state. He hoped to go to the national competition. The steroids he'd used to build muscle had made his features swollen, his face puffy and round, with an exaggerated nose and thick lips. The other guys he lifted weights with had nicknamed him Moon Pie, and he'd made the mistake of complaining about it to Shirl. At least Shirl hadn't spread the nickname around police headquarters.

Moon Pie went outside where the smaller crate still sat and picked it up. He stopped in the doorway, a concerned look on his face.

"Well, bring it over here."

Moon Pie stood perfectly still. "The camel jockey said not to put these with the explosives until we were ready for the fireworks."

"Who?"

"The camel jockey," Moon Pie said. "He said not to put these things together."

Officer Shirley West hated it when Moon Pie opened his mouth and denigrated entire races of people. Not that Shirl was comfortable with Iranians or Iraqis or whatever the hell nationality the guy was who had delivered the crate—9/11 had made everyone distrustful.

"Give me those," Shirl said and yanked the box out of Moon Pie's hands and pried the top off. Inside were several items wrapped in wax paper and then bubble wrap. He unwrapped one, revealing a small brass tube the size and shape of a pencil, with a flat piece of metal protruding from one side.

Shirl said, "This is a pencil timer. Think of a blasting cap with a time delay switch. The Semtex is sticky, kind of like clay. You unwrap the Semtex, press it against whatever you want to blow up, then you stick this timer in it, and pull this tab off." He mimicked pulling the metal tab out of the timer.

"And then run like hell," Moon Pie added with a snort.

"Yeah. You run like hell." Shirl wrapped the timer up and placed it back in the box. He pounded the lids onto both crates. "Put this in the trunk and let's get the hell out of here. We've been off the air long enough."

Moon Pie picked up the crates and there was the sound of a loud pop. Moon Pie almost dropped the crates, then realized the sound came from outside. It was a gunshot. Getting to his gun, Moon Pie juggled the crates, and the top came off the one with the pencil timers. He pulled his gun and went into a shooter's stance, pistol shoved in front, swiveling his body and pointing the gun in every direction. Shirl had barely moved; he was just listening.

"Put that away, dummy!" Shirl growled and shoved Moon Pie's gun down. He scanned the street. Then the surrounding buildings. Shirl then moved to the other side of the doorway and repeated the procedure. Nothing was moving. It was a gunshot, but it was muffled. Maybe it had come from the warehouse across the street, or down the street.

"Sounded like it was close," Moon Pie whispered, still in a shooter's stance, but the barrel remained pointed toward the ground.

"No shit, genius! Now put that away." Shirl's voice had a sting to it.

"Screw you, man," Moon Pie mumbled and holstered the gun.

"Aw, look what you've done now." The pencil timers were scattered across the floor. "If those are damaged, I'm gonna stick 'em up your ass."

"Don't worry about it," Moon Pie said, but he dropped to his knees to gather them up.

Shirl watched and listened in the doorway, and said, "Be sure you got it all and then put the crates in the trunk."

Moon Pie grumbled and tried to stand, but his legs went weak at the unmistakable hardness of a pistol muzzle being jammed behind his ear.

"Hello, Moon Pie," Mr. Smith said and pulled the trigger. The hammer dropped on an empty chamber.

CLICK!

Moon Pie's head jerked so hard he bit his tongue.

"Next time you mess up . . . Do you understand?"

Moon Pie's head bobbed up and down, but Smith didn't think Moon Pie understood. It was tempting to go ahead and rid himself of this one, but there was a better use for him.

Shirl had turned when he heard the unmistakable sound of the trigger being pulled and his hand had instinctively gone to his own sidearm. He saw Mr. Smith with a gun up against Moon Pie's head and lowered his arm to his side.

Smith said to Shirl, "I thought you would have checked out the surrounding area."

Shirl threw an angry look at Moon Pie, whose job that had been.

"The delivery went without a hitch, Mr. Smith. It won't happen again," Shirl said.

Moon Pie licked his dry lips, but remained kneeling. "We thought we heard a gunshot," he said.

"How perceptive of you."

The gun barrel moved away from Moon Pie's head and pointed at the pencil timers. Moon Pie hurriedly picked them up.

Smith said, conversationally, "Someone was in the building across the street."

Shirl glared at Moon Pie but said nothing.

"An ATF agent, according to his credentials." The pistol disappeared inside Smith's suit jacket and his hand came out with a tiny blue piece of plastic, flat and less than one-inch square. "He was taking pictures of you." He handed Shirl the SD card from Killian's camera. "A souvenir of your incompetence. I suggest you burn it. Completely."

A quiet "Oh shit!" escaped Shirl's lips. They were part of a murder now. And not just any murder. The murder of a Fed. If they were caught, they would face the death penalty.

"We have two days, gentlemen," Smith said. "I'm sure I don't have to remind you what's at stake."

"Don't worry, Mr. Smith," Moon Pie said.

Shirl studied his partner's moronic face and, not for the first time, had the feeling he'd gotten himself into something that might get him killed.

"We'll be ready," Shirl said. He hoped it was true.

Chapter Six

The pier at Two Jakes Restaurant and Marina was designed for river travelers to tie off and enjoy fine dining and an assortment of wines, imported beers, and whiskeys that would make an Irishman weep with joy. The walls of the restaurant were mostly floor-to-ceiling tempered glass so the visitors could keep an eye on their boats and have a scenic view of the Ohio.

Jack jumped from the *MISS FIT* to the dock, and Vinnie, the bartender and part-time cook, came down the dock to help him tie off.

"How's it hanging, Jack?" Vinnie asked.

"They don't call me Peter Gunn for nothing, Vinnie," Jack said.

Vinnie laughed and followed Jack inside. "Hey, Jack. Who's Peter Gunn? He a rapper?"

Jack said, "Peter Gunn was a television private eye in the late fifties. He shot all the bad guys and got all the babes."

"I was just kidding. I know who he is and that's you to a T, brother," Vinnie said.

Jack knew Vinnie had a bit of a past, but he didn't look dangerous. More like a pot farmer. Definitely a pot consumer. In any case he was loyal to Jake Brady and had a heart as big as the outdoors.

Jack sat in the far corner of the room where he had a clear view of the doors and the outside.

"What do you want to eat, Jack?" Vinnie asked.

"Got any pizza?"

"You want a Guinness with that?"

"Vinnie, I'm surprised at you. When have I ever not wanted a Guinness?"

"You got it, my man," Vinnie said and went to the kitchen.

Jack sat back and took in the view. To the west he could see all the way downriver to the Blue Star Casino Riverboat with its two-story pavilion surrounded by a park-like setting. The riverboat reminded him of the old 1800s paddlewheel gambling boats made famous by Mark Twain's books. His stories had always conjured up images of riverboat gamblers with walking sticks, stovepipe hats, women on their arms wearing bright-colored gowns and parasols on their shoulders, strolling the decks and grounds. Instead, as he watched now, he saw several fat guys in too-tight bowling shirts leaning on the upper rails of the riverboat. A poorly dressed granny-apple-faced woman was looking Jack's direction, sucking down cigarettes and swilling beer. *Would Mark Twain have written about this? I don't think so.*

A tugboat was across the river, pushing several barges mounded with coal, no doubt heading to the Alcoa plant in Yankeetown. Jack again wondered what life was like back in the days when Evansville was newly settled. No cars. Fewer people. But no pizza.

Vinnie came back and set a beer on the table.

Jack said, "Vinnie, did you know that Guinness Brewery was founded in 1750-something?"

"No, but I can see you take your beer seriously."

"The Guinness family signed a nine-thousand-year lease at forty-five pounds a year on a brewery in Dublin."

"You don't say. Be back with that pizza in a few minutes. I put one in the oven just the way you like it."

A deep voice bellowed from the kitchen doors, "Pizza, my ass!"

Jake Brady stood in the doorway. A flower-patterned apron loosely hung around his bull neck. At sixty-five-plus years, Brady wasn't an old man by any standards. He stood well over six feet tall with a full head of curly, reddish gray hair and huge, hairy, freckled forearms. He had more hair on his neck than most men had on their heads. It was almost comical seeing this giant wearing an apron and cooking mitts. Then Jack saw that Brady was holding an iron platter with a sizzling sixteen-ounce sirloin and baked potato. Brady's specialty.

"Saw you coming up the river," Brady said, and put the platter in front of Jack.

"Save the pizza for me, Vinnie. I'll take it home." Jack said.

Half a dozen customers were in the restaurant, and most were startled when Brady announced in a booming voice, "Hey. Everybody. This is Detective Jack Murphy. The man's a hero no matter what the papers are saying. And, by God, in this place a hero gets a special meal!"

Scattered clapping broke out, and all the attention embarrassed Jack. He didn't know what he was more uncomfortable with— praise or hatred. But his discomfort was forgotten when he cut into the steak. All he'd had this morning was the beer-eal with a side of Guinness.

Brady slid into the seat across from him.

"You really don't have to do this," Jack said.

"Sure I gotta do this." Brady frowned at Jack like he was scolding a truant child. "This place is half yours. Your dad would've done it for you. God rest his soul. Best partner I ever had. He would've told you that this would all blow over. That girl would have killed you if she had half a chance."

"I know," Jack said, and cut into the steak. It sliced like butter and tasted like a bit of heaven.

Brady watched expectantly.

"Orgasm," Jack said.

"Enjoy." Brady stood to leave but Jack stopped him.

"Sit a while. I can use the company." He pointed at the flowery kitchen mitts and said, "That is, if you're not too busy in the kitchen. Or hanging your frilly panties to dry on the clothesline."

"Why, you young pup!" Brady blustered. "I was a cop when you was still messin' your diapers."

"Phone call," Vinnie yelled from the kitchen door.

"Eat your steak . . . hero." Brady picked up the mittens and apron and headed for the kitchen.

Brady was carrying a steaming mug of coffee when he returned. "Better drink this, lad." He set the coffee in front of Jack and picked up the Guinness. "It's your friend, Killian," he said, and brushed a hand through his thick hair.

Jack was confused at first by Brady's shocked expression and then it sank in that Killian wasn't the one on the telephone.

"What?" Jack's jaw clenched. "What's happened?"

"Liddell's coming to pick you up. Killian's been shot. It doesn't look good for him."

Chapter Seven

The Franklin Industrial Complex consisted of abandoned buildings surrounded by a ghetto. Most of the homes were condemned, and waiting for bulldozers to finish what neglect had started. Sheet-metal- and wood-sided buildings lined both sides of the street. The parking and delivery areas had long ago turned to rubble and weeds. The once bustling industrial complex had been sentenced to death by the creation of the new Lloyd Expressway. The expressway budget wouldn't allow for exit and entrance ramps to access Franklin Street, and the life-giving traffic artery to the warehouse district had bled out.

Like grapes on a dead vine, businesses dried up overnight, and many hundreds of workers found themselves unemployed unless they moved to Mexico or some other less-taxed country. Some made the move, some found other jobs, and some were left unemployed and forced on food stamps and public aid. The poor had to survive, and so crimes like burglary, theft, and robbery skyrocketed citywide.

The mayor said the city wasn't to blame and that the building of the expressway was inevitable if Evansville wanted to grow. Putting in a ramp at Franklin or Highway 41 wouldn't fit in the budget. However, money was found for a cloverleaf where the Lloyd intersected with Fulton Avenue . . . a direct route to the Blue Star Riverboat Casino. Jack and probably everyone in Evansville knew the driving force behind the Expressway was to satisfy the interests of the Blue Star Casino, which in turn, increased the casino's revenue exponentially, and by doing so, had lined a few pockets. Politics at its finest.

Jack and Liddell were directed to the back entry, where Officer

Fellwock stood alone in the doorway of the building holding a clip-board.

"Hiya, Jack."

Jack took the clipboard, signed in, and then handed it to Liddell.

"How're the kids?" Jack asked.

"Fine. Just fine," Fellwock said and shook Jack's hand. "Good to have you back. ATF's in there with Captain Franklin. I heard your friend Double Dick's on his way."

"He's not my friend," Jack said. He didn't know why everyone said "your friend." Double Dick hated the very air Jack breathed and the feeling was mutual. Since the victim was a federal agent, Jack had expected some extra pressure, but if Double Dick showed up the crime scene would break down into utter chaos. The entourage of news media that followed Dick around would trample evidence.

Fellwock took the clipboard and said to Liddell, "Nice job with that robbery. You drive like my wife."

"It seemed like the right thing to do at the time," Liddell said.

The officer grinned and waved an arm toward the open door. "As punishment you're stuck with Murphy again. My condolences."

The building had appeared immense from the outside, but it was absolutely cavernous inside. The floor was concrete, the walls were corrugated sheet metal bolted to a framework of steel I-beams curving upward to a pre-engineered roof. Jack could see outlines on the concrete floor where large machines had once been bolted down, but now were gone, dismantled, packed up, and moved to a new location, wherever businesses were fleeing to these days. Maybe, with enough incentives, Japan or India or Russia or North Korea would buy up the land and hire a few Americans. It was ironic how the President's PR crew talked about the number of jobs his term had created and never talked about the number that were unemployed due to outsourcing, not to mention their paying higher medical insurance rates.

A half-dozen crime scene technicians dressed in blue jumpsuits worked the grid. Crime Scene Sergeant Tony Walker was concentrating on an area on the north side of the room. A number of orange and yellow plastic cones created a pattern on the floor. As Jack and Liddell walked in that direction bits of broken glass crunched under their feet.

Liddell got Jack's attention. "Who's that with the captain?"

"SAIC Lenny Misino," Jack said. "The new ATF boss. Killian introduced us. I only know what Killian told me about him, which isn't much. He came from D.C. so he must have done something wrong to get his ass posted here." Jack couldn't hear what the captain and Misino were saying to each other, but the captain's stiff posture and Misino's arm waving and pointing told him the discussion wasn't going well.

Franklin and SAIC Lenny Misino seemed to have come to an agreement and walked over. Captain Franklin made introductions.

Jack shook the ATF chief's hand and said, "Killian introduced us when you first came here."

Liddell and Misino shook hands and Jack asked, "Any word on Killian's condition?"

"Not so good," Misino answered. "Bastard shot him in the face. He's at Deaconess Hospital. Might be in surgery already."

"Let me walk you through what we know," Captain Franklin said. He pointed to a spot where two crime scene techs were working a grid.

"We think Killian was meeting someone," Franklin said, and this caused Misino to scowl. Jack could sense this was what the two supervisors had been arguing about. "He was shot point-blank. Paramedics stabilized him, but he had almost bled out."

Misino took over. "No witnesses, as you might guess. His gun was still in its holster and wasn't fired. His credential case and money were taken, so it might have been a robbery."

Franklin said, "Or someone wanting it to look like a robbery. We've been discussing it and it doesn't make sense. If it was a robbery why didn't they take his gun?"

Jack agreed with the captain, but suggested, "Guns can be traced. Maybe whoever did this knows that. But why take Killian's credentials? Maybe for a trophy. Maybe someone really had it in for him." Jack turned to Misino and asked, "Was it a contact wound?"

Misino said, "I didn't see him before the ambulance took him. But your officer said it looked like a real close-up. Like someone put the barrel just inches from his face."

Jack digested that. If it was a contact wound, or just about, it would rule out a homeless person. Killian wasn't stupid enough to let them get that close. Captain Franklin's opinion that he was meeting someone made better sense. They could get close enough. It was someone Killian trusted. Or maybe he was just blindsided.

"If his ID was taken how did you identify him?" Jack asked.

Franklin answered. "Officer Fellwock spotted a car back behind the building. The driver's door was standing wide open. He thought it was suspicious, ran the plate, and it came back as a government number. Fellwock looked inside the car, found registration and some papers with Killian's name on them. He knew Killian was with the ATF. It crossed his mind that Killian might be working something, but he didn't think he would leave his car door open. He looked around and found the door over there open. Came in. Found him. Called for EMS and backup."

Misino said, "Officer Fellwock saved Killian's life. If he'd gotten to him ten minutes later we would have a murder on our hands."

"Evidence?" Jack asked. Franklin's expression said the answer was no.

"Did anyone properly search Killian's car yet?" Liddell asked.

Franklin said, "Fellwock said the driver's door and the glove box were open. The registration and the papers he found were in the glove box. Crime Scene is processing it, but we don't know if anything is missing."

"Anything else?" Jack asked.

The ATF chief said to Captain Franklin, "I want Murphy on this, Captain. I'll give you any help you need. Resources, men, you name it."

"And Deputy Chief Dick?" Jack addressed the question to Franklin, but Misino answered.

"He won't be a problem. If he gets in your way you call me."

Jack wasn't so sure Misino could deliver on that promise. Dick was more of a politician than a cop. Politicians take care of their own.

"You'll be going to the hospital?" Misino asked.

"I need to check with Sergeant Walker," Jack answered.

"You know his wife, Barbara?" Misino asked.

"I do." Jack had spent a few nights at Killian's house sleeping off a drunk after a fishing trip.

"I personally notified her and had Agent Pons go by her house to take her to the hospital."

"They have two sons," Jack said. "The boys will need to stay with someone a while."

"Taken care of," Misino said. "Agent Pons will meet you at the hospital." He gave Jack the agent's cell number.

Jack was glad Tony Walker was in charge of this crime scene. Tony had been Jack's partner for a couple of years, but he was transferred to Crime Scene when he made sergeant. Jack thought the move was a waste of a brilliant detective, but it proved to be the best of both worlds having a crime scene sergeant who was a helluva detective as well.

"This wasn't a robbery," Walker said.

Liddell said, "I think the ATF chief was embarrassed he didn't know why Killian was here."

Walker stood with arms crossed, his chin propped in one hand. "His car doors were found open. If Killian left them open it means he was pursuing someone and chased them in here and got shot. My guys are going over the car."

Jack didn't buy that. Killian would have called it in if someone was fleeing from him. That reminded him to see if they had found Killian's cell phone or radio. "Suppose Killian was already here— for what reason we don't know. He gets surprised. Shot in the face, close up, which means he probably knew the shooter, which in turn means he was probably meeting someone here. Then the shooter searched Killian's car. Or . . . Killian was made to drive here by someone, then forced out of the car, and taken in the warehouse and shot. But if that were true why would they leave his car doors open? And why not take his gun?"

"Sergeant Walker," a woman's voice called from above them on the catwalk. "I think you should see this."

Jack and Liddell followed Sergeant Walker. Jack said, "If you find his cell phone or radio let me know."

"Will do," Walker said and led them up the stairs to a railed catwalk. The flooring was made of heavy metal mesh, and it ran around the entire upper portion of the warehouse. This was encircled by windows. A tech, an athletic-looking brunette, approached them and indicated she'd found something.

She took them about twenty feet away from the stairs where a single window was open. Jack looked out the window. Below was Franklin Street. Across the street was a warehouse in most respects identical to this one. The only difference was the wooden shack at the opening of a large parking area. *This must be where trucks would check in and leave or pick up loads.*

"This window was open when I got up here. Check this out," the tech said and pointed with a gloved finger.

She was pointing at the hinge for the window. There were signs that it had been lubricated recently.

"Can you open a window on either side?" Jack asked her.

"I tried, but they are pretty stiff. I think I've got some latent prints on this one."

Liddell said, "Killian's fingerprints should be in the database. If you get prints, run his for comparison."

"Will do," the tech said. "But that's not all." She leaned down a little and pointed across the street. "I think those are tire tracks leading up to that little guard shack across the street. Right there," she said, and Jack saw where she was pointing.

Remnants of a tall chain-link fence and posts lay on the ground on either side of the shack where the gates must have at one time stood. The wooden four-by-four posts had been shorn off to the ground, but even from here, Jack could see the tops of them looked disturbed. There were distinct lines running from the street up to the door of the shack where the weeds and rubble had been disturbed.

"Tony, can you ask if any of our people parked there or turned around there?" Jack asked, hoping to rule that out.

"My guys would know better than to do that, but I'll spread the word." He turned to the tech and said, "Good work, Wanda. The crime scene just got bigger. You found it, so go over there and secure it."

Wanda seemed pleased and gathered her gear.

Walker said, "And take a couple of uniform officers with you to check out the shack. Just in case."

"Yes sir," she said. "You want me to finish up here first?"

"I got it," Walker said, and she hurried down the stairs.

"Wait here," Walker said to Jack and Liddell. Digging in a pocket, he came out with paper booties and latex gloves for them. He then walked the catwalk, playing a flashlight beam right, left, up and down, over every surface as he went. He stopped beside a vertical steel I-beam, examining something, then lifting his digital camera and snapping pictures. He motioned for Jack and Liddell to join him.

"Someone was standing here. See." He trained the flashlight on the I-beam. The dust was disturbed at about shoulder height. "Someone rubbed against it. I'm guessing it was someone taller than Killian."

"We're going across the street and then to the hospital," Jack said. "Oh, and let me know about the phone or radio."

Walker said he would.

Jack and Liddell waited in the street across from the guard shack until Wanda, the crime scene tech, had roped off the outside area with yellow tape and motioned for them.

They carefully avoided the trail she had marked where there may be evidence and stepped to the side of the doorway, staying outside.

Wanda said, "I found one small section where I can take a cast of the tire marks." She pointed to a set of colored markers. Then she led them just inside the shack. "There are no surfaces in here to fingerprint, but look at this." She squatted and held a flashlight near the floor, playing the beam horizontally across the dusty surface.

"Boot prints?" Jack asked, and Wanda agreed.

"And something else, right here," she said. Orange crime scene markers were laid out in a large square. "Something was sitting on the floor. A box maybe. See the outline?"

They did. "Can you lift the sole prints?" Jack asked.

She grinned and said, "You bet'cha. I'll get the ESD from the Jeep if you'll stay here and keep everyone out."

Jack agreed and the tech hurried away. He got on his radio and called for a uniform officer to guard the shack and start a second crime scene log.

Jack then called Walker to fill him in on what they had discovered. Wanda came back carrying a small suitcase.

Jack and Liddell walked back to their car, and Jack said, "I need to run by my cabin. I need a few things."

"Gun?" Liddell asked.

Jack patted his waistband. "Never leave home without one."

"Better get some breath mints while you're at it."

"I swear, I only had two beers, Ossifer," Jack said, mimicking a drunk.

"Can you drop me off at my car? I want you to go to the ATF office and go through Killian's desk."

"You're lead detective on this. I'm yours to command, O Wise One."

"I'll go to the hospital after I get cleaned up. I need to ask Barbara some questions. It might be better if I talked to her alone," Jack said.

"Anything else I should do, boss?"

"Yeah, try not to wreck the car. And go the back way. I don't want to run into you know who."

"Yow'sa, boss," Liddell said.

Chapter Eight

Khaled Abutaqa was pleased with himself. He'd make another small fortune from the man who was coming to visit in a few minutes. The delivery he'd made this morning went, as Americans are so fond of saying, "without a hitch." America may be the land of the free, but it was a country where nothing could be had for free.

In his homeland, Abutaqa would be just another mid-level government worker like his father, or a soldier like his three brothers. In his country, he would not be allowed to manipulate the legal system against itself, as was his right—indeed his duty—to do here in America.

In his many years doing business in the U.S., there had been only one small setback. He'd sold explosives to an undercover ATF agent, and Semtex is not exactly something that can be bought at Home Depot. But with the right amount of money, put in the right hands, he'd all but avoided going to federal prison. Even though his attorney was very good—and very well paid—Khaled had served two years. Those years in an Indiana prison were nothing compared to the prisons in Oman. One year there would be a lifetime.

Six months of parole left and then he would be a free man. No more troublesome visits to the parole office. He would get his passport back. Maybe visit his family in Oman. Or maybe bring some family to the U.S. His business was growing, and soon he would need some help.

The ATF had seized his weapons and assets when they had arrested him, but they hadn't found everything. He knew he should just stay off the radar and appear to be going legit, but there was still a need for his particular talents, and he was not afraid.

When he had come to the U.S., he first sold small arms—mostly handguns, ammunition, and cheap assault rifles—and mostly to local gangs or those who could not, or did not wish to, purchase a weapon legally. His contacts in Oman and Afghanistan had given him almost unlimited access to weaponry. He had even purchased U.S. military weapons stolen by less-than-patriotic soldiers. It was exhilarating. Khaled found he could supply anything that was asked for . . . if the price was right.

Many compatriots from home were now living in the U.S. Most had a business enterprise of some sort that gave them a collective pool of resources. With counterfeit traveler's checks supplied by one contact, he could buy shrimp in Louisiana and have it delivered to a restaurant in Indiana owned by another contact. With the proceeds, he would make large purchases of the harder-to-find military items from Afghanistan and Iran and have the items smuggled into the U.S. via a family member's fishing business in Florida.

Mr. Smith had represented himself as someone from a homegrown militia, but Khaled intuited he was nothing of the sort. He had dealt with militants of one sort or another his entire life. Khaled had a nose for the real thing, and Smith was not who or what he said he was. The items Khaled had secured for Smith had piqued his curiosity. Khaled had the feeling from past dealings with Smith that this American was planning something larger than arming a small militia.

Khaled knew a little about Americans and their history. They supposedly fought for freedom for all their peoples, but he knew that only the elite were truly free. He probably knew more about America than most of its citizens. It was always wise to study the enemy, and though he had lived here for many years, he still considered Americans to be infidels, rich pretenders who kept the masses enslaved.

A flicker on one of the monitors built into the wall across from his desk caught his eye. He watched the small white car approaching the house. He checked the other camera views.

Seeing the visitor was alone, Khaled went to greet him.

"Please," Khaled said at the door and motioned for his guest to enter.

Smith entered and came straight to the point. "Do you have the items I requested?"

"It is more comfortable in my office. Please, we will go there and I will make some tea."

Smith followed Khaled into his office. He pulled the door shut and sat in front of the desk. "Do you have them?" he asked in a flat tone.

Khaled moved behind the desk and sat. "Of course, of course, you are a busy man. Let's get down to business. The special items you requested are very hard to come by. My source demanded more money for them and so . . ."

Mr. Smith silenced him with a look.

"Of course there will be no extra cost to you. It will be my gift. If we can do business in the future . . . ?" his words were left hanging in the air.

Smith sat silently, one leg crossed over the other, his eyes never leaving Khaled's. When he spoke, the question surprised Khaled.

"The photo behind you. Are they family?"

Khaled swiveled his chair. "Those are my brothers," he said and tried to smile. The black-and-white photo was of a much-younger Khaled with four other men, all with dark skin, dark wavy hair, full beards, all sharing a strong resemblance. The men were kneeling in front of an armored combat vehicle, each holding an assault rifle and smiling as if this were a family picnic.

"The oldest is studying law at Yale," Khaled said. He tried to point but noticed his hand was shaking and put it back in his lap. "He is on the far left. Next is me, and to my right is the brother who was killed in Afghanistan." Seeing no sympathy in Smith's expression, he continued, "The brother on the far right is the youngest." The youngest one was making a gang sign with his free hand. "He wants to be a rap star. A rapper." Khaled shrugged. "Anything is possible in America, no?"

Khaled opened a desk drawer and brought out a plastic shopping bag with Macy's logo on it. He pushed it across the desk.

Mr. Smith opened the bag. Inside was a matching pair of Smith & Wesson .40 caliber handguns with the barrels threaded to accept a suppressor. There were four fifteen-round magazines, also.

"There are suppressors?"

"Ah, yes," Khaled said, and removed two polished metal tubes from the credenza. He handed one to Smith and laid the other on top of the desk. "As you can see, they are works of art. Very expensive."

Smith said nothing.

"At no extra charge, of course," Khaled added.

Smith picked up one of the pistols and threaded a suppressor onto the barrel. He worked the slide a few times without dropping the hammer, and each time pointed it at Khaled's face and said, "It isn't good to dry-fire a weapon. Did you know that, Khaled?"

Khaled swallowed. "Yes. Yes. Please . . ."

"Relax, Khaled. If I wanted you dead, you'd be dead."

Smith removed the suppressor and examined it. There were no identifying numbers or stamps in the metal, but he was familiar with the model.

"Made by the Israelis for the Mossad," Smith said.

Khaled scowled at the mention of the hated Israeli scum who were so successful at killing his brethren. He hated the Israelis, but they made the best silencers in all the free world.

"These will do for my associates," Smith said, "but I prefer my own."

Khaled shifted in his seat at the sight of the Smith & Wesson pistol that appeared in Mr. Smith's hand. A compact suppressor was already threaded onto the muzzle.

"As you know, truly silenced weapons are a myth. Subsonic ammunition helps, but . . ." Smith shrugged. "And there is a distinct disadvantage of a suppressor. Once it's attached, the normal sighting system doesn't work."

Khaled's eyes never left the gun pointed his direction. The top of the suppressor on Smith's weapon was flattened slightly.

"I modified this one, myself." He sighted down the front of the pistol at Khaled's face and said, "I know what you're thinking. It's not as big as yours. Am I right, Khaled?"

Khaled didn't know how to answer. If he said yes, would he be saying his was bigger than the American's. If he said no, the American might take offense that he was being argumentative.

"It really doesn't matter what you think, Khaled. Mine is much quieter. Shall I show you?"

Khaled's eyes widened. "Please. I have done everything you have asked," he said.

"Have you told anyone? Your brothers perhaps?" Smith asked.

"Wha . . . what?"

"Does anyone know of our deal?" Smith asked, enunciating the words as if to a child.

Khaled felt his face flush. Smith would have to be insane to harm him. After all, he hadn't completed the shipment yet. Regardless, his mouth went dry. The large bore of the suppressor stared like a sightless eye into Khaled's own eyes.

"I swear! No one knows of our arrangements," he said in a pleading voice. "I have the last item ready for you. It's not here. I give it to you. Please!"

There was the barest whisper as the pistol discharged and Khaled felt something sting his ear. His hand went to the side of his head and came away sticky. His shock barely registered when there were two more whispers, and this time he heard glass falling behind him. He turned and saw that each of his brothers in the photo had a bullet hole through the face . . . all except the likeness of Khaled Abutaqa.

"And now no one knows. Do you understand, Khaled?"

"I understand," he said, holding a hand to his bleeding ear.

Chapter Nine

Murphy's Law says: "If finding something is important, you will never find it." Jack hoped Liddell would find something in Killian's office, but his ATF agent friend was the most secretive and independent investigator he had ever known. Even the man's own boss hadn't known what he was working on. Finding anything useful in Killian's office, or at his home, or from talking to his wife, was a crapshoot at best.

Back at his cabin, Jack changed clothes, made Cinderella go out to do her business, and fed her a whole can of Alpo. As he drove his Jeep down Lynn Road he saw the place where his old Chevy truck had been destroyed by two psychos. The truck was now in that great salvage yard in the sky. May it rest in peace.

He pulled into the always packed hospital lot, drove around to the side, and parked in a "Doctors Only" space. He put a placard on the dash that said "FBI." He'd borrowed it from an FBI agent and somehow neglected to return it.

He knew Killian's wife but he dreaded seeing her under these circumstances. It was one thing talking to a victim's family, but Barbara was a friend. He'd eaten in her kitchen. Played poker and drank beer with Killian at their kitchen table. No way could he distance himself from her pain.

He stepped inside the ER doors and felt déjà vu. This was the second time he'd been here in just about as many days. It wasn't him this time, but it was another law enforcement officer. Cops like to think they're invulnerable. It's the lie they tell themselves at the start of each shift. They joke that they are a "force to be reckoned with." Hence, the saying, "If you run from the cops, an ass-whipping is coming along right behind them."

He shook the feeling off and asked after Killian at the security desk. He was told Killian had been taken to surgery. The off-duty cop working the desk hadn't heard yet if he was out of surgery but he suggested that was a good thing. When a cop didn't make it, news spread like wildfire.

Jack stepped off the second-floor elevator and saw a man with dark shaggy hair and dark eyes, maybe thirty, about Jack's size. The man's nose was slightly crooked like it had been broken, more than once, and scar tissue puckered the skin under his right eye. Either he was an undercover cop or a boxer. Jack surmised it was Agent Pons.

"Murphy?" the man said, and they shook hands. "Special Agent Greg Pons."

Jack had heard Pons's name, but most of the ATF spooks were just that, spooks. "Your boss, Misino, said you'd be here," Jack said. "How's Killian doing?"

"He just got out of surgery. Barbara's talking to the surgeon," Pons said.

"Barbara?" Jack asked. He wished he had gotten there sooner. She needed someone to stay and support her. He would call Bigfoot and see if Marcie would come. Maybe she'd call Katie, although he didn't think Katie was up for this. Fear that Jack would be killed was the exact thing that had always gotten between them.

"She's barely spoken," Pons said. "I was able to work in a few questions while we waited, but she doesn't know anything. The kids are with her sister. They don't know about their dad yet."

Jack sat down and Pons continued. "The surgeon said Killian has massive swelling around the brain. The bullet passed straight through his right eye and out the back of his skull. The good news is there are no fragments. He lost the right eye and will maybe lose both. MRI shows a fracture on the left side of the skull. Killian may have permanent brain injury."

Jack grimaced. "It's a miracle he's alive at all."

Pons gave him a look that said, "If you call that being alive."

"Your guys find anything?" Pons asked.

Jack filled him in.

"Sounds like he was either meeting someone up on the catwalk and they shot him, or he was watching the shack across the street and some bastard snuck up on him," Pons suggested. "It would be hard to sneak up on him. Whoever it was must have known he would be up there and was waiting for him."

Jack had come to the same conclusion.

"Any evidence in the shack why Killian was in that warehouse?" Pons asked.

"I was hoping you knew. Any guesses?"

Pons said, "Killian talked about you. You were friends, so you know it's not unlike him to go all Lone Ranger."

Jack said seriously, "At least the Lone Ranger had Tonto. He should've called me or said something to someone." He remembered Killian had called this morning. If Liddell hadn't shown up at the cabin maybe Killian would have told him what was going on. Maybe not. "So Barbara had no clue what he was up to?" Jack asked.

"She's as in the dark as we are," Pons said.

Jack sat down beside Pons and thought about how he could ask the question on his mind without sounding suspicious or derogatory of the ATF, but he decided he had to ask. Pons seemed like a solid guy. Jack said in a quiet voice, "Have you had problems with cases? Leaks in the office? That sort of stuff?"

"You think that's why Killian didn't tell anyone what he had?"

Jack could tell some horror stories about things getting leaked.

Pons said in a firm voice, "Our office doesn't have any of that shit. Killian would know that none of us would say anything—to anyone."

"Is he having any kind of troubles with anyone?"

"You mean in our office? You think one of us shot him?" Pons was becoming angry.

"Not necessarily. I'm asking if he had problems outside of work. Anything any of you noticed. Threats? Debts? Was he acting different? Problems at home?"

"Screw you, Murphy," Pons said and stood.

"Hey, I'm investigating this. I have to ask these questions. You know that. Right?"

Pons seemed to cool down, but his hands were opening and closing as if they couldn't decide whether to punch Jack in the face or put themselves away. "I get it." He sat down again and put his head in his hands. "Sorry. It's just . . ."

"I had to ask," Jack said to smooth things over. Jack remembered a new secretary coming onboard the ATF at about the same time Lenny Misino was taking over as chief. She was cute, blond, curvaceous, and, according to Killian, a little too nosy. But Jack didn't pursue it. He didn't want to appear to be placing the blame on the ATF any more than he had already.

"Are you going to stay?" Jack asked.

"I am. Someone named Marcie is coming up shortly. She's going to stay with Barbara while I go back to the office and see if I can dig up anything. I'll go through Killian's computer files."

"My partner's doing that right now, and Marcie is his wife. But I'm sure he won't mind a fresh set of eyes. His name's Liddell Blanchard." Jack took out a business card, wrote his and Liddell's personal cell numbers on the back, and handed it to Pons. "Anything . . . anything at all, you call me first."

Pons put the card in his shirt pocket.

"I'm going to get a couple of uniformed officers up here," Jack said.

"You think someone might try to finish the job?" Pons asked.

"Until we know what Killian was working on, we won't know," Jack said.

A black-and-white patrol car was parked behind his Jeep. An overweight older cop named Karp was standing beside the Jeep, writing a ticket. Officer Karp saw Jack and said, "I should'a known." He flipped the ticket book shut and stuck it in his back pocket. "You here about that ATF guy?"

Jack said he was. Karp was about to ask something when Jack's phone rang. He didn't recognize the number. He listened a second and said to Karp, "I've got to take this."

"Go ahead, Jack," Karp said. "To hell with a bunch of doctors. You can park here long as you want. I was only writing the ticket because you had that FBI placard in the window" Karp got in his car and drove away.

Jack held the phone to his ear. "Barbara, how are you? I was just up there to see you."

"Greg told me," she said. "He's in a coma, Jack. He . . . he . . . his face . . ."

"I'm so sorry, Barbara. I know now is not a good time, but can we talk? I've got a few questions if you feel up to it."

"I've already told Greg that Killian wasn't supposed to be working today. But I'm sure he was." Jack heard her take a deep breath.

"I have to ask, but I can come back later. I'm sorry to bother you right now. You'll be okay. Killian's one tough ba . . . guy. Do you need anything?"

"I know you're trying to help. I was told Marcie is coming to stay but I don't know if I feel like company. Of course, Greg is here. He and Killian worked together." She gave a halfhearted laugh and said, "I don't know what I'm saying, Jack."

Silence. Jack could only imagine the thoughts going through her mind. "I would sit with you if I could, Barb, you know that."

As if she hadn't heard him, Barbara said, "When he left this morning I had the feeling something was on his mind. You know he didn't talk about work. He didn't want me to worry . . ." Her voice broke and she began crying. Through the tears she said, "But I notice things. He was wearing his fatigue jacket. The one he always wore when he was on the job. He said it brought him luck. I just knew he was going somewhere he wasn't going to tell me about."

Jack had a dozen more questions, but she'd answered his main one. She obviously didn't know anything, but she had a wife's instinct.

"Barbara, I promise you I'll find whoever is responsible for this."

"A nurse is coming. I've got to go."

"Barbara, wait a second. If you see a police officer sitting in the hall, don't worry. I'm posting a man there. You're not in any danger. I'm just doing it because—"

"You're a good friend, Jack. Thank you," she said.

Jack thought she'd hung up but she said, "You know, he did say something strange yesterday. We planned to take the neighbor's kids with ours to the zoo, and he said he had to do something first."

The neighbor Barbara was talking about was a drunk, abusive, asshole according to Killian. Those kids would be wearing tattered clothes and starving for both food and attention, if it weren't for Barbara and Killian.

"I asked him where he was going, and he said he was going to church. It was Wednesday, and he was wearing his fatigue jacket. I take the kids to church every Sunday, but he never comes with us."

"Jack knew Killian had grown up Catholic, but he never talked about religion fondly. He'd once told Jack that he'd gone to Mass enough in grade school that he was all paid up. It was strange he would tell her that he was going there.

Jack drove to headquarters. He had to get his unmarked car and meet with Captain Franklin and SAIC Misino. He called ahead and they were already waiting in the chief's conference room. Franklin told him he'd just dispatched two police officers to the hospital and there would be round-the-clock security. He had just disconnected when his phone vibrated in his hand. It was Sergeant Walker.

"Tony, tell me you have something," Jack said.

Chapter Ten

Property taxes in Warrick County were half those of neighboring Vanderburgh County, and that alone was a huge draw for the little community nestled around Honey Creek in Paradise. Its proximity to Evansville's super-malls, five-star restaurants, playhouses, and world-class hospitals didn't hurt either. And then there was the Honey Creek Country Club and Golf Course, private boat slips, and Knob Hill Marina, which sat on the north bank of the Ohio River.

Jim Ellert's house was on the lakefront and came with its own covered dock. He and his wife had moved there when they were both pulling down good paychecks, she as an accountant and he as security chief at the Blue Star Casino. Life was good. They owned a thirty-foot cabin cruiser, were members of the country club, held parties and cookouts, and were the talk of the community.

Then a six-figure misunderstanding with one of his wife's clients cost her job. But he assured her it would be okay. He would work double shifts to pay for their accustomed lifestyle. And he did, but it wasn't enough. The homeowner association fees alone ate up a quarter of his earnings, and still his wife continued to spend as if nothing had changed. He filed bankruptcy and was lucky to keep the house, but all the furnishings—and his boat—were gone. For Jim Ellert, Paradise had become a prison.

But he still had his job. He was chief of security and held the rank of major, the highest rank attainable among the small security force onboard the casino. Most of his crew were under twenty-three or over sixty-five years of age and their IQs fluctuated just as much, with some of them dangerously close to being illiterate.

By state law, the Indiana state police kept a contingent of troopers on the boat, so they could handle arrests, but as far as all other security matters, Ellert had final say. He represented the casino. As far as he was concerned, if his security guards were able to do what they were told, they were smart enough. He actually preferred the slow, steady ones to the college kids he was forced to hire recently. The slow ones never asked questions. The college kids always wanted to know why they were doing something, or, worse yet, they tried to make decisions.

Last year, the casino had hired Ken Taylor, a Purdue University dropout but one of the casino owner's family members. Ellert remembered the rude summons he'd received to come to the operations manager's office, where he'd been hastily introduced to Taylor. Ellert was informed that he would still be the ranking security officer, but Taylor was now in charge of security operations.

Taylor had said, "You're dismissed for now, Ellert." Not Major Ellert. Not Mr. Ellert. Not even Jim. Taylor's first act in his new position was to cut Ellert's hours. There would be no more double shifts. As if to rub his face in it, Taylor had given the overtime available to the new guys he had hired. Most of them were Taylor's college buddies, and most were screwups.

Just when things had become unbearable at home, Ellert's wife informed him she had been offered a job. He was ecstatic until she told him the job was as administrative assistant to Ken Taylor.

He couldn't tell her not to work because they were too deep in debt. She took the job and as his hours were cut, she worked extra. The real rub came when she went on "business trips" with her new boss. She was bubbly and exuberant at work, cold and distant at home and in bed.

Then came the divorce and the realization that she was cold and distant only in his bed. Taylor was getting all of her now, and Ellert was getting snickering remarks made by Taylor's college buddies.

The casino offered him a small severance package to leave. He knew they could fire him, and he would get nothing, but he had hinted that he would go to the newspaper with the story of the affair. One thing that was common to all major corporations was fear of bad press. But he was considering the casino's offer. It would give him a new life in a new town and a decent amount of money to start over. That was when chance had brought him to the attention of Mr. Smith.

As he sat alone in his kitchen, he looked around at the yard-sale décor of antiquated appliances and windows with no curtains. One word could describe his current lifestyle: pathetic. How had he sunk to this level? He was always an honest man and a true patriot. When his country needed him, he'd been anxious to serve. He wasn't like that bunch of trash who had come into the service of their country merely for the financial benefits. He truly had believed in JFK's famous words, "Ask not what your country can do for you, ask what you can do for your country."

Smith was offering a windfall of cash, but there were drawbacks. Shirl and Moon Pie. Those two were definite losers. One was a washed-up alcoholic and the other a phobic, steroid-eating idiot. Where he was earning a full third of the take, Smith had bought Shirl and Moon Pie for a song. In Ellert's eyes they were no better than traitors. Shirl and Moon Pie were committing more than just a crime. They were forsaking an oath to protect the public and uphold the Constitution. He had never taken such an oath, and he owed his employers no allegiance.

Why shouldn't he get some of the gravy for a change instead of the shit he had been served? He deserved more money. He was more important to Smith than those two "sellouts." Without him, the job didn't have a chance of success.

He rolled up the papers on his kitchen table and shoved them in a cardboard tube. He thought about the bass boat he'd bought from an estate sale for next to nothing. It was worth every penny he'd paid for it. Meaning it was crap and he felt sick about losing his cabin cruiser, but it got him to work and back for half the gas his car took, and in half the time.

Just a few more days and he would be rich beyond his wildest dreams. Of course, he would have to play it smart, continue to work for a month or so after it was done. And during that month he would love every single minute, watching Taylor take the blame for the failure of security, seeing the defeat and humiliation on that jerk's face. What would his cheating ex-wife think of Taylor then?

Chapter Eleven

Jack parked his Jeep on Sycamore Street along with a line of marked police units. No personal vehicles were allowed but everyone knew it was his Jeep. He left the FBI placard on the dash and crossed to the street.

Walker and Liddell were waiting for Jack outside the executive offices' entrance in the front of the police department and they went in together.

Jennifer Mangold, the chief's secretary, sat behind her desk. She was forty, going on fifty, with a year-round dark tan and deep lines around her mouth from years of chain smoking. Her ability to find out secrets had kept her in her job through three administrations. Her face seldom showed any expression other than boredom or disdain, no doubt from several decades of dealing with the public.

"Hey, Jennifer," Liddell said.

"Are you in trouble, Jack?" She motioned down the hall with her head.

"Does the Pope shit in the woods?" Liddell remarked.

Without expression she said, "No. He doesn't. But there's undoubtedly some of it waiting for you in there. The ATF chief is here and he's not happy. He just came out and asked if 'Murphy' was here yet. You can go in."

When they entered the conference room, Jack saw ATF Chief Misino alone in the room sitting by the door.

"About time," Misino said.

"Sorry," Jack said. *My ruby slippers are at the shoe shop, asshole.*

"What do you have?" Misino demanded.

"Let's wait for the captain," Jack suggested.

"My bosses are asking questions, and I don't have answers," Misino shot back. "The only thing stopping the FBI from taking this case over is because I asked them to give you some time. Except for Killian being one of mine, I don't have a dog in this fight. We can't even say he was working an ATF case."

Jack knew that the FBI didn't investigate murders unless the crimes were multistate or of federal officers. The shooting of an ATF agent would get their interest, but it was still the jurisdiction of the City of Evansville. His jurisdiction.

Misino glanced at his watch. "I thought your boss was supposed to be here."

The door opened again and Captain Franklin came in. He sat at the head of the table. "Sorry, gentlemen."

"There's been a development, Captain," Jack said and turned to Walker.

Sergeant Walker addressed the group. "I've got a couple of things. We found a window open on the catwalk . . ."

Misino rolled a finger in the air, as if to say get on with it.

Walker took a plastic evidence bag from his pocket. It appeared to contain a slender metal ink pen.

"Let me see that," Misino said.

Misino turned the bag over in his hands. Pulling a pair of reading glasses from his pocket, he examined it closely and then looked at Jack. "I've seen one of these. What you have here is a World War II–type detonator. It's a timer used with explosives. There's a vial with acid inside. You crush the vial, stick it in whatever explosive you have, and clear out. They used something like this to try and blow up Hitler's bunker." He asked Walker, "Where?"

"The guard shack. It was stuck in a crack in the floorboards."

Misino scowled at the device as if blaming it for his current troubles. "Any idea how long it's been there? A day? A week?"

Walker answered. "I saw a thick film of dust on everything around it, but the detonator was clean."

"Now, at least, we know part of the reason Killian was up on that catwalk," Misino said.

"He was watching a deal going down across the street," Jack said, but didn't add that it still didn't explain why Killian didn't tell anyone at the ATF what he was doing.

Walker opened a manila folder and took out several 8x10 photos. He spread them out on the table. "In front of the guard shack we lifted tire impressions from two distinct vehicles. One was a car tire. Specifically a Goodyear P225/60R16 Eagle RS. Those are the same type of tires that are bought surplus from the government for police vehicles."

"You think one of our guys parked there?" Captain Franklin asked.

"I asked everyone," Walker said. "None of our guys were parked there, or even turned around in front of there, Captain. And those tires aren't exclusively sold to police departments."

"They might be from Killian's car," Misino said. "That doesn't prove anything. He might have pulled in there and turned around."

Walker said, "I checked Killian's tires, and they are different. The second set of tire impressions came from a van, but they're a common tire. I can tell you that both vehicles were backed in." He pushed the photos in front of Misino. "You can keep those."

Walker took another set of photos from the envelope. "These are from the inside of the guard shack. We found three sets of shoe prints. Two are boot impressions, different sizes, and the soles match Rocky boots." Walker held up his boot. "I wear Rocky brand boots," he said. "You can see the pattern is identical."

Misino waved a hand in a dismissive gesture. "They could be anyone's boots, for Christ's sake. My grandma probably wears Rocky boots. Are you trying to say cops are involved in this? It sounds like you're saying a cop shot Killian. Hell! Our cars probably use those same kinds of tires, and I'm sure some of my guys wear Rocky boots. Killian might have checked the building out the day before the deal."

"There were two sets, Chief," Walker said patiently. "And they were different sizes. I already checked Killian's shoes against these. He was wearing lace-up shoes, not boots."

Captain Franklin spoke up. "Lenny, we're not saying anything. Sergeant Walker is just telling us what he found."

Misino was angry, and Jack couldn't blame him. One of his guys went down, and he didn't want to think a cop or one of his own guys was responsible. But it was one explanation of why Killian wouldn't say anything to anyone.

"The evidence is what it is, Lenny," Franklin said.

"Tony, you said there were three sets of shoe sole impressions," Jack said.

"The third set of shoe prints are from a smooth-sole dress-style shoe. Size ten. The boots were sizes eight and a half and ten. Killian's shoes are eleven."

The ATF chief examined the photos. "You guys have a K-9 cross-trained for drugs and explosives, don't you?"

"Johnny Hailman's dog, Captain," Jack said. "Johnny's off duty today."

"I'll call him in. One of you meet him at the scene, Jack. Tony, get someone over there and tell them what's going on."

Misino said, "Killian wouldn't have been there for a drug deal, Captain. If you don't mind, I'll get one of my guys to meet your K-9. My guy was previously Army EOD in Afghanistan." EOD is the Army's designation for Explosive Ordnance Disposal.

"Of course," Franklin said. "Anything else, Sergeant Walker?"

Jack didn't think it was such a good idea to send an ATF guy, considering what they thought might have happened. But there are EPD people all over the scene still, and it could as easily have been one of them. He said, "Tony's got more."

Walker took two evidence bags from his shirt pocket and passed them down the table. Inside one was a brass shell casing. In the other was a small lump of brass and lead.

"I found the shell casing on the catwalk. It was stuck in the mesh floor." To Jack he said, "Remember that I-beam where it looked like someone had brushed against it? The casing was about five feet farther on. It's a Winchester .40 caliber."

"I think the shooter was standing up against the back of the I-beam. While Killian was looking out of the window, the shooter would only have to take a few steps to shoot him."

Everyone thought about that and agreed it was very likely what happened.

Walker said, "Assuming that was how it went down, I had my people search the other direction we thought the shot had come from and no luck. Then we found the smashed bullet on the floor under the catwalk stairs. We haven't run ballistics yet, but I'm guessing the bullet is a .40 caliber. Like the shell casing suggests."

"Can you send this evidence off to the state police lab, Lenny?" Captain Franklin said. He knew the ATF would get a faster turnaround. Misino put the evidence bags in his pocket.

Walker said, "That's all I have for now."

"Jack? Liddell?" Captain Franklin said.

Jack said, "I talked to Killian's wife. She said a couple of days ago he was leaving the house, and she asked where he was going. He told her he was going to church."

Misino's head came up. "You sure that's what she said? Church?"

"Barbara's exact words. Does it mean something?"

Misino said, "That's what my guys call it when they go talk to a resource—'going to church.' I'd never heard that phrase before, but they said it was because they were always praying the snitch had something solid. If Killian said that to his wife, then he was going to meet an informant."

Jack said, "Barbara said he always wore a tattered Army fatigue jacket when he was doing surveillance or something outside the office. Said it was his lucky jacket. He was wearing the fatigue jacket yesterday when he 'went to church.' And he wore it today when he left the house. Killian may not have told anyone about the information because he didn't trust the source."

"We're just making assumptions," Misino said. "Maybe he was in the wrong place at the wrong time. Or someone lured him there. We need proof. We need something solid."

"Anyone have anything else?" Franklin asked. "Then let's get back to work." He put a hand on Misino's shoulder. "Thanks for the help, Lenny."

"I'll show this detonator to my guy and then get all this stuff sent to the lab pronto and make sure it's a priority. My guy will meet your guy at the guard shack," Misino said on his way out of the room.

Before everyone left Franklin crooked a finger at Jack. "I need you in my office," he said, and left Jack and Liddell alone in the room.

When the captain was out of earshot, Liddell said, "If he fires you, can I have your Captain Midnight super-secret-decoder ring?"

"Bite me, Bigfoot. Get your own." Jack said.

Franklin was sitting behind his desk. "Shut the door. Have a seat," he said to Jack, and slid a police report across the desk.

Jack shut the door and sat. The police report was about an armed robbery. Eddie Solazzo had been arrested.

"Solazzo's dead," Jack said.

"Look at the place I've marked."

Jack saw a pencil mark under the words ".40 caliber Smith & Wesson." He remembered Eddie Solazzo had used that type of gun in a couple of robberies.

"Thanks, Captain," Jack said. "You should be a street detective."

"No thanks, Jack," the captain said. "I've got enough trouble with Deputy Chief Dick. And by the way, he's pursuing the complaint that Nate Cartwright's attorney filed on you with Internal Affairs."

Jack felt a knot in his throat. All he needed right now was an Internal Affairs investigation. But the good news was that if Nate Cartwright was filing it with IA, maybe they weren't going federal with the complaint.

"I'll do what I can," the captain said, "but I think he may have you this time, Jack. Honestly, you are your own worst enemy."

The captain seemed to be finished so Jack got up to leave. At the door he turned and asked, "What would you have done, Captain? With Cartwright, I mean."

Without hesitation, the captain answered, "Exactly what you did, Jack. That's why I could never be a street detective again."

Jack found Liddell leaning against the wall next to Jennifer Mangold, arms folded across his chest, eyelids slitted, pretending to snore.

"You're a riot, Bigfoot," Jack said.

Mangold pointed back down the hall and said, "The captain's not going to think so when he sees that."

Jack turned around and saw a Styrofoam cup taped to the captain's door like a crude listening device. Taped to the door underneath the cup was a piece of typing paper with the words "Quiet—Spanking in Progress" written in Magic Marker.

Jack tore the note and cup off of the captain's door. "He doesn't have a sense of humor, Bigfoot."

Liddell's grin grew wider, giving him dimples in his cheeks. "Of course he does. He made us partners, didn't he?"

"You got me there," Jack admitted. "Tell me you found something in Killian's office."

Liddell said, "I was listening at the door. I heard what Franklin said about Double Dick having your ass."

"I can't worry about that now," said Jack. "Tell me about Killian's office."

"Nada," Liddell said. "Agent Pons showed up and helped. I found a piece of paper that had gotten stuck in behind one of the drawers. It had one word written on it. 'Coin.'"

"Coin," Jack repeated the name. He was glad Liddell hadn't said anything about this in front of the captain or the ATF chief. Coin was homeless, dirty, smelly, and a source of information for anyone who gave him some loose change. That was how he got the nickname "Coin." Jack didn't know his real name and doubted if even Coin knew it. Coin's information wasn't usually very accurate because he had killed his brain with alcohol, but now and then he had something solid. They would have to talk to Coin.

"I've got to make a call," Jack said, and dug his phone out of his pocket. The local parole office phone number was on his speed dial, but he no longer knew who would answer. His ex-girlfriend, Susan Summers, had been the chief parole officer but she was now in Indianapolis. He could call her there but it was complicated.

When they had dated, it had started to get serious, but when he was with Susan he was thinking about his ex-wife Katie, and comparing them. Maybe Susan intuited his feelings, and that was why she had left. He had to admit he hadn't tried to argue her out of going. He changed his mind about calling her.

The parole office was just down the street. A walk might clear his mind. Maybe the new guy in charge would let him look at Solazzo's files, and see if they had the name of the person that supplied him the .40 caliber handgun.

"You going to call Susan?" Liddell asked. "I heard the captain say something about Eddie Solazzo using a .40 caliber handgun. I forgot about that."

"You can meet the ATF bomb guy at the guard shack. I'll walk over to the parole office. Meet you back here in a bit," Jack said and added. "I don't want to bother Susan."

"You sure you don't want to call her?" Liddell asked.

"You can call her if you want. I need to take a walk and think."

"Do you trust me to meet the ATF guy all by my lonesome?" Liddell asked.

"Bite me," Jack said.

Chapter Twelve

Jack walked down Main Street toward the river and cut through a gangway between DeJong's Fashions and the law offices of Wee, Cheatem, & Howe—his nickname for the law offices of Brockman and Associates.

The Indiana state parole office building was crammed between Ye Olde Wig Shoppe and Williams Jewelry. Oddly, Williams Jewelry had no history of being broken into, but the Wig Shoppe was a different story. It had been burglarized, robbed, and set on fire. No one had ever been arrested, but Jack had always believed the perp was a bald guy with deep hair resentment.

The parole building was fronted with a stylish blend of glazed yellow brick and ornate Bedford stone. Large slabs of stone over the doorway and windows were engraved with images of horse-drawn wagons pulling heavily laden flatboats. In the 1800s and early 1900s, the building was an office for river-trade companies. He couldn't help thinking that if gas prices kept going up, we might be going back to that type of transportation.

The thick glass door was emblazoned with the Great Seal of the State of Indiana and, underneath, painted in gold lettering: INDIANA STATE PAROLE DIVISION. The Great Seal of the State of Indiana is a gold circle with a picture inside of some guy with an axe chasing a buffalo through the woods. Jack had never seen a buffalo until he went kayaking in Montana, but he guessed, at one time, there must have been buffalo in Indiana. Guys with axes must have chased them all out of the state.

When Jack pulled the door open he had to step back as a large burly male came out. The man was somewhere in his thirties and wearing a tank top. His body was covered with a thick mat of dark hair and decorated with prison tats. He was really big. He needed a really big bath. The man bumped into Jack on his way out of the door that Jack had held for him.

"Hey, Chuckles," Jack called after the big man.

The head swiveled, and then the smelly body turned and he gave Jack the evil eye.

"You didn't say thank you," Jack said.

"And," the man said in a surly tone.

"And, I'm having a very bad day. I want you to thank me for holding the door for you. Think you can manage that, Chuckles?"

The man spit a wad of chew on the sidewalk and raised a nicotine-stained finger and pointed it at Jack. Jack pulled his sport coat back to reveal his badge and gun. He could feel heat building behind his eyes. The man saw the .45 on Jack's hip. He lowered his finger and swallowed hard.

"Uh. Thank you . . . Officer," the man said through clenched teeth.

Jack made a dismissive motion with his hand. "You're welcome," he said and walked inside, wondering why he'd tried to pick a fight with the man-mountain. Maybe he needed to feel in control of something, even if it meant getting his jaw broken. Maybe he really wanted to get suspended. Maybe he was deflecting his anger when he should really be punching Double Dick in his Adam's apple.

The parole office building was as austere on the inside as the outside was ornate. The floors were carpeted with the same dirty indoor-outdoor carpet that was there when he was dating Susan. A stained path still ran down the middle of it from the trooping feet of the walking dead. The walls were painted a puke-green.

Several parolees, both men and women, sat around surfing their cell phones, texting, or making drug deals, and pretending not to notice the cop in the room. He walked to the glassed-in countertop and saw that Miz Johnson-Heddings was still there. She was a hatchet-faced woman of about sixty or ninety, bony and wrinkled with the leathery skin of a reptile.

"You're looking especially lovely today, Helen," Jack said with what he hoped was a disarming smile.

She said, "Do you have an appointment?"

Thinking that her hair was pulled back so tight that it might have caused some brain damage, Jack said, "It's me. Jack!" He smiled and pinched his own cheek in a grandmotherly way. "You know—your favorite son. Little Jacky?"

"What do you want?"

If looks could kill, you'd be dead, lady.

"I come in peace," Jack said. "I need to talk to the Chief Parole Officer, so if you'll tell him I'm here . . ."

"Everyone's busy . . . as you can see," she said.

Jack looked around the lobby. There were four ex-cons pretending not to hear the conversation. He stared at her until she picked up the phone. "Detective Murphy to see you," she said. "I told him you were busy." She listened, and then said, "I'll bring him back."

"Don't bother," Jack said. "I know the way." Before Miz Johnson-Heddings could get up, he let himself through the door marked "Employees Only" and turned left at the hallway. Susan's old office was the second door on the left.

Jack rapped on the partially open door and could hear music of Gershwin or Chopin or one of those dead guys coming from inside. He pushed the door open and saw the office décor had changed dramatically. The room was still filled with books from floor to ceiling, but they were now neatly arranged in piles on the floor in front of the overfull bookshelves. Where the chairs were once covered with folders and books and boxes, a comfortable loveseat was pushed against a far wall. An Amish-made electric fireplace sat in a corner. Just inside the door was an antique hall tree with an IU baseball cap hanging from a hook.

He rapped on the door again. Still no answer. He walked in, and a head popped up from behind the desk.

"Susan?" Jack said, surprised. "What are you doing here?"

"Hi Jack," she said, and smiled at him.

"I didn't know you were back," he said.

"Actually I'm not. Back, that is. I'm filling in for the new guy, Stan Guzman. He's had surgery and will be out for a while."

"Miz Johnson-Heddings led me to believe . . . well, never mind. It's good to see you." He had a hundred questions he wanted to ask. He wanted to ask if she was back in town for a while or for good. He wanted to ask when she had come back and why she hadn't called to let him know. He wanted to ask why she was really here. As the chief parole officer for the entire state of Indiana, it was within her authority to assign someone else to this task. Had she come back to see him? If so, he didn't know how he felt about that.

She preempted his questions by asking, "So, what can I do for the famous Jack Murphy? Or should I say infamous?" She motioned for him to sit, and her expression told him part of what he wanted to know. She hadn't intended to let him know she was here, and although he didn't know why, it bothered him.

He was going to let it go, but he couldn't help but ask, "You weren't going to call me, were you?"

"I was," she said too quickly. "I wanted to call but it's been busy here. Mr. Guzman has been sick for weeks and things have piled up and . . ."

"And you weren't going to call," Jack finished for her.

"Okay. You got me. I wasn't going to call. I was only going to be here a couple of days at most. I've moved on, and I hope you have too, Jack."

She was right. They had both moved on. He didn't know why he felt, what? Betrayed? Hurt? It didn't matter. He was there on a case.

He said, "I didn't know you were a classical music person."

She hit a button on the laptop and the music stopped. "I wanted something to fill the quiet in here. This is the only music Guzman has on his computer."

"I need your help," Jack said. "Did you hear about the ATF agent who was shot?"

"Are you working on that?"

"Yeah. Me and Bigfoot were assigned this morning."

"How are Liddell and Marcie doing? I haven't talked to her for days."

Days? So Liddell knew you were in town and didn't tell me either.

He got back to his reason for being there. "You remember my fishing buddy, Killian?"

"Killian George? He's the ATF agent? Barbara must be beside herself," she said. Susan knew Killian and Barbara through Jack. They had all gone to dinner a few times. "What can I do?"

"Captain Franklin reminded me Eddie and Bobby Solazzo used .40 caliber handguns in some of their heists. Killian was shot with one."

At the mention of Eddie Solazzo, she gave an involuntary shudder. Eddie had taken her and Katie hostage not too long ago. He was going to kill them in front of Jack to punish Jack for killing his brother, Bobby. Jack had saved the two women, but the way he had saved them was one of the reasons she had left town. Not the only reason, but a big one.

"I don't remember anything in the files about the guns they used, but Mr. Guzman was updating all of our files. He's a very meticulous man. Much more organized that I ever was. Be right back."

When she went to find the files Jack walked around the office. Kicked up under her desk were running clothes and two pairs of dirty running shoes. *You still aren't organized, Susan.* He scanned the books on the shelves. One book was pulled partially out. It was old, and he ran his finger over the lettering on the spine. *Don Quixote* by Miguel de Cervantes.

"That's Mr. Guzman's," she said, coming back into the room with a stack of file folders.

"Miz Johnson-Heddings says Guzman is a *Don Quixote* addict. Supposedly he quotes the book all the time and fancies himself as being of a similar mind to the errant knight because he is always 'fighting windmills' with our clientele."

She handed Jack one of the folders, and they both sat down and read. The files were thick. When the Solazzo brothers were still alive they were in and out of prison like it was Walmart.

Jack tried to concentrate on the file, but Susan's coming back to Evansville had thrown him for a loop. He stole a glance at her and remembered when he'd first met her: sitting behind the same desk, piled high with books and folders and paperwork. He remembered getting up and standing behind her, like any warm-blooded man would do—and sneaking a peek down her blouse to see if she was hiding a weapon, which, it turned out, she was. Two of them.

"Did you find anything?" Susan's voice pulled him back to the present.

"Still reading," he said.

She smirked and said, "You've been on the same page for five minutes. Did you go to sleep?"

"I'm a slow reader," he said, and reminded himself he was in love with Katie. Susan was in love with some dentist. And besides, she wouldn't be staying.

"Here. I've got something," Susan said. She handed the file to Jack and said, "Back in a minute."

This was Eddie Solazzo's file. Stuck in the back was a report from the U.S. District Court in Washington D.C. about a guy called Khaled Mohammed Shaliq Abutaqa. *Bet you can't say that five times fast.* Mixed in with the legal mumbo jumbo he read, "illegal sale of weapons and explosives." Jack scanned through the pages but it didn't mention Solazzo until well into the report. Several years ago, Khaled had sold several Smith & Wesson .40 caliber handguns to Eddie Solazzo. Jack found a notation that Solazzo had confessed to purchasing the weapons but the report never said that Khaled was charged. Eddie would know, but he couldn't ask Eddie because questioning during a séance wouldn't hold up in court.

"I've got the file on Khaled Abutaqa," Susan said, coming back into the room. "He was one of mine." She flipped quickly through the file. "I even wrote a note in the margin about Khaled's connection with Eddie and Bobby Solazzo. Guzman must have taken some interest in Khaled recently but he doesn't say why. Maybe there's something else in the file. He wrote under my note about the deaths of the Solazzo brothers and he mentions you."

"Did he say what a stud I am?" Jack said.

"That's not exactly what he called you," she said. "Okay, here's Guzman's worksheet. Khaled was released from federal prison and . . . this is strange." She flipped another page, and then flipped back to the worksheet. "Khaled was transferred from a federal prison in San Pedro, California, to Indiana Department of Corrections and paroled in Evansville. Khaled listed his employment as manager for his uncle's restaurant. Ubhar Omani."

"Is that the uncle's name?"

"The restaurant. The Middle Eastern place down by the casino. It's one of the best in Evansville. Always a crowd."

"It's the only Middle Eastern restaurant in Evansville. Hey, isn't that the place where they lock you in a room and then you have to guess what country you've been taken to, and then wait to be ransomed?"

"You should be open to new experiences, Jack. Eat something different besides frozen dinners."

"I'm open to new foods, but I don't want to eat something that is meant to be ridden. Camelburgers, or shish-ka-yak. Sheep testicles will never pass my lips."

"I can see you need to go back for a refresher in sensitivity training," she said. "Let's move on."

He tapped the folder. "Khaled lives out in the county. When's the last time he's been talked to? Not for a while, I'd guess. Well, I need to talk to him. So do you feel like taking a ride?" He gave her his best smile.

"Let me get my purse. I'll drive."

Ba-da-bing!

Susan still owned the baby-blue two-seater Honda Del Sol. It was a tiny car, made even tinier with the hardtop stowed. From the passenger seat Jack was about eye level with the tailpipe of the truck in front of them. The Del Sol was cramped, but had one thing in its favor—Susan's skirt rode high on the thigh. Not that he was interested.

She turned west onto Lloyd Expressway and drove past the razed lots where the old Sterling Brewery had once stood. The hundred-year-old brick building should have been made a historical landmark, or a museum, but the land was needed for the expansion of the Lloyd Expressway to channel more traffic to the Blue Star Casino. The brewery had to go. All that was left of its history was a rubble-filled lot and two stainless-steel brewing vats, each bigger than the tank of a concrete truck.

Khaled's house was a twenty-minute ride from downtown, so Jack used the time to peruse the file. Stapled to the inside were front and side view photos of a dark-skinned man. The file said he was from Oman. There was another set of pictures loose in the file of the same man but with a full dark beard.

"Put a turban on this guy, hand him a mountain rifle, and he could be the poster boy for Al Qaeda. 'UNCLE OSAMA WANTS YOU,'" Jack said.

"You do know Osama bin Laden is dead?"

"Yeah. They say the same thing about Elvis," Jack retorted. "Says here Khaled Mohammed Shaliq Abutaqa came to the U.S. on a student visa, attended the University of Chicago for three semesters majoring in engineering, then dropped out of school, and his student visa was pulled, but he signed up for classes again and his visa was reinstated. He spent some time in California but everyone out there has a tan. So he moved back to Chi-Town, where he got busted for dealing weapons and explosives."

"It doesn't say all that in there," Susan said, glancing at him.

"I'm reading between the lines. This guy's interesting for two reasons. One, we have the .40 caliber ammunition. Two, we found a timing detonator in the guard shack across from where Killian was shot," he said. "Khaled was convicted and sentenced to five years in a federal penitentiary for selling explosives."

"I remember him slightly. He was very polite. You'll like him."

"Says here he did two years and was paroled. He transferred his parole here because his uncle owns a restaurant and yada, yada. His uncle bought Khaled a house on the outskirts of Vanderburgh County. And . . . the best part. He's on parole for another year. That means we don't need a warrant to search his house," Jack said.

"There is no 'we,' Jack. And 'we' won't be searching his house based on anything you've given me. I have the authority, but I still need a reason."

"Killjoy," Jack said.

"Did Killian arrest him?" Susan asked.

Good question. Killian was posted in Atlanta until about five years ago, so it wasn't likely. Jack read the file more carefully. "No. Killian didn't bust Khalil. Khalil has been clean since he got here, according to the file. The State Department wanted to deport him as an undesirable, but his family must have some kind of oil connection in Oman." Jack asked her, "Where is Oman?"

"What were you doing during geography class?" she asked.

"Probably fighting someone from Oman," Jack said straight-faced. "We had terrorists like Khalil in kindergarten. But the nuns were even worse."

"Khaled," Susan corrected.

"Sorry. I get confused when someone has four or five names."

"If you're really interested, Oman is next to Yemen."

Thanks for clearing that up, Mrs. Wizard. Jack wasn't sure where Oman was, much less Yemen, but it didn't matter. Khaled was *here* now, and like most cons he probably hadn't stopped selling weapons. Susan was right, of course. Jack couldn't get a search warrant issued based on Khaled's past, and she would need more than a hunch to search pursuant to her job. When these idiots get out on parole they sign a paper giving up their constitutional right not to be searched. Maybe a surprise visit by someone from the parole office would yield something.

"Khalil is a loose thread," Jack said.

"Khaled," she said.

"Yeah."

Chapter Thirteen

"His name is Khaled. Please don't call him Khalil. In fact, don't say anything at all to him. You're just a ride-along."

"Yes, ma'am." It felt strange to be working with Susan again or even to be with her again, but he was glad she was around. He had better luck with his cases when he could discuss them with her. She had a way of pointing out things he'd missed. She also had a way of getting on his nerves when she pointed out things he wanted to deny.

Susan made the turn onto McDowell Road. Farm fields stretched out on their right, chest-high cornstalks and then lush green blankets of soybeans and wheat fields that swirled in the winds.

In a few minutes they reached the turn for Khaled's place. The road was gravel and hard-packed earth. She eased to a crawl and said, "Keep an eye out for the number." In the county the mailboxes were across the street from the houses.

They drove past Khaled's address and had to turn around. A rotted post stuck out of the ground where a mailbox belonged. A gravel drive disappeared into groves of pecan trees. She turned down the drive. To keep the dust down so Khaled wouldn't see them coming, she kept her speed down. Jack saw something mounted on one of the trees that made caution inconsequential.

"He has surveillance," Jack said, pointing to the trunk of a poplar. About ten feet off the ground, a small camera was pointed toward the driveway. Susan sped up.

The house was in a circular clearing, and the drive ran around to the back of the house.

"There's another one." Jack gestured to the east side of the house under the roof's overhang. The camera was pointed at the front porch and probably part of the front drive. A small green light glowed on the camera indicating it was active.

She parked in front, and they walked to the door. Susan brought out her badge case, held it up, and knocked firmly.

"Open up, Khaled," she said with a practiced singsong voice. "Parole officer."

No answer.

Jack walked around the side, stepping in front of the camera and waving. "There's a Chevy panel van back here."

Susan knocked insistently. Jack came back and the door opened.

Khaled was a man in his early thirties with dark skin and black wavy hair almost to his shoulders. His hair was slicked back with something like petroleum jelly. He was wearing a bright red western-style shirt with silver and pearl snaps and little horses embroidered on the cuffs and pocket flaps. A red-and-white-checkered bandana was tied around his neck. Tommy jeans, a rodeo-size belt buckle, and expensively tooled Western boots finished the look.

"John Mohammed Wayne," Jack said aloud to Susan.

Khaled looked at Jack like he didn't understand what he'd said. Then he turned his complete attention to Susan's badge and ID. "I do not know you. Only a man comes here," he said and gave Susan a swarthy smile that showed a mouth full of perfect, white teeth. "Please to come in. Come in, Miss . . ."

"Chief Parole Officer Susan Summers," she said.

Khaled looked at Jack and the smile died. Jack expected him to say something like, "Infidel, you die," but he asked Jack, "And you are?"

"Not your concern, Khalil," Jack said.

Might as well piss him off and get it over with.

"Khaled. My name is Khaled."

"Whatever," Jack said.

"Of course. Both come in. Please," Khaled said. His smile was pasted on as he stepped back with a little bow to allow them to enter Casa Khaled.

Khaled motioned toward a well-appointed living room and offered coffee or tea. Susan said, "That would be nice, but no thank you, Khaled."

Jack said, "Nothing for me, Duke." The furnishings looked expensive. The living room was spotless. Khaled either had a maid service, or he had hidden his apron and can of Pledge in a closet with his mountain rifle.

"I see you've noticed my Chippendale," Khaled said, seeing Jack's gaze fix on an ornate secretary desk.

"The dancers? Where?" Jack asked.

"No. Not dancers, Mr. uhh . . ."

"Oh, you mean the furniture," Jack said.

"Yes. What you call a secretary I think. 1940s, mahogany finish, excellent condition." He grinned like a Bedouin pimp at a camel convention.

We're getting along swell.

"Are you a collector, Mr. . . . . uhhh?"

"Yeah. I collect assholes," Jack said, and Khaled's smile vanished. "You could say I'm an expert on assholes, and I think—"

Susan interrupted and stepped between the men. "This is Detective Jack Murphy,"

Khaled expression changed to one of recognition. "Ahhh. You are that Detective Murphy. The one on the news." The Colgate smile was back. "The one that killed two alleged suspects at a bank. One of them young. A female. I am correct?"

"That's me," Jack said. "I think the alleged suspects had half a mind to kill me . . ." He made a gun with his finger and thumb and pointed it at Khaled. "But now one of them has half an alleged mind."

Susan said, "Khaled, I'm here to ask you some questions. Detective Murphy is here unofficially."

"Of course, Miss Summers," Khaled said, once again the gracious host. "But again, may I offer you something? Tea perhaps."

Yeah, get me a can of roach spray and stand still. Jack asked, "Is it true the women in your country are made to cover their faces?"

Khaled was surprised. "You know of our culture?"

"I know enough," Jack said. "For example, you can burn your wife in the street for not obeying you. Or stone a woman for having sex outside of marriage. Of course the men have all the fun and do the stoning. It must be in place of Saturday night football."

A fire burned behind Khaled's eyes, and his jaws clenched. He turned to Susan and said, "Please have a seat, Miss Summers, and tell me what you want of me."

She declined the seat he offered and pointed toward the couch. "I want you to sit down and answer a few questions for me and Detective Murphy," she said.

Khaled sat but Jack could tell that being told what to do by a woman really chafed Khaled's nuts. While Susan asked questions, Jack walked down a hallway to what he thought would be bedrooms. He found three doors, all closed. It was his duty as an officer of the law to make sure no one was lurking inside those rooms with guns or swords or WMDs.

Susan, as Khaled's parole officer, was within her rights to walk through the entire house to make sure Khaled wasn't violating the terms of his parole by hiding weapons, having sex with farm animals, keeping murdered people in the fridge... things like that. Jack thought he could explain his stroll as looking for a bathroom.

From the living room Khaled said, "What are you searching for, Detective Murphy?" To Susan he asked, "What is he doing back there? He has no right to search my house."

Jack came back to the living room. "Can he have a sheep tied to a fence back there?"

Susan turned toward Khaled and asked, "Khaled, are you in possession of weapons or drugs? Or any explosive devices?"

Khaled's eyes turned into slits, and his posture stiffened.

"Is that a no?" she asked.

"No," Khaled said.

"He says he doesn't have any of those things," she said unnecessarily.

"Why didn't I think of that? We could have saved some time and just called him on the telephone, or sent a text message."

She said to Khaled, "I'm going to do a walk-through and if I find any of those things, I can do more to you for lying to me than for being in possession. Do you understand?"

Jack didn't know that she could charge a parolee for just lying. Good thing to keep in mind. "Smart thinking," Jack said. "I agree, you should go through the place. I'll come along to protect you."

Khaled got halfway up then remembered Susan's warning and sat down heavily. "I protest," he said. "This man is not a parole agent. He cannot be in my house."

"Under Title 3, paragraph 14b, a parole officer can enlist the assistance of any law enforcement agency or officer for purposes of conducting a search of a parolee's domicile, et cetera," she said. "Do you want me to take you back to the office and show you the statute? I'll be happy to do that, and you are within your rights to demand that I do so. Of course it might take me several hours to find the code and then to find a witness to swear that I read it to you, and that you understand . . ."

Khaled threw his hands up. "Okay, do what you must. There is nothing here."

She said, "You will remain seated until I'm finished."

Khaled said nothing.

Jack led her to the hallway with the closed doors. He said quietly, "You were impressive back there."

She whispered, "I thought so."

"Will you marry me?" Jack whispered back.

"Don't push your luck," she said.

"I seemed to have hit a nerve with him by being back here. Let's take a peek in these rooms and then see if he has a basement."

"I think you hit a nerve because he doesn't like you."

"What? He doesn't even know me," Jack said. "He'll warm to me. Everyone does."

The hallway had two doors on the right, a door on the left and an archway farther along on the left. The archway probably led to a kitchen. They entered the door on the left. It was a small bathroom with the little white tiles on the floor that were popular in the sixties. The linen closet was stuffed with white towels. A claw-foot tub with a dirt ring took up most of the room. There was a toilet that was missing the seat, a sink attached to the wall, and a medicine cabinet with mirrored doors. She opened the medicine cabinet and read the labels of several bottles of medicine. "He has high blood pressure. And he's taking Zoloft, Bupropion, and Lamotrigine."

"Poor baby is depressed," Jack said. He pulled the towels out of the linen closet and threw them in the bathtub. Susan looked angry, and so he said, "He'll accuse me of trashing his house anyway. I'm just being proactive."

They left the bathroom and opened a door on the right. This was an undecorated bedroom with a simple four-inch-thick mat pushed against one wall. A small rug was spread in front of a window facing east. No closet. A garment rack on rollers held an assortment of white robes, scarves, and other items.

They moved on. The next bedroom was colorful as though someone had used a paint cannon. Walls and ceiling were splotched with uneven patterns of various fluorescent colors. A king-size waterbed took up most of the floor space in the center of the room, and a mirrored disco ball hung from the ceiling. Jack flipped the light switch, and the ball turned. Lights reflected around the room. He turned it off.

"I assume he goes in the other room to pray, then comes in here and . . ."

Susan held her hand up. "I get the picture."

"What would Khaled's imam think?" Jack asked and led the way through the archway into the kitchen. To their left was the doorway that led back to the living room and to their right was the back door leading to a small yard.

"I think you can reach the river from here," Jack said. "Maybe we should see if he has a pirate ship tied up out there."

Susan sighed and opened cabinets while Jack searched the refrigerator. He dumped the ice trays in the sink, dumped a box of oatmeal on top of that, and was about to empty a bottle of spice when she grabbed his wrist and mouthed, "Stop."

He shrugged and screwed the lid back on the jar. Apparently Khaled liked to cook because Jack could smell the lingering aroma of spices. A platter on the table was filled with some kind of mystery meatballs covered with plastic wrap. Susan pulled up one end of the wrap and sniffed the contents. She made a face and quickly replaced the covering.

"Maybe that's yak-berries," Jack said. "You know. From yaks."

Susan pushed him toward the living room. Khaled was still on the couch, arms crossed in defiance or maybe resignation. Jack spied a beaded curtain hanging on the wall behind the entertainment center. There appeared to be another door behind the beads. The base of the entertainment center cabinet was on wheels. Jack rolled it away from the wall, pushed the beaded curtains aside, and opened the door.

"My office," Khaled said.

"No shit," Jack said. Susan followed Jack through the doorway. This room, too, was sparsely furnished. A wood desk sat in front of a heavily curtained window. The chair behind the desk was right out of a cowboy's wet dream. The desk and chair were made of the same dark hardwood, but the chair seat and back was upholstered with brown and white cowhide. On the wall across from the desk was a wall hanging, an intricately carved Western scene of cowboys riding horses hell-bent for leather. Directly in front of the desk was a plain wooden visitor chair.

Jack went to the window and pulled the drapes open. They were heavy blackout drapes, the kind used in bedrooms. *Strange.* An alarm system was on the window. *Maybe the chair is John Wayne's and worth a mint.*

On the wall behind the desk was a knock-off Monet painting and next to it, an American flag. They seemed out of place among all the expensive furniture. The wood carving on the opposite wall seemed out of place as well. It set too high on the wall. Katie would have centered it on the wall. The top of the desk was empty except for a closed MacBook computer.

"It is an ordinary office. There is nothing in here," Khaled said. He was standing in the doorway.

Jack asked him, "If it's so ordinary, why did you hide it? Why didn't you tell us about it when we were searching the house?"

"It is not hidden," Khaled insisted. "You didn't ask about the office, so I didn't tell you."

Jack asked, "Why do you have an alarm on the window? Why the blackout curtains?"

Jack watched Khaled and noticed his eyes didn't blink even once. Jack flipped the computer open and Khaled hurried across the room to shut it.

"You need a warrant to search my personal computer," Khaled said.

"Is there something you don't want us to see, Khalil?" Jack asked.

Khaled stood ramrod straight, arms to the sides, hands made into fists. "I know my rights."

"Sorry. This is a very nice desk. And look at this chair. I mean . . . WOW!" Jack said. He plopped down in the chair and leaned back against the wall with a thump.

"Please, Detective . . . do not sit in the chair," Khaled whined.

"Why shouldn't I sit in the chair? Is it expensive or something?" Jack rocked forward and bumped the arms of the chair into the desk.

"Yes! Yes! Neiman Marcus. Very expensive."

"Does all your furniture have names?" Jack asked. "Americans usually just give names to their kids and their pets. Sometimes guys name their privates. Do you have a name for your little thingy down there? Like Jihad Joe?"

"Jack," Susan said, "out of the chair." To Khaled she ordered, "Get back on the living room couch and stay there. Don't make me tell you again, or we'll be taking that trip I told you about."

Khaled glared at Jack, bowed his head at Susan, and left the office. Jack examined the desk. It probably cost more than he made in six months. "How does some dirtbag like Khaled afford this kind of furniture?" Jack opened the drawers and found them all conspicuously empty.

He looked around the room again, got Susan's attention and asked, "Do you think he has sex in the chair?" and earned a small giggle. He'd forgotten how nice her giggle was.

"I wonder where he got the money for all this." Jack said. "I don't know much about antiques, but he must have a hundred thousand dollars worth of furniture sitting around."

Susan said, "I'll ask him."

"What's missing from this picture?"

"What do you mean?"

"We saw at least two surveillance cameras outside. Unless the cameras were dummies, they were recording, because I saw a little green light glowing on each of them. And there is an alarm on the window here. Maybe Mohammad Wayne has a first-class security system because of the antiques. Or maybe he's back in the illegal-arms business. In either case, where are the monitors? And why is there nothing in the desk?"

"Maybe the cameras really are just to scare away burglars," she suggested.

"If I were a monitor, where would I be?" Jack said and gave the room a closer inspection.

The hardwood floor was immaculate. He lifted the flag and found nothing. He examined the engraving. It was at least two by two foot and an inch thick. He saw it was hinged on one side.

"Lookie here," Jack said, and swiveled the engraving away from the wall. Behind it were three flat monitors built into the wall. Two of them showed the front approach to the house. The third showed a stretch of grass and trees.

Susan opened the computer again and the screen came to life but there was a prompt for a password.

"What's he doing that he needs this type of security?" Jack asked.

"I can't get a warrant for the computer just because he has cameras outside," she said.

She was right. ACLU lawyers and a gaggle of misguided law students were busy attempting to castrate law enforcement and protect the criminals.

Jack considered taking the computer, but he wasn't supposed to be searching the house so it would be hard for him to explain in court later.

"Can I ask him a few questions?" he asked.

"Sure. But remember this is just a routine parole checkup."

Khaled's demeanor was calm when Jack and Susan reentered the living room. Susan sat on one arm of the sofa but Jack stood behind Khaled and just out of sight. He'd found this was an unnerving interviewing position and a calm Khaled wasn't a talkative Khaled. People let things slip when they were nervous or mad.

Susan went first. "Khaled, have you had contact with any felons?"

"Miss Summers, you know I am good citizen," Khaled said, once again reverting to broken English. "I have been, eh—the straight arrow."

The phony accent was too much for Jack. Khaled's English was just fine when he was informing them of his rights. Jack put a hand on Khaled's shoulder and dug his thumb into the nerve bundle behind the neck. "What she's asking, Khalil, is if you've been contacted by any of your old customers."

Khaled twisted away and came to his feet, squaring off with Jack, his face a mask of hatred.

"Answer the question, asshole," Jack said, and came around the couch to stand face-to-face with Khaled.

"What is this shit?" Khaled demanded of Susan. "You don't have a warrant. He isn't a parole officer, and he doesn't even have jurisdiction outside of the city. I don't have to tell him shit! I'll get a lawyer and sue your asses off. This is America. I demand my rights."

"Well, well, your English has—how you say—improved," Jack said. "Remember, if you lie to your parole officer, she can make you go away for a very long time. You won't have a house, or security cameras, or Tommy jeans, or your John Wayne chair. There won't be any more parties in your disco room." Jack backed up a step ready to fight. "And if you threaten me again, you'll have to talk to your lawyer via séance."

Susan pushed between them and faced Jack like he was the problem.

"You didn't answer the question," Jack said over her shoulder.

"You come into my home and offend me with your vile comments."

"Well, your sense of fashion offends me," Jack said. "And I'm sure there are several health code violations in this zoo you call a home."

"Detective Murphy! Leave. Now. Wait for me in the car." Susan shoved him toward the front door.

He gave Khaled a wink and left the house, slamming the door behind him.

Susan emerged from the house two minutes later. Jack leaned against the side of her car with a sheepish grin on his face.

"Good cop, bad cop," he said. "Did he tell you anything?"

"No," she said. "Get in."

When he was in the car, she said, "Good parole officer. Bad cop. Bad, bad, psycho cop. I can't believe I let you talk me into bringing you with me."

"I'm sorry, Susan. I appreciate you doing this. I really do. Maybe I went a little overboard."

"Ya think?" She gripped the wheel so hard her knuckles were white. She started the car and drove in silence. Only when she turned onto Martin Luther King Jr. Boulevard did she speak. "You don't have the right to physically abuse my parolees. What the hell were you thinking? Are you always like this?" Before he could speak, she said, "What am I saying? I knew you were crazy. Now I think I'm crazy."

Jack said, "In my defense I'm a huge John Wayne fan, and Khalil was starting to piss me off."

She parked behind the parole office and sat staring out through the windshield. When she was really angry, she got a slight tic at the side of her mouth. Jack saw the tic was a jackhammer now.

He said in his best imitation of John Wayne Khaled's voice, "You are . . . how you say . . . pretty when mad, tiny infidel woman. Wuh huh."

She tried not to smile but couldn't help herself. She put a hand on Jack's arm and said, "If Khaled calls an attorney and this gets reported up the line, how am I supposed to explain your behavior? I could get fired, you know."

"Look. Susan. You know what I'm investigating. If I hurt Khalil's . . . I mean Khaled's . . . feelings, I apologize."

"Shut up."

"Yes ma'am," he said. "What did Khalil tell you after I left?"

She reached across him and pushed his door open. He started to get out when she said, "Okay. Khaled did business with Eddie Solazzo in the past. He wasn't charged with it, but Khaled says he has a deal in place with the federal prosecutor. I'll have to check on that. He said he sold a .40 caliber Smith & Wesson to Eddie and a shotgun to Bobby. He said Eddie didn't seem to know one type of weapon from another except for big and bigger. Eddie just wanted something that would go 'bang' real loud. Khaled said no one has approached him since he was placed on parole. But we'll never know if he's telling the truth, because I had to cut the interview short when he threatened a lawsuit again. I almost had to grovel. Thanks for that."

"We both know he's lying," Jack said. "But what can you expect a convict to say? 'Yes, small infidel woman, I sell many guns with hope you put me in prison. I miss . . . how you American dogs say . . . decorating cell with Bubba.'"

"Any other observations, Detective Murphy?" Susan asked.

Jack noticed her tone had turned sarcastic, dismissive even. He said, "I think we should have searched that van outside his house while we were there."

"Good-bye, Jack."

"I'm just saying . . ." Jack looked up to see Miz Johnson-Heddings glaring at them from the back door of the office. She seemed to be wearing a different head. This one had barbed wire for a mouth and eyes that glowed like red-hot coals in hell.

He asked Susan half kiddingly, "Does she bite?"

"Not unless you show fear. She can smell it. Are you afraid, Jack?"

"Damn right," he said. He was a little serious. Their day together started out a little rocky, but he got the distinct impression that she enjoyed getting angry at him again. He was growing on her.

This is where she'll say, "I want you so bad, Jack. I get off in a few hours, but I'll always 'get off' for you." Then she'll go inside, and Miz Johnson-Heddings will smile and blow me a kiss.

Susan said, "Well, Pilgrim, the next time you feel the need to abuse someone, please don't call me. Better yet, just kick in their doors and go in guns blazing. Who needs a Constitution anyway?"

Miz Johnson-Heddings now had a mushroom cloud billowing from atop her head. She stepped outside. The date was over.

Chapter Fourteen

Khaled paced his office, cell phone in hand. He'd punched in Mr. Smith's number four times, but each time changed his mind before hitting the send button. He needed answers, but what would Smith do if he even had a hint that Khaled had talked to the police?

Never had he been treated so badly! Who did these crazy Americans think they were? He rubbed his shoulder, and was glad he had hidden his wound under his long hair. The ear had quit bleeding, but he felt the raw flesh from Smith's bullet. At least he'd had the presence of mind to place the cheap oil painting over the bullet holes in the wall. It pained him to burn the photo of his brothers. Maybe he should burn the laptop too. If that woman came back with a warrant it wouldn't just be his computer that would go up in smoke.

He tossed the phone on his desk. "Damn! Damn! Damn!" He had one more delivery to Smith. The thought of the money he would make brought a smile to his face. The pain was forgotten.

Whatever plans Mr. Smith had must be related to why the crazy cop had come. Too much for a coincidence. Smith had ordered two .40 caliber pistols, and then this cop wants to know if he has sold a .40 caliber pistol to anyone. He remembered the name Jack Murphy. He was the one that killed Eddie Solazzo. Murphy had made the connection because Khaled had sold a gun to Eddie. But Eddie was dead. There were no other connections. Khaled was careful to sell only in other states.

He would make this last delivery. Then if Mr. Smith contacted him again, he would kill him. Or he would make an anonymous call to the ATF. It was an empty threat, he knew that, but he was sure that Smith had a lot more to lose than did he, Khaled Ahmed Shaliq Abutaqa.

In one year, he would be free. He would leave the U.S. Go back to Oman. His cousin owned a computer store there and also a nice nightclub with a Western theme and karaoke.

As he sat at his computer deleting everything from the hard drive, he wondered what it might be like to live in the Old West. He had ridden a horse in Afghanistan. He was quite adept actually. And he could shoot equally well with either hand. He would have a leather gun belt made. One with a holster on each side that would strap to his legs. When he got to Oman, he would take his cousin to the desert and practice shooting. But now he would destroy this computer and buy another later. He silently thanked Allah that the parole officer had not taken it.

Chapter Fifteen

Liddell was waiting in the front lobby when Jack returned to police headquarters.

"I met the ATF's explosive expert," Liddell said. "He's so laid back I thought I'd have to take his pulse."

"Did he find—?" Jack asked.

"Not anything useful."

"Did Johnny—?"

"Hailman thought the K-9 indicated on a few places for explosives but we came up zip."

"What did the—?"

Liddell said, "The ATF guy confirmed the detonator was what Misino thought it was. He didn't think anyone used those nowadays and didn't think you could buy it in this country. He said we were lucky it didn't detonate when we picked it up."

"Would you stop finishing my sentences? You don't even know what I was going to ask," Jack said.

"Do too."

"So what am I going to say next, Bigfoot?"

"I don't use that kind of language, pod'na."

"Do you want to hear what I found out?" Jack asked.

Liddell put his hands on his hips. "Well, I was going to ask you, if I can get a word in edgewise."

Jack told Liddell about Khaled, who was on parole, and had supplied the .40 caliber handguns to the Solazzos and that he had a past record of selling explosives. He told Liddell about the visit to Khaled's house and finding the hidden office, the surveillance cameras, and how Khaled had gotten nervous about the computer.

"I'm telling you, Bigfoot, this guy is hiding something. My gut is telling me he's involved in the shooting.

"So now we go talk to Coin," Liddell said. "I know where he's been and where he's going to, but I haven't found him."

"Coin's not usually too hard to find," Jack said.

"I know. Right? Anyway, I got to talking to Johnny Hailman when we were finished at the guard shack and we got to sharing jokes and stuff. Then I tried to chase Coin down but was one step behind him until I found out where he's going to be in about twenty minutes."

"Well, let's go," Jack said. He was still a little hurt that Liddell hadn't told him Susan was back. He wondered who else knew about it and had kept it secret.

On the way to the car, Liddell said, "Let me tell you one of Hailman's jokes."

Jack sighed. "Do I have a choice?"

"No. Okay. Here goes," Liddell said. "A guy leaves his divorce attorney's office and storms down the street to a bar. He sits down, orders a triple Scotch, slings it back, orders another and slings that back and orders another.

"The bartender asks, 'Hey buddy, why so angry?'

"The man says, 'Goddamn lawyers! They're all a bunch of assholes!'

"A customer at the other end of the bar stands up and says, 'Hey! I resent that remark!'

"The man asks, 'Why? You a lawyer?'

"The other customer says, 'No! I'm an asshole.'"

Jack stared at Liddell.

"Get it? He's an asshole and . . . well, I thought it was funny."

"You're driving a bright red Crown Vic. Now that's funny," Jack said.

Coin bopped along the alley, a stained wooden box tucked under one bony arm. He was freakishly tall and emaciated. Thin gray hair grew in patches across a flaking scalp. The fingers of his right hand were permanently stained yellow-brown from smoking. Unfiltered Lucky Strikes when he could get them, stubs and bits of cigarettes from trash cans and street gutters and the floors of toilets when he was desperate. He hustled down the alley with a purposeful lope, panting like a dog, with lips falling back from toothless gums as he stepped over and around things that only he could see.

The box under his arm was as dirty and worn as Coin. It not only held all of his earthly possessions, but doubled as a shoeshine stand. He divided his time between the tiny park on Main Street in downtown, where he offered to shine shoes for two bucks, and sitting on the curb outside the new South Side police substation in Haynie's Corner. He was homeless but not afraid of the police like most of his kind. Hell, he gave information to most of them and a professional shoeshine to boot. He discovered a lifetime ago that when he was asked a question by a cop, it went easier for him if he cooperated and went even better if he had information. If he didn't have any information, he made something up to turn a few coins. That, and shining shoes, was how he got the nickname Coin. No one knew his real name. No one cared.

Over the years he had burned too many cops with "doctored" information, and now he mostly made money by shining shoes. Sometimes though, he could make a little money by witnessing for attorneys in civil injury cases. He saw whatever they said he saw. This was usually good for a bottle of hooch and a couple of nights in one of the cheap motels on Fares Avenue, sometimes with a hooker and he didn't care how old, what they looked like, and he didn't even think about venereal disease—his or hers.

He was small enough to slide in a basement window, so he spent most of his summer nights in the abandoned Riverbend Playhouse on Haynie's Corner. Then the Riverbend had burned down and he was forced to spend a night or two under the Pigeon Creek Bridge sleeping on a piece of cardboard, but in the end he returned to the Riverbend. It smelled charred after the fire, but it was better than sleeping on the wet ground or going to the mission, where they lectured all the time about drinking and the hobos stole his booze and stunk even worse than he did.

Coin was approaching his basement window when he noticed the cop leaning against the wall watching him. By instinct, he turned to walk the other way and bumped into someone that had come up behind him.

"Excuse me," Coin said and tried to move around the man, but a strong hand closed around his arm.

"Hold on, Coin," Jack said.

Coin's eyes widened. "Oh. It's you. Uh, you need a shine Detective Murphy? I'm pretty busy now, but I can get to you later."

Jack held Coin's arm and said, "I'm not looking for a shine, Coin. We need to talk."

"Uh . . . what about, Detective Murphy?" he asked and licked cracked lips.

Liddell pushed away from the wall and said, "Lookie here. We need to know what you and the ATF guy talked about."

"AT what? Oh you mean those guys. I don't know any of them personally . . . like I know you guys," Coin said. "I've seen some of them around, a' course. Can I go now?"

"His name was Killian," Jack said. "Black guy. You talked to him a few days ago."

Coin dropped his precious box and bolted down the alleyway. The sole of one shoe was loose and made a desperate "flap, flap, flap" noise each time it struck the ground. He hit loose gravel and went down hard, rolling head over heels and landing against a brick wall.

"Shit!" Jack said. He and Liddell walked over and checked him for injuries.

Coin had only scrapes. It was the luck of the drunk. They never seemed to get hurt. He tried to get to his feet but Jack pulled him into a sitting position and put a hand on one bony shoulder.

"What's the matter with you, Coin? Why'd you run?"

Coin's eyes shifted right and left like a trapped animal. His long arms wrapped around his chest and he rocked. "I don't know nuthin', Detective Murphy. I swear. I ain't done nuthin'."

Jack pulled Coin to his feet and asked, "What don't you know, Coin?"

"I don't know nuthin' about that black guy. I didn't even know he was what you said."

"ATF?" Jack asked. Coin's Adam's apple bobbed up down while he tried to swallow. "Talk to me, Coin."

"Just leave me alone! I don't hurt no one. I just drink and don't bother no one." His face scrunched up but there were no tears, only true panic in the expression. "I won't say nuthin' to no one. Honest. I won't say nuthin'."

"What won't you say to anyone?" Jack demanded.

Tears ran down Coin's dirty cheeks, leaving trails like a flash flood cutting down a dusty ravine.

"I promise," Coin cried louder. "I won't say nuthin' to no one! I swear to God, Murphy. You know me, Liddell. Tell him I won't talk."

"What won't you say?" Jack yelled. He grabbed Coin by both shoulders and shook him like a rag doll.

"About the cops!" Coin yelled. Then, he put a finger to his lips and in a whisper, said, "I won't say nuthin' about the cops."

Jack let him go. "It's okay to talk to us. It'll be our secret. Tell us about the cops, Coin."

Coin's eyes darted from Jack to Liddell. "I can't, Murphy. They'll kill me."

Jack stayed with Coin while Liddell went to buy a bottle of Wild Turkey. When Liddell returned, Jack sat with Coin on the side steps of the Riverbend Playhouse. He uncapped the bottle and said, "Okay, Coin. Talk."

Coin wiped at his mouth and said, "It was me. I lied to the black guy . . ."

"Killian. The ATF Agent," Jack said.

"I don't know what that is," Coin said. Jack asked him to describe 'the black guy' he had talked to. It was Killian, no doubt.

Coin's eyes shifted from Jack to the bottle, to Jack, back to the bottle, like a game of tennis until Jack screwed the cap back on the bottle.

"Okay. Okay. I lied to him and said I heard it from a hobo. I was the one that heard those two cops in the shack. You gotta get me in the Witness Protection thing."

"Tell me, and I'll make sure the bad guys don't get you," Jack said.

Out of habit, Coin nervously rubbed the fingers and thumb of a hand together.

"I'm asking nicely," Jack said with a scowl on his face. "Tell me or we go downtown and I tell everyone that you talked."

Coin swallowed hard. "Well. It was hotter'n it is today. I was sharing a bottle with a guy I met over by that garage door place. You know the place?"

"Overhead Garage Doors on Kentucky Avenue," Liddell said.

Coin's head bobbed. "I was sharing a bottle with this guy and it was hotter'n blazes. He said he knew a place where it'd be cooler. Se we went to those empty buildings by the train tracks . . ."

"Where? What buildings?" Jack asked. Coin stretched out a bony arm pointing.

"Over there. The big buildings. I used to sleep in them but the cops kept running me off, so I came over here."

"Coin, what about the buildings and the guy?" Jack asked.

"That's where my buddy said he came in town from." He grinned and said, "I ain't never met a real hobo before. I mean I'm homeless n' shit, but he ain't got nuthin' but the clothes he was wearing and . . ."

Jack unscrewed the cap again. Coin's eyes were drawn to it like a moth to a flame. "Coin, focus," Jack said. "Tell us what you heard at the shack, and I'll let you have some."

Coin's words came out in a blur. He told them that he had followed the guy to a wood shack, and the way he described the area, it was the old warehouse district.

"We climbed over the fence," Coin said. "I tore my jeans on it. He showed me a spot in back where we could crawl down in the underneath. It was cool down there in the dirt. We drank and then my buddy went to get some more an' told me to stay where I was. So I did, and that was when I heard someone coming. They was up in the shack over top. I heard heavy footsteps an' talking. Then they stopped talking an' I thought they was gone. I started to crawl out, but I heard laughin' an' they started talking again. I was curious an' there was a board missing up there so I scooched over and took a peek. There was two of 'em, an' they was police. I hoped they wasn't lookin' for me. They talked a little more, then they left. My buddy, he never come back, an' I was worried the cops was there for me so I ran away."

"When did you tell Killian all this?" Jack asked.

"I don't know. It wasn't long after is all I know. He always gives me money an' don't even expect nothing. So I told him what I saw. He's a real generous guy, ya' know that, Detective Murphy? A real gentleman."

"Did you know the two policemen?" Jack asked.

Coin said, "Naw suh. I just saw uniforms an' guns, an' I scooched back so they wouldn't find me."

Jack didn't believe him. Coin knew every cop in the city. But he was scared. Jack didn't blame him for not telling whom he'd seen, but he needed the information. He handed the bottle to Coin, who tipped it up and had half of it drunk before Jack could wrest it away from him.

"Tell me exactly what you heard them say," Jack said, holding the booze just out of Coin's reach.

Coin told them what he'd heard but it wasn't much, or his memory was gone with his alcohol-riddled brain cells. Jack and Liddell took turns running the old guy through his story, but it never changed much. Jack gave him the bottle and watched him slouch off toward the South Sector office where he would sleep it off in the park.

The got back in their car and Liddell said, "Modock, Moonie, Moon, or something like that, right?"

"Those might not even be names. Coin's half a pound short of a brain, Bigfoot."

"Do you believe him?"

Jack thought about it. "Yeah. He was really shook up when he saw us. I've never known him to run from a cop. You think what he heard were nicknames, or was he just making this shit up?"

Liddell thought about that, then said, "I believe that Coin *was* at that shack and heard or saw something. And with what Walker said about the boot prints, I believe there were two guys in uniform in there. Coin should know the difference between cops and security guards, but he was drunk. Plus, he could only see them through a crack in the floor."

"If that part about the policemen is true, it kind of makes sense that Killian didn't tell anyone what he was doing. Two cops talking about getting explosives. Killian was probably afraid—and with good reason—of a leak."

"I get that," Liddell said. "He wanted to check Coin's info out first. Maybe it was just bad timing."

"No one on our department carries a .40 caliber handgun, Bigfoot. We have to carry the Glock .45s."

"Maybe they weren't on duty when they shot Killian. It was a couple of days ago that Coin saw them. Maybe today they were off duty and caught Killian spying on them. Maybe they saw him roll up behind the warehouse."

Jack thought Bigfoot was right, but that meant they weren't much further than they were this morning. "Maybe Coin didn't remember everything . . . or maybe he didn't tell us."

Jack's phone rang and he answered. He listened for a few seconds and disconnected.

"Shit! Better take me downtown, Bigfoot."

Chapter Sixteen

Jack sat in the captain's office. Franklin was in his usual place, behind his desk. Chief of Police Marlin Pope sat in a chair against the wall. Deputy Chief Dick paced directly in front of Jack, hands laced behind his back, nose in the air like Franklin Roosevelt, barely containing his glee.

"You've done it this time, Murphy," Deputy Chief Dick said. "I want your badge and gun. I will be insisting on your termination from service."

"Chief, I don't—" Captain Franklin said, and Chief Pope cut him off.

"Is Nate Cartwright pressing criminal charges, Captain?" Pope asked.

"No, sir. He claims Detective Murphy beat him while he was handcuffed, but at this time he's only making a complaint with Internal Affairs. His attorney is making a fuss and wanting his client's charges dropped. Personally, Chief, I don't think it will go anywhere. The prosecutor will make some concessions and that will be the end of it."

Chief Pope sat silent, staring at the floor. He knew Jack had a temper, and most likely had punched the guy out, but not while he was handcuffed. That wasn't Jack's reputation.

Deputy Chief Dick interrupted. "I don't care what the prosecutor does or does not do. We have witnesses to Murphy's abuse of a prisoner. Internal Affairs assures me the complaint will be substantiated. The victim could change his mind and file charges against this . . . this . . ." he motioned toward Jack, "*rogue* at any time."

Pope asked Jack, "Where are you on Killian?"

Jack's heart sank. He said, "I guess Liddell can take it over. We think Killian was on a clandestine stakeout." Clandestine—meaning unapproved in this case.

Not surprisingly, Chief Pope said, "Jack, I'm going to have to suspend you with pay until IA can look into the complaint. Or until the prosecutor gives us more information on what is happening with the charges against Cartwright. You know that even if Cartwright is tried and convicted, it won't stop the IA investigation?"

Jack sat silent. He was in a bad spot and he knew it, but Deputy Chief Dick acted as if he'd been slapped in the face.

"Chief Pope," Dick said. "I most strongly disagree with that decision. This man should be fired. This isn't his first violation of department policy. I remind you he shot two alleged suspects only days ago and. . . . He's out of control. His partner is out of control. Blanchard intentionally drove . . ."

"Your objection is noted, Deputy Chief," Pope said. To Jack he said, "Leave your badge and gun here with the captain. Liddell can take over any of your cases that are ongoing. Be sure you catch up your paperwork before you leave the building. Stay in touch."

Jack stood and brushed past the deputy chief on his way out, muttering, "Bite me."

Dick turned toward him. "What did you say?" He asked the captain, "What did he say?"

"He said, 'Excuse me,'" Captain Franklin answered for Jack.

Liddell was waiting for Jack in the police department lobby.

"This is getting to be a habit," Liddell said. "In the last three days we've been chewed up and spit out by the brass. What's the plan now?"

"You're in charge, Bigfoot. I'm suspended pending further."

"What? They can't do that. Not now."

"They can, and they did. I need to clear my head, Bigfoot. I'm going for a walk. I'll call you later. Let me know what the reverend tells you."

Liddell stood, mouth agape as Jack wandered down the hall and outside without any clear destination in mind. He'd already forgotten about Double Dick. He was angry with himself for letting his temper get to him. If he had to do it all over, he would never have hit Cartwright—at least not several times.

He meant to tell the captain about Khaled, but he had to get out of there before he did something else he'd be sorry for. He'd tell the captain about Khaled when he had something more than conjecture. He called Liddell and told him not to mention Khaled for now and hung up. Jack was suspended, but it didn't mean he couldn't ask a few questions. He still had some rights.

He walked down the busy Evansville streets and thought about what he'd learned so far. It wasn't much. He hadn't implicated or eliminated Khaled. Two police officers were involved if Coin was to be believed. And Coin said the two cops were talking about explosives and using names like Modock or Mooney or Moon. They were white, male, and cops, and that was basically all Coin knew. Coin told Killian all of this a few days ago, and then Killian pulls a clandestine stakeout and gets shot. Jack wondered if the shooter thought Killian was dead. Maybe he didn't intend to leave Killian alive.

Jack called the security number at Deaconess and was assured there were two police officers setting outside the ICU. When he stopped walking, he was surprised to find himself back at the parole office.

Oh, what the hell. I need to talk to someone.

He hesitated at the front door because he didn't need any more attitude from Hatchet Face, so he walked around to the back door and found it unlocked. He'd have to mention the safety issue to Susan. Anyone could walk in.

Susan's office door was open, and he could hear her humming. She saw him in the doorway, and in a voice that wasn't particularly welcoming, said, "I suppose you need another favor? Who are you going to abuse this time?"

Her words hit a nerve and she saw him wince.

"What happened? Sit down," she said.

Now that he was here, he didn't know what to say. He didn't even know why he'd come. But that wasn't completely true. Susan wouldn't turn away a stray, and that was what he felt like now. He was surprised to hear himself say, "I got suspended."

Instead of a shocked expression she gave him a smile, said, "Oh," and laughed.

He had forgotten how nice her laugh was. "I'm suspended with pay until Internal Affairs is done with me. Double Dick wants my head on a pike as usual, and I guess I'm giving him all the cause he needs."

"I won't ask what you did. If you want to make any further confession, you can go to church. If you want coffee . . ." she said, and seeing the way Jack stared at her she asked, "What?"

"You're a genius."

"Of course I am," she said. "What did I say?"

A few minutes later they were in her Honda again and headed southeast. Jack called Liddell.

Liddell said, "The IA guy caught me when I dropped you off at headquarters. I just got through talking to him."

Jack told him about meeting with Susan again. He said, "Reverend Payne might know something about this. I'm headed there with Susan now."

"The church remark. I get it," Liddell said. "Are you and Susan . . . you know?"

"Shut up," Jack said. "I think Payne will talk with her present. He's a ladies' man."

"Oh, that's the reason you're with Susan. I get it."

"Call Walker to see if there's anything new. Then call the ATF and see if they can hurry the ballistic tests. I'll call you when we leave the reverend's," Jack said and disconnected.

"Are you going to tell me what's going on? And why are we going to see the reverend?" Susan asked.

"I'm taking your advice. We're going to church," Jack said. They were soon in an area of Evansville known as Rosedale—the second oldest section of town—the oldest being the riverfront along Riverside Drive. It was named Rosedale because in the forties and fifties, yards were filled with rosebushes of every variety. It was a beautiful and a prosperous residential area then, but by the late fifties with the end of the war and the overflow of returning, unemployed soldiers, the area became one of the city's poorest and least-maintained communities.

The houses in Rosedale were built in a hurry and set on tiny lots with just enough room for a gangway between them. The rosebushes were gone. The front yards now collected detritus and discarded syringes. Because of the widening of the streets, the side-walks were gone and the homes were only separated from the curb by a narrow dirt walk. The affluent had moved west, outside of the city limits, not wanting to be reminded of what the war had cost them.

These days, you could measure wealth in Rosedale by the sur-veillance cameras, chain-link fences, heavy metal bars instead of screen doors, and pit bulls. Of course that money came from dope dealers and pimps, but they were still the most respected people in the neighborhood. Respectability depends on your point of view.

Most corners were gathering places for business. Drugs were sold in the open to pedestrian and vehicle traffic. Drive-by shoot-ings were commonplace; robberies were a natural by-product. Any time you put poor people, guns, and quick money in the same equa-tion, you are asking for problems. A punk here could make more money taking down a drug dealer than robbing a bank and know that the FBI wouldn't hunt him down. The police figured death was the cost of doing business.

Most of Jack's informants lived here. Driving down most other city streets wouldn't have generated much attention. But in Rosedale, they were getting the treatment. You could feel the hatred and fear. But he didn't hate them back. He knew that under other circum-stances, given different parents, he might be one of them.

"Turn here," he said. She turned onto Line Street. In the middle of the block was a converted, three-story home that now housed the "Church of the Disciples with an Evangelical Witness in Christ." The sign out in front was hand painted, black letters on a white four-by-four sheet of plywood. The "church" housed dopers and con-victs and didn't discriminate on the basis of sex, religion, or crime.

He didn't really like bringing her to Payne's because she cod-dled the old man. And the house was full of degenerates who would lust after her.

He said, "Maybe this was the 'church' Killian was talking about when he told his wife he was 'going to church.'"

"You're not as dumb as you act," Susan said and parked in front. They walked onto the rickety wooden porch. Jack knocked on the door, and it was opened almost at once by the man they'd come to see.

Reverend Payne was hunched over a cane and skinny as a rail. His white hair was picked into an Afro that stood out in stark contrast to his ebony skin. The knuckles of both hands were twisted with arthritis.

"Detective Murphy," Payne said, paused only a second, and added, "and Susan. So nice of you to visit." His voice was deep and confident, belying his seventy-seven years on earth. "Come inside." He turned and shuffled into the foyer. "To what do I owe the pleasure?"

He directed them to a sitting room that reminded Jack of a lobby of a small hotel, a decrepit one, but a hotel nonetheless. Velvet upholstered divans and massive couches and chairs of all sizes spotted the room in no particular plan. Old men and some women occupied most of them. Some read papers or books, and some simply sat and stared at nothing.

"I'm blind, but I can smell your perfume," he said. "Not your perfume, Detective Murphy." He laughed at his little joke.

"Now that you're in a good mood maybe you can answer a few simple questions for me. For us," Jack said. It was stiflingly hot inside the "church," and Jack saw a window open in the large front room. A floor fan ran full blast in front of it. Payne wore sandals on feet whose toes were as twisted as his knuckles. Susan helped Payne sit down, and he let out a hiss as his legs buckled and he dropped the last foot or so onto a cushion.

"Thank you," he said and put his hands on his knees, where they visibly shook. To Jack he said, "You're here because Killian George was shot. And you think I know—what exactly, Detective Murphy?"

Payne had been in and out of prison—mostly in—for a multitude of financial crimes, including counterfeiting payroll checks. Jack made it a habit of never sharing case information with a convict, but there didn't seem to be any choice in this case. He needed Payne's help.

"The investigation is stalled. I need to know about one of your 'flock' that Agent Killian was talking to," Jack said.

Payne shifted uneasily. "You put me in a difficult position, Detective Murphy. My flock relies on my discretion. But my heart tells me you are doing God's work." Sightless eyes stared straight ahead, and he said, "I'll put you in touch with the man that talked to the ATF agent. He can tell you what you need to hear. I'll do what I can to help."

Jack said, "I've already talked to him, Payne. I just need to know if you yourself talked to Killian. Or if you talked to Coin."

"It would mean a lot to us," Susan said.

Chapter Seventeen

As they walked back to Susan's car, Jack went over everything Coin had said and the evidence Sergeant Walker had found in the warehouse and guard shack. They also went over Payne's information. Bouncing ideas off Susan seemed to help him think.

"So Coin lied to Killian. And he lied to you and Liddell," Susan pointed out.

"Yes. But do I believe that two cops have turned terrorist? No. Do I believe some crooked cops are buying explosives? It's possible. Do I believe a cop shot Killian?" He hesitated.

"You think it was a cop that shot Killian?" she asked.

"Let's just say, I'll keep an open mind."

"That's a scary thought," she said as they got in the car.

"I'm glad you came with me," he said.

"You see how I got him to tell us everything. Nonthreatening questions. No rough stuff. You ought to try it sometime."

Jack grunted and leaned back as Susan steered onto Riverside Drive toward downtown.

"What do you make of the names Coin and Payne gave us? Modock?"

"Coin told Payne that one cop called the other Moon Pie," Jack said.

"I used to eat Moon Pies when I was a kid," Susan said. "They were like s'mores."

Jack said, "So we have a cop that's addicted to s'mores or Moon Pies."

They reached police headquarters and Susan stopped in the street near where Jack's Jeep should have been parked. It was gone. "Thanks for the help. I'll let you know what happens," Jack said.

"This is just getting interesting. You aren't getting rid of me yet."

"Susan, I don't want you to get in trouble. How about this? You go through your files again and look for any of the names Payne supplied. Then give me a call."

"That's a man for you. Take, take, take. Not even the offer of a meal."

"Are you asking me out, Miss Summers?"

"Not on your life, bud. But I think I deserve to be kept in the loop. After what you did to my parolee and . . ."

"Okay. I get it. Susan, I would like it if you met me at Two Jakes for a late lunch." He didn't want to get all this started again. Re-girlfriending never ended well. It would be the same old story. Boy meets girl. Boy can't commit. Girl doesn't like that the boy shoots people for a living. Boy loses girl, and she moves to Indianapolis and dates a dentist.

"Do you want to pick me up at my office? Or does Miz Heddings scare you too badly?"

"I'll meet you at Two Jakes. My bulletproof vest is in the cleaners, and I didn't get my Miz Heddings vaccination this year."

Susan glanced at him. "She grows on you, Jack."

"I'm sure she does." *Like a fungus.*

She left and Jack walked across the street to headquarters. Liddell was standing outside by the detectives' entrance, grinning.

Jack told him, "Payne was the one who called Killian a couple of days ago. That's how Killian got on to Coin. Payne said Coin had come to see him and was scared out of his wits after overhearing some policemen talking about explosives. He even said something about an Arab gentlemen being mentioned."

"Could be the Khaled guy," Liddell said.

"We've got names, maybe, but no way to connect the dots."

Liddell raised an eyebrow. "Well, I've got some good news for you."

"I'm fired? And Double Dick was so happy he had a heart attack?"

"Just the opposite," Liddell said. "Captain Franklin said to tell you to get back to work. The IA complaint was dropped, and the prosecutor is filing seven additional counts of rape and aggravated assault against Cartwright. The defense attorney is removing himself as the attorney of record. As of now you're unsuspended, pod'na."

"You don't say?"

Liddell grinned. "I do say. And when Double Dick heard your good news he looked like he had swallowed a porcupine. Someone told him your Jeep was parked in a police spot, and he had it impounded. He's trying to get the FBI to charge you with impersonating a federal agent. He went back to the chief and filed another complaint."

"The FBI placard," Jack said.

"Yeah. Your buddy, FBI Agent Page, told the chief that he had given you the placard and told you to use it. Chief Pope dismissed Double Dick's complaint."

Jack would have to remember to buy Page a fifth of Glenlivet.

Liddell said, "The bad news is that your Jeep was already towed away, but I called Mike's Towing and they're taking it to Two Jakes for you. No charge."

"Sorry for causing a problem, Bigfoot. I should have known better right now."

"Well, you can make it up to me by feeding me."

"I guess I owe you a late lunch. I'm going to get my badge and gun back from the captain and check a few things here. Meet me at Two Jakes in a half hour, and I'll buy."

"Good. I'm hungry," Liddell said and patted his ample belly. "No point in both of us driving. I'll wait for you. I suppose your girlfriend, Susan, will be joining us."

"Susan's not my girlfriend," Jack said. "It's over. She's seeing some dentist in Indianapolis."

"Man oh man! You home wrecker you. You can invite Susan to dinner at my place tonight if you want. I'll talk to Marcie. But it might be kind of crowded with Katie coming and all."

"Oh Christ! I forgot about dinner."

"Its okay, pod'na. When I tell Marcie that you and Susan are back together again she'll understand."

"We are not back together. She's just helping us with the case. I know what I'm doing," Jack said.

"I hope so, pod'na."

Chapter Eighteen

Khaled circumnavigated Evansville by driving the nondescript white rental van north on Highway 69 to Interstate 64 then east to Interstate 164, where he turned south toward the Ohio River. He had decided to stay well outside of Evansville city limits on the way to his destination. The Lloyd Expressway had a reputation for ticket-writing motorcycle cops. It wouldn't do to get stopped.

His pride wouldn't allow him to admit it to himself out loud but he was still shaken by the day's events. First Mr. Smith asking, "Does anyone know of our deal?" and then the whisper of bullets passing beside his ear, and the emptiness behind the man's eyes. His hand unconsciously went to his ear, and his fingers came away sticky. It was bleeding again.

The memory of those eyes would not go away. Khaled had known many types of killers in Afghanistan and Oman and Iraq and Syria. He had worked with jihadists, sold weapons to rebels, explosives for suicide bombers, but this one—this one carried death in his eyes and only darkness was within.

"Relax, Khaled. If I wanted you dead, you'd be dead," Smith had said. Khaled knew the only reason he was still alive was because of the cargo. He was paid handsomely for the handguns and silencers and Semtex, but this last delivery would bring many times that amount. He only had to stay alive long enough to enjoy it.

He patted the handle of the handgun that was half-hidden under his leg and thought about what was in the back of the van. The crates contained items that belonged only in a war zone. What is Smith up to? Is he going to start a war? But the answer to those questions didn't really concern Khaled unless it somehow meant more money or the loss of it. He was involved in gunrunning, money laundering, even a little white slavery, and the people he dealt with were always dangerous. Some were lunatics, religious fanatics, mercenaries, or all three.

He would gladly have missed the chance to meet this psycho. As lucrative as the deal was, something about Smith stank of evil. Yes, this one had the stench of death upon him. He found himself saying a prayer from the Koran that his mother had taught him when he was young. She would pull on his ear until he thought it would fly from his head and make him say a prayer of penance every time he committed some act she viewed as unacceptable. Strange that he would be thinking of that now.

As he exited toward the river camps, he thought about the money he had made and how he would have to stop now that the woman parole officer had found his office. He would have to get another computer and take his to his uncle's office. Then there was the storage room. Thankfully he had cleaned it out to make this delivery. He would have to get rid of the doorway to the basement. He would get that done right away. Some drywall and paint would do the trick.

It was inconvenient, but the house was only temporary. He would complete his parole and move to Florida, where he had family who had assured him that the parole officers and police were more pliable. Anything could be had in America for the right price.

Looking in the rearview mirror, he ran his fingers through his curly black hair and smiled at his image. After the delivery, he would stop by the riverboat casino and flirt with the cocktail waitress who thought he was so handsome. He would have some fun gambling and then later she would favor him with her body. American women were so . . . uninhibited. And when you had a lot of money they were even more so. He felt himself becoming aroused. Tonight he was going to become a very rich man.

Khaled made a sharp right turn onto a narrow tree-lined gravel road, more of a path really. Above the trees he could see the twin bridges that connected Indiana and Kentucky. The gravel ended and the path turned into a rutted trail that wound through towering scrub and rangy trees.

After a half-mile of jouncing, kidney-numbing jolts, Khaled spotted a red flag tied to a branch. He stopped and stepped down from the van. On closer inspection he saw the flag was tied to a freshly cut sapling that was placed across a narrow side trail. He thought it a very clever job of hiding the trail from the curious.

Back in the van, he'd felt anxiety, a chill, what his family would call an omen, but he was not superstitious. He sat up straight and muttered, "To hell with the American!" He spat out the window, drove over the flag and the cut tree. He wouldn't be here long enough to be discovered.

Reverting to his native tongue, he cursed under his breath as he again jarred along the rutted path toward the river. He would meet Smith, unload the cargo, get his money, and get out of here, Allah be willing.

Khaled didn't notice the opening to the trail was being covered with more branches behind him.

Khaled rounded a corner and jammed the brakes hard. His seat belt stretched tight across his chest. He was thrown forward and his gun went flying under his feet. Directly in his path was a black Suburban with the Department of Natural Resources shield on the door. He caught movement in the side mirror. A man had appeared behind the van. He was wearing the dark green jumpsuit that DNR officers wore. His green ball cap partially hid his face as he approached Khaled's door.

Khaled couldn't believe his bad luck. He apparently had stumbled into one of the checkpoints the DNR used for poachers.

"Shit," he hissed, thinking that now he and his van would be searched. He could see the handle of his Beretta 9mm handgun near his feet and tried to kick it under his seat. What would the wildlife officer think when he came across the cargo in the back of the van? It would be a bad thing to shoot this officer, but he couldn't allow the van to be searched.

Khaled leaned as far forward as he could, fingers scrabbling on the carpeting, but he couldn't quite reach the gun before the officer's shape appeared at his door. Khaled tried to look calm as he said, "Have I done something wrong, Officer?" and found himself staring into the silenced barrel of a gun. Then a blinding light.

Quinn picked up a checkered bandana from the seat beside the body and wiped the bloody tissue and detritus from the silencer of his pistol. "And now no one knows," he said.

* * *

Jack got his gun, credentials, and a short lecture from Captain Franklin before Liddell drove them to Two Jakes.

Jack went to his Jeep and searched under the front seat. He found what he wanted and put it in his back pocket.

"Let's eat," Liddell said as they walked toward the building, but when they neared the entrance Jack continued down to the boat dock where the *MISS FIT* was still tied up.

"I thought we were eating here," Liddell said.

"We will. Hurry up."

"Oh boy. I love pic-a-nics."

They saw Susan's little car pull into the parking lot and park beside Jack's Jeep. Jack waved and got her attention.

She walked over and asked, "Are we going somewhere?"

Jack helped her climb onboard. She was wearing cut-off jean shorts, a shirt that tied at the tummy, and cork sandals.

"I thought we were going to eat," she said.

"Me too," Liddell remarked.

"Bigfoot, you could live for a week on what you probably ate for breakfast."

Susan smiled. "Are we stopping somewhere along the way?" Susan asked.

"Yes," Jack said. It wasn't a complete lie.

"Well, it's nice of you to take us out on the boat. So this is what you do when you're suspended." To Liddell she said, "Can you come with us? I thought you were working on a case."

Liddell said, "I am working the case. So is Jack. Let's get going before you piss someone else off. It's been at least a few hours since someone suspended you."

"He's not suspended?" Susan asked.

"Nah," Liddell answered. "Double Dick tried to get him fired today. Twice."

Jack slipped the lines, started her up, and eased away from the pier.

"Things haven't changed," Susan said.

"Well, Captain Jack," Liddell said happily and picked up the sack. "Where we heading for the picnic? That little sandbar across from your place?"

Susan said, "You mean the one Jack's always watching with binoculars? I call it Bikini Beach."

"Both of you just stop," Jack said.

"Where are we gonna eat?"

"Sorry, Bigfoot. We don't have time."

Ten minutes later Jack throttled back and eased into the entrance to a slough. The opening between fingers of land was barely wide enough for the *MISS FIT*. Twenty yards in the *MISS FIT* began to scrape bottom. Thornbushes covered the bank and an uprooted river birch had toppled into the water. Jack threw a line to Liddell and said, "Tie off to that tree."

Liddell tied a line to the birch and asked, "This is where we're going to picnic? Are you kidding?"

"You're fishing if the river patrol or a conservation officer comes by. You two get out the fishing rods. If anyone comes by give a toot on the horn. But don't leave me."

"Jack, this isn't a good idea, pod'na. I mean you almost got fired once . . . twice today. This can't be good. Tell him, Susan."

Susan said, "We're at the back of Khaled's property, aren't we?"

Jack took a pry bar and a flashlight from a compartment under the seat. "I'll be back in ten minutes. Then I'll take you both to Two Jakes for a real meal if you're still hungry."

Liddell began unpacking the fishing gear.

"Aren't you going to stop him?" Susan asked.

"Can anyone?" Liddell said.

Susan picked up her handbag and took her cell phone out.

"Don't call anyone, Susan. If you want, Bigfoot will take you back right now. He can come back for me." Jack stepped out onto the dead tree trunk and wove through the branches toward land.

"I'm coming with you," she said, put the phone in her pocket and stepped out behind him.

"No. You're staying here," Jack said in a firm voice.

"Try to make me?" Susan said.

"Ah, ain't you two cute? It's your first fight. In a while at least." Liddell said.

"Shut up," Susan said.

"You even sound alike," Liddell said and chuckled.

Jack walked the tree trunk and dropped off onto the ground. Susan did the same. "I think it's straight ahead," Jack said. "I remember seeing that big dead poplar from Khaled's office window."

They pushed north through heavy brush to a clearing and stopped. Susan moved up beside him and whispered in his ear, "You still haven't told me what the plan is."

"I have a plan," Jack said. "You don't have to get involved. This is on me."

"We're just going to surprise him, right? So he can't prepare for us like last time," Susan said.

"Absolutely," Jack answered, not really lying. Khaled would be surprised.

The undergrowth around the river wasn't as heavy as Jack expected. They soon came to a clearing just behind Khaled's white clapboard house.

"I'm not stupid," Susan said. "So don't treat me that way."

"Why are you saying that?"

"Well, you brought a pry bar for one thing. Why did you bring it if you aren't planning to break in?"

Jack hefted the pry bar. "It was a gift from my Aunt Lucy. I always carry it for good luck," he said.

"What are we going to do if he's home? Are you going to hit him over the head? Please, Jack. Let's go back to the boat and feed that partner of yours a real meal."

Jack started into the clearing.

"I should have known you—" She stopped talking and wrinkled her nose. The wind had shifted and a distinct odor was in the air. "Something's burning."

Jack smelled it too. "Shit!"

They ran to the back of Khaled's house. A steel fifty-five-gallon drum was being used as a burn barrel. Jack could see flames rising from inside. "We're too late," he said.

"Maybe not," Susan said. "You know we're on camera, right?"

"I can always say I smelled smoke and was checking to see if the house was on fire."

"Yeah. You just happened to be walking from your boat to the back of Khaled's house. He might be home," Susan said. "Let me go up and knock."

"And say what? Excuse me, are those s'mores on the fire?" He didn't want to tell her that he knew Khaled wasn't home. He had been calling Khaled's home phone every ten minutes or so.

He kicked over the burn barrel and looked around for something to put out the flames. He couldn't find anything. He saw something in the fire and kicked it into the grass. It was a laptop computer. "Is that Khaled's computer?"

"Looks like it," Susan said. "It's ruined."

"See if there's anything else." He used his foot to roll the barrel around in the flames to put most of the fire out. Then he noticed a picture frame in the ashes. He kicked it to the side and turned it over with the toe of his shoe.

"Look, Susan."

She pulled the frame farther away from the hot ashes and saw it was a photograph of some kind. The glass was broken, but part of the picture had been spared the flames. She carefully lifted it from the frame and held it up for both of them to see. There were four men in the photo, all squatting by a military vehicle. All four were holding rifles. Three of the men had holes where the heads should have been. One man was smiling into the camera.

"Recognize anyone?" Jack asked.

"Is that Khaled?" Susan asked.

"Yeah, that's Khaled," Jack said. "And these look like bullet holes where the other heads should be."

"What could that mean?" she asked.

"Listen, Susan, if Khaled's in the house, surely he's seen us by now," Jack said. "Why isn't he out here screaming at us?"

"What are we going to do?"

Jack lifted the pry bar and headed for the back door.

"What if he's home?" Susan whispered.

"If he's home, yell 'Surprise!' and hope it's his birthday." He thought Khaled had gotten spooked by their visit, burned everything, and was on his way to Oman.

As it happened, he didn't have to pry the door open. It was unlatched. They entered and went to the office. The desk drawers were scattered around the floor. The American flag hung by one corner, the engraving had been pulled from the wall, and the monitors had been smashed.

"It looks like a tornado touched down in here. Khaled must have gone crazy," Susan said.

Jack pulled back the drapes covering the window. Chips of drywall were on the floor behind the desk, and there was a large hole in the drywall behind where the cheap paintings had hung.

Jack examined the drywall and said, "Someone put their fist through the drywall."

"Maybe Khaled did it and used the paintings to cover it up."

Jack didn't think so. The chips weren't there on their earlier visit. He pulled a small flashlight from his pocket and shined it inside the hole in the wall. "Look. Someone was digging in the studs." He used the pry bar to make the opening bigger.

"See that," he said putting his finger over a round hole in the wall stud. "Have you got a knife?"

"I must have left my utility belt at home," Susan said.

Jack focused the flashlight beam down inside the wall but he couldn't see much.

"Look, Jack," Susan said. "The house was burglarized when we got here, and there was a fire outside. We were just making sure Khaled was okay. We can leave now and come back with the sheriff's department."

"Well, now I'm checking to see if Khaled's in this hole," Jack said and stabbed and pried at the wood with the pry bar until he opened the tiny hole and pried loose a small metallic object.

He put it in his pocket and said, "Okay. Let's go."

She was more than agreeable. When they got outside Jack sifted through the ashes again. From inside they heard a loud popping and then a whoosh, and flames billowed out the office window and the back doorway. A split second later Jack heard an engine start up.

"Shit!" Jack said, and tossed Susan his cell phone. "Call 911!" he said, and ran around the side of the house. He made it to the front yard just in time to hear an engine screaming away. He could make out the outline of a small car, maybe white through the cloud of dust it had raised. It may have been Khaled's.

Susan came up beside him. "Was that Khaled?"

"It wasn't Khaled."

"Are you sure? Did you see?"

"It wasn't Khaled," he said again. "He wouldn't have left his disco ball."

Liddell piloted the *MISS FIT* back to Two Jakes while Jack and Susan examined the partially burned picture and melted mess that was once a laptop. They had climbed back on board while Liddell stowed the fishing equipment and had barely spoken a word to each other or to him.

"So, are one of you going to tell me what happened back there?"

Jack handed Liddell the picture. "The guy that still has a face is the one we talked to this morning. Khaled Abutaqa."

"These look like bullet holes," Liddell said.

"We found that and the computer burning in a trash barrel out back. We saw the computer on Khaled's desk when we were there earlier and he was very protective of it."

"You think he burned it?" Liddell asked.

"I don't think so. I don't know. But I found this," he said, and handed Liddell the bullet fragment he'd dug out of the wall stud. "I found it in a wall stud behind his desk. Someone had knocked a big hole in the drywall. I think they were trying to recover the other bullets." He held up the picture again. "I don't think Khaled would burn his computer, or shoot a picture he was in. I think someone was sending a warning to Khaled."

"Or maybe he's dead," Liddell offered.

Chapter Nineteen

Quinn had parked the Toyota in the side yard, and now sat at the kitchen table. He had found the car in the "for sale" advertisements in the *Courier & Press* newspaper. The recently widowed owner had asked more than the ten-year-old Toyota was worth, but he hadn't planned on paying.

The house was secluded, probably early 1900s, surrounded by fields of corn and soybeans and wheat. The nearest neighbor, Khaled Abutaqa, lived less than a mile away.

He'd come to see the car early this morning and the owner had made him coffee and offered him a slice of freshly made zucchini bread. It was delicious. Maybe the best he'd ever tasted. He told her so and she'd smiled and cut him another piece. She chattered on about her dead husband, her son who had been killed in Iraq, her arthritis, and other uninteresting things. He felt sorry for her. So alone. So abandoned by the advancement of time. He snapped her neck like a dry twig and dropped her down her basement steps.

He'd removed the DNR decals, but he'd needed a place to store the rented Suburban. It had been a bitch to unload Khaled's van and fit the items in the back of the Suburban, and he'd barely been able to manage it alone. He hadn't realized how heavy and bulky some of the things would be. That was his second mistake. The first was in shooting the picture behind Khaled's desk. It had given him momentary pleasure to see the Arab squirm, but then he'd had to go back and remove all traces of his earlier visit.

After he killed the old woman he'd driven the Toyota and parked it in the trees a short distance from Khaled's house and walked the rest of the way. When Khaled's body was found, the authorities would come to his house. Quinn thought to make it look like a home invasion robbery, or a burglary gone badly. When he got inside Khaled's he found the computer. He also found the remains of the picture of Khaled with his brothers. He couldn't leave these behind.

He had noticed a burn barrel behind the house. He'd dumped Khaled's trash can in the barrel, poured gasoline on the computer, and threw it in. The picture went in after that.

With that done he'd turned his attention to the bullets he'd fired into the wall behind Khaled's desk. Shooting the picture was a mistake, but one he could correct. Khaled wasn't a person of interest to the police yet. At least he didn't think he was. The police wouldn't look at the house very hard to try and solve his murder, but if they saw the bullet holes in the wall they would get nosy. He tried to dig the bullets out of the wall, but he had just gotten started when unexpected company had shown up. A man and a woman. The woman was cute. She reminded him of Pamela, from his days in D.C. It was a shame he'd had to kill Pamela.

His first thought was to kill them, shoot them both, but he didn't know if they were alone or if others were coming. And that would leave even more evidence behind. He decided to wait and watch.

He hid in the bathroom, leaving the door cracked. If they discovered him he could dispatch them easily enough. He heard them come in and go to Khaled's office. The woman called the man "Jack" and he discovered the man was a police detective. That was the deciding point. He would have to kill them now. And what better way than another fire?

He made his way quietly out of the front door, set the timer on the incendiary device for thirty seconds, and tossed it into the front room. He was in his car and backing onto the road when he saw the fireball behind him. Now there would be no evidence, and no nosy detective.

And now, sitting here in the old woman's kitchen, he was even more curious why they had come to Khaled's. Quinn didn't think they were looking for him—or even aware he existed. These weren't Agency people. But he hadn't expected some local yokels to interfere, whether intentional or not. Maybe they were looking for

Khaled for some other crime. He hated loose ends but there was nothing to be done now.

He knew the owner wasn't expecting any company. The house would just set empty. He decided to stay the night. Why not? He had an early meeting in the morning.

Chapter Twenty

Jack tied off the port lines, and Liddell and Susan stepped onto the dock at Two Jakes.

"What do we do now?" Liddell asked.

Jack said, "Ballistics on the slug. The computer's probably a waste of time."

Liddell said, "If you ask for that they'll need to know where this stuff came from, pod'na."

"I know someone who'll do it off the books," Jack said. Sergeant Walker would do the comparison without asking any questions.

"Jack, you should turn the computer and the bullet over to the sheriff's department."

"Not going to happen," Jack said. "Khaled's house wasn't a crime scene. As far as anyone is to know it was just a house fire."

"I agree with Susan, pod'na. If Khaled's the guy, we don't want to lose the case. What if the bullet fragment and the computer are the only pieces of evidence that could have convicted him?"

"Point taken, Bigfoot. I need a ride downtown." Now that he wasn't suspended he would need to collect his department Crown Vic.

Liddell didn't argue with him. "I'll wait in the car," he said and walked toward the parking lot.

A smile played at the corners of Susan's mouth. "Is Liddell under the impression we're dating again?"

"The mind of a yeti is a mystery," Jack said.

Susan turned away, looking out over the river. "I've got to say, Jack, there's not a dull moment when I'm around you."

"Yeah. I guess this has been stressful."

"What are you thinking about, Jack?" she asked.

He had forgotten how perceptive she was. "I was thinking about us. The way we used to be and the way we are now. I'm assuming you're still dating your dentist, and I'm still in love with my ex."

"What's wrong with that?" she asked.

"Well, for one thing, Katie won't talk to me."

"Have you even tried, Jack?"

"Look. I'm sorry I brought it up. I've still got a lot of work to do, so . . ."

"Oh no. You're not getting off that easy. If I know you, Katie hasn't answered your telephone calls and you're pouting."

She was right. He was pouting. It was his duty and right as a man.

"Take her flowers. Take her candy. Take her in your arms and tell her you love her, Jack."

"I understand what you're saying. But I don't even know where to start. You know me. I'm a klutz when it comes to that kind of stuff." She should know. When they were living together, he had bought her a jogging outfit for her birthday and left it on the kitchen table. No note. No box even. Being the person she was, she had thanked him, kissed him, and then . . .

"Jack, I'm going to talk to you like a shrink. You're attracted to me. Hell, who wouldn't be," she said. "But you have always been conflicted between anyone you've dated and Katie. You push everyone you date away from you. You use Katie as a convenient excuse to not have a real relationship, or, God forbid, think about getting married. Hell, remarry Katie if that's what you want, but do something. Police work can't be your whole life. It will destroy you."

She turned her head away. "Sorry, Jack. I didn't mean to say all that."

Jack turned his back and said, "Well, I've got to get going. People to kill. Rights to violate." And he left.

"Shit," Susan said.

Liddell turned down Sycamore Street and pulled to the curb by the carport behind the police station. "Want me to wait and see if Double Dick is waiting for you?"

Jack got out and waved him off. "I think Double Dick is off somewhere licking his wounds."

"I think he has someone do that," Liddell suggested and they laughed.

"I'm going to take your advice and see the sheriff," Jack said. "I'll call you in a bit. You shouldn't be there when I meet them. No point in both of us digging a hole."

Liddell tried to argue but Jack insisted. He wasn't sure if he was really going to give all the stuff to the sheriff's department, but it was the sensible thing to do. He would need the county sheriff's help in trying to find Khaled.

"It's late. Let's knock off," Jack said. "I'm going to see the sheriff right now and get rid of this stuff. Then I'm going home. Eat, drink, and go to sleep. You should too."

"See you early," Liddell said and drove away.

Jack was walking along the back of the carport when he heard voices on the other side. He hoped it wasn't Double Dick. That asshole usually spent the afternoon in his office, wearing his dress blue uniform, saluting himself in the mirror.

He stopped and peered around the side and saw it was Captain Franklin, smoking, talking to two men in suits. One of the men was about Franklin's height, older, overweight, with thinning hair, and his sport coat was held open by an ample stomach. The other man was young, with a dark suit, dark tie, and dark perfectly groomed hair. He was right out of a fashion magazine.

Franklin threw the cigarette butt on the ground, crushed it underfoot, and led the men inside.

Jack had never seen these guys before, but they were unmistakably government types. He stayed where he was until he heard the door shut then hurried to his department-issued car. He pulled out onto Sycamore Street and turned left on the ramp leading to Lloyd Expressway.

Chapter Twenty-one

Jack smelled the smoke before he turned onto Boberg Road. A two-tone brown car—VANDERBURGH SHERIFF marked on the side—blocked the entrance to Khaled's long driveway.

Jack pulled onto the shoulder and a deputy approached. His name tag said, "D. Thene." Jack recognized the face but had never really talked to him.

"Is one of your detectives here?" Jack asked, and flashed his badge.

"Sergeant Elkins is down there," Deputy Thene said, pointing down the lane.

Jack knew Sergeant Elkins. He was an old-timer who had come up under the patronage system in a day when you just paid the going rate to the current political party to make rank. He'd asked Elkins one time why he was just a sergeant. Why not a lieutenant or chief deputy? Elkins had replied, "To hell with a bunch o' ball-less brass."

Deputy Thene keyed his shoulder mic and said, "Detective Elkins, EPD Detective Murphy's here to see you."

Jack heard the response. "Okay. Send him down. Tell him to leave his car there."

Jack walked down the long gravel lane feeling a little guilty. He made his mind up that couldn't turn the evidence over. He'd come out here thinking he could pretend to find it in the charred remains. But as he got closer he saw that the house had burned to the ground, and there were too many deputies, firefighters, volunteer firefighters, and civil defense personnel combing through the ashes. He looked at his watch and was surprised to see how late it had gotten. In another hour it would be dark and he wasn't much further than when he'd started. Of course, being in Double Dick's sights all day didn't help matters any.

Elkins was leaning against a German Township Fire Department truck, the stump of a black cigar wedged between his teeth.

"Is that a cigar in your mouth or are you just happy to see me?" Jack said.

Elkins watched him, unsmiling. "I quit smoking," he said. "Goddamn brass made me. The entire department is going 'smoke free.' Bunch o' pussies."

Jack grinned. "You know what Freud would say about that."

"Screw you, Jack."

He'd forgotten how crotchety Elkins was, or how outspoken. The man had nothing but disdain for political correctness. He was a man after Jack's own heart.

"What are you doing here? You didn't come to try and talk me into retiring, did you?"

"Why would I do that? I hadn't heard you were thinking about it."

Elkins took the cigar from his mouth and pitched it in the smoldering remains of Khaled's house. "I ain't never going to retire." He chuckled and had a coughing spasm that sounded like a garbage disposal.

Jack said, "I'm here about George Killian's shooting." He told Elkins what had led up to Khaled as a "person of interest" in the investigation, saying he had interviewed him this morning, but leaving out the part about his breaking in before the fire had started. When Jack was finished, Elkins gave him the stink eye.

"You didn't ask if Khaled was in the fire," he said.

This old bastard is shrewd.

"I assumed you would have more detectives here if a body was found," Jack said.

"We didn't find him or his vehicle. A white Toyota RAV is registered to him. I put an 'attempt to locate' out for him and his car. If we find him, do you want to talk to him?"

"Yeah," Jack said. "I have some more questions for him." Jack started to leave and seemingly as an afterthought, asked, "You didn't find any weapons by chance?"

Elkins shoved his hands in his pockets. "Are you holding back on me, Jack?"

"I've told you everything," *that I'm going to.*

Elkins pointed at the smoking heap that had once been a house. "In the first place, I knew this Khaled guy was on parole for dealing weapons—and explosives. These guys found a concrete room under the kitchen. No weapons. Nothing. Of course, we're still sifting through all of this."

"A hidden room," Jack said. "Huh."

"Did I say it was hidden?" Elkins asked.

"I'm a detective," Jack said. "I suspect it was a grease fire. He had enough in his hair to power a diesel engine."

Elkins broke a smile. "Bet he smoked Camel cigarettes."

Jack walked back to his car wishing he hadn't taken the evidence. It was too late now. He'd wait until after they found Khaled. He might be dead. You can't violate a dead guy's rights. Now that he'd told Elkins that Khaled may have been involved in Killian's shooting, Elkins would kick the search into high gear.

Jack drove west and called Sergeant Walker's cell phone. They talked for a minute and Walker said he would find someone to examine the hard drive and the bullet fragment on the QT. He didn't ask any other questions.

Jack headed for his cabin. He had to feed Cinderella. He'd stop somewhere and get a couple of hamburgers for them both. He'd tell Bigfoot about talking to Elkins in the morning. Liddell would understand. Then they had to get busy and find Khaled. He was sure Khaled was the key to this.

The wind picked up, and the skies grew dark and threatening to the south. He saw a McDonald's ahead, and was in luck, the drive-through was empty. He bought four double hamburgers with cheese. Cinderella liked all the condiments. He bought two supersize fries and pigged out on them as he drove towards home.

Jack turned off Highway 41 and reached his cabin just as the skies opened up and rain came pouring down. He ran through the downpour with the bags of food. He went into the kitchen and used paper towels to dry. Cinderella sat, staring up at him, licking her chops.

"Can you say, 'supersize me'?"

Cinderella bared her teeth and then let out a howl.

"That's pretty good for a mangy mutt." Jack unwrapped two of the hamburgers and dropped them in the dog bowl. He didn't have a chance to give her any fries because he didn't want to get close enough to lose an arm.

The telephone answering machine showed thirty-three messages. "Why didn't you answer the phone?" he said to Cinderella. "I work. I bring home the food. I clean the house. I do the dishes. And what do you do?"

She stopped scrounging in the bowl long enough to look at him and squint. He was sure she could understand English.

He unplugged the answering machine. He didn't feel like listening to anyone. The media and Double Dick had worn him out about the bank robbery, and he didn't want to answer questions about how it felt to shoot a kid. He didn't feel like talking to his mom, who probably was wondering why he hadn't called his brother. In fact he didn't want to talk to anyone.

A flash of lightning lit the kitchen and made him think of the concussion grenade that had almost ended him. He thought of the incredulous expression on the face of the teenage girl. "You shot me," she had said. It was as if that possibility had never entered her mind.

He felt a wet nose on his hand. Cinderella stared at him with a manic look in her eyes. If she could speak she would be saying, "You asshole!" He took what was left of the fries and dumped them in her bowl.

"You can say thank you," he said to her.

She stopped munching and let the biggest fart he'd ever heard. She sniffed the air and then continued to eat.

"Ungrateful. That's what you are," he said, and then, "Why am I talking to a dog? Am I nuts?"

Cinderella chuffed and finished off the fries, and licked the empty bowl.

Jack found a bottle of Scotch where he had hidden it from himself, in a cabinet over the refrigerator that required a chair to make the reach. His thinking in putting it there had been that if he was too drunk to stand on a chair he'd already had enough. His dad had said, "The harder you work for something, the more you'll appreciate it when you get it." He'd appreciate this.

He poured a generous amount in a dirty coffee mug and sipped. Wonderful. He remembered an older detective telling him that Scotch had an essential vitamin—Vitamin Alcohol.

His thoughts turned to Susan and he poured a little more Scotch. They'd been good together. Not the Scotch and him. Susan and him. The way she had looked at him when he first saw her today, and the way she'd smiled at him at Two Jakes, he could tell she was interested. He was attracted to her sexually. *But is that enough?* He *had* loved her in his own way, but he had also loved Katie. He still did. Didn't he? After all, he and Katie were happy until she'd lost the baby and . . . The baby. My child. His eyes grew moist and his throat tightened. *What am I doing?* He took a long swig from the Scotch bottle and put it on the counter.

He reminded himself that he was working Killian's case. He didn't have time for this. He shouldn't even be drinking. He picked up the phone and dialed a number.

"Hello."

"Katie. It's me," he said. It sounded lame, even to him. He didn't know what to say next. Susan was right about him needing to talk to Katie, tell her how he felt, what his thoughts were. He missed her. He should say he was sorry and would do anything to work this out. He should say he loved her and wanted her back in his life. But the words stuck in his throat and wouldn't come out.

"You sound exhausted, Jack," Katie said. He thought *she* sounded tired.

"I'm fine," he lied. "I just wanted to see if you'd heard about Killian." Another lame remark. Of course she'd heard. Killian was one of his fishing buddies from back when they were married. Katie and Barbara had gone on fishing trips with them. He and Killian would fish and drink, the girls would spend the time chatting or watching "girl movies."

Katie was quiet.

"What's the matter?" Jack asked.

"I'm at the hospital, Jack. Killian is in surgery. Jack. Jack, are you there?" she said into a dead line.

Chapter Twenty-two

The tan Crown Vic jumped the curb in front of the ER and parked. Jack rushed inside, took the stairs two and three at a time, and hurried down the hall to the surgery waiting room.

Katie sat on a padded bench with her legs drawn up, her head resting on her knees. She saw him coming and said, "I didn't mean to worry you, but I'm glad you came." She forced a smile.

"How is he?" He sat down beside her, and saw that she looked as tired as she had sounded on the phone.

"His fever spiked and he started seizing about an hour ago. They rushed him back into surgery. The surgeon told Barbara it was something to do with the swelling around his brain. He's out of surgery and stable for now."

Jack looked down the hallway and saw a uniformed officer sitting on a chair outside the recovery room door. The officer raised a hand and Jack nodded.

"How's Barbara?" he asked Katie.

"They let her be with him."

"Do you think there's any chance I can go in for a few minutes?"

Katie's expression turned sad. "No. The surgeon barely let Barbara in."

"I should stay," he offered.

"No offense, Jack, but you look like hell. You push yourself too hard. Marcie was here for a while. She's coming back so we'll keep Barbara company. I'm fine. I can sleep on the couch here."

Her eyes were soft, and something inside him felt like it broke. "Katie, I . . ."

"Please go home and rest. Take a hot shower." Her nose wrinkled.

* * *

The temperature had backed off the ninety-degree mark due to the heavy rain. It was now hovering in the mid-seventies. Jack called Sergeant Elkins and gave him an update on Killian's condition, thinking it might spur Elkins to look even harder for Khaled.

Jack turned onto Sycamore Street with the rain outpacing his windshield wipers. Dispatch had called. Captain Franklin wanted him at HQ. He dreaded it because he was at a dead end until Khaled could be found. He couldn't call Narcotics or Vice or any other intelligence-gathering unit to run the names Moon Pie and Modock. If Moon Pie was a cop, it might tip his hand. No rumor spread faster than a cop under investigation.

He parked and was getting out of his car when a strong hand gripped him by the shoulder.

Jack spun around, knocking the hand away, and reached for his gun.

Franklin and the two guys in suits Jack had seen earlier stood there staring at him.

"Hold on, Quickdraw," Captain Franklin said, trying to make light of Jack's reaction. The two men were holding papers over their heads against the rain.

"Sorry, Captain," Jack said. He cleared his throat and looked at the two suits.

"This is the detective who's working the shooting of the ATF agent. Jack Murphy," he said and made introductions. They were FBI agents from D.C., and both were named John something or other.

The younger agent was square jawed with a buzz cut and a day's growth of hair on his face. He was wearing a smart suit that looked like it had its own name, like Valentino or Bill Blass or the whole family of Brooks Brothers. Jack was sure the suit had a price to match the pedigree. The FBI generally hired attorneys or accountants and not fashion models.

The other guy was more mature, a little more overweight than he'd originally thought, and he looked every bit like a Walmart shopper. His $49.95 sport coat, checked shirt, too-wide tie, and cheap slacks said it all.

"You boys are a long way from home," Jack said. "Why is the FBI from D.C. in little E-ville?"

"Be nice, Jack," Captain Franklin said. "They just drove a long way. What have you been doing?"

"Just checking for leads," Jack answered, truthfully.

Franklin said, "Do yourself a favor and don't give the deputy chief any more to hang you with."

Jack had parked in one of the city council parking spots that were usually vacant. The city council only met once a month, but they had five much-needed parking spaces directly behind the detectives' office.

"Don't worry, Captain. He won't catch me," Jack said. "Do I need to go inside?" He wondered what the hell he'd done now. Or rather, what had the captain had heard. And he wondered if the captain smelled the alcohol.

"Not necessary," Franklin said. "I just wanted to make the introductions. You will be working with the FBI now. You'll want to get together and exchange information."

"Sure," Jack said. *Not.*

The FBI agents just stood there, not offering to shake hands, not speaking, not even flashing their badges like in the movies. Something about them was off, and Jack couldn't put his finger on it. He liked the local FBI and always—well, most of the time—enjoyed working with them. FBI agents prided themselves on being inscrutable, unreadable, large-and-in-charge. But these guys seemed different somehow. He took an instant dislike to them.

"So, Jack," Franklin asked, "did you find something new?"

"So far you know what I know. Nothing worth talking about." *Or that I'm going to tell these bozos.*

"Give these men your contact info and then you should go get some sleep." Franklin said.

"I'm heading home. I'll stay in touch," he said to the agents.

They exchanged business cards and Jack got back in his car to leave. As he drove away he looked in his rearview mirror. The younger agent was watching him. Jack suddenly knew why he didn't like them. Especially the young one. He was too arrogant. Too cocky. Too much like Jack.

Why would the FBI send two agents from D.C.? And why was he feeling these guys weren't really FBI? Maybe he was seeing conspiracies where there was nothing. He was tired, and a little drunk if he admitted it. But his gut was telling him to keep these two at a distance.

Chapter Twenty-three

He must have been driving in circles, on autopilot so to speak, his mind playing and replaying everything from the conversation with Killian this morning, up to meeting with the captain and fashion police, putting a puzzle together with most of the pieces missing.

When he zoned back in he was on Riverside Drive near the Blue Star Casino. Old-fashioned cast-iron street lamps lined the street and created a scenic greenway walk that stretched for five city blocks. Colored lights adorned every inch of the Blue Star Casino riverboat. Its towering smokestacks were lit up like the Vegas strip, and it would be so until late in the morning when the majority of partygoers and gamblers, both casual and professional, drunkenly returned to their homes.

Across the street Fast Eddie's restaurant was grinding out live band music, the head-banging, kill-'em-all, garage band type that wouldn't make it anywhere else in a civilized society but was preferred by the singles crowd inside the meat market, which was always packed beyond seating capacity. The ones that couldn't get inside Fast Eddie's hung around outside and drank and partied and revved motorcycles and sometimes fought. With several large colleges in the area, the place drew a plethora of nubile young women competing to show off ample chests in whatever wet T-shirt contest was going on—inside Fast Eddie's and outside. This in turn brought out a crowd of gawking young, and not so young, men. And women.

On the east side of the Blue Star Casino was the Evansville riverfront esplanade. It was built at a cost to the taxpayers of nearly five million dollars. Several acres of beautifully landscaped commons normally filled with sound systems, raucous bands, and summer bierstubes, were empty tonight.

Jack parked in the casino pavilion driveway and put the FBI placard on the dashboard. He pushed through the pavilion doors and was deafened by the jukebox. He bypassed the bar and took the stairs to the second level. The motto of the casino was "A Party Every Day." Photos of lucky winners lined every inch of wall space on the stairway. Jack surmised that if they put photos of the losers on the walls they would have to use all the walls of every building on Riverside Drive.

At the top of the stairs was a balcony that drew one's eye down to the main floor of the pavilion, where people were drinking, smiling, staggering, smiling, and drinking. Not necessarily in that order. Many customers, including several in wheelchairs with oxygen tanks on their laps, were gathered around a new Corvette sitting on a rotating pedestal with a sign that proclaimed, "One lucky winner will drive this away." Marketing at its finest.

Jack turned from the balcony view and headed toward the security office. He passed a kiosk that sold "Fine Cuban Cigars." Off to his right was the Garden Club, the most expensive restaurant in the city. The money spent in there could feed all the hungry children in the world, or save all the mistreated and abandoned animals in animal shelters. Jack remembered taking Katie to the Garden Club once. He'd had to sell a kidney to pay for one entrée and a lung to buy dessert. He had to do CPR on his wallet afterward.

A bored-looking uniformed police officer named Jack Daniels was standing at the side of the cigar kiosk. Jack Daniels was his real name and to Jack he was standing in the perfect place. Jack Daniels and Cuban cigars. What could be better?

Daniels said, "Hi'ya, Jack."

Jack asked, "See much action up here?"

Daniels grinned. "Just waiting for the food to go bad. The onions always go first, and then it gets a little dicey with the tomatoes." He turned serious. "Sorry about Killian, Jack. He doing okay?"

Daniels was a day-shift motor patrol officer. About half of the city police force worked off-duty jobs to supplement their meager salaries. Being a cop was a job you had to save up for.

"He's holding his own," Jack said, and the officer ogled a blonde walking by in a short skirt.

"Seen Stu around?" Jack asked.

"You'll be lucky if he is," Daniels said. "He spends about as much time in there as Congress spends in Washington."

Jack left Daniels to try and chat up the blonde and walked down a small side hallway. He stopped outside an unmarked metal door with two peepholes, one at eye level and another at belly button level. Maybe the lower one was for crawling drunks. He knocked on the door and yelled, "Vice! Open up. Let the little girls go and come out with your hands off your pecker."

Sergeant Stu Sanders opened the door. "Come on in, old man."

Stu and Jack had grown up in the same neighborhood, gone to the same schools, fought the same bullies and each other, and even dated some of the same girls. Then Stu was seduced by the dark side and became an Indiana state trooper, while Jack did what any respectable Irish Catholic son of a cop would do and joined the Evansville police force.

Stu was a scrawny kid, but you'd never believe it now. He was into weightlifting and bodybuilding big-time. With his smartly parted hair, round steel rimmed glasses, and baby face, he resembled a cross between the Hulk and Harry Potter.

Jack stood by Stu's desk, mimicking bodybuilder poses and grunting like he was taking a dump.

"Up yours, Murphy," Stu said and chuckled.

"You wish." Jack sat on the edge of the desk. "I was just driving through the neighborhood."

Stu answered, "You think I work 24/7?"

"Truthfully . . . yeah. What else are you going to do? Lift weights, hang out here, lift more weights, pose, lift again, and pose again."

"You're just jealous, Murphy."

Jack grinned. "Actually I need you to find someone up in your system or ask around for me."

"This about Killian?" Stu asked.

Jack said, "This is a long shot, and you have to keep it between you and me. I have info that says maybe two cops are involved in the shooting."

"No shit?" Stu said.

"Can you look some names up for me?"

"You have their names?" Stu asked.

Jack gave Stu a brief rundown of the investigation to date, including the two names Coin and Reverend Payne gave. Stu cocked an eyebrow, and a smile crept over his face.

"Did I say something funny?" Jack asked.

"No. It's just that I finally know something you don't. I can tell you who the cops are. One of them at least."

Jack felt his heart beating fast.

Stu went to a filing cabinet and took down a 5x7 photo in a cheap frame and handed it to Jack. It was taken at a weightlifting event. Several muscle-bound apes stood around in the background, while Stu, wearing a Speedo, was deadlifting about a million pounds.

"This is making me uncomfortable, Stu. Maybe we should have a chaperone?" Jack handed the photo back. "I thought you were going to tell me about Moon Pie and Modock. You know I'm not interested in guys. And besides, I'm dating someone. A girl. Well, a woman really. Very feminine. With developed . . . woman parts . . . and stuff."

"Sure, sure," Stu said and handed the photo back to Jack. "Word has it you can't get a date, but that's not where I was going with this. Take a look at the guy in the background. To the left of me." He pointed to a squat figure looking directly into the camera.

"That's Moon Pie," Stu said.

Stu was pointing at a guy about twenty-five years old with a pale complexion, light blond hair, close-cropped. He had the exaggerated features of a serious muscle head; round face, lips too thick, and eyes like marbles in that oversized head. They were the kind of features that gave the word oxymoron a double meaning. Jack had seen him around the police station.

Stu said, "With that head everyone on the weight-lifting circuit calls him Moon Pie. His real name is Skippy Walker. And before you ask, I don't know who his partner is. Moon Pie complains about working with an old man."

"I know who his partner is," Jack said. "Shirley West."

"West was a Detective Sergeant, until he shot that kid by mistake. Right?"

"Yep," Jack said, thinking, Coin couldn't describe the two policemen very well, but here were two policemen. He'd have to check them out.

"I heard he was an alcoholic too. How does a guy like that stay on the force? Why would he want to?" Stu asked, and his desk phone rang. He answered, listened briefly, and put the receiver down. "A sixteen-year-old male got onto the boat somehow. They don't know what to do because he won big at the slots and wants to cash out. How he got on board I don't know, but I'm going to find out. I've got to go and spank him. I mean the guard, not the kid. The problem with the boat is that it hires just about anyone for security guards. There are three Indiana state policemen assigned to this tub, which means only one of us is on each shift. How the hell can we babysit these guys? Why don't you come with me and tell me some more? I'll give you the nickel tour."

Jack had never been in the casino area of the boat. His idea of gambling was dating. Jack went to the escalators, but Stu, being a fitness nut, insisted they take the stairs. When they reached the pavilion, Stu went into tour-guide mode.

"Blue Star Casino covers twenty acres, not counting the two hotels. The pavilion's main floor is one massive room with two entire walls constructed of glass. Near the center of the room is Hoosiers Lounge, an open bar/entertainment area separated only by wood railings. Hoosiers Lounge features free entertainment every weekend with name acts. Crystal Gayle was just here, and Eddie Money will be here next week. Tonight is a local fifties band. The Duke Boys," Stu said as if he was reading off a cue card.

They crossed the pavilion floor, and Jack saw a young security guard sitting behind the podium at the entrance of the boarding gates. He didn't appear to notice as they entered the double glass doors. Stu hooked a thumb over his shoulder as they walked into the long enclosed ramp that led to the boat. "See what I mean about spanking these guys? Jeez!" He told Jack to wait a minute and walked back to the guard. Jack could hear Stu chewing out the young man, and then he returned. As if nothing had just happened, he continued narrating the tour.

"The Blue Star Casino Riverboat consists of three levels providing one thousand plus slot machines and forty table games. Mechanical, boiler room, et cetera, are in the lower level. Most nights during summer the outside upper deck is elbow-to-elbow people, with live entertainment and a plethora of free alcoholic beverages. And don't ask me to spell plethora."

Stu explained the outside upper deck was inaccessible to customers right now because it was undergoing reconstruction after an inspection revealed there were only two lifeboats for the entire boat. Then he whispered, "The only reason the casino wasn't shut down during this 'refitting' is because of the millions of dollars in revenue the state draws from the boat's operation."

Stu gave a brief synopsis of the history of the Blue Star. In July 1993, Indiana Governor Evan Bayh approved a bill that resulted in the Indiana Riverboat Gaming Act. The law, he explained, was supposed to spur job growth and help develop economically depressed areas in Indiana. Apparently, the economically depressed areas referred to in the bill were only along Indiana's waterways, because the bill mentioned only counties along Lake Michigan and the Ohio River.

The Blue Star Casino was the first to apply for and receive a gaming license from Indiana, but it took two years for this to become a reality in 1996, after a citywide referendum resulted in a fifty-one to forty-nine vote in favor of the casino. "I'm sure there was a separate secret vote behind closed doors with a lot of political handshaking and palm greasing," Stu said.

The same year the Blue Star opened its doors in Evansville, the Argosy Casino & Hotel riverboat in Lawrenceburg, Indiana, received its license. That was the floodgate the gaming industry was waiting for. Four more riverboats received gaming licenses in 1996, and now ten riverboats operated in Indiana.

"Under Indiana Gaming Commission rules, the riverboats were required to sail for several sessions each day. Boarding was every two hours for a thirty-minute window. That all changed recently and now there's continuous boarding."

They entered a door on the second level. Jack was hit by the smell of cigarettes and cigars, and the raucous noise from the slot machines and talking. It was like walking into a festival—only inside. Slot machines and table games filled most of the space, and there wasn't an empty seat. People were lined up waiting for their turn to play. A plump lady bumped into Jack, said, "Excuse you," and waddled off into the smoke-filled room.

"So this is where my Medicare money goes," Jack remarked, surveying the elderly clientele.

Stu's laugh sounded like a snort. He pointed to one elderly woman sitting alone at a slot machine.

"That's Agatha Barning," he said. "She's eighty-five and spends at least thirty thousand a week here. She was worth about five million is what I heard."

Agatha's appearance was that of a bag lady, not a multi-million-aire.

"Is she married?" Jack asked straight-faced.

"She's mine," Stu said and laughed.

"Does she have a sister?" Jack persisted.

"Not one that's alive."

Stu led him to the aft stairway where a security guard stood post. This one was young with a face cratered by acne.

They walked through the fire door and down a set of stairs. "We'll skip the first deck," Stu said. "It's a repeat of this one." They walked down another set of stairs to a locked door that opened into the bowels of the boat.

They were in a maze of hallways, and as they passed doors, Stu explained what was in the various rooms. Stu pointed to a heavy steel door and said, "That's the surveillance room. I can't show it to you, but there are over fifty monitors in there. Everything is recorded. Of course, most of the monitors are dedicated to the ticket counter, the money rooms, and the dealers. Pretty impressive, huh?" Stu asked.

"How much money is here on a given day?" Jack asked.

"Fifteen to twenty million. There'll be even more money with the Thunder on the Ohio boat races coming up this weekend."

"And here I have to squeeze George Washington until he spits out his wooden teeth," Jack said, and Stu snorted again.

"You and me both, brother," Stu said.

Jack hadn't noticed any special security at the money rooms. A countertop with bars that ran to the ceiling and a sturdy-looking door were all that separated the cashier from the customers. He'd seen one security guard so far, and he was unarmed.

This seemed a little slipshod to Jack considering the kind of money at stake. On the starboard side of the boat, they passed several doors marked ELECTRICAL, MECHANICAL, ENGINE ROOM 1, and so forth. The lower deck had an unreal feel about it. The air didn't feel quite right. Sound didn't travel well. He was glad when they reached the starboard stairs and headed up.

"The elevator doesn't work?" Jack asked.

Stu patted Jack's stomach. "Just trying to get you some exercise, buddy."

"Thanks for your concern," Jack said.

They went up several flights of stairs to the third level and through double steel doors that led to the outside upper decks. The air out here was like standing in an oven. He wasn't surprised to find it was empty of customers or even crew.

A dozen or more steel boxes were being welded to the deck but there was no construction going on tonight. Stu explained that the metal boxes were for emergency inflatable boats. Dozens of large wooden crates were piled up here and there.

As they approached the wheelhouse, Jack saw two crew members in blue jumpsuits standing near the railing. They were smoking something pungent and passing it back and forth. When they saw Stu, they flicked it over the side and made themselves invisible. Stu didn't seem to care. Except for the marijuana involved, the crew's actions reminded Jack of his own office when the chief of police would come in. Newspapers would go in desk drawers, and people would suddenly be on the phone or remember an interview they had to go to. Thankfully, he'd never had that problem. It's not that he didn't goof off from time to time. He just didn't care who saw.

The wheelhouse had an unremarkable door. Not even a name on the outside. He thought it should at least have a big, wooden ship wheel attached to the outside, or maybe the head and bust of Dolly Parton.

"I'll introduce you to the captain. If you behave, maybe he'll let you drive," Stu said and winked.

"I don't really have the time to go out on the river, Stu," Jack objected.

"Then you'll have to start swimming," Stu said. "We left dock right after we got on the boat."

"Well, I guess since I've been shanghaied, you can lead on."

Stu entered the wheelhouse without using a key, and Jack wondered if this was a breach of security. He wasn't exactly worried about a terrorist hijacking—Stu had explained that the riverboat traveled only ten knots at top speed—but he didn't want some irate or drunken gambler taking the boat for a joyride while he was onboard.

"Hello, Captain Bruce." Stu shook hands with a man about Jack's age.

The ship's captain was wearing something similar to an airline captain's uniform. He was of average height and had a sturdy look about him that inspired confidence. Jack assumed he was a fitness nut like Stu, so he was surprised to see the captain light up a huge black cigar.

"Jack Murphy," Jack said and shook the captain's hand. His grip was firm.

"I know who you are," Captain Bruce said. "You were in the paper a while back."

"I'm a legend," Jack said.

The captain smiled and asked, "You smoke these?"

"Not for a while."

Captain Bruce took a glass cylinder from his shirt pocket and handed it to Jack. It was marked Black Cohiba Gigante. Jack shook the cigar out into his hand and used the pointed end of his handcuff key to poke a hole in the tightly wrapped end of the cigar and bummed a light. They smoked in silence for a minute.

Stu—always the health nut—opened his mouth to say something, but Captain Bruce cut him off.

"I know. I know. My body is a temple, and I shouldn't abuse it. Well, consider this a little incense for the temple. So what brings you all the way up here?"

"Jack's an Evansville police detective, Captain, and a good friend," Stu said.

A deep voice said from the door behind them, "I didn't know you had any friends, Stu."

Jack turned around and saw a giant black man somewhere in his forties, tall and even more muscled than Stu. He was dressed in a uniform similar to Captain Bruce's.

"Jack," Stu said with a huge grin, "meet John Keep."

"That's First Officer Keep to you, Sanders." Keep took Jack's hand in a viselike grip. "I'm the navigator."

"Did I mention I'm armed?" Jack said, only half-joking as he rubbed the ache out of his hand.

"I'm giving Jack the fifty-cent tour," Stu said. "Maybe Captain Bruce will continue."

"Anything for a hero," Bruce said and pointed to the elaborate control panel in front of them. "We use radar and navigation just like in larger bodies of water." A black screen was backlit with fluorescent green lines and marks like square objects. He pointed to one of the objects. "That's a barge coming at us at five knots." Other gauges showed the river depth, water temperature, and so on.

"This boat is an exact replica of *The Robert E. Lee* steamboat, a side-wheel racing boat that was built about one hundred and thirty years ago. *The City of Evansville*, she's called, and she's three hundred foot long by seventy foot wide and weighs in at 1,589 tons. Without passengers of course."

"That perfectly describes my partner," Jack said. "I named him Bigfoot because he weighs in at full-grown yeti."

Stu rolled his eyes. "Sorry, Captain Bruce. Jack's brain is oxygen-deprived from walking up three flights of stairs."

The captain let Jack put the boat into reverse and lock on the autopilot to take her back to dockside. He explained that Mister Keep would do the final docking.

They thanked the captain and First Officer Keep for their hospitality, shook hands, and headed down to the second level.

"Well, you didn't sink the boat," Stu said.

"And I didn't have to swim back either."

Stu got serious. "What's going on, Jack?"

Jack told Stu about the FBI agents. "They had FBI badges but they seem more like NSA or CIA or one of those other three-letter agencies. They got here way too quick if they really came from D.C. Why wouldn't they just use the FBI agents here? I don't trust them."

After they docked, Stu made a Xerox of the 5x7 photo of Moon Pie and gave it to Jack.

"Can you tell how much someone has spent gambling, Stu? Or do I need a subpoena?"

Stu laughed. "I can run that for you, but it will take a bit. You want it on West and Moon Pie, right?"

"Thanks, Stu."

Jack headed for the detectives' office. He needed to look into the background on Skippy Walker and Shirley West. His drowsiness had passed and he was wide awake. Possibly a result of the nicotine in the cigar.

* * *

As Jack drove to headquarters, he felt a thrill of excitement. He finally had a lead. He hoped he wouldn't run into the Feds again so he decided not to use the computer in his office. It was between shifts so he could use the computer in the empty motor patrol workroom. He pulled up the files on Skippy Walker, aka Moon Pie, and Shirley West. He got their addresses and telephone numbers along with photos of them in uniform. Skippy definitely had the whole Jay Leno thing going. Shirl had the appearance of a Marine drill sergeant with his short stiff buzz cut of gray hair.

He had worked with Shirl years ago when Shirl was still a detective sergeant. When Shirl wasn't drunk he was a good investigator. But like many alcoholics, booze finally got him. Shirl was shit-faced drunk and on duty when he'd shot a kid who was holding a cap gun. Shirl was lucky he wasn't fired and/or charged with manslaughter. The kid's family received a huge monetary settlement from the city.

Jack called Susan from the workroom phone. Her answering machine picked up on the third ring. "Hello," the disembodied voice said. "If you have dialed correctly, you have reached the person you were calling . . ."

Jack recognized the voice as that of Miz Johnson-Heddings— Susan's receptionist. Her tone was funereal and reminded him of something from a horror movie. Before the rest of the message could play, Susan picked up the line.

"Hello."

"Is this Miz Johnson-Heddings?" Jack asked.

"Don't knock it. Her voice discourages salesmen and other evildoers."

"Good choice. Almost discouraged me," Jack said.

"Must be an important call then, huh? And you remembered my home phone number."

"I know who Moon Pie and the other cop are," Jack said.

Chapter Twenty-four

By the second half of the nineteenth century, Evansville was a major trading port for steamboats and flatboats hauling goods along the Ohio River. Then the railroads came, and the need for the waterway diminished. Three of Evansville's most iconic buildings, the old post office, old courthouse, and Willard Library were built as monuments to the geographic placement and abundance of natural resources found in the bend of the river. Hardwood lumber from the area fed the Reitz Sawmill that resulted in a growth of Victorian-era homes along the riverfront. Susan lived in one of these.

Susan had inherited a three-story, brick and Bedford stone Victorian home that faced the Ohio River. Across the street was a spacious park with a children's playground and a grand view of the riverfront. Behind the house sat an old carriage house with heavy iron hinges and old-fashioned carriage lamps high up beside the massive doors. When Jack had first met Susan, she was fixing this place up to be a bed-and-breakfast. But when she took the job in Indianapolis she had stopped the renovations. The last he knew she hadn't decided whether to complete renovations or just sell the house. He didn't see a Realtor's sign in the yard.

Jack parked in the drive where a cobblestone pathway led to the vintage front door. Mounted in the middle of the door was an ornate lion's head knocker. The door opened as he approached.

"Come in, but watch your step," Susan said. She was shoeless and wearing a knee-length painter's apron with a pink T-shirt and on her head was a once-white painter's cap. The legs below the apron were bare. She was a runner, so her legs were as spectacular as he remembered.

"Let's go back to the kitchen table," she said. "I have some news for you."

Jack followed her into the kitchen and let out a whistle. "Wow! This is different," he said, taking in the new appliances, cabinets, tile flooring, and brightly painted walls.

She smiled and motioned him toward a chair at the table. She poured two cups of hot coffee and they both sat. "Do you want cream or sugar?"

"I like my coffee like I like my women," Jack responded. "But enough about me, tell me your news first."

"No, no. You first."

"Okay," Jack said. "I have a friend with the State Police that is assigned to the Blue Star Casino. His name is Stu Sanders. I just talked to him and found out this is Moon Pie." He showed her the photo of Skippy Walker. "And this is Moon Pie's partner, Shirley West. Shirley's a guy, by the way."

She studied the pictures. "I've seen this guy before," she said, tapping Shirl's photo. "But I've never seen the other one. Are you sure that's who Coin and Payne were talking about?"

"Stu's into weightlifting. He showed me a picture of one of his competitions, and Moon Pie was in the background. Shirl is tall, thin. Shirl's sixty-two and has to retire in three years. Sixty-five is mandatory retirement age for EPD. Moon Pie is short and muscular, twenty-five. I don't know much about Moon Pie's past, but Shirl is an alcoholic. He was almost fired a few years ago. He shot a kid that he thought had a gun. Shirl was a sergeant in detectives at the time, and he was dead drunk. Now he's a patrolman and working with Skippy Walker."

"We probably have the right guys that Coin said were policemen. And I'll bet you a dollar to a donut that Khaled is Modock. What are the chances that Khaled's not involved?"

She took a sip and made a face. "Oh, that's bad." She sat her cup down. "Just playing devil's advocate. All of this hinges on Coin. And Reverend Payne. If Coin is lying or maybe he's just mistaken, then this is all conjecture."

"I agree that Coin could be lying or mistaken, but there's just too many coincidences," Jack said. "And my gut is never wrong."

Susan got up and took Jack's hardly touched cup and poured

both coffees in the sink. "Okay. Since you put it that way I believe you. But why is this going on?"

"Beats me. If I knew that I'd have the shooter's throat in my hands. Now it's your turn to spill."

"Mabel called me just before you did."

"Who's Mabel?"

"You know her as Miz Johnson-Heddings," Susan said. "Mabel was very upset and that's not her nature. She said that after I left work two FBI agents came in asking questions about Khaled and demanding to see not only his file, but Eddie Solazzo's file as well. Mabel tried to call me, but the agents wouldn't let her. She got them the files but they didn't even look at them. She said they just took the files. She tried to stop them but they threatened to arrest her."

Jack couldn't imagine Miz Johnson-Heddings being bullied by anyone.

"Let me guess," Jack said. "The FBI agents were from D.C. One was an old guy dressed badly, and the other was a younger guy straight from the cover of *GQ* magazine."

"So you already know about these creeps. Excuse me, I mean these federal agents."

Jack told her about Captain Franklin introducing him to the suits. "They don't act like any FBI I've ever known. I'm not sure they're really FBI."

"What do you mean, not FBI? Who are they?"

"I don't know," Jack said. "I mean, they could be the real deal, but it's just too strange."

He told her about the timing of the agents showing up, and questioned again why the local FBI wouldn't be involved.

"Jack, do you think those guys know we were at Khaled's? I mean, why would they pull his file?"

He thought about it. "I don't know. If they do, they haven't said anything. Maybe they're interested in Khaled for some other reason. Maybe Khaled poses a biological threat because of all the grease in his hair."

"Oh, come on, Jack," she said.

"What? You didn't think that greaseball was a threat to public health? And who knows what he was up to in that disco bedroom. Okay, here's our bigger problem. The FBI took Eddie Solazzo and Khaled's files. They are putting things together, just like we did.

Miz Heddings doesn't know anything, but you do. If they contact you and ask anything about this just tell them I had you take me to Khaled's house. You don't know why. If they know we went back to Khaled's you tell them I made you. Tell them I'm unhinged."

"So I should tell them the truth."

"Yes." *Bitch.*

"Listen to me, buster. These guys took files from *my* office and abused *my* receptionist. They're the ones that should be scared to see me."

He raised his eyebrows.

"You always get your way, don't you? Of course you do. What was I thinking?"

"So what now?"

"I've got to find Khaled," he said. "I'll call you when I've got him. Okay?"

"Okay."

Jack sat in his car out front, thinking about where to go next. He couldn't believe she hadn't insisted on going, but he was relieved. He needed to call Liddell, and he needed to check on Killian, and he needed to find Khaled, among a dozen other things. And he was bone tired.

There wasn't much else he could do tonight. Shirl and Moon Pie weren't very good suspects in Killian's shooting, and Misino or Franklin would laugh in his face if he asked to bring them in for questioning. His case was circumstantial. Shirl and Moon Pie patrolled the sector where Killian was shot. A drunk, unreliable snitch (Coin) had told Reverend Payne he'd seen two policemen in the shack across the street from where Killian was shot. The policemen were talking about explosives, but Coin couldn't remember anything in detail. Coin had come up with the names Moonie or Moon Pie and Modock. Jack had stretched the rest of it to fit what he knew about Khaled and Shirl and Moon Pie.

Until Khaled could be found and made to talk, this wasn't going anywhere. And to boot, he now had two funky FBI agents from Washington, D.C., messing around. He'd had to talk to them about Khaled because they were already on to him. But he hadn't told them about Shirl or Moon Pie or Coin or Reverend Payne. Information was power.

His cell phone vibrated and he didn't recognize the number but he answered, "Murphy."

"Ask and you shall receive," Sergeant Elkins said. "We found your guy. Khaled Abutaqa."

"Did he come in to report his house had burned down?" At last something was going his way.

Elkins responded merrily, "No. Actually he wanted to report that someone murdered him. I wasn't real interested, but you know, I thought about how you were looking for him and I didn't want your brass screaming at me like a bunch of old women."

Jack shut the engine off and listened. Sergeant Elkins told him that two boys were down at the river under the Twin Bridges to set off fireworks when they stumbled across a body. The sheriff was called and when the deputy arrived they showed him where the body was, and the deputy found a van nearby.

Elkins said, "The plates were removed, but we traced it back to Avis on Franklin Street. They're closed but I'm trying to get someone to come in and give me some info."

"Have someone drive by Avis and see if Khaled's Toyota RAV is in the lot or parked nearby."

"No shit, Jack. Why didn't I think of that?"

Jack knew Elkins wasn't pissed at him. He was mad because this would put him in the spotlight, and that's not where he ever wanted to be. He was like the opposite of Double Dick, who would do anything to put his face in the public.

"How did he die?"

Elkins said, "Here's the summary. Kids find the body. Our Crime Scene finds the van."

"You can skip ahead if you want."

"Okay. I will," Elkins said. "Khaled was about twenty feet from the van, faceup on his back on the ground, one or two bullet holes in his right eye."

"Was he shot anywhere else?" Jack asked.

"I'm not done. Sheesh! Okay, so we figure two bullet holes because there are two exit wounds on the back of his skull. My crime scene guru is under the impression that one shot was fired while Khaled was sitting in the driver's seat of the van. Then he was drug out on the ground onto his back, and shot again through the same eye. Forensic evidence shows the head was moved and someone dug into the ground beneath the skull. My guru thinks they dug the bullet up. We didn't find the bullet—either bullet—and there are no shell casings. That would mean a revolver was used, or the killer picked up his brass after he killed this guy."

Elkins told Jack they identified the body by the Indiana driver's license in his wallet. Cash and credit cards were still in it. They could rule robbery out. Khaled's body had been taken to the morgue at the coroner's office.

Jack said he would meet Elkins there, hung up, and punched in another number.

"Bigfoot. What are you doing?"

"I'm talking to you, pod'na," Liddell answered.

"I need you."

"You charmer. Where am I going?" Liddell asked.

Chapter Twenty-five

Jack told Susan about Elkins's call and where he was going next. She agreed to wait for his call. He then went straight to the morgue.

The morgue was in the Vanderburgh County Coroner's Office building, a squat, ugly, tan brick structure. The flat-roofed building had the personality and appeal of Hillary Clinton and that was being generous. The woman standing at the front door was short and ugly like the building.

Lilly Caskins held the front door open and motioned for Jack to get moving. She had been chief deputy coroner since before Jack was a gleam in his father's eye, or so she said. She was a diminutive woman whom everyone called "Little Casket." It was a nickname that suited her well, for she was evil looking, with large dark eyes staring out of extra-thick lenses inside horn-rimmed frames that had gone out of style during the days of Al Capone. Think Wicked Witch of the West, but smaller and nastier tempered. But the thing that bothered Jack most about Little Casket was her bluntness at death scenes. She had no compassion for the dead or patience for the living.

"I wondered when you were going to get here," Lilly said. "The FBI called. They want an immediate autopsy on this guy. I told them our pathologist couldn't parachute in. They said they'd be here in an hour, so we'd better get this party started."

Jack again wondered what the FBI had to do with Khaled, and how they knew about this murder so quickly. Khaled's house was in the county, so the arson was the sheriff's case. His murder was in the county also, although barely, so again, it was the Sheriff's Department's jurisdiction. Jack wouldn't have known about the murder so quickly if Elkins hadn't called to tell him. Who was the FBI getting their information from?

"And your captain is coming with them," Lilly added.

"You could have told me that first," Jack said. He hadn't yet told Captain Franklin about the possible link between Killian and Khaled. He hadn't mentioned that he had visited Khaled's house twice today. Or that he had found a bullet lodged in a wall stud or about the computer or picture or that he was in Khaled's house when it was set on fire. At best he was withholding evidence of arson and now a murder investigation. At worst, he might become a suspect in both events.

Little Casket puffed up and said, "You're a detective. I thought you knew everything. How am I supposed to know who's got you in their sights this week? You make enemies like cockroaches make babies." She walked inside, and Jack followed.

"So what's up the FBI's twat?" she asked Jack. "They ordered me not to touch the body until they got here."

"Am I going to get a look first?"

"FBI don't pay my salary." Her almost lipless mouth tightened. "You don't pay it either, for that matter, but you're already here and they're not."

For once, Jack was glad she was such a bitch. "Is Dr. John here?"

Lilly stopped and turned around. "No. Our starship transporter thingamajig is being repaired so he won't be able to beam in. He'll have to drive here like the rest of us. He's been called."

Jack almost asked Little Casket what was up her twat, but he didn't want that mental image. They entered the autopsy room and when the door shut behind him the air seemed to be sucked from the room, and with it all sense of hope and life. The room was spotless, every stainless steel surface shining, but even with the air scrubbers on full tilt the air smelled of strong disinfectants with the stench of death mixed in. This wasn't a place for the living.

Laid out on the autopsy table was the naked body of Khaled Abutaqa. A square of wood propped up what was left of Khaled's head, and his normally dark Middle Eastern complexion was as pasty as floor wax. There were several scars on his legs, stomach, and chest that might be old bullet wounds. His right eye socket was a pulpy red mass; his left eye sightlessly stared at the ceiling. The back of his skull had flattened or was missing, giving his head the look of a cake that had fallen.

On a gurney nearby were a pair of blue jeans, a red and white-checkered shirt with fake pearl snaps for buttons, and a pair of hand-tooled Western boots. Rolled up on top of this pile was a wide leather belt with an oversized brass steer-head buckle.

Jack heard a toilet flush and Sergeant Elkins came out of the restroom in back. "Hi Jack," Elkins said. "I heard the FBI's coming. Little Casket has been cleaning the place and putting on makeup. She was going to run home and bake some cookies for the Feds, but I told her you might want to see this guy first."

"Kiss my ass, Boy Wonder," Lilly said.

Jack had never heard anyone call her Little Casket to her face.

Elkins said, "She calls me Boy Wonder because we were an item once. I prefer Man of Steel, but hey . . ."

"I call you Boy Wonder because—boy do I wonder how the hell you ever got hired," Lilly's tone was light and she was almost smiling.

"Speaking of wonder, I wonder if this guy's right now standing in line for his seventy-two virgins," Elkins said.

The door opened again and Dr. John walked in wearing tattered jeans and a black AC/DC T-shirt that had seen better days. His blond hair was sticking up on one side like he had slept on it. Coming in the door with him was Liddell.

"Ladies. Gentlemen. You too, Jack," Dr. John said.

Jack and Liddell listened as Elkins gave the pathologist a quick rundown of the scene where Khaled's body was found. He told about finding the van near the body, and bits of bone and tissue and blood on the inside passenger window. He concluded with the position of the body when they arrived and the obvious gunshot wound to the right eye. He gave Dr. John the Indiana driver's license they'd found in the victim's wallet.

During this monologue Dr. John had been examining the body. He looked at the Indiana driver's license picture and read the physical description from it aloud.

"Well, I would say this is his identification. The physical description matches even though the face and skull are a bit deflated. Does this Khaled guy have fingerprints on file?"

There was no hair, skin, or tissue left on the head; the hands had been skeletonized, burned almost to ash. "The feet are pretty much intact," he said to Elkins. "Your crime scene guys take his boots off at the scene?"

"Fire department got there before us. They used foam to put the fire out, and when they pulled the body out his boots must have come off."

"Is that the seat belt buckle?" Dr. John asked, tentatively poking at the hunk of melted metal on Khaled's stomach.

"I think that is—was—a brass belt buckle," Jack said. "He was into cowboys."

Dr. John looked at the burned clothing, then back at the body, and said, "Hunh."

Jack said, "The FBI and our captain are coming fairly soon. Bigfoot and me would like to be gone by then. Can you give us a quick tour? Was he shot? Strangled? Burned alive?"

Dr. John manipulated the head, examined the sides of the skull, the backside, and then the X-ray film that Little Casket had already taken.

"He was shot in the face through the right eye. I don't suppose your crime scene techs found anything at the scene?" Dr. John asked Elkins.

"Do you mean did we find the bullet? No. Wasn't much left from that fire."

Dr. John felt the back of the skull again. "There's an exit wound. Was he in the driver's seat?"

Elkins nodded.

"I'm guessing—this is not for my final report—that he was facing his killer. He was shot point-blank in the right eye. The trajectory of the bullet could be consistent with the shooter standing outside the van. The bullet traversed the brain and exited the back of the skull slightly left of center." He examined the X-ray again, then turned Khaled's head to the side and examined it. "Yeah. That would make sense. Someone walked up to the van and shot him in the face."

Jack traded a look with Liddell. *Policemen.*

Elkins asked, "Did you tell me that Killian was shot in the right eye? Maybe that's the shooter's signature."

Jack asked him, "Does the van belong to Khaled? I thought he owned a white Toyota RAV4."

Elkins said, "We haven't found the Toyota yet. The license

plates are missing from the van and Khaled doesn't have a van registered to him."

Dr. John said, "Large caliber bullet." He looked over at the X-rays Little Casket had already taken. "Here's some bullet fragments inside the skull. Not a whole bullet, mind you."

"Khaled knew the shooter," Elkins said.

"Possibly," Jack said. *Or he thought a policeman was legitimately stopping him.*

The front door buzzer sounded.

"That's the FBI," Lilly said. "I'll have the secretary get it."

"We don't have a secretary," Dr. John said.

"That's right," Lilly said in a mocking voice. "And we don't have anyone to help with autopsies, and we don't have a vehicle worth a damn, and I could go on and on. Damn county council." She headed to the front of the building, saying over her shoulder, "And now I have the FBI giving me orders like I'm some kind of waitress."

Jack heard Captain Franklin's voice in the hallway introducing the FBI agents to Lilly. He heard Lilly made some sarcastic remarks and then they came into the autopsy room. Lilly first, followed by the older agent, John Walmart, and then John Armani, who even at this hour was dressed as though for a cocktail party at the Waldorf Astoria. The captain came in last.

John Armani glared at Jack with eyes that seemed to cloud over with a shark's nictitating membrane.

Captain Franklin asked Jack, "Why are you here?"

Elkins spoke up. "I called him, Captain. I understand Khaled is a person of interest in the shooting of Agent Killian."

Uh oh.

Captain Franklin asked Jack, "How—when—did you establish that?"

"I checked out that lead you gave me about Eddie Solazzo having a .40 caliber gun when he was arrested. The parole office said Khaled had supplied a .40 caliber handgun to Eddie before Eddie got dead. So naturally I was interested in talking to him. And here he is." He didn't want to lie to the captain about being at Khaled's house, but he didn't want to admit that he was there—twice—and didn't report the fire at Khaled's. The two FBI agents didn't ask anything, but the younger one was looking at Jack, smirking.

Asshole.

Jack said to Elkins, "Well, I'll let you get back to your work. I guess Khaled isn't going to tell me anything now."

As Jack and Liddell left, he could feel the young agent's eyes following him.

Outside the morgue, Jack said, "You were awful quiet in there."

"Waste of breath, pod'na," Liddell said.

"The young one reminds me of a girl I dated in high school. She rarely talked, but she was always watching me with those dead eyes. Creepy."

"Did she wear a suit and carry a gun?" Liddell asked.

"Only to the prom. We went as the Men in Black."

Chapter Twenty-six

Jack and Liddell called it a night and agreed to meet early in the morning. Jack had just seemed to get to sleep when he heard an insistent banging noise at his front door. He squinted at the bright sunlight coming in through his window. It was morning already and he couldn't quite remember going to sleep. He was on his stomach, naked, and he looked at the empty bottle of Glenmorangie on the floor with a pile of clothes beside it. Cinderella had pulled his pillow off the bed and lay on it, one eye cocked at him, the other half shut.

The banging stopped and he thought maybe he had been dreaming. His bed was near the window on the front porch, and he had forgotten to close the curtains, again. Living in the bottoms like he did, there wasn't much reason to close curtains. There were no neighbors to worry about. He lay still soaking up the sun when the banging started again, this time on his window. He grabbed the sheet off the bed and wrapped it around himself, then looked out the window. No one was there.

He got up, twisting the sheet into a knot at his waist, and made his way to the front door. Whoever it was had most likely seen him in his birthday suit and knew he was home. If it was a pair of Jehovah's Witnesses he would invite them to get naked with him. Have a "come to Jesus meeting," so to speak.

He yanked the door open.

"Surprise," Katie said.

He was so shocked to see her that he didn't notice he'd dropped the sheet until she put a hand to her mouth to cover a grin. He grabbed at the sheet but he'd stepped on it and it was tangled around his feet. "Damn," he said, and then "Not you. Sorry. Give me a sec."

He shut the door and ran to the bedroom, where he put the pile of clothes on. They still smelled from wearing them all day yesterday, and a little of Scotch. He came back to the door buttoning his shirt and noticed his pants were still unzipped. "Damn! Shit."

Katie pushed the door open and came in. "Jack, I come in peace," she said with a smile. "Just take your time. I'm going to put some coffee on and get you awake."

He pulled at the zipper and the tab came off in his hand. *Oh, screw me!* He went back in the bedroom and found a pair of sweatpants and pulled them on. He finished buttoning the shirt and went to the living room, where he could hear Katie in the kitchen, opening and closing cabinets, the refrigerator, the oven, and the microwave. A little more clattering and he smelled the aroma of freshly brewing coffee. Katie was a great cook. And she could make a hell of a cuppa.

"I can see I should have called first." She said, coming from the kitchen. She stopped in the kitchen door and was looking at his crotch where his sweatpants were tented. She made no attempt to avert her eyes.

"Oh . . ." Jack covered himself with his hands. "Just a minute," he said and ran to the bathroom.

He was speechless and angry at the same time. He'd tried to talk to her for months without any success, and now she was here, she was beautiful, and she'd seen him in a state of arousal. He wanted to take her in his arms and kiss her. He also wanted to shove her outside and slam the door in her face. These emotions played tug-of-war but he said, "Coffee ready?"

Katie laughed and asked, "Are you?"

He didn't know what to say. How do you talk to a woman you've been intimate with, but who recently despised you, and now you had shown her a stiffy? Bad start to the day.

Katie said, "Liddell tried to call last night and again this morning. I tried to call a while ago and you didn't answer either of your phones." She went into the kitchen again and Cinderella padded into the kitchen after her, no doubt expecting to be fed. This all had a surreal feeling. Katie being here, rummaging around the kitchen. She had never liked the cabin. That was the reason for the house in town. The cabin was his for fishing trips.

"You don't have any food," she said and came back into the living room.

"I eat at Two Jakes," Jack said and reached for his cell phone on the coffee table. The battery was dead.

"There's nothing in there. Not even dog food." Cinderella stood at Katie's side. Jack could swear the dog was giving him an accusing stare.

"I brought food home last night. We ate. That dog will eat all day long if you let her. We had . . ." He suddenly thought of why Katie might be here.

"Killian . . . ?"

Katie sat beside him and put a hand on his arm. "Killian's resting and Marcie is there with Barbara. Marcie insisted I check on you. She said you don't listen to anyone else. Jack, are you in trouble at work again?"

The "again" is mostly what this visit was about. When he and Katie were married, he had spent so much time in the captain's office he should have had a chair with his name on it. Katie had warned him perpetually about what she called his "flippant attitude" toward his superior officers. He had always responded by telling her they weren't his superiors. In most cases it was true. In Double Dick's case there was no contest.

"Where did you hear that?"

"You're deflecting, so it must be true."

He hated it when she psychoanalyzed him. Deflecting? What the hell did that mean? "Yeah. I guess I might be in Double Dick's sights again," he admitted. He wasn't going to tell her he'd been suspended and then unsuspended. She'd probably heard all about it from his bigmouthed partner.

Jack remembered his father saying, "Hard work is what a man should expect out of life." Jack did his job, and he got results. He didn't care about credit or political correctness. He did what he did to help people. The rest was fluff. He didn't want promotion. He didn't care if everyone liked him. He worked for the citizens of Evansville and not Double Dick or even the mayor.

She squeezed his arm, and Jack saw worry in her eyes.

"Katie, don't worry about it. It's okay. I'm okay. I'll get some groceries. I'll take the dog with me and get her a hamburger before I go to work." She leaned close and put the back of her hand on his cheek. He could smell her perfume. The warmth of her touch brought the past back with a rush. The first time he had kissed her, the first time they made love, the taste of her. He pushed the thoughts away.

"Jack, I still care about you. You know that, don't you?" Katie said, and the lump he'd expected in his groin was growing in his throat. "You need to change, Jack."

"You're probably right. I guess I should try at least."

"No," she said. "You really need to change."

"Oh . . . Well, I have to get ready for work." He got up and walked her to the door.

"You will be careful, won't you?" Katie said and gave him a hug.

"I'm always careful." He walked with her onto the porch. "That's why you never knocked me up, muffin."

She smiled at his stupid joke and it was beautiful to see.

He admired the view from behind while she walked off the porch. Then he reminded himself that he had things to do, miles to go, and all that Robert Frost stuff.

He went back inside and took a cold shower. He was drying off when the phone rang. Cinderella was curled up on the pillow on his bed. He wrapped a towel around his torso and tried to shoo her away but she snapped at his hand.

He snatched the phone up and yelled at the dog, "Stay off my damn bed," and then into the receiver, "What?"

"Jack?"

Shit. "Sorry, Captain. I was asleep," he lied. He grabbed the smelly couch pillow and threw it at Cinderella. She didn't budge.

"I know it's early, but I need to see you in my office. ASAP."

The Sugar Creek Inn sat across the highway from John James Audubon State Park, in a wooded setting of its own. True to its name, a small creek flowed under concrete bridges built to allow guests to stroll the beautifully landscaped grounds. The large conference rooms welcomed businesses, conventions, and dinners. The hotel wasn't cheap, but it was more than accommodating for entertaining business clients and their every need. It was out of place and time in a small town like Henderson, Kentucky. Quinn felt he had chosen well.

He was a successful assassin because of his instincts and positive attitude. He wasn't a pessimist, or an optimist, not a glass half full or half empty. The glass was his. He would do what he wanted with it, and when he wanted. He used whatever resource or weapon presented itself in order to complete his task. In his line of work, winning wasn't just everything, it was life or death.

One more day and he would be on his way to Belmopan, a tiny city in Belize, a place with no extradition, a place where he would be untouchable. The local drug cartel would protect him in exchange for a few favors. Then, with a few smart investments, minor plastic surgery, he could live anywhere. Seeing the woman with the detective at Khaled's house had started him thinking about Pamela. He remembered something he'd heard Pamela say. "Money makes the world go 'round." Even though she had betrayed him, played him, turned on him, he still thought about her. It had hurt him to have to kill her, but she left him no choice. It had been easy to believe her lies. He supposed, in his own way, he had loved her.

Smith sat in the atrium and watched the balcony across the courtyard. He had no doubt that the men waiting for him, especially Moon Pie, intended to blow their entire "share" of the money on cars, women, and toys. He had no doubt they would draw attention to themselves, and one by one they would be captured. And they would spill their guts. Greed was a terrible and debilitating motivator. Greed and sexual lust were the downfall of great empires. He wasn't ruled by emotions. He was driven by his ability. He killed because he could. He took what he wanted because he could. Did what he wanted because no one could stop him. He had proven this in Chicago.

He watched a little longer before crossing the courtyard and taking the stairs to the second floor.

"Sit down, Moon Pie," Shirl said.

Moon Pie alternated between pacing the floor and peeking through the peephole in the hotel room's door. A wooden crate and a cardboard tube sat in the bottom of the open closet.

Ellert snorted, and said, "Will you stop? You're making me dizzy."

"Shut up, Tin Man." Moon Pie said.

"Can't you do something with this little shit?" Ellert yelled. "Tin Man" was a derogatory term that police officers used to describe the casino's private security. Ellert had heard it all in the past. He had been immune to their disrespect. But now that he was no longer

Chief of Security, now that Kenny f-ing Taylor had stolen both his job and his wife, he was more than sensitive to the slightest disrespect.

"Both of you shut up. For Christ's sake!" Shirl said. "Come over here and sit down," he said to Moon Pie. "If someone is in the room below, they'll hear you stomping around up here and arguing. They may get suspicious and call the police." Shirl knew what he just said wasn't true, but his paranoid partner might think so. People in this kind of hotel didn't give a shit what anyone else did.

Moon Pie sat on the arm of the couch, pouting, and Shirl wondered again why he had gotten involved in this. But he knew exactly how he had come here. Four years ago, on a sunny day a lot like this one, he had gone to his favorite watering hole, the 711 Tavern. It was a cops' hangout, so he didn't care that he was on duty and no one in the place cared either. He'd had a few. A few too many, but it was near the end of his shift. He was almost home free. But then his radio squawked out a run. "A man with a gun." He was close. He did his duty. And his whole life had come apart.

He didn't know it was a kid. Didn't know it was a cap gun. He'd heard a pop, saw a tiny flash, and he had responded.

He hadn't lost his job, or gone to jail like some people thought he should. But he had been demoted to patrolman, to uniform patrol, and partnered up with Moon Pie. The last four years he had gone through a lot. He'd lost his wife because of his drinking, and had become so depressed and broke that he had considered . . . He'd considered doing a lot of things he would never do. Suicide was the top of the list. And then he'd gone back to the 711 Tavern. He felt at home there. Surrounded by other losers like him.

And that's where he met Mr. Smith. At first he'd figured Smith for a cop, maybe from another town, hanging out where he felt comfortable, around other cops. He didn't figure Smith was his real name, but then a lot of cops, especially ones from out of town, ones with problems like his own, didn't want to give a real name.

After a few drinks, Mr. Smith confided he was retired from the Central Intelligence Agency. A spook. A black ops guy. The conversations seemed innocuous enough at first. Just venting, like "So and so ought to get blown away," or "We ought to have 'scumbag tags' instead of 'deer tags.'" That kind of talk.

Shirl found himself confiding in Smith about the accident that had cost him his rank and his public humiliation. Smith said cops would never get paid what they were worth. The public didn't appreciate them. And that eventually led to talk about how a cop could make more money being a criminal. Maybe rob a bank. No one would ever catch them.

Shirl wasn't sure who brought it up, but the talk got around to how much money casinos made; how they were profiting from the addictions of good people, how they were cleaning out the life savings of those who could afford it least. That led to the discussion, a "what-if?" discussion, purely theoretical mind you, of how a robbery could go down. What it would take to actually pull it off. Smith had made comparisons to Robin Hood. Shirl liked the idea. The more they drank the more appealing it sounded. The idea moved from improbable to possible to doable.

At first Shirl acted like he thought his new friend was joking. Like this was still just harmless banter. But he knew better. Each time they met, the subject of the gambling boat came up sooner and was more thoroughly examined. In less than a week, the casino was all they talked about.

It would feel great to be rich. To get even with a system that hadn't rewarded Shirl's dedication and service properly. He had risked his life for what? So he could be the target of activists, scumbag attorneys, and even his own department. And yet the rich were still getting richer for doing absolutely nothing. Hell, he'd even stopped voting. The world had changed and left him behind, broken him.

The idea had gelled, become a plan, taken on a life of its own. Smith said they would need another guy to make it work. Moon Pie was Smith's idea. Shirl tried to talk him out of bringing Moon Pie in. He'd explained how the steroids had obliterated what few undamaged brain cells Moon Pie had. But Smith insisted they would need someone like Moon Pie for certain parts of the plan. Just what those parts were, Smith hadn't shared with Shirl, but Shirl knew just the same. There were some dangerous things, some risks to be taken. Shirl knew what Smith was really saying was they would need a fall guy if it came to that. If Moon Pie were killed during the robbery it wouldn't be any sweat off Shirl's ass. He was so sick of the little prick he'd agreed to add Moon Pie to the team.

Smith also recruited the casino's ex–chief of security, James

Ellert. Shirl knew a little about Ellert, and he'd heard other things. Ellert had gone from being the top dog to a position that paid just a little above "squat" to supervise a bunch of malcontents. Ellert's wife was a knockout, so it was no surprise to Shirl that she had ditched him and was shacking up with his boss. Shirl got the feeling that Ellert was expendable for the same reason as Moon Pie.

He was pulled from his thoughts when Mr. Smith came in the room with a finger to his lips. "Keep your voices low. I could hear you down the hall."

Moon Pie asked, "You want me to keep watch, Mr. Smith?"

Smith ignored him and said, "Do you have it, Mr. Ellert?"

Ellert opened the closet and took out a cardboard tube, popped the cap from one end, and spread several large diagrams across a small desk. The men gathered around.

"These are the locations and name of the rooms on all levels of the casino," Ellert said.

"Did you bring the other items, Officer West?" Mr. Smith asked.

"It's all here," Shirl said, and took the lid off the crate, exposing the sticks of Semtex and the pencil timers.

"I've explained to Major Ellert his part of the plan. He will being the items on board that we need. He will show you officers where you will retrieve your items."

Smith directed his next comment to Moon Pie. "This will be the last time any of us meet, so listen to Major Ellert closely."

Ellert shuffled through the drawings and selected a diagram labeled BELOWDECKS. He pointed several places on the diagram. "This is the engine room. And here are the fore and aft ballast tanks."

He let the diagram roll up and spread out another. "You won't have to worry about any of those unless something goes wrong."

Moon Pie asked, "What do you mean if something goes wrong? If we don't need to know what those are, why are you telling us?"

Shirl put a hand on Moon Pie's shoulder and shushed him. "Go ahead, Major Ellert," he said.

Ellert took three sticks of Semtex from the crate and laid them on the diagram. "I've used this stuff before in the army. I'm going to blow up three of the ballast tanks and disable the boat."

Mr. Smith took over. "The explosions will happen simultaneously. All three at precisely eleven p.m."

Shirl squeezed Moon Pie's shoulder to keep him from interrupting.

"Five minutes before the explosions," Mr. Smith said, and turned his attention to Moon Pie and Shirl, "you two will go to the restroom by the cashier's cage on your assigned deck. You will retrieve a weapon and a mask from the paper towel dispenser. You will then pull the mask over your head, go to the cashier cage, and force them to open the door. You will get as many bags of money as you can carry and bring them to the top deck. That's the extraction point, gentlemen."

"You said the paper towel dispenser, how do we . . . ?" Moon Pie said, and Ellert handed a small shiny key to Moon Pie and one to Shirl.

"Those unlock the paper towel dispenser. Don't lose the key or you'll have to force it open, and, believe me, that'll make a lot of noise," Ellert said.

"Are the masks are gonna be presidents' faces? Like in that movie *Point Break*?"

"Sure," Ellert said.

"Who am I gonna be?" Moon Pie asked.

"Just listen," Shirl said.

Smith took a deep breath and continued. "Each of you will have just two minutes to collect the money, another minute to make your way to the top outside deck. I'll meet you by the wheelhouse. If you're not there you may be left behind."

"How are we gonna get off the boat?" Moon Pie asked.

Mr. Smith ignored him and produced a .40 caliber Smith & Wesson handgun, silencer attached, from inside his jacket.

"You will have one of these. They will be loaded. Shoot anyone who interferes with you. Chaos is your friend. Your only task is to get the money and take it to the upper deck. Remember, you have two minutes to get the money, one minute to get to the top deck. Bring the money to the wheelhouse." He addressed Moon Pie, "Mr. Walker, I have a way to get off the boat, but you must be on the upper deck no later than eleven-o-three. Do you understand?"

Moon Pie was still ogling the weapon in Smith's hand. "Mr. Walker, repeat what I just told you."

Moon Pie slowly said, "Two minutes . . . to get the money. Be up there by eleven-o-three."

Shirl felt a chill. He knew Mr. Smith didn't really intend to leave anyone behind. That is, anyone alive.

Without another word, Smith left. Ellert sat on the sofa and pulled the table near him. "I'll go through this again if you want."

"Won't the ship's captain make a distress call? What if some of the passengers or crew use their cell phones?"

"Mr. Smith said he would bring a jammer on board. No calls in, no calls out. He will make sure the wheelhouse is secured so we won't have to worry about the captain or first mate. The ship will be dead in the water in the middle of the Ohio. In answer to your next question, I don't know exactly what Smith's plan is to get us off the boat, but I'm inclined to trust him."

Shirl thought, then you're a fool.

Chapter Twenty-seven

Jack called Liddell on his way to see Captain Franklin. Liddell had not received a call. They agreed to meet at HQ after Jack met the captain. If he still had a job.

Jack took his time dressing and drove to police headquarters. Franklin sounded pissed off, so he wanted to give him some time to cool off. If he got lucky, someone else would screw up and get him off the hook.

He arrived at headquarters. The hallways were empty except for one uniformed officer dragging a drunk toward the booking lobby. The drunk was singing at the top of his lungs and was actually pretty good, but he'd never make it to *American Idol*.

He would pass by Central Records on his way to the captain's office. Central Records was staffed by a gaggle of civilians, mostly women, and gossip was measured in half-lives. The rumor mill was headquartered in Central Records and their Supreme Commander was a fifty-something blond dynamo named Penny Pepper. She knew everything there was to know about everything and everyone. Penny was the ninja master, the Red Power Ranger, and the Xena, Warrior Princess, of rumors, and Jack was in luck. She was sitting at her desk behind a counter protected by bulletproof glass. The precautions were necessary for the public's safety from the civil servants inside.

"Hi, Penny," Jack said, and he saw a Cheshire Cat–like smile spread across her face. "What's Franklin want with me?"

She said, "I wouldn't know anything about that, Detective Murphy."

He noticed she had called him by his title and not just "Jack" like she usually did. His mother had done the same thing. When she was mad at him she would call him "Mister Murphy." As in, "Mister Murphy, you take your hands off that boy's throat this instant and get in this house."

Jack leaned against the counter and waited. Penny leaned against the other side of the counter and, in a conspiratorial voice, said, "The captain is in his office with two FBI men. They've been in there for an hour and forty-two minutes. They asked for some personnel files. One of them was yours."

She shuffled some papers on the counter, but he knew she was dying to tell him the rest. Being a nice guy, he asked, "What does the FBI want with me?"

She dropped all pretense and decorum. "I overheard them talking about the murder last night. The one by the twin bridges. That's out by your place, isn't it? What did you do, Jack?"

His hopes sank. She had said, "One of the files . . ." suggesting there were others. He hoped the Feds weren't on to Moon Pie and Shirl. Killian's case belonged to him, not these two Federal dickheads. He didn't want them pulling Moon Pie and Shirl in and ruining any chance he had at finding Killian's shooter. Khaled was dead; Moon Pie and Shirl were the only ones left.

Penny feigned a look of concern and asked, "Seriously? Are you in some kind of trouble? You can tell me."

He could swear she was vibrating with excitement. She wasn't interested in Jack's problem, only the stories it would provide. She could see the Spew-litzer Prize or even the Busy-body Award for Gossip Excellence within her reach.

"I'm not in trouble, Penny," Jack said, and she deflated like a weather balloon. He decided to cheer her up and said, "I do know something, but you have to promise you won't tell anyone what I'm going to tell you."

She mimicked a zipper going across her pencil line of a mouth.

"Okay. Don't tell anyone, Penny, but I heard that Detective Jansen is . . ." he whispered the next words, "*coming out.*"

"Oh . . . my . . . God!" she mouthed, a hand covering her smile.

"Shhh. That's what this is about. Jansen hit on me and some other detectives. You didn't hear it from me. Right?

She hugged herself with glee, saying, "Don't ask. Don't tell."

Jack watched Penny disappear into the inner recesses of Rumor

Central and he went to meet Captain Franklin and the FBI. He felt a little better.

Jack was buzzed into the inner sanctum by the captain and then followed him into his office. The captain shut the door. They weren't alone. The two Feds sat in chairs they had pulled back against the wall on either side of the door. The older guy hadn't changed clothes. Either that, or he owned a closet full of Walmart suits. The younger agent sat to Jack's right and he, also, was dressed in the Armani suit he had worn yesterday, which was probably a mortal sin in the fashion world.

Franklin sat behind his desk. His usual black suit, white shirt, and red tie were accentuated by a pissed-off expression. An empty chair had been placed in front of the captain's desk where the captain would be to his front and the two Feds behind him on either side.

Jack's mind raced. The worst scenario he could imagine was *What if they thought he had killed Khaled?* He must have left some evidence of his visits to Khaled's house. But it had all burned to the ground. And he hadn't killed the man. Still, he might be wise to shut up and ask for an attorney. He'd worked within the system long enough to know not to trust it.

"You wanted to see me, Captain," Jack said, and sat down. Franklin introduced the federal officers again and Jack had the same feeling as before, that their names didn't fit their faces. Franklin asked the one question Jack had hoped not to hear.

"Why were you at Khaled's house?"

"Why was I *where*?" Jack asked, as if he had misunderstood the question. He turned his chair sideways to keep an eye on John Armani. If he was going to get out of this, he would need a diversion. A fistfight should do the trick, and this guy was the biggest prick and probably the easiest to piss off.

"Don't make this any harder than it has to be," said Walmart, who was being the good cop.

Armani glanced over at his partner and leaned toward Jack and said, "If you don't answer our questions, Murphy, we'll charge you with interfering in a federal investigation and slap your ass in prison so fast you won't have a chance to pick out drapes." In a more professional tone he said, "Do you know what they do to ex-cops in prison?"

On television, this is the part where the suspect—that was Jack—would break out in a nervous sweat. But this wasn't television. He stared Armani straight in the eyes without answering or blinking. That's a Jack Murphy interviewing tool. In body language it means, "Bite me; shoot your best stick."

Walmart—the good cop—continued as if Armani hadn't interrupted. "Jack, we went to the parole office. We got the files. We talked to the sheriff—what's his name—Elkins. We know everything."

If they know everything, why are they talking to me? Getting an attorney was looking better and better.

Franklin leaned back waiting for an answer. Armani gripped the arms of his chair, feet flat on the floor, like he was going to leap up and make the biggest mistake of his short life. Walmart seemed amused. Jack knew they were fishing, or they would have placed him under arrest. He wished Armani would come at him so he could make a necklace out of his teeth.

Jack hung his head as if he was giving up, then stood and walked to the door.

"Sit down!" Franklin ordered.

Jack locked the door and put his back against it, facing the men head-on. John Armani leapt to his feet and grabbed Jack's wrist. His grip was strong; so was his cologne.

"If you want to keep that hand," Jack said, "take it off me."

Captain Franklin said, "You gentlemen are guests here. Unless you're arresting my detective, I suggest you take your hands off of him and sit back down."

Walmart said, "That's enough."

The younger agent gave Jack a menacing glare before releasing him and taking a seat. Jack upgraded his assessment of John Armani. The man was insane . . . and dangerous.

Jack rubbed at his wrist and sat on the edge of the captain's desk. "Let's make a deal. I've got some questions, too."

Franklin said, "Jack—" but Walmart held a hand up.

"Let him continue, Captain."

"Let's lay our cards on the table," Jack said. "I'll tell you what you want to know, and you tell me what I want to know. I'll even go first."

"Let's see what you have to offer," Walmart said.

Sergeant Walker had gotten the ballistic report back on the slug Jack gave him last night. It matched the slug retrieved at the warehouse, and was a .40 caliber. Walker had given it to Liddell and Liddell to Jack. Jack now placed the bullet fragment he'd dug from Khaled's wall on top of Franklin's desk.

The older agent took a plastic evidence bag from his pocket and tossed it on Franklin's desk. It was sealed with red evidence tape that bore the logo VCS. This was evidence from the Vanderburgh County Sheriff's Department. Probably compliments of Sergeant Elkins. Inside that bag were two misshapen metal slugs. They were a large caliber just like the one Walker had found in the warehouse.

"Elkins knew about the slugs before Khaled's autopsy?" Jack asked. It wasn't really a question, but he wanted to be clear before he kicked Elkins in the nuts for not telling him.

"These match the one from the warehouse where the ATF agent was shot," John Armani said. "I'm sure the one you have matches as well, and we know you got it from Khaled's house."

"Silvertip hollow-points," Captain Franklin said.

"The type Killian was shot with," Jack said. "Proof that Khaled was involved in some way with the shooting."

"Okay, Detective Murphy," the older agent said. "Your turn."

"Okay," Jack said. "But I have one more question."

Walmart seemed to be running out of patience, but he held his temper and spread his hands in a magnanimous gesture.

Jack said, "I want to know why you're interested in Khaled. The truth. And none of this national security shit or I walk."

Neither agent said anything.

Jack got up and made for the door.

"Wait," Walmart said and reached inside his jacket, pulling out some pictures. He stood and handed them to the captain, who examined them and passed them to Jack.

The photos were less than useless. The quality was blurry and grainy; worse than a child's Etch-a-Sketch drawing. The person in the photos was probably a man somewhere between fifteen and one hundred years old. Jack couldn't even tell what color the man was.

Armani said something about a "specialized unit" and "anti-terrorist activities," before Walmart interrupted and said, "We are tracking a man who is an explosives and weapons expert. We think he's working for terrorists now. He obtained military-grade explosives and weapons from Khaled Abutaqa. All we are allowed to tell you, gentlemen, is that he is a person of interest to the United States government."

Jack shook his head, "I told you if you pulled that secret shit I was gone. I'm out of here. Good luck—gentlemen," Jack said and rose from his chair.

"Sit down, Detective Murphy," Walmart ordered. He and Armani exchanged a look and both reached in their jackets and produced a new set of credentials. Walmart said, "We haven't been completely honest with you." They handed Franklin their identification. Walmart's identification now showed him to be Paul White of the Central Intelligence Agency. Armani was Allen Thompson, CIA. They had badges to go with the IDs. When they opened their jackets to retrieve their credentials Jack also saw they were carrying guns. Forty-caliber Smith & Wesson's if he was right. *Hmmm.*

Paul White, the older agent, said, "I'm sorry for the subterfuge, Captain Franklin. Believe me, it wasn't a matter of trust. We thought it would be easier for you if you were working with an agency you were on more familiar terms with."

To Jack he said, "You really are observant, Jack . . . I mean, Detective Murphy." There was that smile again like a con man spotting a mark. "He should be working for us, Allen," he said to the younger, more psychotic agent.

"What the hell is this about, gentlemen?" Captain Franklin's cheeks were red. It wasn't a good color for him.

"I truly apologize for not being up front with you, Captain Franklin," Paul White said, and put his credentials back into the pocket of his cheap suit.

CIA Agent White continued, "This investigation truly does have national security implications, and I'm going outside my authority to even tell you this much." He looked from Jack to Franklin to make sure they understood the seriousness of what he was telling them.

"Captain Franklin, we're here because we need your assistance. Again, I'm sorry for the deception. Believe me, I would be angry too. I can see now that the deception was unnecessary," White said and looked to his partner to support him.

"You have our apologies," Agent Thompson grudgingly added.

Franklin seemed mollified. Jack wasn't. He was still on the hook.

White said, "Detective Murphy has done excellent work. Even if his methods are slightly, how do I put this . . . ?"

"He's irritating as hell," Franklin suggested and just like that they were all friends again. Except Jack. He was once again low man on the scrotum pole. Satisfied that he had made his point, White pulled a different picture from his jacket and passed it around. This photo was much better than the blurred ones they had shown earlier. The guy in this photo was scary looking, with eyes that were empty, soulless. He was like Allen Thompson on crack.

"This is John Quinn. Not his real name," White said. "He was in our counterterrorist unit but he no longer works for the CIA. Or for any other U.S. government agency. We were telling the truth when we said he may be working for terrorists."

"In other words he's gone off the reservation, and he's in Evansville," Jack said.

"He's here all right," White said. "About six months ago a shipment of military equipment was stolen. Fort Hood army base. Do you know about the incident in Chicago a month ago? You may have read about it in the papers."

"Are you talking about the bombing? The financial district?" Franklin asked.

White nodded. "That's the one. Over two hundred dead. Hundreds injured. Millions of dollars in damage. Suspected terrorist attack. Most major train stations, subways, and airports closed for hours. More millions of dollars lost. All because of Quinn."

Jack asked, "You think Khaled supplied the explosives to Quinn?"

Thompson gave him the look and said, "That's why Khaled is dead. He was a loose end."

The rest of their information was brief. There was no mention of Shirl and Moon Pie. So maybe the assholes were lying again.

They had finished their part and were all looking at Jack. So he lied. "I'm trying to run down Killian's snitches, but those ATF guys keep their sources close to the vest. Like I told you, I got on to Khaled because he sold a .40 caliber handgun to Eddie Solazzo a few years ago."

Allen Thompson asked, "We knew that, but we didn't know police detectives could enter someone's house illegally and dig around in a wall to recover evidence. Isn't that against the law?"

"I'd say bite me, Allen, but I don't know if there's a vaccine for that."

White put his hands up and said, "Stop. It doesn't matter at this point who did what. From now on, I expect Detective Murphy to turn everything he comes across over to us. Even if it is just remotely involved."

Franklin said to Jack, "We'll talk later about your 'visit' to Khaled's."

Jack responded, "Yes, sir. I won't let you catch me pulling a stunt like that again." To Thompson he said, "And if you ever lay your hands on me again, I'll make you into a real spook. Capish?"

Captain Franklin made a show of looking at the wall clock and said, "I suggest we all get to work. That is, unless you have something else you want to add, Jack."

"No, sir. I'm meeting Liddell in a few minutes. I don't suppose I can have a copy of the photos to show him," Jack said. To his surprise, White handed the pictures over.

"I'll keep you informed of anything we find, Captain," Jack said, and as an afterthought he added, "And I won't keep these guys in the dark."

Captain Franklin said. "If Deputy Chief Dick was aware you had 'visited' this weapons dealer's house he would finally have you."

Screw Double Dick. Twice.

Chapter Twenty-eight

The meeting hadn't turned out well, but it was better than a sharp stick in the eye. Jack didn't intend to share squat with the CIA. His sworn oath was to uphold the constitution and protect the citizens of Evansville. He would do things his way. His dad had said, "Doing the right thing isn't the best thing to do. It's the only thing to do."

He drove west to Donut Bank. Liddell stopped there each morning before work and was probably in a sugar coma by now.

John Quinn. Not his name, the CIA said. If the CIA were to be believed, Killian was a casualty of an arms deal gone bad, Khaled had supplied the arms, and Quinn had killed Khaled. But that didn't explain the two policemen Coin saw. Quinn must have had accomplices that the CIA hadn't found. Or did they know about Shirl and Moon Pie?

Quinn was a killer who had gone off the reservation and was setting up his teepee in Evansville. Jack could almost forgive Quinn for killing Khaled—hell, he wanted to kill Khaled himself—but he couldn't forgive him for shooting, or allowing to be shot, a good man, a husband, a father, a dedicated ATF agent. They had left him for dead.

Jack found Liddell sitting in a corner booth at Donut Bank. On the table in front of him were a small plate with two cinnamon twist donuts and an extra coffee mug for Jack.

Jack eyed the two twists and asked, "Has Marcie got you on another diet?"

"She don't need to 'cause I can eat all this stuff and still be built like Arnold, or even the Rock." Liddell stuffed a cinnamon twist in his mouth and talked around it. "But I'm much better looking—and taller too." He pushed the extra mug at Jack and said, "Get some coffee. I already paid."

Jack was going to say he was proud of Liddell for showing restraint, but he knew it wouldn't last the week. Liddell was just pacing himself like a horse in a pastry race.

Jack took the cup to the counter and filled it with black coffee and sat down.

"Thanks for the coffee, Bigfoot."

Liddell inhaled the last cinnamon twist. "I control the donuts, they don't control me."

"Where'd you hear that?" Jack asked.

"Donut Eaters Anonymous," Liddell said. "We meet a couple times a week."

Jack filled his partner in on the meeting with Captain Franklin and the two phony FBI/CIA guys. He told Liddell about Quinn and handed him the photos of Quinn the CIA had supplied.

Liddell studied the pictures. "So these guys were CIA masquerading as FBI? And they say Khaled was getting guns from a military base and Quinn was behind it."

Liddell slid the pictures back to Jack and said, "I'm just thinking out loud, but it seems to me that if they knew about Khaled, they would have had someone watching him before the gun deal. Maybe they were there when Killian was shot. Shouldn't they have at least tipped the ATF off about the guns or explosives? I mean, this guy blew up Chicago, for Christ's sake!"

Jack said, "I thought about that. Killian got the information from Coin. He wouldn't have had any idea the CIA was interested. They didn't exactly say they were part of an antiterrorist outfit, but they did say that Quinn had gone rogue. But, you're right. If they knew this activity was taking place here, they should have warned someone. Us or the ATF. I don't know if they were there when Killian was shot, but they are indirectly responsible."

Liddell licked his finger and wiped up the leftover cinnamon sugar on the plate. "I vote for Quinn doing Killian and Khaled. Both of them were shot in the same way. The shooter may have thought Killian was dead. The shooter is probably Quinn."

"I don't think the CIA wanted Quinn stopped by us. Or by Killian,"

Jack said. "The younger one, Allen Thompson—isn't geared right. I don't think they're here to arrest Quinn." He didn't want to think the CIA had shot Killian to keep him from interfering in the gun deal, but it was possible. The only thing he knew about spooks was what he'd read in books or seen on television, and none of it was good.

"So. What are we doing today, pod'na?"

"Elkins is apparently convinced these guys are FBI agents, so we can't contact him anymore. I've been ordered off by the captain, and I don't trust Elkins not to go to the phony FBI and pass on whatever we ask him or tell him. I guess we're on our own."

Liddell finished his coffee and stood. "I'll talk to the ATF. Maybe they can check out the CIA guys and see if that's who they really are."

"Not a good idea, Bigfoot. Whether these guys are FBI, CIA, NSA, or anything else, they're here, and must already have serious connections. If the ATF starts making inquiries the CIA will find out. I don't want us getting shut down."

"So, where are we going?"

Jack said, "You're going to find a motor patrol assignment sheet. I need to know when Moon Pie is working today?"

"You're going to look around Moon Pie's place while he's out?"

"You think I'm a burglar or something, Bigfoot?"

"Yeah."

"Well, keep it to yourself," Jack said.

Clouds drifted across a perfect blue sky. Kids played in the little park across the street from Susan's house. A young blond woman sat on a park bench staring at nothing and sipping from a paper cup, ignoring the perilous acrobatics being performed on the jungle gym. Susan's Honda was in her driveway.

Jack had decided that between Moon Pie and Shirl, the little muscle head was the weak link. Maybe he'd left something in his house. Like a diagram of a bank with pictures of bombs drawn on it near the safe. Liddell had found out Shirl and Moon Pie were working the day shift. Liddell had also discovered—and Jack was embarrassed to admit he himself hadn't thought to check—that Moon Pie and Shirl's patrol district included the warehouse where Killian was found. He didn't think they would show up on the North Side of Evansville, but . . . So Jack needed a lookout.

He needed to keep Liddell out of as much of this as possible.

The fact that the CIA hadn't wanted him at this morning's meeting was a good sign that they weren't focusing on him. Besides, with Liddell at headquarters, he could help out in other ways.

So Jack's options for a lookout were Katie, her sister Moira, or Susan. Katie would never go for what he had in mind, and Moira was a deputy prosecutor. Susan had already helped with one burglary, and look how well that had turned out.

Jack Murphy's Law says: "In for a penny, in for a pound." He was in luck. Susan's Del Sol was parked in her driveway. He parked on the street. Before he could ring the bell, the door opened and she stood there smiling.

"Come here often, sailor?" she asked.

"Actually I have . . . that is, I have something to ask you."

"I saw you pull up out front. I've got coffee."

"Coffee would be great," he said, and hoped it was from the Keurig. Her brewed coffee had the flavor of swamp water. They went to the kitchen and sat on bar stools. She handed him a steaming mug of black stuff from an old cofffee percolator. The kind with water in the bottom, a basket of ground coffee on top, and it was heated on the stovetop. He looked into the mug and thought: *This ought to be interesting.* He took a sip and it was surprisingly good.

"I found my aunt's old percolator in the attic. Pretty good huh?"

"Very good," he admitted. "This is quite impressive," he said.

"You're just saying that."

Not. "No, I'm serious. This is a great cuppa Joe. My only talent is pissing off my bosses."

"That's not true, Jack. You piss other people off too. So, what's your question?"

He skipped over the part where Katie visited while he was naked, told her about his six a.m. call from Franklin and his little talk with the FBI-turned-CIA.

"Those two FBI guys that were messing with Miz Johnson-Heddings yesterday were actually CIA," he said.

Here's another difference between men and women. Susan was angry the CIA guys had lied, whereas Jack objected to them even breathing the same air he was. She expected the truth, whereas, he expected to be lied to by his government. In fact, he considered it his right as a taxpayer and it was about the only thing he got from the government for free.

When he finished telling her about the two bullets the Sheriff's Department had recovered from Khaled, she asked. "Do you think the CIA shot Killian? And Khaled?"

Jack shrugged, but said, "They want us to believe that Killian was shot by Khaled, and Khaled was then killed by this Quinn guy. They brought up the bombing in Chicago not long ago."

"That was Quinn?" Susan's eyes widened.

"According to the spooks, anyway," Jack answered. "But, yeah. I can believe that one. And I think Khaled supplied him with the explosives. Maybe he just came to Evansville to eliminate Khaled as was suggested."

"But you don't think so"

"I'm not sure," Jack admitted. "But my gut is telling me that he needed Khaled—at least one more time. Thus the arms deal Killian was looking into. Maybe Quinn killed Khaled after he got what he wanted. The CIA wants me to believe Quinn's done here, so why are they sticking around?"

"Khaled is—was—on parole, so it follows that if the CIA was interested in him they would know to come to my office. But how did they know about Eddie, and why take his files from the office?"

"Exactly," Jack said. "Captain Franklin was the one that thought of Eddie Solazzo, and the CIA are pretty much embedded in his office. Big Brother is listening and all that shit. But I think Quinn has accomplices. Moon Pie and Shirl for starters. The CIA hasn't talked about anyone helping Quinn, except for Khaled, but I'm sure they know something. They've known everything else."

"So we need to find Quinn. He's the ringleader. Whatever he is planning can't be good," Jack said, remembering the news stories about Chicago. Bodies everywhere. *A terrorist attack?*

"These guys aren't going to let us anywhere near Quinn," Jack said.

"But shooting Killian—the attempted murder of an ATF agent—how can they get away with that?"

"The CIA has covered their asses. Quinn or Khaled will be blamed for shooting Killian," he said.

"Jack, if we're right there are more loose ends."

She was right. Moon Pie and Shirl may be targets when they lead White and Thompson to Quinn. And then maybe Jack and Susan and Liddell might disappear. "Why would Quinn involve policemen in whatever he is or was doing? I should have asked the spooks if he did that in Chicago."

"What if Moon Pie and Shirl think they're working for the FBI or CIA? Maybe Quinn fed them a line just like these two CIA guys did with the captain and you."

Jack hadn't thought about it from that angle.

"So what do you suggest we do next, Detective Summers?"

She shrugged. "We know there are stolen military weapons involved. They never said what type of weapons. For all we know they have rocket launchers. Quinn was in their antiterrorist unit and we know he is an explosives expert. If we knew more about what happened in Chicago maybe we could get a handle on all of this."

"I agree. But I think these guys told me more last night than what is even in the official reports."

"A personal agenda, maybe? Quinn, I mean. Not just to cover his tracks by eliminating Khaled. Maybe he has a personal score to settle with the CIA," Susan suggested.

"Quinn is an embarrassment to them, but maybe he is going after them. Maybe he has deliberately drawn the CIA here like you said."

Jack knew in his gut these guys were here to kill Quinn. He was an embarrassment? Maybe he was selling secrets? John Walmart didn't look like a hit man, but then Ted Bundy didn't look like a serial killer. The cocky young agent . . . he was a different story.

"Maybe you should try the direct approach," Susan suggested. "If you think Shirl is the smarter of the two, you should talk to him. Tell him you know what he's involved in. Who he's working with. How dangerous and crazy Quinn really is. How Shirl may be in danger from these guys. Maybe Shirl will spill the beans."

"Not a bad idea," Jack said, but he thought it was a horrible idea. Shirl was a cop, and an ex-detective. If someone even asked him what he'd had for breakfast, he'd ask for an attorney and invoke the Fifth Amendment. Moon Pie was out of the question. He was probably on steroids, and that makes you paranoid. If Moon

Pie thought they were found out, he might become violent and Jack would have to hurt him in a permanent way. The thought of getting in some licks for Killian was appealing.

"So what do we do next?" she asked.

"That's why I'm here."

Chapter Twenty-nine

"I'm going to start charging the city for my gas if we keep this up," Susan said. She was once again driving because Jack's Crown Vic would stand out on Moon Pie's dead-end street. She parked a block over from Moon Pie's house on a street that ran parallel. The houses were close together, but Jack could look between two of them and see Moon Pie's front door.

Jack had insisted that they drive around the neighborhood a few times, and he got a good look at the dump Moon Pie called home. Moon Pie's house was a run-down ranch style covered in oxidized aluminum siding. The gutters were missing and the insides of the windows were covered with newspaper. In his backyard, one of a string of sixty-foot-high electrical towers marched off to the east and west like a row of giants.

Jack's cell phone rang.

"Did I interrupt anything?" Bigfoot asked. "Like a burglary or something?"

"Has the ATF called?" Jack asked. He thought they would be wanting an update, if the CIA hadn't put them on a leash.

"Pons called and said his boss was on the warpath. Misino apparently received a visit from the spooks. He's super pissed off that he had to hear it from the CIA about the Chicago disaster's possible connection to Killian's shooting. He told Pons to tell you to, 'take a flying leap.' But less politely."

"Did he mention having his EOD guy take a crack at Khaled's house?"

"ATF's had a vasectomy, pod'na. I told you something like this would happen."

"No you didn't, Bigfoot."

"Did too. You're the senior partner and lead investigator. You're always to blame."

"I'm with Susan. Is he working?" Jack asked.

"He and his partner are working. Their district has been getting a lot of drug complaints. Kids hanging outside. That kind of stuff. I suppose they'll be busy today."

"I'll get back to you," Jack said. He didn't want to talk over an open line. Big Brother *was* probably listening by now.

Susan said, "You're going in there, with or without my permission, aren't you? Once again you lied to me about just doing a drive-by." She mimicked Jack's voice and said, "Let's see where he lives. His house can say a lot about him."

"I don't sound like that."

"Well, that's what you said," Susan argued. "You want me to be the lookout again, don't you? Well, this time I'll let you go it alone."

"Do I look like a burglar?" he asked.

"Yes."

"Okay. But think about this. Shirl's not going to tell us shit if we talk to him. Moon Pie's crazy. Quinn might have already offed Khaled. The fire at Khaled's house wasn't a coincidence. The burned computer, the bullets in the wall, the picture. I've got to get in Moon Pie's house and hope I can find something."

An older Cadillac Seville came down the street toward them, the bass from its speakers making the Del Sol pound and vibrate. It pulled alongside and the music died. The arm outside the driver's window was as thick as a tree trunk, heavily tattooed, with every finger on the huge hand bedecked in gold jewelry. The driver was a white male in his thirties, and his head turned slowly to glare at Jack. "Wha'chu doin' in my territory, Murphy?" the driver said, "I ain't got no warrants, and you don' have enough he'p to bus' me." He smiled and showed a row of gold-capped teeth, some with carat size diamonds embedded in them.

"I'm on a date, asshole," Jack said. "I thought I'd show her what a sewer looks like. Why aren't you still in prison, Ray Ray?"

Ray Ray was a white pimp and a drug dealer among his other hobbies. He claimed membership in the Crips gang in Los Angeles, and wore the "black act" like an extra skin. But Jack knew it was Ray Ray's only avenue to respect. He knew Ray Ray wasn't such a bad guy while you were armed. They'd even exchanged bullets last Christmas. The two men glared at each other, then both broke into smiles and bumped knuckles.

"I heard you shootin' girls now, Murphy. You one mean motha' fuckah." Ray Ray said.

"Yeah," Jack held his .45 up where it could be seen. "If you don't stop interfering with police business—and my date—I'll shoot you . . . again." He'd ended the Christmas festivities by shooting Ray Ray in the left cheek of his ample ass.

Ray Ray laughed and cast a glance at Susan. "You a nice lady, Miss Parole Officer. If you wanna stay that way you watch yourself around this dude. He bad news." Ray Ray drove away.

"Real classy guy," Jack said. "Nothing for you to be concerned about."

"I know him." Susan's hand came out from under her leg. In her hand was a stainless steel Smith & Wesson .38 Chief Special.

"He violated parole twice, and I was the one that sent him back," she said and slipped the .38 in her purse. "You two seem friendly."

"It's a long story," Jack said. "The short version is we shot at each other one night. He went to the hospital. We called a truce, and now we're BFFs."

Jack turned his attention back to Moon Pie's house. "Moon Pie's working right now, but if you see a police car, toot the horn and duck down."

Susan put a hand on his arm as he started to get out and he saw a new burgundy colored GMC 4x4 truck pull into the driveway of Moon Pie's shack. A short, squat figure with no neck emerged. "That's Moon Pie. He's supposed to be on duty," Jack said.

"I guess he took the day off."

Moon Pie's truck was so big he had to hang on to the door to step down. He walked to the back of the house, and only seconds later came back to the truck. His head swiveled like a turret as he looked up and down the street. He then dropped the tailgate, reached in the bed of the truck, and carried a very large box behind the house.

"Did you see what he just carried in?" Susan asked.

"Yeah. A new Bose Home Theater system."

"I priced one for what will be the common room of my bed-and-breakfast." She rubbed her thumb and fingers together.

"Pricey, huh?" he asked.

"A couple of grand at least. You don't hook one of those up to a thirteen-inch black-and-white television."

As if to prove Susan's words, Moon Pie got up in the truck's bed and wrestled a large flat box to the tailgate. He could barely get his arms wide enough to hold it. Jack saw it was a big-screen television before Moon Pie carried it around the back.

Moon Pie came back, climbed into the truck, and pulled out. As he drove out of Jack's view, Jack could see the license plates.

"He has temporary plates on that monster. Thirty grand easy. How can he afford all of that stuff on a cop's salary? I mean, ignore the dump he's living in," Jack said. Getting inside the house was no longer necessary.

Susan pointed out, "Maybe he cashed in a 401(k)."

Jack didn't buy it. Image was everything to someone like Moon Pie. If he had that kind of money, why was he buying these expensive items and still living in a shack like that?

"So what now?" Susan asked.

"We're going back to your place. I've got some errands to run," he said.

Jack left Susan's house and drove his Crown Vic to Reverend Payne's. Seeing Moon Pie with all the new toys gave him an idea. Payne had a relative who worked for a credit bureau and could get financial reports, which Payne didn't mind sharing for a small fee.

If he'd brought Susan with him, Payne would have insisted on making coffee and having a chat. Jack was in and out in less than five minutes, and a hundred dollars lighter than when he'd arrived.

He left Payne's place in Rosedale and called Liddell.

"I'll meet you in your office," Jack said and hung up. If the CIA were listening they would either think Jack was on his way to police headquarters or they wouldn't have a clue where he was going. He hoped Liddell could avoid being followed.

Jack sat at a table in Donut Bank where they couldn't be observed from the street, and had coffee waiting when Liddell showed up. Liddell turned up the collar of his sport coat and comically looked left and right, hands jammed into the coat pockets.

"You're a riot," Jack said.

"Do I look like a spook?" Liddell asked.

"Yeah. I couldn't see you unless you turned sideways and stuck your tongue out. Then you look like a hernia."

"I went by Shirl's place," Liddell said. "He's living with an exotic dancer named—get this—Angel. According to court records Shirl got divorced about two years ago. His ex took her maiden name back and is now Kathy Malbon. Shirl must have been boffing Angel while he was married because before the divorce Angel filed a couple of complaints on him. Stalking, harassment, the usual stuff. Then, shortly after the divorce Angel dropped the complaints. Guess they kissed and made up. I couldn't find anything on Shirl's ex-wife, Kathy Malbon. No address, no record, nothing."

"What about Angel?" Jack asked.

"Five-foot-three, strawberry blond, a hundred pounds, green eyes, busted nine times for prostitution and twice for possession. She's no angel. All her addresses were 'pay-as-you-go' motels, but after the divorce, she used Shirl's apartment in Parkside Terrace for her address, and voilà, no more arrests. There's no way to get inside, Jack. The complex is huge and people were coming and going like fleas to a circus."

Jack had made arrests at Parkside Terrace Apartments. It was like one of the housing projects, but populated by more criminal types. If Shirl was living there he was either getting a hell of a deal to work off-duty security for the place, or he was really on his way to the bottom. Jack told Liddell about his trip to Moon Pie's, the expensive toys, and his visit to Reverend Payne. "Payne should get in touch soon with financial histories on everyone. You owe me fifty dollars, by the way."

"Put it on my tab, pod'na. We've got the right cops," Liddell said. "Now we just have to sit on them and hope they lead us to Quinn."

Jack said nothing.

"What? You have another plan," Liddell asked.

"No. You're right, Bigfoot. But I have a feeling we're running out of time. These two CIA guys blew their cover for some reason. Maybe they thought they could keep better tabs on me and that we might get lucky and lead them to Quinn," Jack said.

"Maybe they've heard about your reputation for pissing every-one off and hope you'll take this heat if this all goes south and we have another Chicago incident."

Jack said, "I don't trust either of them any farther than they can blow me. And, by the way, you know who was off work today." He meant Moon Pie.

"His partner was probably off too," Liddell said. "The schedule must have been wrong. I'll run home and put on a disguise then we can split up and follow them both."

"Seriously, stay there. I may need some help later. I got this."

"I'm getting into this spook stuff," Liddell said.

"I'm going to the hospital and check on Killian before I do any-thing else."

Chapter Thirty

Jack pulled the Crown Vic into a "Doctors Only" parking space and went to the hospital's gift shop, He bought a couple of magazines for whoever was staying with Killian and a bottle of Evian water for himself.

Through the glass wall of the gift shop, he saw CIA Agents White and Thompson step off the elevator. He got behind a rack of magazines and books—not knowing why he was dodging them—but something about their purposeful stride told him to stay out of their way. If he hadn't gone to the gift shop first he would have run right into them.

When they were out of sight he got on the elevator they had come from. It still had the smell of strong cologne. Eau de Spook. Kind of a sissy smell for a G-man.

Getting off at Killian's floor, he could hear Katie's voice coming from the area of the intensive care unit. She was yelling at someone to "Get the hell out of here."

He ran down the hall and turned the corner. The first thing he noticed was that the police guard was not at his post. Then he saw Katie squaring off with a woman in a white coat.

"That's my gal," he said under his breath and took Katie's wrist before she could threw a punch at the doctor—or nurse.

"Whoa. Let's all settle down now," Jack said, and struggled to control Katie.

"Mrs. Murphy," the woman in the white coat was saying, "you'd better think twice before you assault a federal agent."

Jack gave the woman a second look. She was wearing a white jacket that was easily mistaken for a lab coat. Her blond hair was cut in that severe chop that most women in law enforcement seemed to favor.

"What's going on here?" Jack demanded and noticed that two nurses were staying behind the nursing station counter. He had always thought nurses were tough. They dealt with unruly patients and lifted people into and out of beds like they weighed nothing. If you messed with them, they would clean you off the bottom of their white shoes. But these nurses were showing unusual restraint.

The female agent pulled a badge from her pocket, but didn't have a chance to show it or say anything before Katie got in the woman's face. Katie said, "This bitch and two other goons threw us out of Killian's room!"

Jack was surprised at her language. Katie was a sixth-grade teacher and he had never heard her use a curse word.

Katie continued to invade the other woman's space and said, "Killian was barely conscious, and these assholes pushed their way into his room and . . ."

Jack almost yelled, "He's awake?" He was so pleased to hear that news, he had to fight the urge to slug the woman himself and rush to Killian's room.

The agent again tried to speak, but Katie was a step ahead of her.

"Just shut up. I'll explain this to my brother, Alan," Katie said.

The agent gave Jack the once-over. He was fairly sure she wasn't falling for the "brother" routine.

Katie took Jack's hands and said, "Alan, Killian regained consciousness about twenty minutes ago, but two Gestapo agents waltzed in here like . . . like . . . like they owned the hospital or something and ordered us out of the room. Then this bitch shows up and tells us we can't see him. Barbara is complaining to the hospital administrator."

She wasn't done. "I refused to leave and they threatened to arrest me. And now this one . . ." she said, pointing a finger in the woman's face, "is accusing Killian of being part of some terrorist plot."

Katie turned toward Jack and squeezed his hand until it hurt.

"She's looking for Detective Murphy, too," Katie said. "Apparently he's a part of the plot."

Jack was stunned. He might have violated a few department

policies, maybe pissed these guys off, but he wasn't involved in a criminal conspiracy and definitely wasn't a terrorist. But, under federal law they could lock him up for days without charging him. Was that their plan? Were they trying to get him out of the way? If so, why? He thought they had all agreed to play nice. Apparently the CIA had put this bullshit plan together so fast that they had neglected to show this agent a photo of him. If they had she would have pulled a gun instead of a badge.

"What the hell is going on, Agent, uh . . . ?" Jack asked, hoping he sounded genuinely incredulous. He held his hand out and demanded, "Let me see your identification."

She flashed her credentials and said, "FBI Special Agent Crenshaw. And you are?"

Her badge said Federal Bureau of Investigation, but if she was working with the other two numbnuts, she was CIA.

"Alan Connelly," Jack said. "So you're FBI but that doesn't give you the right to threaten my sister." He could immediately see that Special Agent Crenshaw wasn't buying it.

"I wasn't told you had a brother," she said to Katie, but kept her eyes on Jack.

"Can I see your identification again, Agent Crenshaw?" Jack demanded.

She pulled out the badge case and handed it to him. He examined the creds closely while he tried to come up with a plan. And he wondered if the other two were coming back.

"What could the FBI possibly want with Killian or Jack?" he asked, handing the ID case back to her. "Don't you people chase mafia dons and bank robbers?"

"Do you have some identification, Mr. Connelly?"

Oops! Self-righteously he said, "Killian has never done anything dishonest in his life. He's a hard-working public servant, Miz Crenshaw. He's not a terrorist, and for damn sure he's not a criminal. He's a federal agent just like yourself. And Detective Murphy is a hero around here."

Barbara Killian came around the corner with a nurse who looked like a Russian wrestler.

"Katie?" Barbara's voice was filled with concern. The nurse was on her telephone talking to hospital security, and not in a gentle tone. Barbara was looking from Katie to Jack to Crenshaw.

"What is going on?" the nurse asked, cell phone still up to her face. "Security is on its way. I suggest you vacate this floor. You have no authority here."

Barbara got in Agent Crenshaw's face. "Those two men shoved me out of my husband's room. Who do you people think you are?"

"Let's get you back in there," Jack said. He put an arm around her shoulder and led her toward the doors to the ICU.

"Just a minute, Mr. Connelly. I'm not done with you," Crenshaw said, but the large nurse placed herself between Jack and the agent, and Katie got back in her face, arguing loudly.

Crenshaw reached into her handbag, and he didn't think she was reaching for a breath mint. He hurried into the ICU and could hear Katie saying, "This is bullshit. I'll complain to your superiors. I'll call the governor, who happens to be a close friend of mine." Crenshaw was threatening physical violence if they continued to interfere.

"I've got to find a way out of here," Jack said to a confused Barbara. "No time to explain."

"I can help you," came a soft voice from behind them.

He turned around. A cleaning lady with a name tag that said "Ruby" grabbed his hand and led him to a doorway. She unlocked the door and handed him the set of keys. "Down the stairs. Turn left at the bottom. Follow that hall until it ends and turn right. You'll come to another locked door that leads outside. Leave the keys in the door. I'll get them later."

He went through the door and took the steps two and three at a time. Behind him he heard Ruby say, "Good luck," and then the door above closed.

Agent Crenshaw couldn't shoot them all. At least he didn't think she could, but he other things to worry about. Did the Feds put an APB out on him? Were they right now at Susan's? Had they arrested Liddell?

He'd come too far to get benched. Murphy's Law says: "The degree to which you look on the bright side is directly proportional to the amount of misfortune that will befall you." He had earned some good luck.

Agent White's cell phone vibrated. White didn't answer. The only people who had his number were Thompson and now the female agent on loan to them from the FBI's antiterrorist squad. He hadn't asked for her, nor did he want her. Crenshaw had deliberately been kept in the dark and hadn't a clue what their mission was. She didn't even know who they really were.

White wasn't accustomed to working jobs inside his own country against American citizens. He was from the old school. The new operatives like Allen Thompson were in it for the power and thrill that went with being labeled a "spook." Thompson would obey orders but he would never understand what honor and duty really meant. Guys like that were saving the world by killing it, one person at a time. White's big concern now was how Agent Crenshaw would handle it when they had to start eliminating people. He had his orders. If she got in the way . . . well.

White answered the phone.

"Sir, this is Crenshaw."

"Go ahead."

"Jack Murphy is here in the hospital."

Her voice was calm, controlled. He had to admit she was cool headed. Maybe she would perform well, but she had let Murphy slip away. One strike.

"Where exactly is he, Agent Crenshaw?"

"He was trying to visit the ATF agent, sir. I pursued him into the basement of the hospital but lost him. My orders, sir?"

To her credit she had made no excuses.

"I don't have to remind you how important this is."

"No, sir."

"We're on our way."

"Yes, sir."

"And Crenshaw?"

"Yes, sir."

"Don't alert hospital security. You find him and call me."

"Yes, sir," she said.

Jack came to the exit door, opened it, and poked his head out to see where he was. He hadn't seen or heard Crenshaw, so he must have lost her. Several cars were moving in the lot but none of them were police cars

His mom always said that if an Irishman didn't have bad luck, he'd have no luck at all. It was true, because he'd walked less than ten feet when he heard the sound of an engine revving behind him, and he was lifted off his feet, over the hood, and slammed into the car's windshield.

His head hit hard, and he rolled off the hood, unable to protect himself as he hit the blacktop hard. Agent Thompson pulled him to his feet and threw him against the car's hood. Thompson twisted Jack's arm behind his back and shoved his face against the hot metal surface. Lightning bolts of pain exploded through Jack's brain. His shoulder was definitely out of its socket.

After what seemed like a lifetime, the pressure eased and he was struck in the back of the head with something hard enough to make his knees buckle. Thompson crowded against him to keep him from falling to the ground and began punching him in the back and the side of his face.

Jack heard a ringing inside his skull and could smell Thompson's too-sweet cologne. Thompson slammed Jack's head into the car again and it was all Jack could do to remain conscious.

"What's the matter, Jack? Don't you have a snappy comeback for that?" Thompson said and shoved Jack's arm further up behind him. Starbursts of pain exploded in Jack's shoulder, and he heard himself gagging.

He's not going to arrest me. He's going to beat me to death.

Thompson yanked Jack's .45 from his holster and threw it over the hood of the car. He then drove all his weight into Jack, crushing the wind from him, twisting his arm.

"What's that, Jack?" Thompson said and drove an elbow down into Jack's spine. "You say you're going to do what to me?"

Jack's pain was unbearable and then it was gone. His mind focused on one thing—revenge. Time stopped for Jack Murphy . . . and ran out for Allen Thompson. The pressure on Jack's shoulder eased, and Jack realized that he had taken the CIA man's scrotum in a death grip with his hand.

Thompson began sucking in air like a faulty vacuum cleaner and Jack squeezed with all his strength. Thompson was trying to move away, but Jack shifted and yanked back and forth, playing scrotum Ping-Pong. He wanted to rip his balls off, but he lost his grip. Thompson fell into him, still sucking air, and Jack turned and brought a knee up—hard—under Thompson's chin. He heard Thompson's teeth crack together, or maybe his jaw had broken, he didn't know. He just knew Thompson had crumpled to the ground and lay in a fetal position, hands cradling his groin.

Jack propped himself against the trunk of the car, not feeling the hot metal anymore. Gorge rose in his throat, and he didn't try to fight it back. He doubled over and threw up on Thompson's thousand-dollar Armani suit. Jack took some deep breaths, tried to stand, and another wave of nausea hit. This time he dropped to his knees and hurled straight into Thompson's face.

He fought back the dizziness, lifted his head, and scanned the parking lot. Crenshaw and White were still out there. A half-dozen cars were moving around but none were coming in his direction.

He took more deep breaths and saw that Thompson was starting to move around. Jack kicked Thompson in the face and when the agent's hands came up to protect his head Jack kicked him in the crotch. He could see Thompson's jaw was at an odd angle, maybe broken. "I warned you, asshole."

Jack staggered to the door of Thompson's car and tried to get in, but his damaged shoulder screamed with the effort. He knew what he would have to do. He'd seen it done a hundred times on TV. It looked easy. It wasn't.

He positioned himself near the doorpost and slammed his shoulder against the body of the car. The pain was excruciating one second and gone the next. He didn't have time to hurt, so he slid into Thompson's still running car and drove to the Mary Street exit. He hoped White or Crenshaw wouldn't find Thompson for a while. He hoped he'd broken the bastard's jaw.

Chapter Thirty-one

Vinnie, the bartender, was standing on the wooden deck behind Two Jakes smoking when an unfamiliar car lurched across the delivery drive and came to a stop. Jack fell out of the car onto the concrete drive. Vinnie threw the still burning stub into the parking lot and was already yelling, "Jake! Jake!" as he rushed to the car. He helped Jack up, putting an arm around his waist, and met Brady at the door. Between the two of them they half-carried, half-dragged Jack through the back entrance and into a small storage room that was converted into a bedroom. They laid Jack on a cot and Brady hurried out of the room. He came back with a steaming coffee mug but Jack waved it away.

"The car," Jack muttered and tried to sit up. Brady put the mug to Jack's lips and said, "Drink some of this."

Jack got a couple of sips down and pushed it away, sputtering and coughing, "Are you trying to kill me?" He lay back, still coughing.

"This will help you rest," Brady said. He tried to get Jack to drink some more, but he just shook his head and made a face.

"We'll take care of the car. You need a hospital, lad."

"No hospital," Jack said, and reached for the mug and drank down whatever nasty concoction was in there. He would vomit again, but the pain was worse than the drink. He felt woozy. Then he passed out.

Jack opened his eyes, and Brady was standing over him.

"Here, take these and wash them down with another toddy." Brady dropped some pills in Jack's hand and helped him sit up. Jack popped the pills into his mouth and barely tasted the bitterness before some of the lukewarm alcohol-laden liquid was poured down his throat.

"Jesus Christ!" Jack swallowed and sputtered. "What is that stuff? It tastes like lighter fluid."

"It's an old family recipe. You'll sleep for a while. When you wake up, you'll feel better."

"Can't sleep right now. Got to find Susan and Liddell," he said, and was gone again.

Jack was asleep for several hours. When he opened his eyes, Susan was sitting on a chair beside the cot and holding his hand. His head and shoulder were sore as hell, but he'd live. On the other hand, Agent Thompson might have to get a sex change.

"You should see a doctor, Jack," Susan said.

"You should see the other guy," he said, and winced when he tried to smile. He put a hand up to his cheek and felt puffiness. *Bastard!*

"She's right, you know," Brady said to Jack. "But he's hard-headed like his old man was."

"I'm fine," Jack lied. "Where'd you take the car?"

"You're feverish, boy."

"Honest, Brady, I'm fine." Jack flexed his injured shoulder a few times. It hurt, but not as much as before. His head was another matter. "I've got to call Katie and Moira and make sure they're safe. These guys don't play around. Where's Liddell?"

Brady said, "We can't reach him. His cell phone is switched off. Katie and Moira are somewhere safe. I didn't tell them much. Hell, I don't know that much. But they are going to stay put. I've worked out a code for them to answer the phone so they'll know it's one of us."

"Where's the car?"

Brady grinned.

"What's so funny?" Jack asked. He was worried about Liddell.

Brady said, "Well, I parked it in Double Dick's parking spot," he said with a sardonic grin. "Don't worry, I wiped it down so there's no fingerprints."

"You didn't," Jack said.

"You bet I did."

That was very risky, old man.

Jack's run-in with the CIA had shaken things up a bit. Not knowing who was involved in this conspiracy—and that's all it could be called at this point—created more questions than answers.

Susan said, "After Vinnie came for me and explained you were here, I didn't think I should call anyone. What are we going to do?"

Jack tried to think. The fiasco at the hospital had surely brought the police into it. Hell, he had assaulted a federal agent, stolen his car, and fled the scene. "Guilt by fleeing" is the unofficial police terminology. But he didn't think Thompson would file charges— for the physical injury or the stolen car. Likewise he didn't think Crenshaw would arrest Katie or anyone else who helped him escape from the hospital. They would, however, spirit some of them away if they got the chance.

"I've got things to do," Jack said and made it to his feet this time.

"Not without me," Susan said. "I've probably lost my job. I want to finish this."

Jack said, "We need wheels. We have to assume they've flagged all the vehicles available to us."

Vinnie pulled a set of keys from his pocket and put them in Jack's hand.

The keys were to a motorcycle Vinnie kept under a tarp behind the marina building. There was even an extra helmet for Susan. Brady promised to let them know as soon as Liddell checked in.

The Honda Gold Wing had no plates, but Vinnie assured Jack it couldn't be traced back to Brady or Vinnie. Jack didn't ask how Vinnie came by the bike. He started it and was surprised by how quiet it ran.

"Where are we going?" Susan asked. "I got a call from Indianapolis before Vinnie came to get me. They wanted to know why I was impeding a federal investigation."

"It's going to be okay," Jack said.

"My boss sounded shaky on the phone. Somebody must have rattled him good." She said, "He said there's going to be an internal inquiry of my handling of Khaled Abutaqa, and his subsequent death."

Jack knew it was only a matter of time before they'd be pressuring Brady and Vinnie. He wasn't worried about Brady. He was a tough old bird. Vinnie would never talk, but Jack knew Vinnie had some kind of shady past. He hoped it wasn't something that would land Vinnie in prison.

"We have nowhere to go."

"Only one place I can think of right now," Jack said. He put the bike in gear and headed for Rosedale. A few minutes later, Jack pulled down the alley and stopped behind Reverend Payne's church. A large wooden shed-like garage sat at the back of the property. Sliding barn doors were secured with a heavy chain and padlock. There was wood privacy fence with a gate to the right.

"This is where we're going to get help?" Susan asked.

"Payne will let us stay for a while. At least until I can figure out what's next." Jack said.

"Don't even think about leaving me here, Jack. After everything I've done, those guys will find me and put me in jail. It's safer for both of us if we stay together."

She had a point. The CIA held all the cards now.

She hopped off the Gold Wing and put her shoulder to the gate and forced it open. Jack dismounted and pushed the motorcycle into the back yard. The yard looked like an auto graveyard. Rusted hulks, truck tailgates, motorcycle frames and engines, tires, and hubcaps made up the bulk of the mess. The motorcycle would fit right in.

Susan picked her way through the junk and knocked on the back door.

Payne came to the door and invited them in. He didn't seem surprised to find them there.

"I haven't had a woman come to my back door for quite some time," he said and smiled.

"I don't usually have CIA agents chasing me," Jack said.

They sat at Payne's kitchen table and Jack rubbed his injured shoulder. The pain felt like a charley horse galloping toward the finish line. He said to Payne, "I don't think these guys will cast their net very wide, but just in case, don't talk to anyone here about us." He was hoping Payne would insist on Susan staying there.

"What happens here, stays here," Payne said. "One of my boys came back from the parole office this morning and said some men were talking to your secretary. He said she was giving those men hell."

"Those are the guys who are chasing us," Jack explained. "I had a little run-in with two of them at the hospital."

Payne stared sightlessly in Jack's direction. "When you have a run-in with someone, they usually get dead."

"No one was killed, but one of them was singing tenor when I left."

"I should call Mabel. She would have called me about this morning if she could. I think she might be in trouble," Susan said.

Jack agreed, but there wasn't anything they could do for her now. "Susan, I don't think she's in physical danger. We'll try to call her from a pay phone. I don't think we should use our cell phones. As a matter of fact, I think we should turn them off." He couldn't remember if the phone could still be tracked, even turned off, but they both powered down their cell phones anyway.

Jack asked Payne, "What did you find out for me?"

Payne sat back. "Skippy Walker has a bank account with Old National Bank. Or at least he did. He withdrew all of his money three days ago. Fifteen thousand, two hundred and thirty dollars. He also borrowed against his 401(k). Thirty-five thousand dollars. In other words, he has no savings."

"That explains the new truck and toys," Jack said. "And what about Shirley West?"

"Shirley West has quite a bit put away in a couple of banks. Nothing that he couldn't of earned though. He hasn't made any large deposits recently. He hasn't touched his 401(k) and there's a bunch of money there. The only withdrawal he made was a year ago. He pulled out five thousand."

"He got divorced a year ago," Jack said.

"That's all I could get," Payne said.

"That's plenty. Thanks for your help. I owe you one."

"And I'll collect someday too," Payne said.

"Well, we have two choices now," Jack said to Susan. "I can turn myself in. Or you can hide out here with Payne while I find this Quinn guy. If I catch him first, the CIA will most likely go away."

Her answer surprised him. "Maybe you should turn yourself in. This is the federal government we're dealing with, Jack."

He noticed she said "we" and not "you." "I'm not sure who they are," Jack said. "But there's no way in hell I'm sitting around while Killian's shooter is still out there."

Susan picked up the motorcycle keys from the table. "Let's go," she said.

"Can you ride a motorcycle? I mean, you want to drive?" Jack asked.

Payne cradled his crippled hands in his lap. "I think you should both stay here where you are safe. But if you're bent on going, you'll be less conspicuous in my car."

Payne's car turned out to be a seventies model MG Midget. Jack couldn't imagine why a blind man needed a car, but it was a welcome piece of luck. Payne unlocked the chain holding the garage's sliding doors and pulled them open. Susan got behind the wheel and drove the MG into the alley while Jack put the Gold Wing inside the shed. She seemed at home in the cramped car but Jack had to duck his head and pull his knees up to his chin. Payne closed and chained the doors behind them.

"Where to?" Susan asked.

"Let's go to Moon Pie's," Jack said. "But first, let's stop at a pay phone. You can call Mabel and I'll see if I can reach Liddell." He patted his pockets and asked, "Do you have some change?"

Susan rummaged in her purse. "I've got plenty of change, but you have to promise me, no more burglaries."

"I promise," Jack lied.

They went to a pay phone on Riverside Drive near an insurance building.

Susan tried several phone numbers for her receptionist and finally reached her. She was fine, but concerned, and Jack could hear her voice from five feet away and with traffic going past. She sounded like the witch in *The Wizard of Oz*. He imagined her saying, "I'll get you, my pretty. And that detective of yours too." And then she would cackle and he would wet himself.

Susan hung up and only had enough change left for two phone calls.

Jack called Stu Sanders's work number and didn't get an answer. He only had change left for one more call. "To hell with it," he said, and tried Stu's personal cell phone. Stu answered on the second ring.

"Stu, I'm glad I caught you. Have some guys come by asking about me?"

"What are you talking about, Jack? What did you do now?"

He told Stu about the run-in with Crenshaw and the fight with Agent Thompson in the hospital parking lot. "If they ask, you should tell them what you know. I don't want to be responsible for you being arrested for helping me."

"Are you kidding? I'd never go to jail for you."

"That's the spirit, Stu."

"Listen, pal, stay safe. Call if you need anything, and good luck."

Susan said, "I thought you were going to call Liddell. I don't have any more change."

"We'll be on the move," Jack said, and turned his cell phone back on. "Let's drive around. I only need to talk to him for a minute. I'll shut the phone off again after."

They got back in the MG and Susan drove through the downtown streets in a crisscross pattern.

Jack tried Liddell at work. No answer. He was about to call Liddell's cell when the phone vibrated in his hand. The number displayed was from a detective's desk, but not Liddell's or his own work number. He answered.

"Where have you been? Can you talk?" Jack asked.

"The captain called me in and ordered me to stay in the office. I'm not supposed to talk to anyone. He said you'd gone out of town for a couple of weeks, but he didn't say where or why and I didn't ask. I had to turn Killian's case over to him. There were two guys with the captain and one of them looked and smelled pretty bad. Is that the guys you were telling me about?"

Jack said, "I just wanted to make sure you were safe." He told Liddell about the fiasco at the hospital.

"Well, that proves they're not CIA," Liddell said.

"How's that?"

"Because the CIA would have just shot you and hid the body," Liddell said.

"Do what the captain says and stay out of this. I might need you later," Jack said, and Liddell reluctantly agreed. Jack powered the phone off.

"So?" Susan asked.

"Obviously these guys planned to put me on ice for a couple of weeks. The captain told Liddell to stay in the office and keep his mouth shut. Liddell had to give our case file to the Feds."

Jack looked up and down the street. He didn't like being so exposed.

Chapter Thirty-two

Susan drove down First Avenue. Before they reached Moon Pie's street, they saw him pull out onto First Avenue heading south. Susan made a quick U-turn and caught up with Moon Pie's truck.

"Stay several cars back," Jack said.

"Hey, who's driving?" She slid into the left lane and stayed three cars behind Moon Pie.

Moon Pie stopped for a red light at First Avenue and Franklin Street. Jack could see through the back window that Moon Pie was jamming to some music. The light changed, and he went straight ahead, through the light at John Street and onto 4th Street. Moon Pie hung a right on Court Street. There was very little traffic, so Susan backed off.

"Where do you think he's going?" Susan asked. She allowed a Toyota truck to get in front of her.

"You're pretty good at this tailing stuff," Jack said.

"Thank you. I saw it on television."

"He's not going to Shirl's," Jack said.

When Moon Pie turned into the parking garage for the Blue Star Casino, Susan pulled to the curb next to the abandoned building that had housed the Indiana State Employment Office a few years earlier. The same people who owned the Blue Star now owned the building. They were gobbling up as much property and land as they could before people woke up and realized that gambling was bad.

They left the car on the street and walked into the parking garage. After passing tour buses parked near the visitor entrance, they went inside and up the escalator to the second floor, where a skyway connected the casino's hotel with the pavilion. Jack could see Moon Pie a hundred feet ahead of them on the skywalk.

Jack and Susan looked like a couple on their way to get fleeced. Inside the pavilion, Jack went to the railing and watched Moon Pie show some kind of card to the guard. He headed toward the boarding gate. Moon Pie was wearing a straw porkpie hat. He had on chinos with a lime green and tan bowling shirt and tan boating shoes with no socks.

He was a man on a mission.

Jack and Susan followed. At the turnstiles, the security guard stopped them.

"You have member cards?" the guard asked. It was the young guy with acne Jack saw on the boat during his tour with Stu. The kid's eyes traveled Susan's body from stem to stern.

"We've never been here," Susan said, smiling at the young guard whose scraggy beard was fighting for life in the craters on his face. "Is it a lot of fun?" she cooed.

"Well," the guard said with lust in his eyes and a stick shift in his groin. He wasn't sure what to say, so Jack helped him along.

"Don't you make an exception for visitors from out of town?" Jack suggested.

The guard's full attention was on Susan as he motioned for them to go ahead. The wall clock next to the boarding gate showed 5:30.

Jack was curious and asked the guard. "How did the guy in front of us get through without a ticket?"

"Gold VIP Card." He smiled and Jack noticed he had no teeth. Either that or they were hiding from the man's bad breath.

Susan asked, "A what?"

"Gold VIP Card, capital G-O-L-D, capital V, capital I, capital P," he spelled for them.

"How does a feller get one of them there cards?" Jack asked, and Susan nudged him in the ribs.

"When yo're a reg'lar, you apply fer one, an' they sen' it to ya," he answered. And, still smiling, added helpfully, "If yo're lookin' fer that fella just come through, you'll pob'ly find him in the Crystal Room. Deck two."

"Why is that?" Jack looked at his name tag, "Why is that, Clete?"

"Cause that's where all them high rollers go," he said.

"Thanks fer yore hep'," Jack said and handed the security guard a ten-dollar bill. He thought of something else and asked, "Clete, is the boat sailing?"

"Nope. In a couple weeks it won't be sailin' ever agin. They got a new law that the boat don't haf'ta sail no more. If y'all hurry you'll pob'ly make it. Boat's almost full up."

They thanked the guard and headed down the gangway and entered the riverboat casino. The lights inside the room were more annoying and the noise louder than he remembered from last time. And the patrons were more inebriated. People tend to get louder as they get drunker. It wasn't even three thirty and some of them were already half-past drunk, going on stupor.

"Let's get tokens," Susan said and nudged him toward the cashiers' cage.

"I don't gamble. Besides, I only have eleven dollars."

"Well, I have money." She pulled the wad of bills from her bag. "I'll get a few tokens so we can blend in."

Before he could stop her, she was gone. She came back with a bucket of tokens, gave Jack a fistful and headed toward the slot machines. Jack saw the Crystal Room to his left and went to find Moon Pie.

The Crystal Room lived up to its name. The ceiling appeared to be inlaid with gold, and above every table hung sparkling, crystal chandeliers. Dancing lights filled the room like a scene from *Saturday Night Fever*. Little dangly things made of glass and brass hung from every wall fixture. The effects would be dizzying even if you weren't drunk.

At a craps table, a frail gray-haired woman was yelling at the pair of dice in her hand, "C'mon, baby, c'mon, baby." Jack hoped she didn't say, "Baby needs a new pair of shoes" or "Grandma needs some new teeth" or some other nostalgic phrase.

Colorful characters skulked around the perimeter of the room waiting for someone to give up a machine. Everyone was drinking and pulling slot handles or staggering about like creatures from the gambling laboratory of Doctor Frankenstein.

He was about to give up on this floor and try to find Susan when he saw Moon Pie coming out of the starboard stairwell. He was with a security guard, and as they got closer Jack could see the guard was wearing the oak leaf insignia of a major on his shirt collar. The boss.

Moon Pie and the guard stopped near the slot machine Jack was pretending to play without even glancing in his direction. Jack saw "J. Ellert" embossed on the guard's name tag.

J. Ellert and Moon Pie were having an animated discussion, and Ellert was none too happy. Jack heard Ellert say, "Listen, asshole. Stay away from me." This surely wasn't the way a security chief should be talking to a V.I.P. customer. Especially when the customer was an off-duty city policeman.

Jack decided he would follow Ellert. Moon Pie should know who Jack was, but maybe he was in "gambling mode" and incognizant of anything but throwing his money away. When they split up he started to follow Ellert but Susan rushed up and nearly bowled him over. She had a death grip on a large plastic cup with the Blue Star logo on it and it was overflowing with tokens.

"I won! Look. I won." He could see that he would have to get her into therapy if she came here often.

"Wonderful," he said with a plastic smile. "Come on." He took her by the arm, led her in the direction Ellert had gone, and explained what he'd seen and heard.

"How did Moon Pie react?" she asked.

"Moon Pie didn't say anything to Ellert, but Ellert was coming unglued. I don't think Moon Pie recognized me."

"What with you being a rock star and all," she said.

Moon Pie was following Ellert, his new un-friend, to the aft stairwell. The two men disappeared behind a metal door that said TO DECKS.

Jack held Susan back. "Let's give them a minute to get away from the door." They were rewarded for not being hasty by the sudden reappearance of Major Ellert, who shot out of the doorway, brushing past them without so much as an "excuse me" or even a "get out of my way."

"Boy," Susan said under her breath, "that man is pissed!"

It was an understatement. Ellert was taller than Jack and had a few extra pounds on him, with a lot of them hanging below his belt line. Jack said, "It's a safe bet he isn't one of Moon Pie's friends from the gym."

Susan leaned in, kissed him on the cheek and said, "You go after Moon Pie. I'll see what's eating Ugly."

Jack entered the stairway and heard a door below shutting. He hurried down the stairs. At the bottom, he cracked the door open to be sure he wouldn't run into Moon Pie or anyone who was looking for him. He didn't see any CIA guys wearing black trench coats and Boris Badenov hats, so he pursued the elusive flying squirrel... Moon Pie.

Moon Pie stopped at a five-dollar slot and was feeding it bills by the fistful. Jack kept a respectful distance and played a poker machine. He lost about a dollar fifty in the same amount of time Moon Pie fed several hundred dollars into his machine. Moon Pie was a loser. What a surprise.

Moon Pie moved on to a craps table where Jack watched him for a couple of minutes. Losing at this too, he was about to move to a roulette wheel when Jack saw Major Ellert crossing the room. Moon Pie must've spotted Ellert too, because he disengaged from playing roulette and locked on target. Then something strange happened. Ellert saw Moon Pie coming, did an about-face, and almost ran to the nearest stairway and disappeared. It was as if Ellert was afraid of Moon Pie. Either that or he didn't want to be seen with him.

Ellert being afraid of Moon Pie was unimaginable. It was like a bear avoiding a gerbil. Ellert had the size advantage and, unless Moon Pie was the next Jackie Chan, Ellert could squash him like a bug.

Susan came up beside Jack and put her arm in his and whispered in his ear, "We need to talk somewhere private." She led him to the stairwell Ellert had disappeared into.

Once there, Susan let go of his arm and pointed to a pay phone on the wall on the next landing down. "The big ugly one was on that phone. He punched in a number several times and would say about two words, wait a few seconds, then hang up. He was very agitated."

Jack put his hand out for change and Susan dug in her purse again. They descended the stairs to the pay phone. Jack fed some coins in the phone slot and punched a series of buttons and waited. The phone rang and was answered by a tired female voice, "Sugar Creek Inn, how may I direct your call?"

Jack hung up.

"What did you do?" Susan asked.

"In college I dated a girl at the phone company. She told me how to do a redial off a pay phone. Ellert was calling the Sugar Creek Inn."

"Why would Major Ellert be so angry at Moon Pie?" Susan asked. "And why was he calling the Sugar Creek Inn? Isn't that in Kentucky?"

Both good questions that Jack didn't have answers for.

"Let's go to the Sugar Creek Inn," he suggested.

Susan gave him a sly look. "Is this your way of making a pass at me?"

He let that go and said, "We can't go home. We've got to stay somewhere."

"You're joking," she said, then, "you're not joking."

"Well, we can't stay here," he said.

"We don't have any luggage or clothes," she reminded him.

Clothes are the least of our problems. He asked, "So are you in?"

"Absolutely," she said without hesitation.

Chapter Thirty-three

At Sugar Creek Inn they checked in as Mr. and Mrs. Jones, which earned them a smirk from the woman behind the counter. She introduced herself as Millie Hardy. Millie was in her mid-forties, shapely, with curly dark hair that framed her face and lay across her shoulders. She wore a leopard patterned silk blouse that left nothing to the imagination, low cut, skin tight. On her ample bosom was a tattoo of a tree, its leafy limbs seemed to spread across her cleavage.

"You like my tattoo?"

"Very nice," Jack said, and Susan gave him a wink.

Millie explained, "It's the Tree of Life," and leaned across the counter, giving him an arborist's view. "The Celts believe the natural world is the giver and keeper of life. This . . ." she ran a finger down her cleavage, ". . . represents the intertwined desires of man and nature. The branches reach into the sky and the roots," she ran her eyes down to his crotch, "reach into the sacred streams. Deep below. Creating an explosion of life." Her eyes rose to his and she smiled seductively.

Susan looped an arm in Jack's and said to the woman, "That's interesting, but we just need a room."

"Of course you do, sweetie," Millie said and pushed a plastic key card across to Jack. "Room 375."

Jack took the key and said, "A friend of ours was here earlier. He might have been with two other men."

Millie turned all business. "We don't allow employees to discuss guests. What guests do here is their own business."

"Can I speak to a manager?"

"I'm the owner," Millie said. "One of them at least."

Jack and Susan exchanged looks. Jack wondered if she let her other registration clerks wear such seductive clothing and flirt with the guests. This woman really didn't fit his expectation or first impression of the Sugar Creek Inn.

Millie must have interpreted the look they were giving her and said, "I was at a party and one of my girls had to leave unexpectedly. I don't usually work the front. Hell, I don't usually work here at all. Yet here I am."

Jack thought about ditching the Mr. and Mrs. Jones act and pulling his badge. He wanted to ask her how long she had been on the desk. Had someone named Ellert checked in? If so, was anyone with him? Did it hurt like a bitch to have that tree tattooed into her chest? He was saved from a decision when she said, "Anything else I can do for you I'd be more than happy to—Mr. Jones."

She had once again turned into the seductress. Susan took him by the arm and led him toward the elevators. Over her shoulder she said, "I'm sure we'll be just fine."

Jack could see Susan was a little ticked off. He couldn't resist. He turned and asked Millie, "Do you have a list of the movies we can rent?"

This time Susan slapped him on the shoulder and pulled him toward the elevators.

"What? I just wanted to know what kind of place we were staying in," he said when they got out of earshot of Millie.

"I'm not staying here," Susan said matter-of-factly. "You can if you want."

"It might be fun," he said with a playful grin.

"Oh please! She'd eat you for breakfast."

Jack grinned even wider. "You think?"

"Don't make me regret helping you, Murphy," she said. "Do you think Ellert is involved?" she asked, changing the subject.

"I can't think of any other reason Major Ellert would call here right after his run-in with Moon Pie. If he's calling here still, maybe Quinn is here. It's a long shot, I know, but we need a safe place right now, and maybe we'll see Quinn or Shirl or Moon Pie. Two birds with one stone."

"We absolutely can't stay here, Jack," Susan said, glancing toward the red-haired cougar. "Why don't I go back to Evansville and talk to the CIA guys? What can they do to me? They'll question me and let me go. I can be your eyes and ears. I think we should find out what the CIA is doing."

It was tempting. She probably wouldn't be in any danger. After all, he was the one that did the "nut scootin' boogie" with Agent Thompson. But then again, these guys had the power to turn the police department against him and shut down their investigation. There would be too many questions that Susan couldn't answer. And he didn't want them to know about Shirl and Moon Pie if they didn't already.

He said, "You will probably be arrested. Maybe disappear for a while. You know too much." He figured they probably wouldn't get anything out of Millie unless he assumed his cop role, and even then she could tell him to go to hell.

"Did Payne give you Kathy Malbon's address or phone number?" he asked.

Susan dug in her purse and handed him a scrap of paper.

"I didn't get her address but I know where she works," Susan said. "It's a company called Brodstetters. Some kind of accounting firm."

"We'll need some quarters," Jack said and patted his pockets.

"I'll get it. You don't need any more complications in your life," Susan said.

Susan got change and they drove to a pay phone, where Susan made the call to the accounting firm. She held the phone where Jack could hear.

A woman answered, and Susan said, "Miss Malbon, please."

"I'm sorry but she isn't available. Can someone else help you?"

"Can you tell me how to reach her?"

The woman said, "May I ask what this is in reference to?"

"No, you may not," Susan said, and Jack took the phone from her.

"Hello, miss," Jack said. "I'm a police detective. That was my secretary. I'm sorry for her bluntness." He gave Susan a sideways look, and she again slapped him on the shoulder. "I need to speak to Ms. Malbon right away. It's police business. Can you help me?"

The woman seemed to thaw. She said, "Like I told your secretary, Ms. Malbon is not in the office now. Can I—"

Jack interrupted her and said, "It's very important I contact her right now. Her life may be in danger."

"I can call her," the woman offered, and now Jack lost his patience.

"This is life or death. Listen up, if I have to come to your office I won't be this nice."

This seemed to get the woman's attention. "Oh my God!" she said. "Ms. Malbon asked not to be disturbed, but I guess I can tell you. She's at a conference today," the woman was saying and Jack felt disappointed. "She's in Henderson at a CPA conference. I can give you the telephone number for the hotel."

"Can you tell give me the address of the hotel?" *Maybe we just got lucky.*

He listened, thanked the woman and hung up.

"She's at the Sugar Creek Inn."

Susan gaped at him.

Susan stood outside the closed doors to the second-floor conference room at the Sugar Creek Inn. She had peeked in and the room was full. More than half were women.

"We don't know what she looks like. How do we find her?" she asked.

The sound of clapping came from behind the doors. Jack said, "Come on," and pushed the doors open.

People were sitting in clusters, talking, some were milling about, grazing the snack table like a herd of—well—accountants. Only a few women were leaving the room. Jack hoped Kathy Malbon wasn't one of them.

He spotted a short balding man standing by the podium. Jack approached him and saw he was fiddling with the audio and video equipment.

"Before you turn that off . . ." Jack said and the man looked up. Jack flashed his badge quickly, hoping the man didn't notice he wasn't from Henderson PD. "Can you ask Ms. Malbon, Kathy Malbon, to come to the podium?" Jack said.

"That's me," a voice said from behind them.

Like most conference hotels, The Sugar Creek Inn had a business center. Jack, Susan, and Kathy Malbon sat close together with the door shut. Jack thought she was beautiful, in a country sort of way, with a milky complexion that needed no makeup, dark brown eyes, and blond curls falling in soft waves around her face. Jack couldn't imagine Shirl dumping her for a hooker. She was probably close to Shirl's age—he guessed about fifty-something. Maybe Shirl was one of those guys running from his age.

He showed her his credentials again. "I'm Jack Murphy," he said and extended his hand.

"Susan Summers," Susan said.

Kathy shook their hands. She said to Jack, "I know who you are. I've seen you on television."

"We just need to ask you a few questions," Jack said, and watched her for a reaction. She seemed prepared for him, like she knew he would be coming and dreaded it.

"What's he done this time?" she asked. "I haven't talked to Shirl for quite some time."

"He hasn't done anything . . . yet. But I can see you still care for him. He may be in serious trouble" Susan answered. Susan had read her correctly. Kathy Malbon was obviously still in love with Shirl.

"What kind of trouble?"

Jack said, "An ATF agent was shot. A man we think was involved in that shooting was killed last night."

Her shoulders drooped slightly, hands clasped tightly in her lap. "You think that Shirl and Skippy are involved?" she asked.

Jack hadn't mentioned Skippy Walker.

"Tell me what you know," Jack said.

She met Susan's eyes. "Shirl and I . . . what caused our divorce . . . well, he was seeing other women. Quite a few other women, actually. This last one is young enough to be our daughter," she said, and scoffed at the idea.

The barest hint of tears came into her eyes as she began to talk. "Well, I was here, at the hotel early this morning to get things set up for the conference when I saw Shirl come in. I naturally watched to see who he was meeting. Maybe I wanted to see if he was cheating on this one too."

"And . . ." Jack prompted gently. He wanted to cut to the chase, but sometimes you have to let a person tell the story their way.

"I saw Skippy with Shirl. Skippy is Shirl's partner. I met him after Shirl's demotion. I couldn't believe they were sticking Shirl with someone like that. But I guess Shirl was lucky to have a job. Anyway, they were in street clothes, not uniforms, and I didn't know they ran around together outside of work." She looked at Jack and Susan to see that they were on the same page before continuing.

"I was up by the conference room and they were in the lobby, just standing there like they were waiting for someone. Then this other man met them."

Jack took the picture of Quinn from his pocket and handed it to her. "Does this look like the guy?"

She looked at the picture and shook her head, but said, "I think that's the guy that met them later."

Jack let her hold on to the picture. "So four men met? Can you describe the third man?"

She gave an exact description of Major Ellert, minus the security uniform.

"Have you ever heard the name Jim Ellert?" Jack asked.

She thought for a second. "No. I don't think so."

"Okay," Jack said. "You saw a third man meet Shirl and Skippy in the lobby. What happened next?"

"I remember I thought it was strange because they never spoke to each other. Not even a hello. Except for Skippy of course. He looked like he was nervous and said a few things to Shirl and the other man, but they never answered him. Then they got on the elevator. I stayed in the conference room and cracked the door to see what floor the elevator stopped on. It stopped on this floor. I saw them get off and go down the hallway to a room. They must have already had a key because they just went inside."

She gave a nervous laugh and said, "You probably think I'm horrible."

"Not possible," Jack said. "You are helping us considerably."

Susan smiled at her and said, "Please continue."

Kathy Malbon looked even more embarrassed if that was possible, and said, "I didn't know what to do. I thought maybe they were having a party and expecting . . . others. You know?"

"Okay," Jack said.

"I finished setting up for the conference—that took about fifteen minutes or so—and I thought about leaving, but my curiosity got the best of me. I wanted to see if there were other women coming to the room. That's when this man came into the lobby." She handed the picture of Quinn back to Jack, and said, "At least I think it was this man. It's hard to be sure."

Jack's heart was racing. He wanted to grab her by the shoulders and shake the rest of it out of her, but Susan had put a hand on his knee.

"And I saw the guy go to the stairs. He was carrying a big briefcase. Like a catalog case, you know? And he turned down the same hallway and went to the room. He let himself in without knocking."

"Did they leave the room?" Jack asked. He'd talked to enough witnesses to know when they were finished. Now he'd have to help her remember the rest of the details.

"I saw the man in that picture leave," she said. "I didn't stay much longer. No one went in or came out while I was watching."

"How long was this guy in the room?" Jack asked, holding up the picture.

"I'm not sure."

"Just tell us what you remember," Susan said.

"I'm trying. It's just so hard to imagine Shirl being involved with a murder. He was such a sweet man, a good man, and then he changed."

"Kathy," Susan prompted.

"Yes. Yes, that's the man I saw. He was in the lobby and just looked out of place, I guess that's why I noticed him "

"What time was all of this?" Jack asked.

"I got here at five this morning. Maybe around six or six thirty."

"Do you remember what room?" Jack asked.

Kathy Malbon showed them which room she had seen Shirl and Moon Pie enter. Jack thought about searching the room but that would, once again, mean tipping their hand. Besides, on the boat Ellert had tried to call the room several times and according to Susan was unsuccessful, so chances of anyone being in there were slim. Shirl was an ex-detective. He wouldn't leave evidence lying around the room.

Now they were on the Twin Bridges approaching the Evansville city limits. Jack had part of a plan formed in his mind. He would have to find Shirl. Maybe Susan was right about approaching him. Telling him they knew everything. He might not confess to anything, but at least Jack would see if he was lying, and maybe stop whatever they were planning next.

Susan had powered her cell phone on to call Mabel again when the screen lit up.

"Hello, Reverend," she answered.

"You gave him your personal phone number?" Jack asked.

She motioned for Jack to be quiet. Then she handed the phone to Jack. "I called while you were ogling the Tree of Life and asked him to get Ellert's finances for us."

"Thanks. I forgot about him." He said into the phone, "Susan's telephone."

"Detective Murphy?" Payne's voice sounded weak and unsteady. Jack felt a little ashamed of the way he'd treated the old man. In his defense, it wasn't good practice to get too chummy with a career criminal. "So good to hear your voice," Payne said.

"It's just wonderful to hear from you as well, Reverend. Susan's here next to me, and she's wonderful too. So now that we're all wonderful and glad to hear from each other, can you get to the friggin' point?"

Payne's laughter sent him into a coughing spasm. When he composed himself again, he said, "You're a hard man, Jack."

"Bless me, Father, for I have sinned," Jack said. "Now can you get to the point . . . please?"

Again the deep laugh. "I'm old. You must learn patience."

"I'm not real good at patience, Reverend."

Payne was either hooting with laughter or having a stroke. Not that Jack cared, but he wanted the information before the old convict croaked. The laughter was coming in big whoops and Jack held the phone out so Susan could hear, and she started laughing too. She had a nice laugh.

When Payne settled down, he asked for Susan. Jack shoved the phone toward her and she carried on a long conversation, but all Jack could hear were a lot of "uh-huhs" and "yeahs." Occasionally he'd hear an "Is that right?" or an "Are you serious?" but mostly just "uh-huhs."

She punched the end button and put the phone back in her bag.

"You didn't let me say good-bye," Jack groused.

"Are you always like this?" she asked.

"Being chased by the CIA might have something to do with my attitude right now. What did he tell you?"

Susan summarized the call for him. By the time they turned west on Veterans Memorial Parkway, he had a pretty good idea of the up-dated financial picture of the suspects. Moon Pie was spending all of his savings, Ellert appeared to be pulling up stakes, and Shirl was moving all of his money into high-risk investments.

Jack turned around and sped back toward Henderson. He said, "Stu gave me the pieces of the puzzle but I was too stupid to see where they fit."

"Where are we going?" Susan asked.

"To see the Tree of Life again," Jack said. "I want to get to the root of this. Get it? The root?"

Susan groaned.

Chapter Thirty-four

Millie was still on duty at the motel desk, and when she saw Jack she winked. She ignored Susan when they walked up to the desk.

Jack held his badge on the counter. "I'm a cop, and I need to see your register," he said. He hoped she didn't ask to see his identification, because, that would mean giving his real name. As fast as the CIA was working, there may be a BOL out on him and Susan by now.

Millie, who Jack had come to think of as "The Tree of Life," was suspicious now. Allowing them to masquerade as the Joneses to have an illicit affair was one thing, but talking to the cops was another.

Jack pulled his jacket back so she could get a look at his gun and that seemed to do the trick. Murphy's Law says, "You attract more flies with honey, but you get more attention with a gun."

"All of the guests are on the computer," Millie said. "Can I ask *whom* you're looking for?"

He doubted that all of the clientele was on her computer. There were customers and then there were customers. The difference in registration was how many hours they spent in the room. "I just need a name for someone who rented Room 322."

She hesitated, but she probably had dealings with cops before and knew when to clam up and when to cooperate. She rummaged behind the counter and put several stacks of cards on the counter. They were similar to the card he had signed earlier.

"I thought you said all the guests were on the computer?" Jack asked, thinking she was trying to stall him.

"They are. But it might be easier for you to go through the cards for this week than for me to search the computer. And to tell the truth, I truly don't like giving you this information"

"I can lock you up, seize your computer and these cards, search everyone's room and get statements from everyone, and . . ."

"You say Room 322?" She punched some keys and then a confused look crossed her features. "Room 322 is not here. I mean it's not on my system. How did that happen?"

Jack didn't know if she was lying or if the CIA had made the information go bye-bye. He was getting pissed.

"Give me a key to that room then," Jack said.

She made a sour face and said, "You're the second one today asking for that guy."

"What guy?" Jack asked.

"Room 322. Cold-looking bastard," she said, and gave a theatrical shiver. "He rented the room about three weeks ago. Over the telephone, so I never saw him, but I remember when he checked in."

"I thought you didn't usually work the front desk," Susan asked.

"I do when they pay what this guy did. I think I might have the registration card."

She dug through one pile of the registration cards, pulled one out, and handed it to Jack.

"Joe Casper's the name he gave," the clerk said and snorted. "Like in Casper the Friendly Ghost. Get it?" she asked.

"Tell me about him," Jack said. "Is he still here?" Jack took Quinn's picture from his jacket and handed it to her.

"That's the same picture the other guy showed me. Yeah, that's Joe Casper. Least that's what he put on the card."

"What other guy?" Jack asked.

"Some guy come in here before you. He took my key card and went up to that room, but he didn't come down with nothing," she said.

"What did this other gentleman look like?" Jack asked.

She dug down in her bra and scratched, then glanced up to see if Jack was watching. He pushed the picture in front of her again. "Now would be a good time."

Two minutes later, he and Susan were outside room 322 with the clerk's key card in hand. Jack held his Glock by his leg and

Susan had her hand in her purse as he slipped the card in the lock and heard it click. He pushed the door open.

The room was pristine. "I guess the tattooed lady forgot that the room was cleaned," he said. He was more interested in the room now that he had found out Allen Thompson was interested enough to come here. Thompson had found nothing or took whatever there was to find.

They stood in the room, and it was like any other hotel room, only seedier. They went back to the desk. Ellert had made several calls from the pay phone to this hotel. Who was he expecting to be here?

"We know someone called here today asking for that room. A man was asking for someone in that room," Jack said.

She scratched some more. "Yeah. I forgot. I got a couple calls a few hours ago. It was a man. I switched his calls to the room."

"Who did the man ask for?" Jack asked.

"He didn't ask for anyone," she said as if that should be obvious. "He just asked for room 322."

"Was Casper here then?" Jack asked.

"I don't think so."

"Do you know or don't you?" Jack asked. He was tired of pulling information out of her.

"Casper wasn't here because the other guy in a suit came in ten minutes or so before I got the phone calls from whoever."

Allen Thompson was right here when we were on the boat. "Describe the man again. The one that showed you the picture and searched the room," Jack asked.

"He seemed real wore out. Young, big, expensive looking suit, but it looked dirty, and he smelled bad. You know. Like . . ." She mimicked vomiting.

Tired and smelly because I kicked his ass. "Did he show you any ID?" Jack asked and fought the urge to choke her.

"Mister, he didn't have to. He had a piece on his hip just like you."

"That's Thompson," Jack said to Susan. "Let's go."

"Wait," the clerk said. She handed Jack a business card and smiled. "I'm off weekends."

Jack drove, and they were making good time down Vietnam Veterans Parkway. Jack was deep in thought when Susan's cell phone rang again. She glanced at the screen and handed the phone to Jack, saying, "Liddell."

Jack answered and could hear loud traffic noise in the background at the other end. "Liddell?"

"You've got to get out of town, pod'na," Liddell shouted into the phone. "The CIA has everyone convinced that you killed Khaled."

Liddell was shouting so loud that Susan could hear him. "No one will believe that," she said to Jack.

"Jack, I can meet you."

"Not possible," Jack said. "Don't tell me where you are, Bigfoot. Just get off the phone and don't call again. You hear me?"

"Jack. There's a warrant out for your arrest. Captain Franklin gave orders that you are to be detained by any means necessary. Do you understand? They have you as 'armed and extremely dangerous.'"

"Well, they got that much right. Now be a good Bigfoot and go away for a while. I got this. Thanks, partner." Jack punched the end button and handed the phone to Susan and said, "Turn it all the way off."

She did so and said, "The whole police force is looking for you. And me. What can you do against all that, Jack? Maybe Liddell's right. Maybe you should run."

Jack felt the knot on the back of his head and the anger built inside him. He turned a sharp right down Sycamore Street. Police headquarters was only ten blocks away.

Susan said, "You can't be serious. You can't turn yourself in. The CIA—"

"Hell with the CIA," Jack said and gripped the steering wheel tighter. "I'm not turning myself in. The CIA wants to find me, so I'm going to let them."

"Your plan is to turn yourself in to the CIA? And that's not crazy?"

"No. It's not crazy. It's a plan," he said. "I didn't say who I was turning myself over to."

"You can't go to the CIA, or the FBI, or your people. Your partner said everyone is after you."

"I'm going to the ATF. They have less reason to want me out of the picture, and they're considered rebels by the system. They don't always do things by the book, God bless them. I have a friend there who will help," he said. "Not that you aren't my friend." Jack patted her arm. "By the way, have I told you how much I appreciate everything you've done for me? Are still doing. I never would have gotten this far if not for you."

"Now you're scaring me," she said. "You're going to do something reckless, aren't you?"

"What? I can't say something nice? What is it with you?"

"Just promise me that you are going to be okay," Susan said. "Katie would hate me if I let you get hurt."

He was surprised that she mentioned Katie because he was just thinking about her. "I'm going to be okay. I promise," he said. Then he had to ask, "You said Katie would hate you. I hate to ask, but have you and she renewed your friendship?"

"We never stopped being friends. And yes, we've talked quite a few times. Women are like that."

"I'll have to check my woman manual. I guess I missed that part."

"Well, if it makes you feel more like not getting killed, she still loves you. She thinks you're impossible, but she still loves you."

Jack didn't know if Susan was saying that because it was true, or because she was worried about what lay ahead. It did matter to him if Katie loved him. But Katie would know he would do his job. She wouldn't like it, but she'd expect it.

"Thanks for sticking with me," he said and took her hand. "You're my kind of woman." He grinned. "You have money and you carry a gun."

Susan forced a nervous smile. "Very funny. I am, how you infidels say, pretty when angry. Wuh huh."

"John Khaled Wayne," Jack said. "That's a pretty good impression. You're all right for a tiny infidel woman."

"No problemo," she said.

Chapter Thirty-five

The Winfield K. Denton Federal Building was a massive structure built in the early 1950s. The main branch of the U.S. Postal Service was added on to the federal building a few years later, and together they occupied four city blocks.

The building housed the federal courts along with all of the other federal government offices, just as the Civic Center housed all of the local and county government offices. In fact, the buildings were across the street from each other in what could be considered the heart of Evansville.

He'd been inside the federal building many times, but the sight of it was ominous now as he turned onto Sycamore Street. He pulled into the employee lot of the post office, and it started to rain. The rag top on Payne's MG leaked through rips and tears in the fabric. He drove across the lot to the back area of the federal building. He could barely see the parking spots through the deluge. With the wipers on high speed, visibility was cut to those micro-seconds between swipes. Out a side window he could see police and sheriffs' vehicles parked along Sycamore. It was shift change. Everything would be moving soon. He was in the lions' den.

The federal building's windows were mostly dark. It was way past quitting time.

"Now what?" Susan asked.

Jack knew that if they'd gotten there a half hour later they would be sitting in the middle of a beehive of policemen heading to roll call or going home. For now they were safe.

Jack had pulled the battery and chip from Susan's cell phone after phoning Pons. He now put it back together for one short call and then he would disable it again. He hoped it wouldn't be on long enough for a signal trace. He dialed a number. ATF Special Agent Greg Pons answered on the first ring.

"I'm outside." Jack didn't identify himself.

"Go to the door and come on up," Pons said, and the line went dead.

Jack tore the phone apart, opened the car door, and said, "You can take the car back to Payne now."

"No way," she said. She opened her door.

They both stepped out into the pouring rain and rushed to the loading dock of the post office. They were drenched when they reached the steel entry door marked PRIVATE. The locking mechanism clicked, and they entered a hallway where a freight elevator could be seen to their left. The doors to the freight elevator opened and they stepped on.

"There are no buttons. Just key slots," Susan said.

The doors closed. By itself the elevator rose and stopped at the third floor. Jack took Susan by the arm and led her to the end of another long hallway and turned left, went down a shorter hallway to the end, and came to a heavy oak door with the ornate brass emblem of the Bureau of Alcohol, Tobacco, Firearms and Explosives. The door lock clicked. Jack ushered Susan inside.

"I hope this is worth my not arresting you," came a voice from the darkness. Greg Pons stood in the doorway of what looked like a break room.

"This is Susan Summers," Jack said.

"Hi, Susan," Pons said, and offered her a handful of paper towels to dry her hair. Jack noticed Pons hadn't offered him anything to dry off with.

"Ladies' room?" she asked.

"Out the door, down the hall on your right. Knock and I'll let you back in," Pons said.

When Pons heard the outer door shut he pulled up a chair and sat. Jack sat opposite him. They had only known each other for a couple of days, so Jack didn't have any credit built up in the "trust me" department. Pons looked angry.

"Your department wants you on a murder charge. They're saying you shot Killian. Now you're here."

"Greg—Agent Pons—you know it's all bullshit."

"Tell me why I'm not arresting you," he said.

Jack judged Pons to be an honest man. The consideration he'd shown for Killian's wife said volumes for his character. Most street cops considered all Feds a bunch of paper pushers who were eager to grab the glory and headlines. Himself included. By the same token, most federal agents considered the local cops to be lazy and incompetent. In too many cases, both sides were right.

Jack started at the beginning.

"When Killian was shot, I went to the parole office—that's where Susan works—to see where a convict, deceased now, had obtained a .40 caliber handgun. Susan told me about Khaled Abutaqa."

Pons was nodding. "I knew of Khaled. He's the guy you allegedly killed and burned his van."

Jack told Pons how he had used Susan's authority to lean on Khaled Abutaqa and about Coin's information that Killian might have been checking out an arms deal that involved at least two city policemen. He told of the return trip to Khaled's house, what he found there, and about the subsequent fire and the car speeding away. Pons listened as Jack told how the two phony FBI men had gotten into the mix, how they had changed their story and were really CIA. He told Pons about Quinn, and about Crenshaw outside Killian's room, his tussle in the parking lot with Thompson, and his discovery of who the two cops were.

"Susan and I followed Moon Pie, from his house to the Blue Star, where I saw him talking to the Chief of Security, James Ellert. Ellert was angry and wanted Moon Pie to get away from him. Then Ellert went to a pay phone and called a number several times in a short period. I dialed the number back and it was the Sugar Creek Inn in Henderson."

He told about getting financial information on Moon Pie, Shirl, and James Ellert, and their finding Shirl's ex-wife at a conference at the hotel.

"Shirl's ex, Kathy Malbon, saw Shirl and Moon Pie meet another man and enter a room at the hotel. The third man she described sounded like James Ellert. I showed her the photo I have of Quinn," Jack paused and took the soggy photo from his pocket and handed it to Pons. "She thought this man was hanging around the lobby around the same time that she saw Shirl there. We checked Ellert's finances and found out that, suddenly, all three of these guys are doing strange things with their money. Moon Pie is spending like crazy, Shirl is making risky investments, and Ellert sold his house and a boat and is in financial trouble."

Pons said, "Let me get this straight. You assaulted this Khaled guy, then went back and broke into his house and dug a bullet out of his wall, found a burned computer and a partially burned photo?"

"I didn't really assault him," Jack said. "We just had strong words." It wasn't a complete lie.

"And then Khaled turns up dead?"

"I was at the Two Jakes or with Susan most of the day after I left Khaled's. I could provide an alibi if I had to."

"Okay. You threatened a FBI or CIA agent in front of your captain. You assaulted that same agent at the hospital after you fled from a female FBI agent. You and Susan Summers drop off the globe, you find out you're wanted by your own department for murder, and you called me. Is that about it?"

"Greg, I—"

Pons gave Jack a hard look. "You have to see how serious their case is against you, Jack."

Hearing this version of events gave Jack reason to pause. The CIA guys had trumped up a convincing case against him.

"I'm innocent, Greg. If I wasn't, why would I come here?"

Pons picked up a pad of paper and a pen from his desk and said, "I believe you."

Jack breathed a sigh of relief.

"Tell me again about White and Thompson."

When Jack again got to the part outside the hospital, Pons laughed. "So that's an Irish wedgie?"

Susan knocked, and Pons buzzed the door. She came back into the room. "What did I miss?"

"Nothing you don't already know," Jack said.

"What do you want from me, Jack?" Pons asked.

Chapter Thirty-six

Ellert had to admire Mr. Smith. The smudge pot was a nice touch. The tear gas would make it almost impossible to see, much less breathe. Smith had given him a gas mask, but had told him not to tell the others about the tear gas. Maybe Smith had a plan. Maybe he was going to cut those prick cops out of the deal. Smith seemed to have thought of everything. Ellert just hoped people didn't panic so bad that they jumped overboard. He didn't want anyone to die; he just wanted to get even with his ex-wife and that bastard, Ken Taylor. And it wouldn't hurt to be a millionaire.

As head of security he could waltz past every metal detector and hide the guns and masks in the restrooms. The smudge pot was a different story. He couldn't carry something that big past security, but Smith had a brilliant idea. He instructed Ellert to hide the smudge pot in the landscaping near the port railing of the boat. Smith said there was going to be a big commotion near the pavilion doors at the other end of the boat at ten thirty p.m. When Ellert heard all hell break loose, that was his cue to slip off the deck and bring the gas onboard. The smudge pot was the size of a five-gallon bucket so he didn't think he would have any trouble carrying it.

He held two boxes from Donut Bank in his sweaty hands as he approached the turnstiles.

"What'cha bringing us tonight, Major?" said the young guard named Clete. He eyed the boxes.

"Hope you got some tiger tails in there, Major," an older guard piped in. "Those are my favorites."

"Something better, Fred," Ellert said with a wink. "You'll be surprised."

"Make sure those hogs in the break room don't eat it all, sir," Clete chimed in.

Ellert glanced at his watch. "I'll try," he said, and walked past the only security point to the casino. The metal detector beeped but the guards waved him through. He proceeded up the boarding ramp carrying the boxes containing the Halloween masks, plastic explosives, detonators, and silenced pistols. He had thought up this part of the plan himself. Mr. Smith was impressed with his creativity.

The man Smith/Quinn hired sat on the green metal bench outside the doors of the casino pavilion entrance and fingered a wad of new twenty-dollar bills. His shirt was denim, of the kind issued in prison, and hadn't seen a good washing for months. His current residence was a place aptly called the Rescue Mission. It was a squat, one-story building that housed indigents, homeless, and recent parolees. He was tired of bad food. Tired of institutional clothes. Tired of being broke and homeless.

Tomorrow he would stay in a nice motel and treat himself to a nice sit-down meal in a classy restaurant. Maybe he'd go to the Riverhouse Hotel downtown where he could get both. The waiters there wore short-waisted white jackets and served food on huge platters. Prime rib. Roasted potatoes, maybe expensive wine. He fingered the wad of bills again. Hell! He'd order a bottle of champagne.

He thought back to this morning when he was outside enjoying a smoke because the assholes wouldn't let them smoke inside. A nice-looking car came down the street and stopped outside the shelter. The driver rolled down a window and motioned him over. At first he thought it might be another of those damn faggots that hung out around the riverfront parks. He'd just gotten out of prison for beating one of them nearly to death. But this guy didn't talk like a fag. He was all business, and he said he had some work. He said it would pay well.

His first instinct was to walk away. Something about the guy's eyes was scary. The man must have sensed his distrust, because he hauled out a wad of cash that would choke a mule. So he'd gotten in the car and went for a short ride while the man explained that all he had to do was hang out on the sidewalk in front of the casino. At exactly ten thirty he was supposed to pick a fight with someone going in. The man even gave him a watch so he could keep the time. It was a cheapo Timex, but what the hell. He hadn't had a watch since he got out of prison.

He'd thought about asking for more money, but his mama didn't raise no fool. No sir. This wasn't someone he wanted to get acquainted with.

He sat on the bench and watched closely as a rich-looking dude and his girlfriend dropped off their Lexus with the parking attendant. They were coming across the street, holding hands and grinning like the rest of the yuppie bastards he had come to hate. Always looking down their noses at him. He checked his watch again. Ten thirty. Time to go to work.

Major Ellert checked his watch. At exactly ten thirty, Smith had promised to create a diversion at the pavilion entrance. He said it would take care of all the outside security cameras and most of the guards on the boat long enough for him to bring the smudge pot on board.

It was ten thirty now. Ellert hurried down the stairs to the lower level and hid the donut boxes in an equipment closet that only he had a key to. He would have to take the Halloween masks and weapons up to the restrooms after he brought the smudge pot onboard.

He hurried to the portside emergency exit. That door was equipped with an alarm, and would be on the monitors. But he knew the monitors would be drawn to the diversion and he could manually override the alarm. He hoped he had enough time to get the smudge pot, get back on board, lock the door, set the alarm and get downstairs before the cameras were back in position.

He stood by the exit and waited.

At the agreed time he heard screaming and cursing coming from outside. He punched in the code to disable the alarm and opened the door with a key. He hurried out on the port deck and could hear a woman screaming her lungs out in the direction of the pavilion. He walked to the railing, opened a small section of the gate, and jumped to shore. The smudge pot was right where he had left it.

He grabbed it, leapt onto the deck, and carried the pot inside. Then he secured the door and reset the alarm. So far, so good.

He carried the container down the empty hallway to the fan room. Only he and the engineers had keys to this room.

He shoved the canister under the air intake vent and set an empty crate on top of it. The crate was a fire hazard and did not belong in the fan room. He'd discovered it about two days earlier and supposed that one of the lazy engineers was using it for a place to sit and hide. Instead of disposing of it, as he would normally do, he left it just for this purpose. If anyone discovered the canister by accident, it wouldn't matter. The fun would start soon.

He listened at the door for movement in the hall. It wouldn't do to run across that nosy state trooper. The casino security staff may be a joke, but the troopers were all business. Satisfied he was alone, he went back to the room where he'd left the donut boxes. He took the blocks of Semtex out, laid them on the floor, and put the detonators in his shirt pocket. He then carried the donut boxes with the pistols and masks to the aft stairway and up to the second-floor men's restroom. If the surveillance cameras were watching him, he could claim he was doing a routine check of the restrooms.

Two men were inside the restroom sharing a doobie until they noticed Ellert's uniform, flicked the joint in a toilet, and disappeared like cockroaches.

He used his key to lock the bathroom door from inside and set the case on the floor. He unlocked the wall-mounted paper towel receptacle and swung it out on its hinges. It was almost full but there was room on top of the paper towels for one of the silent pistols and a mask. He locked the cover back in place, unlocked and left the bathroom. Now to the third level.

He hoped Moon Pie had remembered to bring the key. He hoped the little asshole wouldn't do something stupid and get them all caught. This last thought caused a trickle of sweat to run down the back of his neck.

Jack called Stu's direct office line but got no answer. He called the number for the casino security office. A woman answered. "Dispatch," she said.

"Stu Sanders, please."

"He's not in his office," the dispatcher answered.

"Find him. It's urgent police business."

"Yes, sir," she said in a bored voice. "Wait one."

In seconds, she said, "Patching you through now, sir," and Stu was on the line.

"My dispatcher said it was urgent, Jack. I hope this ain't a prank, buddy, 'cause I'm kind of busy right now." He sounded agitated.

"Stu, it's not a joke," Jack said. "Listen carefully. I think something is going to happen there tonight. I need to know if you've seen Moon Pie, or if anyone strange has come aboard."

"The boat's always full of assholes. Look, Jack, I got my hands full right now." In the background Jack could hear a woman sobbing and then someone said, "Screw you, cop!"

"What's going on?" Jack asked.

Stu yelled something at one of the security guards that Jack didn't quite catch before Stu answered.

"This jerk-wad just started beating on a guy in front of the pavilion, and now he's pissed off because I'm sending him to jail." Stu snorted a laugh. "I just happened to be walking from the garage and saw the fight, so I grabbed this turd and now he says he's suing me." Stu let out a deep breath. "Can you believe that? The victim and his girlfriend had just turned over their car to the valet, and I guess Mr. Personality here objected to the distribution of wealth."

"Stu, you need to hear this."

"This jerk wad had a ton of money on him. I'm trying to find out if there are other robberies before I bag and tag him." That was Stu-talk for "put him in jail."

"Goddammit, Stu," Jack said through clenched teeth, "you have bigger problems."

Chapter Thirty-seven

The detonators were in Ellert's shirt pocket. Mr. Smith was very specific about how and where to place the explosives and when to set the timers.

Ellert was amazed. When he'd gone through his security training for this job, his teachers had come up with almost every scenario possible for robbing the casino. Smith had outsmarted them all and made their precautions look like child's play.

He wiped the perspiration from his brow. It wouldn't be long now.

Shirl saw the commotion in front of the pavilion as he walked across the skywalk from the hotel garage. The guy sporting prison clothes came off the bench, ran across the street, and started pounding a guy who stepped from a Lexus LS. He knew it was a Lexus LS because he planned to be driving one himself before long.

The girl who had gotten out of the car wasn't bad either. Maybe he'd get one of those too. His live-in, Angel, had become tiresome. Nice body, but she couldn't carry on a conversation that wasn't about dope. Of course, he wasn't interested in talk when he'd let her move into his apartment.

Shirl thought about Angel's body and had to push the thoughts out of his mind. She was getting to be a liability, and he suspected that she was even bringing dope into the apartment. That he wouldn't tolerate. The police department's internal affairs assholes would love to have another go at him.

He'd made a lot of money off Angel, selling her to traveling businessmen; always someone from outside town, but it was time to get rid of her. The thing was, she knew a lot and had guessed a lot more. She had "accidental overdose" written all over her.

He stopped on the skywalk to watch the action down there. The guy was getting a first-class ass whipping. It was fun to watch, but he had to go. He wanted to get on early and make a show of playing the slots and drinking. Hopefully Ellert hadn't screwed up or chickened out. Anything was possible with a rent-a-cop.

He watched as a muscled-up state policeman got into the middle of the fracas below. He recognized Stu Sanders. This would be a short battle. He hoped Sanders wouldn't interfere with them. He ignored the escalators and took the stairs two at a time to the main floor.

At the ticket counter, a cute blonde took his money and handed him a pass.

"They're boarding shortly, sir."

He took the ticket and was about to make a cute remark when a cocktail waitress came by. He turned to watch her ass as she walked by. She had a nice rack too, but her hair was chopped into one of those severe haircuts you see on butch lesbians. What a waste.

He turned back to the cute blonde behind the ticket counter. She was busy with another customer so he moved on.

He didn't trust Smith. His experience told him to be there early and watch. That was why he'd hidden a Seecamp 9mm semiauto pistol in an ankle holster. He would pick up the silenced pistol that Ellert had hidden in the third-level restroom, but he wanted to have his own weapon as well. "Never trust a gun you didn't load yourself," was his motto. He hadn't gotten this old by being stupid.

A line was forming as he approached the boarding gate.

Moon Pie slouched against a wall on the second level by the craps tables. He was watching the cashier's cage. The idea that in the next hour he would be a millionaire brought a smile to his face. He could bet anything he wanted from now on.

His mouth was dry, so he motioned to a nearby cocktail waitress. He wasn't supposed to be drinking, but what the hell. The slim redhead accepted the twenty he gave her for a beer and smiled. She didn't offer any change, and he didn't ask for it.

He downed the beer in one go, thought about getting another, then thought better of it. His mouth was still dry. He licked his lips and ran a hand through his greasy hair under the porkpie hat. His movements were robotic, almost as if someone else controlled his body, but he couldn't help it. He had never been this nervous before, but then, he had never been this close to being rich. There were no clocks on the boat so he looked at his watch.

The restroom was next to the cashier's cage. The silenced pistol would be behind that toilet seat thing. Ellert had gone over the plan with them several times but now, with all the lights, beeping machines, excited chatter, and drunken laughter, Moon Pie's brain was filled with a deafening white noise. He struggled to remember what Smith had told him to do. "What's the damn plan?" he asked out loud.

He looked around the room for Shirl. He'd know what to do next. But Shirl wouldn't be on the second level, would he? Shirl was supposed to be on the third floor. Moon Pie had gotten to his own spot so early he was sure he would have seen Shirl passing through. "Where the hell is he?" he said through clenched teeth. Maybe Shirl had also come onboard early. Or worse yet, maybe Moon Pie was late?

He remembered the plan. Get the gun from the restroom and put it under your shirt. There was to be an explosion belowdecks, and that was his cue to rob the cashier. No. No. Get the gun and mask down. Put the mask on and wait for the explosion. That was it. He moved across the floor in the direction of the men's room.

"Screw Smith. Screw you too, Ellert," Moon Pie said but no one near him noticed. They were so busy watching their money circling the drain.

He went into the restroom and unlocked the metal receptacle on the wall, lifted the cover off, and dropped it to the floor. The blued steel Smith & Wesson, silencer already attached, lay on top of the mask. He took the gun out, stuck it in his back waistband, and pulled his bowling shirt down over it. He took down the mask and rolled it up and stuck it in the back of his waistband, almost down to his crack.

When he came out of the men's room he tugged at the back of his bowling shirt. Having the likeness of Bill Clinton stuck in his butt crack made him smile. "Eat shit, Bill," he muttered with a chuckle.

Wearing masks of presidents was Mr. Smith's idea, but Moon Pie was sure he had seen it in a movie. Maybe that was where Smith got the idea. Maybe Smith wasn't as smart as Shirl thought he was.

"Where the hell is Shirl?" he said out loud. He knew they were supposed to pretend like they didn't know each other, but he'd like to know if the job had been called off. How would anyone be able to tell him if it was? When he'd tried talking to Ellert earlier, that asshole acted like he was shooing a fly.

Moon Pie motioned for another beer, and a cocktail waitress brought it right over. He gave her another twenty. She smiled, but he didn't pay much attention this time. He was looking for Shirl. Or Ellert. Or Mr. Smith. Perspiration dotted his forehead as his mind ground through the next part of the plan. He tipped the beer up and tugged at the back of his waistband.

Chapter Thirty-eight

Pons worked the slide of his Smith & Wesson 10mm and chambered a round. He reached into a drawer of his desk, took two more loaded clips, and put these in his jacket pocket.

"Can you hit anything with that hand cannon?" Jack asked. "Or are you just planning to make a lot of noise?"

Pons slipped the weapon into his belt holster. "Have you got a gun?"

Jack pulled the Glock .45 from his waistband.

"And you're talking about my hand cannon?"

Jack already had a round chambered. A .45 caliber bullet makes a hole about the size of a pencil eraser when it enters a body, but it makes one hell of a mess when it exits.

"If you guys are through comparing the size of your guns," Susan said, "you can tell me what we're doing next."

"Killian was doing his job. Now I'm going to do mine," Jack said. "You ready, Special Agent Pons?"

"Let's do it."

"Wait a minute," Susan said. "What are we doing? I haven't heard any type of plan for us yet."

Jack said to Susan, "I want you to do something important."

"Oh, no you don't," she protested.

"Someone has to alert the troops. Captain Franklin needs to know what's going on. If this goes sideways, I need someone to tell them I didn't kill Khaled. Someone needs to know the truth about what's going on. Give us twenty minutes before you go to the police. Don't talk to anyone but Captain Franklin or Liddell."

Her expression showed it was obvious she didn't like it. But he thought she saw the logic.

She said, "You owe me a lot of money, buster. You'd better be around to pay off."

Pons drove south on Court Street toward the casino.

"The gas pedal is that thing by your right foot," Jack said. The speedometer of the agent's Pontiac showed thirty miles per hour, the speed limit on downtown streets.

"I'd let you drive, but this vehicle is owned by the federal government, Jack, so you'll just have to buckle up and enjoy the ride."

"I could get out and push you faster than this. Hell, we could walk faster." The federal building was a mere ten blocks from the casino, but the distance wouldn't matter if the robbery went down before they boarded the boat. To his credit, Pons passed the parking garage entrance and parked in front of the pavilion.

Jack had called Stu and told him they were coming. Stu met Jack and Pons at the door to the security office. He had the surveillance monitors on his desk cranked up.

"Watch this," he said and hit some keys on the computer. A picture came up of Moon Pie walking onto the boarding ramp. "That was about thirty minutes ago." The camera picked up Moon Pie at different points where he continued onto the second level of the casino. Moon Pie then stood against a wall near the craps tables. He was gazing toward someone or something just out of range of this camera. Stu hit another set of keys and said, "I'm running facial recognition so it will pick him up wherever he is. Now we're in real time."

Moon Pie was coming from a restroom.

Stu said, "See something odd here?"

"He's moving kind of funny. Got something in the back of his pants," Jack said.

"Either that or he's shit himself," Pons said.

"It's bigger than a pistol," Stu said. "Sawed-off shotgun?"

"Are there cameras in the restroom?" Pons asked.

Stu grunted. "If there was, the surveillance crew would ignore the rest of the boat."

"Can you zoom in on him, Stu?" Jack asked.

"Are you kidding? I can put the camera right up his nose."

Stu punched a few more keys and the camera zoomed in on Moon Pie's face.

"That's close enough," Jack said. "He's not watching the craps table. What is he looking at?"

Stu brought up another monitor and tapped the screen. It showed people standing in line at a cashier's cage.

Pons said, "You were right, Jack. They're going to rob the casino." He asked Stu, "Can you find Shirl?"

Stu went to another keyboard and searched for Shirley West in the casino database with no luck. "He's not in the casino's computerized system. That doesn't mean he hasn't been on the riverboat. He just hasn't come to our attention for any reason, like if he has a Gold pass or he's been barred from coming onboard for causing trouble. If you can get me a photo of him I could scan it in, and the facial recognition software might find him."

Jack didn't think they had time to wait for that. Jack looked at his watch. The boat left the dock on the hour so they had about fifteen minutes to board. "Can you get us on the boat?"

"Does the Lone Ranger wear a mask?" Stu said, and headed out the door. "I already called the gate and asked them to stall departure until we get there."

On the way Stu said, "Moon Pie has lost about fifty grand this year. Here and at other casinos."

"I didn't know you guys got paid that well," Pons said.

"We don't," Jack said.

"That's not all," Stu continued. "The Blue Star is holding a twenty-thousand-dollar marker for Moon Pie."

Pons let out a low whistle. "Man, oh man! I joined the wrong department."

As they neared the metal detector at the gate Stu asked, "Are you both carrying?" Jack and Pons said they were. Stu said, "Just don't shoot anyone that doesn't need shooting or I'll be doing paperwork until I'm a hundred."

The lone security guard didn't look up as they passed through the metal detectors and walked through the double glass doors and onto the boarding ramp.

"Did you alert security?" Jack asked, hoping he hadn't.

"This isn't my first rodeo. Besides, none of these guys carry weapons, and half of them are likely to jump overboard if there's trouble."

They entered the second level, and a young crew member said, "You just made it, Stu." The crew member was wearing a stark white coverall with a light blue stripe running diagonally up to the left chest where a prominent blue star was sewn over the heart. Over the star, white embroidery proclaimed "Blue Star Casino & Hotel."

"Where's Major Ellert?" Stu asked the man.

"Haven't seen him," the crewman said. "I didn't talk to no one just like you told me, and I've been right here waiting for you."

Stu thanked the crewman, and they went into the second level. "That was my buddy, Leon. He's probably the only guy I trust. He wouldn't have said anything even if he knew what was up."

The room was crammed with slot machines, blackjack and craps tables, and people. At the far end was the Crystal Room, a private area that was hardly more than an elegantly decked-out sandwich, chip, and drink bar with a few dining tables scattered along the wall. To Jack's left were the big-money slots and the poker room. On the video Moon Pie had come from a restroom that was past the poker room, near the cashier's cage.

Stu nudged Jack and pointed toward the big-money slots. "There's your boy now."

Moon Pie's short stature made him barely visible over the top of an obese, elderly woman. She was melded into a doublewide wheelchair, manically feeding a slot machine. His porkpie hat bobbed up and down when he fed his own machine and pulled the handle.

"Yeah. That's Moon Pie," Jack said. "Looks nervous, doesn't he?"

Moon Pie was lifting his hat and swiping his hand through his hair, and then wiping perspiration from his forehead with the back of his hand. Each time he did this, his eyes would dart toward the cashier's cage and then back over at the slot machine where the woman was playing and then back at his own slot machine. The men moved to a better position. The bulge in the back waistband of Moon Pie's tacky bowling shirt was more obvious than it was on the video.

"What about Shirl?" Jack asked.

"Probably watching the cashier's cage on one of the other floors. I don't really know him. He's older, right?" Pons asked.

"I've got an idea," Jack said.

*   *   *

Paul White watched from where he sat playing a slot machine just outside the Crystal Room. He was impressed, and it took a lot to impress him. He hoped Detective Murphy wouldn't figure it out, but the man was like a dog digging for a bone. Jack had been told to stay out of this and when that didn't work White had Jack charged with killing Khaled. Now, Jack was not only here, he'd brought some friends. White recognized the ATF agent named Greg Pons from his briefing before starting this mission. The other guy was a state trooper.

With Jack, Pons, and the trooper that made at least three other armed men on this boat besides himself, Thompson, and Crenshaw. Shirley West and Skippy Walker were almost certainly armed, courtesy of the deceased Khaled Abutaqa, but he couldn't imagine Ellert being given any kind of weapon. And, of course, Quinn would be armed. He would be the most dangerous of all. It would be a war when it started. People would get killed. But that wasn't his concern. He was here for Quinn.

"Update," White said into a wireless microphone pinned inside his jacket collar. To the casual observer, it would appear he was talking to his slot machine like most of the other players.

Agent Thompson, stationed on the third floor, said, "No change yet." The body mikes they were wearing were space-age technology and worked perfectly, even within the steel-hulled casino. They didn't worry about local radio buffs picking up their transmissions because this system transmitted on such ultrahigh frequencies that anyone listening would hear only a hiss.

Crenshaw's voice came over their earpieces, "You seeing what I'm seeing?"

White looked around and spotted Crenshaw standing behind one of the dealers.

"Jack Murphy, ATF Agent Pons, and a state trooper are watching Skippy Walker," she said.

"Stay put," White said.

Agent Thompson sat at the bar on the third level. He was dressed in jeans and a dark knit shirt, just one of the hundreds of other customers who had come for entertainment and a drink. In his peripheral vision, he watched Shirl sitting at the other end of the bar with a beer in front of him. Shirl had only glanced his direction once, focusing instead on the mirror behind the bar. No one had approached Shirl. No one else paid him any mind, except the bartender, and Shirl had spoken to no one except to ask for more peanuts.

They had known about Shirl and Skippy, or Moon Pie as he was called, for several days. The surveillance devices they had put in Shirl's apartment enabled them to receive more than just telephone conversations. The little gizmos they planted included video capability. Thompson thought about some of the "activity" he had watched over the last two days and smiled. Shirl was a pretty energetic man for his age.

This little piece of equipment had also come in handy while they sat outside that parole officer's house listening to Murphy's discussion of Shirley West and Moon Pie as the men working with Quinn. They knew about Coin and Reverend Payne and Ellert too. They knew about the meetings at that dive hotel in Henderson, although they had come across the information too late to finish their business with Quinn. Murphy had put all the pieces together like a pro. In fact, White was talking about recruiting him into their ranks. That would never happen because he was going to kill Murphy.

He had to hand it to White. The senior agent had read Murphy's personality like a book. White knew that Quinn was planning something sensational, but they needed to know the target. Jack had led them to all the right players and had even guessed Quinn's target. If he didn't hate Murphy so much he'd be impressed.

Quinn had built quite a maze, and Murphy was the perfect rat to run through it. The whole thing was a win-win situation for Thompson. Murphy would lead him to Quinn. Quinn would die. Thompson would kill Murphy and make it look like one of the cops had done it.

In Thompson's earpiece he heard, "Be ready."

"Upper deck. I'm clear," Crenshaw said. Her responsibility was to move around, see what they had missed, and act as backup.

"Clear," Thompson said. He moved to an empty slot machine and watched Shirl enter the restroom.

Shirl came out a minute later and sat at the bar again. He ordered another beer and kept an eye on the cashier inside the money cage.

Thompson wondered if the die-hard gamblers on the boat would place a bet on how many lives would be lost before this was over. He could guarantee a high body count.

Jack knew he couldn't stay where he was for much longer. Moon Pie had competed with Stu in bodybuilding contests. And since he was a VIP on the boat, he probably knew Stu from the casino too.

"Pons is going to the third floor, but do we know where Ellert is?" Jack asked.

"I take it you want me to locate him," Stu said.

"You have the run of the boat," Pons said.

"If I find Ellert, do I watch him or take him out of play?"

"If Ellert tries anything do what you think best," Jack said.

Stu agreed. "You know, when I was taken off the street and assigned to this job I felt my police career was over. I never thought someone would try to rob the casino. I assumed there was a system in place that would prevent a robbery."

"Is there?" Pons asked.

"How would I know? The casino doesn't let us near the money and the upper brass treats us like mushrooms. Covers us with shit and keeps us in the dark," Stu said.

"Our best bet is to take these guys down quickly," Jack said. He didn't want to even think about a shoot-out in there.

"If I find Ellert, I'll disable him, then come back to help you guys," Stu said. "Hopefully they're not in communication. Cell phones don't work worth a damn inside here and not at all downstairs. I'll be back." He turned and headed down the stairwell.

Jack said, "He makes a good point. Think we can take them all at the same time?"

"If we had about ten more guys, maybe. But that boat has sailed, no pun intended."

"I'll stay with Moon Pie. Shirl definitely knows me," Jack said.

"He'll probably be in the same spot as Moon Pie on this floor."

Jack said. "Don't underestimate Shirl. He's been around the block."

"Be careful yourself," Pons said, and headed toward the stairs to the third level.

Chapter Thirty-nine

Ellert tossed the Donut Bank box that had contained the Semtex, now empty, among the clutter of pipes in the plumbing chase. He had planted all the explosives Quinn wanted. He was still a few minutes ahead of schedule. He had no desire to kill anyone, but the more he thought about the freedom the money would bring, the more he thought about getting even with Kenny Taylor and his ex-wife, the more accepting he became of some collateral damage.

He unlocked the door to the mechanical room and found the smudge pot undisturbed. It was directly under the intake vents that drew air from the outside and circulated it throughout the boat's ventilation system. The air exchangers were enormous. They could completely change the air inside the casino every three or four minutes.

Now to light the smudge pot. The gas would hit first, and then the explosions would rock the boat. He would wear the mask until he was sure most of the gas had dissipated. Then he would mingle with the panicked patrons until the cops showed up. He would be a hero for restoring order. His part in this affair was almost complete.

He had only hesitated to place the charges in the surveillance room because it would surely kill the crewmen who were stationed in there. He knew them. Knew their families. But there wasn't any choice. If he tried to send them out of the room before the explosion, they would figure out that he was involved. It was too bad they had to die.

He pried the lid from the smudge pot and was almost overcome by the fumes before dropping the lid back in place. "Holy shit!" he said. He put the gas mask on and pulled the straps tight. He could breathe better but his nostrils and throat still burned from the first whiff. His eyes watered and he could barely read the face of his watch. The first explosion would be in five minutes. It would take at least that long for the gas to do anything.

He lifted the lid an inch or so and saw some type of brackish liquid floating on top. It wasn't like any tear gas he'd seen in his military training, but it was what Smith had given him.

He wiped a cold sweat from his brow and could feel nausea coming on. He focused back on the canister. There wasn't a fuse, so he was unsure how to ignite this thing.

He fumbled in his pocket for his cigarette lighter. As his hand closed on the lighter, he felt a tingling in his nose and throat. A sneeze erupted from him and then another. The inside visor of the gas mask was covered with red droplets. He panicked and yanked the mask off and was immediately sorry when he was hit full in the face by the fumes coming from the canister. He backed into the hall and swiped at his nose with the sleeve of his shirt. His cuff came away bloody.

There was still time to disarm the charges, or at least the one that would almost surely kill the surveillance room crew. But Ellert, the soon-to-be-millionaire, asserted himself again. He used his handkerchief to wipe some of the blood out of the gas mask and was pulling it back on when a fist came out of nowhere.

Stu Sanders pulled Chief of Security Ellert to his feet and locked a handcuff on one wrist. He pushed Ellert against the wall and yanked his arms over his head. He then handcuffed him to an overhead pipe. Ellert's nose was bleeding and he was unsteady, but he would live. A gas mask was on the floor at his feet. "You always were a dickhead, Ellert," Stu said.

Stu held his breath and entered the room where he saw a large canister under the air intake vents. His eyes were burning as he stomped the lid back in place and shoved the container away from the vent.

The chemical smell left in the air was overpowering, but, whatever it was, it wouldn't be hurting anyone on this ship. Stu went back in the hall and shut the door to the A/C room behind him. Ellert was trying to stand. Stu patted Ellert's clothing down for weapons. Finding none, he checked Ellert's pockets to be sure he didn't have a handcuff key hidden on him.

"Wakey, wakey, asshole," Stu said, and slapped Ellert's cheeks.

"What the . . . ?" Ellert said, coming around. Blood was still running from his nose, and he seemed too groggy for the punch Stu had delivered to his jaw. Ellert stood up and tried to yank his hands free and then saw he was handcuffed. Stu could see fear in his eyes. "You can't leave me here!" Ellert whined.

"You should have thought of that before you became a dick," Stu said. If the surveillance cameras caught all of this it would be enough to hang the three of them—Ellert, Moon Pie, and Shirl. And it would get the Feds off Jack's back.

"Your buddies are going to jail, asshole," Stu said, and turned to walk away.

"There are bombs!" Ellert yelled.

Stu walked back. "Where?" Stu asked. Ellert licked his lips but didn't answer. "There are over a thousand people on this boat," Stu said. "And we're in the middle of the Ohio River, for Christ's sake."

"Take the handcuffs off and I'll tell you."

"You're full of shit, Ellert," Stu said, leaving.

"You gotta let me go, Stu!" Ellert turned his head and spit a wad of reddish phlegm on the wall.

Stu said through clenched teeth, "I'll leave you here like a rat. Talk."

"There are bombs, Stu, Sergeant Sanders. I'll die if you don't take these off. We'll both die. Let me go, and I'll tell you everything," Ellert begged.

Stu grabbed him by the neck and drew one huge fist back.

"I'll tell! I'll tell!" Ellert wailed and turned his face but the blow didn't come.

The story Ellert told was ridiculous. So ridiculous in fact that Stu believed him. Ellert told Stu where he had placed the Semtex and the order in which he had set the detonators. Stu ran down the hallway and found three of the charges. He pulled the small cylindrical detonators from them but he didn't know how to stop the timer. He guessed these were like blasting caps. Spotting a sturdy metal trash can, the kind that is fire safe, he dropped the devices in the can, hoping this would contain the blast. He didn't have time to search for the charge that was planted near the ballast tank. The surveillance room was more important.

He ran to that room and pounded on the door.

"We can't open up, Sergeant Sanders," one of the surveillance crew yelled through the steel door. "Major Ellert gave strict orders not to let anyone in until he personally came back."

Stu didn't have time to drag Ellert's ass to the door to give them the okay, so he yelled a warning, drew his gun, and shot at the lock several times. He kicked at the door and still it wouldn't open. "Ellert planted explosives in there," Stu yelled. "Search if you don't believe me, but don't touch anything. Just run."

One of the surveillance crew sounded concerned but still wouldn't open. "You'll have to get the casino manager if you can't find Major Ellert."

"Get your asses out of there. There are explosives in there. Go to the upper decks. Do it now!"

Stu hoped their survival instinct would override their orders, and they would head for the safety of the upper decks. He rushed up the stairs to warn the ship's captain about the explosives.

Jack worked his way across the room to come up behind Moon Pie. He had looked in Jack's direction several times, but didn't give any sign of recognition. The glazed look in Moon Pie's eyes was almost primal, as if he was having an out-of-body experience. Jack was going to give him another out-of-body experience in just a minute when he stroked him with the butt of the Glock.

Jack closed in and reached for Moon Pie's shoulder when someone shoved something hard into his ribs. White said, "Don't turn around. Walk to the stairs or I'll kill you. You believe me, right, Jack?"

"I take it you're not arresting me?"

White shoved the silencer into Jack's spine and pushed him toward the stairwell.

Moon Pie felt sick. He rushed into the bathroom just in time to throw up on the floor.

"Damn it. Damn, damn!" He punched the closest stall door with his fists.

"Hey! What the hell's going on?" a voice said from inside the stall. "Goddamn drunks."

"Shut up!" Moon Pie gave the door a vicious kick and then another.

"I'll call security." The voice said, but the was less angry, more scared.

Moon Pie pulled his gun and put three bullets through the stall door. There was a groan, and the sound of something heavy sliding to the floor. In a rage, Moon Pie kicked the stall door in and shot the dying man in the face. "Stupid jerk!" he yelled.

He pulled the Halloween mask from his pants and took the porkpie hat off. He pulled the mask over his head and checked himself out in the mirror. He put the porkpie hat on top and flicked the brim.

"Let's get this party started."

Chapter Forty

The third level of the casino was busy. There seemed to be more cocktail waitresses, and therefore, more drunks. The atmosphere was giddy. The whirring of the slots and the constant "bing-bing-bing" from the various machines were distracting and alluring at the same time.

Pons had been in the Southern Indiana district office for eight years and before that he worked in ATF intelligence gathering in D.C., but he'd kept in shape and qualified with his handgun three times a year. He felt he could handle this.

His left hand held the pistol inside his jacket pocket; the other he kept free to defend himself if needed. He moved aft, toward the restrooms and cashier's cage, guessing Shirl's actions would mimic those of his partner, Moon Pie. He saw Shirl sitting at the bar but he wasn't drinking. The woman bartender said something to the man, and he silenced her with a look.

A waitress asked if Pons wanted a drink. He asked for a 7UP, no alcohol. She came back with it and gave him a big smile and waited as if she expected a tip. He just smiled back and took his drink to a seat by the craps tables. From there, he could keep an eye on the stairway and Shirl without being obvious. He hoped to seem like just another guy waiting to get into the game. If Jack was right about the timing of the robbery, it would happen in the next few minutes.

Shirl was watching the cashier's cage using the mirror over the bar. Pons studied Shirl. The man was wearing a loose-fitting shirt, outside his waist, but there was no telltale outline of a handgun like he had seen on Moon Pie.

If Shirl pulled a gun, Pons was going to shoot him, but he would prefer arresting him before it got to that point. Then he started second-guessing himself. What hard evidence did he really have that Shirl was planning to rob the casino? If he grabbed Shirl too early, Shirl could say he was just another patron of the boat, and he was carrying a pistol because he's a cop. If he didn't act now, however, and waited for Shirl to pull out a gun, someone could get shot, and Pons would feel responsible.

Pons expected something to happen soon, but Shirl didn't move. "Shit," he said. Shirl was just sitting there, watching the cashier's cage. If he knew how Jack and Stu had made out, and if they had already arrested Moon Pie and Ellert, maybe Shirl would just give up without anyone getting hurt. Besides, it would be crazy to pull a robbery while the boat was sailing. Chances were good they were waiting for the boat to dock before they made their move.

He made his mind up and headed for the stairwell to the lower decks.

Agent Crenshaw had donned the ridiculous cocktail-waitress outfit that was White's idea. Her small automatic was held in place by a special leg holster near her crotch. The outfit was designed to show a lot of skin, and was almost too skimpy to hide anything. A touch of makeup, and she was good to go.

White's orders were for her to take the top deck now. If she saw Quinn, she was to notify him. White was giving the orders but didn't know that he wasn't in charge of this operation. She wasn't really FBI, and she hadn't been loaned to these two goons. In fact, she outranked them both, but it was her plan to let them think she was just another dumb broad.

The three lawmen had split up. The state trooper was heading for the stairs leading belowdecks. He had the run of the boat, so he would be able to lead her places that only Quinn would be able to access. That left White to deal with Murphy and Moon Pie. Pons was headed upstairs toward the third level and top deck. Thompson would take the ATF agent and Shirl. She mentally flipped a coin and decided that Quinn would likely be belowdecks taking out the communication room and anything else that would ruin his plan. She went after the trooper.

She soon got lost in the maze of hallways but didn't see the trooper or anyone else for that matter. Then she heard yelling and crying. She found Major Ellert in a back passageway, handcuffed to an overhead pipe. His front was soaked in blood and he was struggling futilely with the handcuffs.

"Thank God!" he said. "I'm Major Ellert, head of security. I need you to find a security guard upstairs and bring them here with hand-cuff keys." When she didn't move, he said, "I don't know you. How did you get down here? Never mind. Just get one of the security people and hurry."

Crenshaw reached under the bustle of her outfit and pulled out the small handgun. She shoved the muzzle in Ellert's mouth and pulled the trigger.

Ellert's head came apart, and his body went limp. She holstered the gun and started searching again. She found the door to the surveillance room. Of course it was locked. She stood a foot or so from the peephole, retrieved her pistol, and then unbuttoned several buttons on the blouse. She knocked and when the peephole went dark she put the pistol barrel against it and fired two rounds. She fired several more bullets into the lock and pushed the door open. Two men were sitting at a bank of monitors. They were both staring at a third man who had grown a third eye in his forehead. One of the men said, "We're unarmed." The other said, "Don't kill me."

She shot both men in the face, walked closer, and shot them again in the head. She had hoped to find Quinn here. She would find him. Right now she had to destroy any evidence. She walked behind the bank of monitors to see what kind of damage she could do and found two Semtex charges. The pencil timers stuck in them weren't set to go. She pulled the metal strip from each charge, giving her about five minutes to clear out. Someone, probably Quinn, had done her a favor. There wouldn't be anything left in this room.

She pulled the door shut behind her to maximize the effects of the Semtex and looked for a stairwell. She would kill Quinn. Of that she had no doubt. But she would have to kill White and Thompson as well. The U.S. government had invested a lot of money and time in the five-man team that had originally tried to get Quinn. Two had died in Quinn's D.C. town house, and another in the hallway, each shot several times. Because that team had failed, she was given the green light to do whatever she thought best. White and Thompson had been part of the original team, but they didn't know she was the one calling the shots on this op. They had only been told this operation was a chance to clean up their mess. They had made a bigger mess.

White dug the silencer deeper into Jack's spine and shoved him into the stairwell. A solid steel wall was to Jack's right, the metal railing to his left. He wondered if he would survive a jump.

White shoved him against the rail and pointed the pistol at Jack's crotch. "Don't do anything stupid," he warned.

"If I did, how would you know?"

White's response was to fire a silenced bullet between Jack's legs. It splattered on the stairs and ricocheted a few times.

"My penis surrenders. Can I go to the bathroom?" Jack asked.

"You're a smart boy, Jack," he said. "It's that mouth that gets you in trouble. Your captain puts up with it because he's stupid. Do you think I'm stupid?"

"What was your first clue?"

White chuckled, but it wasn't a warm sound. "You have balls, Jack, I'll give you that. Brains . . . not so much, but big balls."

"Now take your gun out of your waistband and throw it over the railing."

"I'd rather not," Jack said, but he reached in his waistband and brought his .45 out with two fingers.

"Now, pitch it over the railing."

Jack did as told but he wasn't going to die alone. He'd take this asshole to hell with him.

White pushed him forward and down a few stairs. "Okay, stop there."

I guess this is it. He was ready to fight, but before he could make a move he heard the sound of footsteps bounding up the stairs. White pointed the pistol at Jack's head and whispered, "Against the wall. Not a sound." Stu Sanders came flying around the corner of the landing heading for them, not seeing them. White struck Jack in the back of the head with something hard. Jack staggered forward into Stu and they fell against the wall at the bottom of the landing. Jack was dazed, Stu started to reach for his gun and stopped when he saw the silencer White had pointed at his face.

"Don't, Stu," Jack said.

Stu raised his hands over his head.

"Please, put your hands down. This isn't a cowboy movie," White said.

Stu looked at Jack and asked, "Who is this guy?"

"I don't have a clue," Jack said. "He says his name is Paul White. First he was FBI and then CIA. But if he was really CIA, he'd know that policemen don't watch cowboy movies, only porn flicks."

"Shut up," White snarled.

"That's the thing about Jack," Stu said. "He never knows when to shut up."

"Another wiseass," White said and again pointed the pistol at Jack's little sailor.

"Agent White," Jack said, "aiming that cannon at my dick doesn't intimidate me. My dick has done nothing but make bad decisions for most of its life. You'd be doing me a favor."

This time White did laugh. "You're funny," he said and leveled the pistol at Stu's chest. "I'm not forgetting you, Trooper Sanders. Jack can watch you die unless you lose the gun."

"Okay," Stu said and slowly began to move his hand towards his gun.

"Use your other hand," White said. "Slow and easy. Throw it over the rail."

Stu removed the 9mm from his holster and tossed it. It clattered down a few stairs. "Listen to me," Stu said. "Some asshole planted explosives downstairs. I got a few of them disarmed but there are more. I couldn't find them."

White's expression didn't change.

Stu said, "I can understand you wanting to shoot Jack. I've thought about it myself. He's a prick. But right now we have a serious problem, and in case you didn't notice, we're in the middle of the river."

"Stu's right," Jack said. "Not about me being a prick, but . . . hello . . . explosives. That's bad. We need to work together."

"You've got more immediate problems right here," White said. "Agent Thompson should be finished with Agent Pons and then we'll get rid of you two. Quinn's not going anywhere."

"Listen to me," Stu said. "This guy—Ellert—had a big canister of some type of gas that he was feeding into the ventilation system. When I found him, his nose and eyes were bleeding. I think it's some kind of mustard gas. We could all die."

"Not all of us," White said.

"Are all of you crazy?" Jack asked. "How are you going to get away if the boat sinks?" Then he understood. "Quinn has a boat, doesn't he?" he asked. "And you knew about it."

White grinned. "See, I told you you're a smart boy."

"Quinn's going to gas everyone and sink us. You knew about the explosives and all of this, didn't you? This was going to be your cover for killing Quinn. Right? You and Thompson and Crenshaw. All in it together. So how were you three going to escape?"

"Nothing matters except killing Quinn," White said. "You're right about him having a boat. We knew about the ordnance Khaled was supplying to Quinn. All we had to do was sit back and watch you running around like a hamster in a cage. What do you think of that, smart guy?"

"I think you'll never get away with it," Jack said.

"Yeah. Well how about this," White said. "You shot Quinn—he shot you and anyone else that gets dead—and when this thing sinks everyone else drowns while me and Thompson leave in Quinn's boat. How's that for an escape plan?"

"What about Agent Crenshaw?"

White smiled. "She won't make it. One of you will have shot her."

"You don't get out much, do you?" Jack said. These weren't regular squirrels playing hide the nuts. They truly believed they had the right, or the duty, to kill for God and country. Even when they were killing hundreds of innocent people."

"Let's all move, like friends," White said. He motioned for Stu to go down and shoved Jack forward. To Stu he said, "Oh. And in case you get any bright ideas—if you run, I'll kill Jack first and then you. I'm a very good shot."

Jack knew he and Stu were as good as dead. White was only keeping them alive until he could get them down to the lower decks where their bodies wouldn't be found right away.

"You can still stop this and prevent all these people from dying," Jack said.

White motioned with the gun. "Get moving."

"Who gives a shit about Quinn?" Jack said, stalling for time. "You guys take him and do whatever you want. We'll help you catch him. I'll even kill him for you."

"I can kill you both right here," White said.

"Okay," Jack said and he and Stu moved down a step. "As long as I'm going to die why don't you tell me about Khaled? Did you guys kill him or did he just fall in some grease solvent?" Jack started to turn. He was going to rush White. All he had to lose was his life.

"Move," White said, and then there was a gunshot.

Jack thought he'd been shot, but then White fell past him and down the flight of stairs.

Blood pooled around White's head, and it was easy to see why. The base of his skull and most of his face were missing.

Pons was standing above them. "I hope that was one of the bad guys."

"Not anymore," Jack said.

Pons came down a few steps, and Jack could see the hand holding the gun was shaking.

"You did the right thing, Greg. This guy's partner is around somewhere, and he's even more psychotic. The partner was supposed to have killed you. What happened up there?"

Pons looked a little embarrassed. "I thought maybe the robbery wasn't going to happen until we docked. So I came to see what you two had found out. It didn't look like Shirl was going anywhere."

Jack found his and Stu's guns at the bottom landing near White's crumpled form and retrieved them. He handed Stu his gun and said. "There's a female with them. I think her name is Crenshaw. She's the one that was at the hospital with these bozos. They were probably going to finish Killian off."

Stu said, "We need a plan, and quick. There really are explosives down there."

"What the hell?" Pons asked.

"Ellert was down below trying to light this big container of chemicals. He said it was tear gas, but whatever it was, it made him really sick. He told me he planted Semtex different places down there to sink the ship. I couldn't find all of them."

"How much time do we have?" Jack asked.

"I don't know. There are new crates of inflatable life rafts on the upper deck," Stu said. "But I don't think we have time to evacuate everyone."

"Moon Pie and Shirl are probably waiting for the explosion. That's their distraction. We've got to stop them. Someone has to warn everyone," Jack said.

"I know the ship better than either of you. I'll go back down and see if I can disable the rest of the explosives," Stu said. "You guys get up there and see what you can do."

"You think that's a good idea?" Pons asked. "If we're going to abandon ship, maybe you'd be better off up here with us?"

"There are crewmen down there. I've got to try and get them out. No one else dies today," Stu said and hurried down the stairs.

Jack and Pons hoofed it back upstairs.

"Do you think we can evacuate this boat in time?" Pons asked.

"Evacuate them to where?" Jack said. "If we try to get them to leave we'll start a stampede. There are only two of us and we don't know how many of Ellert's crew might be involved in this. Let's hope Stu gets the explosives in time. We have to stop Shirl and Moon Pie, or we'll have a lot of dead people on our hands."

They entered the second level of the casino and Jack asked, "How did you know where I was?"

"I didn't."

Jack looked around for Moon Pie but didn't see him. Everything looked normal. If you can call hundreds of zombies throwing money away "normal."

"Where are they?" Pons said. "Maybe I was right, and they're waiting until we dock. Maybe Stu was wrong about the explosives."

"I think the CIA guys were using me to track Quinn," Jack said. "And I led them right to him."

"You mean they were just going to kill him?"

"Yeah," Jack said. "And us."

"So it's just you and me against Shirl and Moon Pie and Quinn and two more CIA operatives."

Jack said, "I'll find Moon Pie. You find Shirl."

"What about Thompson and Crenshaw?"

"They're with Quinn as far as I'm concerned. If you run across any CIA people shoot first, and then say you're sorry."

"That's your plan?" Pons asked.

"You know the old saying, Greg. Better tried by twelve than carried by six. I don't know about you, but I'd rather go to jail than get killed. You got a better plan?"

Chapter Forty-one

A shudder ran through the boat, and Jack felt the floor under his feet tilt very slightly to the starboard side. He hoped Stu had gotten clear. His instinct was to check on his friend, but he feared it was too late.

The passengers had felt the change in the boat's position too. Some exchanged looks that asked: "Is something wrong? What was that?" Even the hardcore had stopped placing bets or pulling levers, but someone hit a big jackpot nearby and Jack was caught in an onrush of gawkers.

As Jack tried to shove through the crowd, he saw Moon Pie coming out of the restroom, wearing that stupid porkpie hat with a rubber mask over his head and a silenced handgun in his hand. The gun was similar to the one Jack had taken from the dead CIA man.

Jack saw Moon Pie stalking toward the cashier's window, but was unable to push free of the throng of people crowding around the "big winner." He hesitated to pull his own gun and bully his way through, fearing that would just make the crowd worse. But then he heard Moon Pie yell over the noise, "Gimme the goddamn money!"

Jack pulled his weapon and clubbed his way forward. Moon Pie pointed the gun into the cashier's room and fired several times. Jack couldn't hear the shots, but he could see the burning gas escaping the barrel as round after round was fired.

Jack was halfway there when he saw Moon Pie stop shooting and heard a bloodcurdling scream.

"Shut it!" Moon Pie screamed. "Shut up or I'll shoot your old ass!" He shot multiple times, and the screaming stopped.

Jack raised his .45 and fired into a chandelier. The chandelier exploded into a shower of sparks and glass, and the crowd to his front ran in every direction all at once. Jack was caught in a sea of panicked bodies, and forced to watch as Moon Pie fired again and again into the cashier's office.

Moon Pie stepped back and kicked the door but it wouldn't give. He swore and was shooting holes in the door by the time Jack was able to free himself from the crush of people. Moon Pie suddenly turned around, and the eyes in the mask stared straight at Jack. The eyes widened and then he fired the rest of his bullets into the crowd. One bullet smashed into a metal support beam inches from Jack's face. Jack dropped to the floor and shot between the spread legs of a woman who seemed to be frozen in her tracks. Moon Pie fell back against the door of the cashier's cage, arms hanging at his sides, while a spot of crimson grew across the front of his bowling shirt. Jack fired twice more. Moon Pie looked like he was dancing as the Bill Clinton mask jerked upward and sideways, and then he collapsed to the floor.

Jack pushed himself up from the floor. The woman was looking down at her legs and feeling down her front. "Was it good for you too?" he asked as he walked past her to Moon Pie.

Moon Pie lay dead on the floor. The rubber likeness of Bill Clinton now had extra nostrils.

"I didn't vote for you anyway," Jack said, and pushed the body with his foot to make sure Moon Pie was down for good. He was.

Chapter Forty-two

Quinn had no doubt that Shirl and Skippy Walker would be tied to the murder of Khaled, the shooting of the ATF Agent, and the casino robbery. He was sure because he had left evidence behind just for that reason. The rubber masks and silenced weapons found with Moon Pie's and Shirl's bodies would cinch the police case. If someone believed there was a mastermind, the trail of breadcrumbs would lead to Ellert, who would be dead from the chemicals in the smudge pot.

Quinn's black Hyperflex wetsuit was complete with hood, gloves, and boots, and he blended perfectly with the dark tree line behind him. The wetsuit had two purposes. It would act as camouflage when he crossed the river, and it would protect him from the cold water if it became necessary. The night had cooled only slightly, but the water temperature was sixty degrees. He was on the Kentucky side of the Ohio, where there were no river cabins or people to worry about. He could make out the city lights of Evansville as he slid the assault raft into the relatively calm waters of the Ohio. The slight hissing noise of the raft inflating was masked by the raucous sounds of a heavy metal band playing outside Fast Eddie's near the casino.

If his timing was right, and if Ellert did as he'd instructed, the riverboat would be disabled and drifting with the current. Nothing like a good old-fashioned jurisdictional fight to slow law enforcement down.

He remembered the shock in Khaled's eyes before he died and was amused. Khaled had thought he was going to be the one making a killing off this piece of equipment. The black assault raft was known as the ERB 310, or Emergency Response Boat. It weighed a little over one hundred pounds and could be inflated and ready to launch in two minutes. The ERB was used by the military but re-designed for police rescue operations when speed and ease of assembly were essential. It had the capability of mounting two engines on the rear motor clamp plates, but Quinn had opted for a single fifty-five HP outboard that was capable of speeds up to twenty knots. Best of all, it was invisible at night.

He made one more trip to the back of his truck, carried the other item delivered by Khaled, and mounted it to the metal plate for the second engine. The Browning M2HB .50 caliber air-cooled machine gun was the same type used in World War II but was in use still. It was a formidable weapon capable of firing a 710-grain 12.7 mm armor-piercing round at almost three thousand feet per second. It fired 550 rounds per minute with an effective kill range of over a mile. The one drawback of the weapon was the weight. Eighty-five pounds and another forty pounds for one hundred rounds of belt-fed .50 caliber ammo.

Quinn inspected his own personal weaponry. Satisfied that he hadn't neglected anything, he finished shoving the raft into the water and climbed inside. He lifted the top receiver of the Browning, inserted the belt of .50 caliber ammo across the top of the bolt, and closed the receiver. He pulled the charging handle and drove a four-inch bullet into the bore of the weapon, then set the safety.

The Suburban was clean. He'd left nothing behind that could tie him to the vehicle. It was clean. It was time. He started the engine, and sped across the water to the riverboat. He pulled alongside, tied the raft off to a steel ladder on the riverboat's side and climbed. His destination was the wheelhouse, where he would take out communications and navigation. He reached the wheelhouse, drew his weapon, and opened the door.

"Where are the keys?" Quinn demanded and struck Captain Bruce in the head with the butt of the gun.

Bruce fell to the floor, bleeding.

Quinn pointed the pistol at the navigator, John Keep. "I won't ask again," he said.

Captain Bruce was a brave man but not a stupid one. The keys were in his pocket. He dug them out and slid them across the floor.

"Good man," Quinn said. "The only hope you have of regaining control of this vessel is to stay alive." He motioned with the silencer and said, "Back there."

The muscles in Keep's forearms rippled. He was a big man, and he wouldn't let anyone treat the captain like this. Keep helped Captain Bruce to his feet, and they did as instructed.

"On the floor. Face down."

Captain Bruce lay on the floor and said, "Mr. Keep. Would you join me, please?"

Quinn said, "Not you, big man. You come here and shut the engines down."

"We can't let him do that, Captain," Keep said.

Quinn pointed the pistol at Keep's head. "One of you. I don't much care which."

Keep clenched his fists and moved fast, but Quinn was faster.

Captain Bruce watched in horror as Keep's head came apart, throwing blood and brains and bits of skull against the back wall. "You bastard," the captain said, and pushed up from the floor.

"If you don't shut the engines down, you're next," Quinn said.

Bruce stood beside his first officer's body and said, "Screw you, buddy."

"Just as well," Quinn said. The end of the silencer spat twice, and Bruce's body lay crumpled next to his dead friend.

Quinn examined the dozens of switches on the panel and found the controls for the engines, shutting them all down. Next, he fired several bullets into the communications console. A hard thud came from somewhere below his feet, and then another. The room tilted slightly. "I believe that was your starboard ballast tank, Captain," he said. "You are now dead in the water." He smiled at his own joke and then left the wheelhouse.

Pons felt the whump of the blast and hoped Stu Sanders had gotten clear.

The explosion was the signal. Why else would they disable the boat? Shirl was nowhere in sight. Someone yelled, "The boat's sinking." Soon other voices joined in and then, inevitably, the shoving.

Pons didn't see any of the casino security officers on the third level. The door to the cashier's cage stood open and a gray-haired woman in a Blue Star Casino shirt stood in the doorway, crying. Pons wondered where the hell security was and then figured they were probably engaged at the exits. At least he hoped they were at the exits.

He headed for the cashier's cage just as the gray-haired woman and a shaky young man fled from there, not bothering to secure the door behind them. The panic was full blown, and people fled in all directions. The exit doors to the stairwells were in total chaos with people jammed so tight no one could move. There was nothing he could do for them. But he could find Shirl and arrest him.

Gun in hand, Pons put his back against the wall just outside of the vacated cashier's cage. He spun around and went into a crouch as he entered and found the room was empty. All of the drawers were open and paper money was scattered around like confetti. He was too late.

He walked to the doorway. He wasn't sure the boat was going to sink, but Stu had said something about chemical agents near the air ducts. It was time to go. He could swim. And so could many of these people.

He ran for the exit that led to the outside deck. He intended to direct people to that exit but had to abandon that plan. Ahead of him was a man in a Halloween mask with a gun in one hand and two large canvas bags in the other. The man was pushing against the doors but they didn't open. He knew this was Shirl.

Shirl took something from his pocket and was fiddling with the lock when Pons came up behind him and shoved his duty weapon against his neck. "Federal Agent," Pons said. "Shirley West, you are under arrest." He took Shirl's gun and slid it into the back of his waistband.

"Now unlock the door."

Shirl used a key and unlocked the door to the upper decks and pushed one open. Pons shoved him outside. The deck was deserted but lit by strings of colored Christmas lights that spanned the length of the top deck.

He shoved Shirl face-first, against a steel wall beside the doors. "Hands on the wall, Shirl. You know the drill."

Shirl said, "You've got my gun. Can I take the mask off? It's like an oven in here."

"Leave it," Pons ordered. "I've never arrested a president before."

"Who're you with? FBI?"

"I'm holding the gun and you insult me." Pons did a quick pat down of Shirl's outer clothing, and then said, "In case you couldn't hear in there, Officer Shirley West, you're under arrest on federal charges. Attempted murder of a federal agent, conspiracy to commit robbery, and illegally carrying a silenced weapon. If that was an explosion I heard, you will be going away for a very long while."

"You don't know what you're talking about. I'm a cop. I'm carrying a gun, so what? And I had the mask on as a joke."

"And you just happened to have a key to the locked exit doors," Pons said.

"Yeah. You're making a false arrest, and I'm gonna sue your ass. If you knew what was good for you, you'd run while you had the chance."

Shirl was very talkative. Before Pons registered this as a danger sign, something slammed into his back and then again. He stumbled into Shirl and fell to the deck.

A black-clad figure approached from the direction of the wheelhouse, and Shirl did a double take.

"Help me move his body out of sight," Quinn said.

"What's going on?" Shirl asked. "How did the FBI get on this?" He pulled the rubber mask off and wiped the sweat from his face with the back of his hand. "Why are you wearing that getup?"

Quinn ignored the questions and asked, "How many of the charges went off?"

"I only felt one. They were supposed to go off all at once, right?"

Quinn said nothing. He had felt two explosions. Ellert hadn't done his job. No surprise. He and Shirl dragged Pons's limp form across the deck and disposed of him behind a metal container that had LIFE RAFTS stenciled on the side in four-inch black letters.

"You killed a federal agent," Shirl said and bent to retrieve his silenced pistol from Pons's waistband. While he was bent down, he felt his ankle for his own hideout piece. The .38 revolver was still there.

"Correction," Quinn said. "We killed him. A jury won't make the fine distinction as to who pulled the trigger."

"What now?" Shirl asked.

"Finish your job." Quinn shoved the rubber mask back into Shirl's sweaty hands.

* * *

Jack passed a cocktail waitress as he exited the stairs onto the third level. Something about her seemed both familiar and wrong at the same time. He turned around to stop her but he was too slow. She was behind him and shoved a compact semiautomatic in his gut.

"Don't move, Murphy," the waitress said, and he saw it was the female agent, Crenshaw.

"You look . . . different. Sorry about the confusion at the hospital, but I didn't feel like being arrested. And what is it with this 'Don't move' shit? Do they teach you that in spook school? When White was still alive, he said the same—"

She head butted him and he staggered back. The blow had taken him by surprise. Before he could recover, she yanked his gun out of his hand.

"You killed White," she said. "Don't think I won't kill you."

"Oh, did you and Mr. Walmart have something going?" Jack asked. He still had White's silenced pistol in his waistband, which was both bad and good. If Crenshaw found it, she might just shoot him. If she didn't, he might have a chance. So far, she had been willing to talk, so maybe she wasn't up to homicidal mode yet.

"White was going to kill me," Jack said. A trickle of blood run down his forehead.

"Shut up," she said. "Where's Quinn? If I think you're lying it will be the last thing you say, asshole."

It took all of his willpower not to knock the dog shit out of her. Well, willpower . . . and the fact that she had a gun stuck in his ear.

"You don't want to kill me," Jack said. "I can help you get Quinn."

"Wrong answer."

He felt the barrel dig into his ear but she didn't pull the trigger. He was getting tired of this game. Either she was going to shoot him, or she wasn't.

"Listen, Crenshaw, there's an ATF agent named Greg Pons up here somewhere. He's trying to stop people from being killed by that psychotic asshole you're looking for."

She didn't say anything or head butt him again, so he continued.

"I know you CIA types think you're all smoke and mirrors and all that happy shit, but White's dead. And after that explosion I think a state police officer named Stu Sanders is dead. For all I know, ATF Agent Pons might be dead. I'm all the help you've got. I can help you get Quinn."

"I should kill you now so you don't get in my way," she said dryly. "But, as you say, you might find Quinn. Seeing you want to arrest Quinn, it might be fun to watch."

And distracting. He didn't think she cared whether everyone on the boat died, as long as she got to Quinn. Jack's best chance was to show her he was as crazy as she was.

"I'm not planning on taking Quinn alive. So if you want to shoot me, get it done or give my gun back and get the hell out of my way," he said.

He felt the pressure against his ear ease and she backed away.

"I shouldn't do this," she said, "but I feel like we owe you something for keeping after Quinn even after he killed your friends. You should be working for us."

Jack's blood ran cold. "What are you talking about?".

"I'm sorry," she said. "I thought you knew." She dropped her arms to her sides and said, "I'm really sorry about your friends. Quinn didn't leave anyone to . . . he doesn't leave witnesses."

Jack's pulse pounded in his ears. He'd been out of touch with everyone for a while. His knees felt weak and he leaned against the wall. Who was she talking about? Killian? Liddell? Susan? Katie!

He studied her face, but he couldn't tell if she was lying. "Who?" he managed to say.

She reached out to steady him, and her act of kindness frightened him more than any gun could. He pulled away.

"Everyone you care about. You can get even," she said. "Help me. I'll fix things with your bosses. Quinn will be dead, and you'll be a hero."

Jack wished she would shut up. She was like the devil whispering in the choir loft. He knew she would kill him the second he was no longer useful.

She went on, "Quinn doesn't care how many people die. But we do."

"We—meaning you. Your partners don't seem to have any qualms about killing. And by the way, where is that other limp dick, Thompson?"

She said, "You make jokes, but we're dead serious about finding Quinn. You were fouling everything up. Thompson and White wanted to kill you back at the hospital, but I just want Quinn."

"Scout's honor?" Jack asked.

She took a deep breath, and said, "You've shown some initiative. So I'm going to tell you what you're up against. His real name isn't Quinn. It's whatever he wants it to be. He doesn't exist. He was one of us, but now he's not. Five of our best agents caught up to him a month ago. Three are dead. White and Thompson are what is left of the team." She smirked and said, "No offense, Murphy, but you're not a pro."

"Yeah," Jack said. "But most of your pros are dead."

"White is a moron compared to Quinn. You have no idea what Quinn can do. He was . . . is . . . one of the best. He trained most of our agents. He trained me."

She surprised him by handing his .45 back. "Regardless of what you decide, you'll need that to get off this boat."

"We do this together," he said. "And then you disappear. I don't tell anybody. And I don't need your help with my boss." *I'm getting fired and I don't give a shit.*

"Oh, I think you'll change your mind about needing my help."

"In that case, you can go first," Jack said and stood back to let her pass. Jack hoped she was as good as she thought she was. Or he hoped she'd catch the round that was meant for him.

"Agent Crenshaw," he said as she moved around him on the steps.

"Yes."

"In case I don't make it out of this, I just want you to know that you have nice legs."

Chapter Forty-three

True to her word, Crenshaw went through the Level 3 doors first. The outfit she had on barely concealed her woman parts, so where did she keep the gun?

Jack scanned the room. He didn't see any law, but he saw plenty of disorder. Money was everywhere. Some people interrupted their own and others' headlong flight in order to pick it up, resulting in a pileup. Jack didn't see Thompson, Shirl, or Pons.

Crenshaw nudged him and pointed toward the doors leading to the outer decks. She yanked the door open. Nothing happened. Jack said, "My turn." He hurried through the opening and something pinged off the steel wall by his head. Chips of paint and lead stung the side of his face before he dropped to the deck and rolled behind one of the metal boxes he'd seen on the deck earlier. Stu had said they were installing more life rafts. They were really lifesavers.

Bullets danced around him like a swarm of angry hornets. Crenshaw came through the door, hit the deck, and crab-crawled the last few feet to cover. Across the deck, Shirl was running, firing over his shoulder, and then disappeared around the wall of the wheelhouse.

Crenshaw fired back, her bullets stitching across the wall of the wheelhouse. Jack knocked her arm down, driving bullets into the deck.

"What the hell are you doing? There are men in there."

"Anyone in there is already dead," she yelled and charged toward where Shirl had disappeared.

Jack knew there could be other threats than Shirl here. For a pro, she wasn't using her head, but all he could do was back her play. Crenshaw had rounded the wheelhouse but Jack stopped at the corner and crouched low. He heard more shots and risked a peek. Crenshaw was standing in the open, like she was on a pistol range, and she was blasting away at Shirl's retreating figure. The loud pops from her handgun were replaced with the splattering and zinging sounds of bullets coming his way—and definitely not coming from Shirl. Time to go.

Jack ran headlong into Crenshaw, knocking her to the left, behind a large stack of wooden crates. He ran for cover behind one of the life raft containers, tripped over something and went sprawling. He saw that he had tripped over Greg Pons. He crouched beside the unmoving agent and felt the brachial artery. The pulse was weak, but his chest was rising and falling. Jack checked for wounds but found nothing. He risked a peek in the direction he had shoved Crenshaw. She was taking a lot of fire.

"You okay?" he yelled.

She pulled a splinter of wood from her cheek. Jack was glad she was on his side . . . for the time being. Crenshaw reached under her skirt, produced a clip, and slapped it in her gun.

So . . . that's where she keeps her weapons.

Jack checked his own gun. Two rounds left. He patted Pons's sides and ankles but didn't find another gun he could use. He still had White's handgun. He wished he'd thought to search White for extra ammo.

The shooting had tapered off, but each time he or Crenshaw tried to move they almost ate a bullet. Quinn or Shirl or whoever was shooting at them wasn't wasting shots. He and Crenshaw were pinned down.

Pons let out a soft groan and opened his eyes.

"Don't move, Greg," Jack said. "You're not behind very good cover."

Pons grimaced. "Shot in . . . back." His eyes shut tight, and Jack thought he'd stopped breathing. Then his eyes opened. "Stupid," he muttered.

"Just lay still, Greg," Jack said.

"Vest," Pons said and tried to grin but it came out ugly. "You?"

Jack had felt Pons's ballistic vest when he'd checked him for injuries. That was why Pons wasn't bleeding much. Still . . . ballistic vests don't protect you from impact injuries. Pons could be bleeding internally.

"Real men don't wear bulletproof vests," Jack said and peeked around the corner. A bullet creased his cheek and his hand went to his face. "Shit!"

"John?" Crenshaw yelled, and to Jack's surprise a voice answered.

"Is that you, Lucille?" The voice sounded happy, almost playful, like old friends reuniting.

"Give it up, John," Crenshaw said.

There was a chuckle. "Sorry, love. You know the drill."

"I'm not alone, John."

"I can see that, Lucille. How much does Murphy know?"

Jack saw Pons was out like a light. He was still breathing though, and that was probably more than Jack would be doing if he didn't get lucky. Quinn had just asked what "Murphy" knew, so that meant he was as good as dead. "He doesn't leave witnesses," Crenshaw had told him. He wondered if that went for her too.

"Why don't you come and ask me yourself, John?" Jack said. "We can swap recipes. I've got one for stuffed spook."

Crenshaw said, "Joe and Billy are here. Have you run into them?"

Jack couldn't keep up with all the names. John was Quinn. Joe and Billy were probably White and Thompson. Crenshaw was Lucille, or maybe this whole thing was looney. Did Quinn know White—was that Billy or Joe?—was dead? Was Thompson still out there or had Quinn already killed him? Or Crenshaw for that matter? Nothing was what it appeared.

"I wouldn't count on backup," Quinn said in that same playful tone.

Jack thought that in psycho talk, that meant that Thompson was dead. And that was a good thing. But the cockiness of the asshole was really pissing Jack off.

Quinn said, "Billy took a little swim, you see. And Joe would have showed himself by now. Did you kill him, Lucille?" Quinn asked.

She didn't answer.

So Thompson was Billy and Billy had been killed by Quinn and thrown overboard. Joe was White and he was killed by Pons. It was all starting to make sense. Not.

Crenshaw caught Jack's attention and motioned for him to cover her. He held his palm out indicating she should stay put. *What the hell is her rush to die?*

"What are you going to do?" Pons asked. He was coming to and his color was better, but he wasn't out of the woods.

"Lie still," Jack said. "You've probably got some broken ribs." The coughing had brought up some blood.

Jack had to make a choice. Stay here and watch Pons die, or take the fight to the bad guys. His dad always said, "You get a lot farther with a kind word and a gun than you do with just a kind word." Or was it Mom who said that?

He made eye contact with Crenshaw, pointed at himself, and then motioned in the direction he'd seen Shirl run. He waved for Crenshaw to go right and flank them, He expected her to argue, but she just nodded "okay." *Bitch.*

He held his gun tight against his chest, took a deep breath, and then before he moved he saw Crenshaw charge straight toward Quinn's position. She was drawing fire so he ran toward Shirl's position. One bullet creased his shoulder. Another burned along the top of his scalp. He hit the deck and rolled behind another metal box. Bullets struck the deck only inches from his face. There was nowhere to go except out in the open. Then the shooting stopped.

He heard a soft moan and looked to his right. Crenshaw was down on her hands and knees, crawling behind a crate. A dark splotch was blooming on the gold silk waist of her outfit. He felt something wet on his own side and his fingers came away sticky. "Son of a bitch," he said, and felt for an exit wound. He'd been hit in the side and didn't even feel it.

The good news—he wasn't going to die. Bad news—this asshole had shot him twice now, three times counting the one across his scalp. Quinn was playing with them. Crenshaw wasn't kidding about Jack not being a match for him.

He made himself a promise. He might die . . . but he would have company in hell.

"Drop the gun, Detective Murphy." Quinn had circled around behind him and now stood a few feet to his left, silencer pointed directly at Jack's face.

"You're going to kill me anyway," Jack said.

"I've won. No hurry."

So he thinks Crenshaw is dead. Maybe he had a chance. Quinn liked to play games. Brag. He wanted something from Jack, and that was the only reason he hadn't already finished it.

"Crenshaw, or Lucille, or whoever she is," Jack began, "said I was no match for you."

Quinn smiled. "Lucille was one of my best. I'm almost sorry I had to kill her."

"Tell me something. Are you the one who shot Killian?" Jack wanted to keep him talking, try to come up with a plan. He couldn't see where Crenshaw had crawled off to, but she was hit bad. She was probably as dead as the rest. As dead as he would be when Quinn got tired of talking.

"Killian was in the wrong place at the wrong time. I understand he lived, although that might change."

"Khaled? Was he involved with the Chicago deal?" Jack asked.

At the mention of Chicago, Quinn's smile grew even wider and the barrel of the silencer lowered a tad. "Chicago. Now that was magnificent. This will be too. You'll see. Well. Maybe you won't."

The silencer came back up. Quinn was finished talking.

"Can I at least stand up?" Jack asked. He would go out fighting at least. He'd already been shot three times. He wondered how many more he could take.

Shots started ringing out, not from a silenced weapon, and Crenshaw came from behind Quinn, running full-out, her semi-automatic thrust ahead of her. Jack was so startled that when he looked over, Quinn was gone. He saw Crenshaw's bare feet run past. She was yelling like a banshee one second and the next she grabbed at her throat. She went down hard and rolled onto her back.

Jack crawled to her. One bullet had taken of a chunk of her cheek and part of her ear. Another had hit her in the side of the neck. Jack tore off the bottom of his shirt, wadded it and stuffed it in the hole. He lifted her hand and placed it on the wound. "Keep pressure on it. I'll get help." *She's going to die.*

"Kill him," Crenshaw said. Her eyes were filled with hatred.

Jack said the only comforting thing he could think of. "It's a good thing you don't have a heart or Quinn would have aimed for it."

She grunted and said, "If you get killed, he wins."

"Hang in there and you can kill him yourself." He couldn't help but feel admiration for this tough but mentally disturbed woman. She was more warrior than anyone he'd ever known. Of course, that didn't make her any less crazy.

He pulled his shirt off and it put under her head.

"Kill him," she said. "He'll kill us both."

Jack wasn't afraid to admit that he was afraid. He was prone to wisecrack when he was under pressure, but he'd never been up against someone like Quinn.

"What do you think my chances are?" he asked.

She squinted her eyes shut but didn't answer.

"Thanks, Lucille. You're a pillar of confidence."

She took a raspy breath and said, "I should have killed you myself."

"Screw you, Lucille," Jack said.

He got into a crouch and yelled, "Hey, Shirl. What's it like to be on the losing side?"

No answer.

"Moon Pie's dead. All that money is still down there. This is going to hell fast."

Still no answer.

"At least Moon Pie faced me like a man, Shirl. He wasn't a pussy like you."

Shirl's voice came from somewhere to Jack's left. "You always thought you were better than me, Jack. But who's the better man now? Huh?"

Now where's Quinn?

Shirl yelled, "I've got four or five million dollars here, Jack. If you weren't such a Boy Scout, I might offer to give you a little. Let you walk away."

Jack knew Quinn would wouldn't leave witnesses. "No one's walking away except Quinn. He's going to kill you, Shirl. Think about it. That's been his plan all along. You and Skippy took all the risks. Ellert was never going to walk out of here. You'll never see any of that money."

Shirl didn't sound as confident when he said, "I've got the money. I'm leaving here and you'll be dead."

"You're smarter than that, Shirl. Quinn killed his own men in Chicago before he came to Evansville. Did he tell you that? He killed three CIA agents. Make that five. How far do you think you'll get?"

Shirl said nothing.

Jack pressed him. "You're a disgrace. A discredit to your badge. Where's your honor?"

"I didn't shoot anyone yet . . . Jack."

"Officer West, take the money to the boat," Quinn ordered.

Quinn's moving around. Smart.

"Yeah, Shirl. Do what Quinn tells you. You're his bitch now. Or you can jump over the side and swim to Kentucky. Let me deal with Quinn. We don't have extradition with Kentucky. Hell, they can't even spell extradition."

A bullet splattered close to Jack. Too close. Jack couldn't tell what direction it had come from. Quinn could be moving around behind him.

"What's he talking about? Who's Quinn?" Shirl asked.

Quinn said, "Don't be an idiot. You know what he's doing. He's trying to turn us against each other."

Shirl said, "He told us his name was Smith. He's the one who shot Killian. He killed that other ATF agent up here, too." Shirl's voice had changed. He seemed less sure of what he was doing. "Jack's right, Smith or Quinn, or whoever the hell you are. We'll never be able to hide from them. The Feds will never quit looking."

"I apologize for calling you an idiot, Officer West. You have to know Moon Pie's death was inevitable. I'm surprised you didn't kill him yourself. The death of the ATF men is inconsequential. I know places where we won't be found. The split is fifty-fifty now. How does that sound?"

Shirl said, "Moon Pie was kind of slow in the head, but bringing him in on this was your idea, not mine. Were you planning on killing him the whole time? Killing all of us?"

Jack yelled, "It's not too late to fix this, Shirl. I'll testify for you. Help me with Quinn, or just get off the boat. Go for help. Save these people."

Shirl was silent, but at least he wasn't shooting.

Jack said to Shirl, "Shirl, you'd better move. Find cover. He's coming for you." To Quinn he said, "What do you say, Quinn? Think you can take us both?"

Quinn didn't answer. Not good. Jack needed to move.

"I'm going to take the money to the raft," Shirl said. "Take it. Take it all."

Again, Quinn didn't answer.

"You better watch your ass, Shirl. You can't spend the money if you're dead." Jack yelled. He hoped Quinn would move in on Shirl being as Shirl had the money. At least Shirl would be out of play.

Shirl balanced the canvas bags filled with money on the railing. He leaned over to see if he'd been lied to about the escape craft. It was dark, but he could make out a dark shape floating next to the hull of the riverboat. He could drop them into the raft and hope Smith would go for the money. Or he could drop them in the river and fight.

"Drop the gun, Shirl," Quinn said. He had come up beside Shirl. Only a few feet between them.

Shirl turned slowly, one arm balancing the bags, the other holding the silenced gun, but Quinn's gun was only inches from his right eye.

"Whatever are you thinking, Shirl? You know Murphy's playing you, and yet you don't trust me. Think of what you are throwing away. Drop your gun and put the bags on the deck. We can still go fifty-fifty."

Shirl made the only choice he could if he wanted a chance to stay alive. He dropped the pistol and put the bags down.

"Now your hideout gun," Quinn said. "I know you old guys carry one."

Shirl bent over and reached for his ankle. Before he could touch the gun's handle a bullet passed through the top of his head. Quinn's pistol spit again and a second bullet struck him. Shirl's body sprawled over the canvas bags as if he was protecting them. Quinn walked up and shot him in the head again. He pushed Shirl's body off the bags with his foot.

"Prison's not a nice place for a policeman. I did you a favor," he said and hefted the bags. He moved down the rail to just above where the inflatable was tied to a ladder. He dropped the bags and heard them plop into the floor of the raft. He had only to climb over the side and disappear. But there was more money on the second level that moron, Moon Pie, had lost by dying. He was torn between going back for the money or making a clean getaway. The only thing that stood between him and the rest of the money was that joke of a cop, Murphy. Everyone else was dead. He made his mind up. It was all or nothing. And, truth be known, he was looking forward to killing Murphy for all of the trouble he'd caused.

Quinn was a dark outline against the blackness as Jack moved in on him. "Drop the gun," Jack ordered.

"Detective Murphy," Quinn said, without turning around.

Jack saw Shirl, facedown on the deck, unmoving.

"That's right, asshole," Jack said. "Now drop the gun, or I'll get my Christmas wish."

"Well, we wouldn't want to disappoint you. What was it you said? 'You can't spend the money if you're dead.'"

Jack hadn't counted his shots, but he guessed he had maybe one or two more before he was empty. He glanced down and saw Shirl's backup gun. Now all he had to do was get to it without getting killed.

"I'm going to give you the chance you never gave anyone else, Quinn," Jack said, knowing in his gut he should just shoot him in cold blood the way Killian had been shot, the way he'd promised Barbara, and himself, and Crenshaw.

Quinn stooped and laid the gun on the deck. "There. We can be friends now."

"Shut up," Jack said.

Quinn made a clucking sound with his tongue. "Detective Murphy. We're professionals. There's no need for hard feelings."

"What feelings?" Jack moved closer to Shirl and said to Quinn. "Turn to your right and kneel down."

"And what if I decide not to?"

"If you don't, it'll hurt."

Quinn had laid his gun in the open between them, but Jack had witnessed how fast the man was. He felt Shirl's ankle and tugged out a little revolver.

"Was he a friend of yours?" Quinn asked.

"Not particularly," Jack said. "But he shouldn't have been killed by a worthless bastard like you."

Quinn got to his knees and put his hands on top of his head. "You know, Detective Murphy, I'm really impressed with your, ah . . . will to survive. I can't seem to kill you."

"I'm Irish. We kill each other."

Quinn laughed at Jack's black humor. "Ah, Detective Murphy. You're quite entertaining. It's really too bad we didn't meet under other circumstances."

"It wouldn't have worked out, Quinn. I like women."

Quinn laughed again and said, "Well, since we obviously can't stand here exchanging quips all day, I'm going to make you a deal."

The deck lurched a bit, and Jack was caught off guard. He saw Quinn dive for the deck and he fired, but his bullet passed through empty space. Quinn scooped up his gun and fired. A bullet grazed Jack's knee and he went sprawling to the deck behind Shirl's body. He pulled Shirl's body close and felt the impact of several bullets as they struck the corpse. Jack tried to return the fire, but this time his gun really was empty. He still had Shirl's .38. He shoved Shirl's body away and pulled himself to the rail, ready to fire, but Quinn was gone.

He leaned over the rail and saw a dark shape moving down the side of the boat. He tried to aim at the figure and saw sparks on the rail beside him. He was being shot at. He held the revolver over the rail and cracked off blind shots. He didn't think he'd hit the bastard. He was about to lean over the rail again when a sound like a jack hammer started and the railing and deck around him sheared off, hurling chunks of metal past his face, and shredding his clothes.

Jack dropped to the deck as green tracer rounds buzzed through the air. Jack back-pedaled and fell over Shirl's legs, which probably saved him. Shirl's body jumped and danced as bullets ripped it to shreds and the air was came alive with stinging bits of shrapnel.

Quinn expended the full belt of one hundred sabot tracer rounds from the Browning .50 caliber machine gun. The armor-piercing rounds had ripped through the steel deck, creating an impressive lightshow. Quinn unclipped the machine gun from its mount and let it drop into the river.

"Well, that should make you think twice, Jack," Quinn said, and stacked the bags of money into the stern. It wasn't as much of a haul as he had expected, but it was what it was. He hoped Jack Murphy was dead. If he wasn't he'd have to come back someday for a rematch.

He slipped the securing line from the ladder and was pushing off when something heavy dropped on him and slammed him to the floor of the raft. He could feel a leg and torso pinning him. He pulled his pistol and pumped rounds into whoever until he was sure they were dead. In the moonlight he saw it was Shirl's body.

Quinn shoved the body over the side, pointed his pistol at the edge of the deck, and yelled, "I think I'll let you live, Murphy. But don't worry. I won't forget you." He was trying to goad Murphy into sticking his head out, but there was no movement from above.

He started the engine just as something else crashed down on him. This body was very much alive.

Murphy's Law says: "Medical costs for bullet wounds: $15,000. Loss of employment and pension for disobeying orders: $250,000, give or take. Dropping twenty feet and landing on your enemy: Priceless."

He had landed on Quinn by pure luck. He rolled off Quinn and over the side, into the river. The sudden submersion in the cool water shocked him and he sucked in a lungful of it before he came up for air.

Jack heard a motor revving and grabbed for the side of the inflatable craft. His hand caught a rope and he wrapped his arm in it before Quinn goosed the big motor to full throttle. Jack was dragged by an arm, hydroplaning across the surface, flipping and slamming face-first again and again into the water like a trapped rodeo rider.

The water tore at Jack's remaining clothing, and he was losing his grip, but somehow he got both hands on the rope and pulled himself close against the raft. With an effort born of panic, he threw one leg over the side and then pulled himself over. Quinn saw him and kicked at his face as he lay in the bottom gasping for breath.

Jack reached for his gun, forgetting it wasn't there. Quinn released the throttle and reached for his own gun. Jack launched himself forward, arms outstretched, intending to take Quinn overboard, but Quinn had anticipated the move and caught Jack's injured knee with a kick. Jack nearly went over the side again. When he righted himself, Quinn was on him. The big outboard ran full out as they struggled, sending the unmanned craft hurtling down the river.

Quinn grabbed Jack's chin and the back of his head, attempting to snap his neck, but the rocky bounding of the boat caused Quinn to lose his balance. Jack drove a knee upward into Quinn's groin, but the blow didn't seem to faze him. Quinn slammed a fist into Jack's face once, twice, and again before Jack's pain-paralyzed brain even registered the beating.

Quinn leaned over Jack and grabbed his head again, but Jack drove the fingers of his right hand into Quinn's throat. The blow should have crushed Quinn's larynx. It didn't, but it was enough to push Quinn back. Quinn reached for his pistol, but he'd lost it in the struggle. He crawled around, searching the bottom of the boat.

Jack lay on his back, feeling around for something to use as a weapon. His hand closed on a pistol. It was Quinn's. The inflatable was bounding across the water, and he couldn't steady his arm. Jack held the pistol against his side and tilted the barrel up, trying to point it at the blurry figure scurrying around. Jack knew he might get one shot off before Quinn took the gun away and killed him. The barrel crossed what Jack hoped was the center of the blurred image and he pulled the trigger.

There was a muted cough; and Quinn grabbed his thigh just below the groin. Jack pulled the trigger again and Quinn collapsed with a shattered elbow. Jack was lining up a shot when the inflatable catapulted end over end and sent Jack flying through the air. Jack would later tell Liddell that he thought he had died and was having an out-of-body experience.

The sensation of flying came to an abrupt halt when Jack struck the ground hard. He regained his senses, but he didn't know where he was, or, more important, where Quinn was. He could tell he was on his back. He tried to move, to get up, and was only able to move his head and his arms and one leg. The other leg wouldn't move. He stared into a dark sky. No moon, no stars. The air was warm, the ground cool, and there was an insistent buzzing noise.

His ears popped and he could hear better, but the buzzing was louder. And where was Quinn? Jack pushed himself onto his elbows and saw that his right leg was twisted at an impossible angle, the toes pointing down and not up. There was no pain, but that wouldn't matter because five feet away, Quinn stood ... swayed actually ... holding a silenced pistol. The assault craft had landed against a tree several feet behind Quinn. The noise Jack heard was the prop churning the air.

Quinn's face was streaked with blood, and one arm hung limply at his side.

"I really should kill you, Detective Murphy," he said and limped forward, clearly in pain. "But I think I'm going to cripple you instead. You can live the rest of your life in a hospital bed with someone wiping your ass."

"Well, you're a little late if you want to cripple me," Jack said. "Look, you're boring me to death. You people all talk like a cheap spy novel."

Quinn's expression changed so fast it was like watching a silent movie. He raised the pistol.

"You really are a piece of work, Jack." Quinn's gun never wavered as he looked behind him at the bags of money near the overturned boat. "I'll have millions, and you...you'll have your pathetic little disability pension."

Jack tried to give him the finger, but he was barely able to remain conscious.

Quinn picked up the bags of money. "On second thought, Jack," he said, a grin on his blood-smeared face, "I think I will kill you."

Quinn looked surprised, the smirk disappeared, and Jack noticed a pencil-thin line of blood trickling from the corner of Quinn's mouth. Then he did the unexpected and fell backward onto the boat's propeller. The spinning blades tore hungrily into Quinn's back, and then threw his chewed-up remains into the sand.

Crenshaw pulled a small inflatable boat onto the bank. "Bastard!" she said. Jack wasn't sure if she meant him or Quinn, but it didn't matter. He was glad to see her.

"I didn't know you served drinks onshore," Jack mumbled through bloody lips.

Crenshaw blew a strand of hair out of her eyes. One arm hung useless at her side, and she had packed and bound the wound on her neck somehow. She was shot to hell and bloody, but still standing, her pistol pointed in Jack's direction.

"I really should kill you," she said

Jack wasn't surprised when, instead, she threw her pistol into the sand at his feet. She stepped over what was left of Quinn, disappeared behind the raft, and the engine shut down. She reappeared with a small gasoline can.

"You take off if you want," he said. "I'll just lie here for a while." He wasn't sure what she had planned, but gasoline and a hot engine were not a good combination.

Crenshaw ignored him and uncapped the can. She poured gasoline onto Quinn's body and all around it and said, "You never saw me, Jack." She emptied the can on the inflatable and tossed the can onto Quinn's body.

She said, "This psycho was robbing the riverboat with a couple of bad cops and tried to escape. You pursued and jumped into the raft with him. He crashed into the riverbank and there was an explosion, but you were thrown clear." She kicked her pistol nearer Jack's hand. "There is the small matter of the bullet I put through his temple but, hey, I can't think of everything. You're a smart guy. You finish the story."

"Why are you doing this?" Jack asked.

"You mean not killing you." It wasn't a question.

"Yeah."

She picked up the canvas bags and tossed them toward Jack. She opened one bag and pulled out a stack of banded $20 dollar bills.

"You'll be quite the hero when they find the money. But you know they will never believe there was a government agency behind all this. Even if they did, the government will cover it up, and you'll look like a nutjob. Spies, assassins, and conspiracy theories are only good for the movies, Jack."

She pulled a Bic lighter from her top, lit the stack of money and, tossed it onto Quinn's body. A whoosh was followed by a blast of heat that crawled across the ground.

"With Quinn turned to ash, you won't have any proof."

Jack asked the question that had been eating at him.

"Quinn didn't kill anyone else did he? I mean, my friends are . . . ?"

Crenshaw held her side with her good arm, and he could see she was still bleeding. She walked her small boat out into the water and gingerly climbed in. She turned and looked at the bonfire she'd made. "You'll see," she said.

"Up yours, Lucy Crenshaw," he said softly.

"Back at you, Murphy," she said.

Jack's eyes closed. An army of darkness came for him and he spun into the void.

Chapter Forty-four

Six days later...

"Where's my gun?" Jack asked, peeking under the sheet. "There you are." He lowered the sheet.

Liddell sat in a chair by the window next to the bed. "Welcome back, pod'na," he said with a big smile.

The light coming through the window hurt Jack's eyes. He turned his head and saw he was sharing the room with another patient. Bandages covered the other man's entire head like a turban.

"Who's the sultan?" Jack asked Liddell.

"You should talk," Killian said. "You've been laying there for six days spilling your guts in your sleep. An' boy I heard me some juicy shit. I didn't know you and Double Dick were having a ménage a duo."

Jack lifted a hand and gave Killian the finger. "You look like someone's mummy. Glad to see you're still in the land of the living."

Killian said, "Your partner here has been filling me in on what happened after my surveillance was so rudely interrupted."

Liddell pulled a chair up and sat. "Not so fast, Killian. I need to ask Jack some questions to see if his memory is intact." He asked Jack, "What was the last thing you said to me before you went and almost got yourself killed?"

Jack turned to Killian. "Ignore him. Too much sugar and he gets this way."

"Wrong. The correct answer is, 'I'll keep you posted.' And did you? No you didn't. You went all commando, and I had to steal your boat to go looking for your ass."

"You took the *MISS FIT*?"

"Well, me and Susan," Liddell said. "She stayed with you while I went back for medics."

"Thank you for saving my life, partner," Jack said.

Liddell cocked his head and said, "Who are you, and what have you done with Jack?"

Killian said, "I recognized Shirl at the warehouse. Then I heard someone behind me, and next thing I woke up here."

Jack asked Liddell, "What happened to Pons? And Stu?"

Liddell said, "Pons was released this morning."

Liddell didn't say anything about Stu, so Jack knew he was dead. He choked up at losing a good man . . . a good friend.

"Tell us about these CIA people," Liddell said.

Jack said, "Not even if you held a gun to my balls."

"Cops don't have balls," Killian said.

Liddell persisted. "C'mon, pod'na. Pons said there was three of them on the boat. None of their bodies were found and the surveillance video was wiped clean."

Crenshaw. You magnificent bitch. Jack didn't know how she did it, but she had wiped her tracks clean. Well, almost. There was the matter of a crispy Quinn.

"We found you because of the bonfire. Fire department said it was gas fueled. The body in the fire was almost cremated. Was that Quinn?"

Jack remembered Crenshaw shooting Quinn, and then setting his body on fire. She had saved his life and disappeared. "It was Quinn. I had to shoot him. I think he burned up in the crash," he lied. "Did they find Stu? Did anyone else die?"

"Stu saved a lot of lives," Liddell said. "The casino paid for his services and made a quiet donation to his family."

Jack remembered that Stu was divorced but had a son and daughter, both serving in Iraq. Killian said Jack had been unconscious for six days. He'd missed Stu's funeral. "Were his kids notified?"

"They came home on compassionate leave," Liddell said. "They came to visit you, but you weren't awake yet. They said to tell you that you weren't to blame. They knew their dad was doing what he always did."

"That he was," Jack said.

"Skippy Walker and Shirley West were found with a lot of evidence that ties them to the robbery, but this Quinn fella is still a mystery. The Feds are trying to identify him by DNA. A couple of passengers died, but most of the injuries were caused by them trampling each other."

"So, the boat didn't sink," Jack said.

"Oh," Liddell said. "ATF Chief Misino sends his regards. He said, and I quote, 'Tell Murphy to quit goofing off and get back to work.' "

Jack laughed, but it hurt. In fact, everything hurt.

"I haven't told you the best part," Liddell said and finished the story.

Crenshaw was correct about one thing at least: Jack was a hero. Not to his own supervisors, of course, and definitely not to Double Dick, who had launched a campaign to have him fired. But as far as the news media and the Blue Star Casino were concerned, he could do no wrong. To the Casino, he and Pons and Killian were national treasures. The casino was paying for their medical expenses, and every inch of space in their rooms was filled with flowers proclaiming each of them to be a "Winner." What else could you expect a casino to say?

Barbara came in and kissed her husband until Jack said, "Enough. Get a room or pull the curtain."

Doctor Goldman came in and was impressed with Jack's improvement. Instead of the white lab coat he wore a brown tweed jacket, light blue button-down shirt, and tan slacks. Golf was definitely on his rounds this morning. Goldman said, "You should stay out of gunfights for at least another week."

Jack asked, "How about something for the pain, doc? Maybe an IV with Scotch?"

"You're already on enough pain medication, detective. Junkies are coming in off the streets and lining up outside your room," the doctor said.

"Good one, Doc," Liddell said with a grin.

The doctor assured Jack that if he survived the hospital food, he could leave in a few days.

Jack asked Liddell the question that had been on his mind since he woke up. "Did Katie get in trouble with the Feds? What happened to Susan and her minion, Miz Johnson-Heddings?"

"Susan is back in Indianapolis and up for a promotion. Her secretary retired, but she sent you her love," Liddell said.

"Right." Jack was glad this was so funny to someone.

"Katie has spent almost every day beside your bed," Liddell said.

"Oh yeah?"

Killian said, "She left about an hour ago with your captain. I had the impression they were, you know . . ." Barbara gave him a harsh look, so he added, "But I'm sure I'm wrong about that. Barbara always tells me when I'm right. It saves time."

At first Jack was a little upset, but then, what had he expected her to do? Say, "Thanks, Jack, for turning my life upside down, and taking up with Susan again, and then running off to get yourself killed. You really know how to show a girl a good time." It was probably for the best. He had a way of attracting trouble and ruining relationships.

He was still brooding when Liddell said, "Hey, pod'na. Look who's here?"

"Hi," Katie said. "I had to go to school for a minute. When I left, you were still asleep."

"Yeah, they told me." *You stayed by my side the whole time.*

Liddell got up and moved Katie into the chair beside Jack. She brushed the hair back from her face and said, "Captain Franklin is coming back to see you later. We just got a call that you were awake."

Jack scowled. Maybe Killian hadn't been wrong. Maybe the captain had worn her down. The bastard had always had a thing for her.

"We?" Jack asked. "Did you know Franklin's a child molester? And a philandering child molester at that?"

"You should be nice to him, Jack," she scolded.

He tried to smile. "You're right. He's a swell guy. You do know that he's the one that was going to arrest me?"

"My, aren't we in a bad mood," Katie said. She sat beside him on the bed and held his hand. Her touch was soft and warm, and her comfort was everything he wanted or needed.

"Yeah, relax, Jack," Jack mimicked her. "Have a rest. Later we can take the captain out for a thank-you dinner or go to a movie and all share popcorn."

"Is that jealousy I hear?" Katie said. He felt his face flush. He didn't know why he was acting like a schoolboy.

Katie leaned over and planted a kiss on his lips. Not on his cheek. Not a hug. A real kiss and a long one at that.

"When you get out of here, you can take me on a date if you want," she said.

"I missed you," Jack heard himself saying.

"We should pull the curtain and give them some privacy," Liddell said.

"Watch it, Bigfoot," Jack kidded him. "I can still take you, even with a broken body."

"Only if I were unconscious, pod'na," Liddell said.

Katie stood and Liddell said, "Hey, don't leave on my account. I'll be quiet as a mouse."

"Not me," Killian said. "I want to watch."

Barbara slapped her husband's shoulder, and said, "Men are all pigs."

Katie agreed, and said to Jack, "I'm not going anywhere." She pulled the curtain around the bed.

Epilogue

Jack sat in a rocker on his porch. The leg with the cast was propped on the railing, and he was watching the bikini-clad young maidens frolicking on the sandbar across the river. He could still see the blackened patch of sand where Crenshaw had built the bonfire using Quinn's body for fuel.

His mind wandered back to that night. Crenshaw had shot Quinn, saved Jack, burned Quinn's body to cinders, somehow arranged the disposal of White's and Thompson's bodies, and all while suffering from several gunshot wounds. The one to the neck alone should have killed her. He wondered if she was even human. She had left little to no evidence of CIA involvement. As far as the police department was concerned, this was a robbery attempt gone wrong. Shirl and Moon Pie and Ellert were dead, so there was no one to arrest. Even John Wayne Khaled and the van he rode in on were dead. The CIA and FBI, of course, denied having sent any agents to Evansville. Jack and Pons had tried to give them the facts but neither the EPD, ATF, nor the FBI or any other agency with initials seemed anxious to go any further with an investigation.

The FBI had cleared Jack and Liddell of any wrongdoing in the bank robbery where the fourteen-year-old girl had been shot, not to mention the deaths of most of her family of robbers. Nate Cartwright, the serial rapist, was believed to have absconded after being bonded out by a mystery woman. Jack believed that was Crenshaw making good on her promise to "fix" things with Jack's boss. The news stories were now condemning Shirl and Moon Pie as crooked cops and praising Jack and Pons as heroes, so it all balanced out. It wasn't the complete truth, but Jack was satisfied that justice had been served. He only wished he had been the one who shot Quinn and not Crenshaw.

He rescued a couple of Guinness from the ice bucket beside him. Popping the tabs on both, he handed one to Katie. She was wearing one of his long-sleeve shirts and nothing else. The cast on his leg came up about mid-thigh and wasn't the only thing that was stiff.

"How's the cast?" Katie asked.

Jack reached a hand out, and she put the yardstick in it. The numbers were worn off from shoving it inside the cast to scratch.

"I can do that for you if you're having trouble reaching it," she said.

He stopped scratching and looked at her. She had changed a little. She was more . . . frisky. "I think you reached everything just fine last night."

"And this morning," she said.

She smiled, and he smiled back. They had spent every night together since he had returned to his cabin a week ago. Her idea of physical therapy was both appealing and exhausting. If they kept this up, he'd be back in the hospital. He could imagine the nurse asking the ER doctor, "What do you think is wrong with him, doctor?" and the doctor would say, "He has a rare condition known as coitus non-interruptus, nurse. In layman's terms, he shouldn't have freed Willy."

He gazed again at the sandbar across the way. A cooler sat smack in the middle of the scorched sand with a beach towel spread over one edge. A young couple was building a bonfire of a kind that didn't require gasoline. Everything seemed normal, sane. It was hard to imagine everything that had begun and ended on this little stretch of the Ohio.

An amateur video shot by a civilian with a cell phone showed the bonfire where a man's body burned brightly. The zoom lens made it of poor quality but the television stations had replayed it over and over, every night for a week. There were interviews with the families of people who had died on the riverboat. More interviews with friends of the family members. And interviews with people who knew the victims in high school or college. Of course, everyone interviewed professed shock and cried. You had to hand it to the news media. They were relentless in pursuit of the truth. Well, they were relentless anyway.

Jack thought it particularly tasteful the way the news anchor apologized each time the station showed the makeshift funeral pyre while zooming in on Quinn's charred body as it was removed by the fire department.

As for Susan . . . she was back in Indianapolis, still dating the man of the perfectly white teeth and no danger in his life except for the occasional lawsuit. Jack consoled himself that at least Susan wasn't dating a lawyer. He was finally over her.

"A penny for your thoughts," Katie said. She eased herself onto the arm of the rocker and was tracing her fingers lightly across his face, her breath moist in his ear.

"Oh," he said, swallowing hard. "I think I need something scratched."

"Do you want me to help you up?" she asked with a giggle and toyed with the buttons on her shirt.

"You already did," he said, and let her help him into the cabin.

ACKNOWLEDGMENTS

This book owes its existence to the talented staff at Kensington Publishing Company. My editor, Michaela Hamilton, has suffered through my numerous mistakes and offered "encouragement," "praise," or "kicks in the pants" as needed. Thank you, Michaela.

A special thank-you to my good friend, Indiana State Police Officer Stu Sanders. Stu was gracious enough to show me around a riverboat casino and introduced me to the ship's captain and crew. Don't worry, the captain didn't let me drive. As you may notice, Stu is also a character in this story and any resemblance is intentional. Any other characters come strictly from my imagination.

A special acknowledgment to one of my readers, Kathy Vonderahe, who named CIA Agent Lucy Crenshaw. Thanks, Kathy. Sorry this book took longer than expected. I hope you approve of the use I made of the name you suggested.

I deliberately changed the layout and other details of the riverboat casino for obvious reasons. I researched the history of many of Indiana's floating casinos in the years prior to their being allowed to permanently dock.

Thank you to my fans, author friends, and family. Detective Jack Murphy is a thriller series thanks to you all, and there is more to come.

Don't miss the next hard-hitting thriller featuring Jack Murphy
and Liddell Blanchard

THE DARKEST NIGHT
by Rick Reed

Coming soon from Lyrical Underground, an imprint of
Kensington Publishing Corp.

Keep reading to enjoy an exciting excerpt . . .

She had been so focused on watching the first man across the street that she hadn't heard the other two come up behind her until too late. Strong arms had wrapped around her from behind while a cloth sack was pulled over her head. She was repeatedly punched in the face and torso with fists that felt like mallets as blows rained down on her. She had tried at first to resist, break free, but something hard struck her in the head.

The next thing she remembered was coming to with a screaming pain in her head, and her jaw felt broken. She had been bound, hand and foot, and had been squeezed into a small space. She could feel it moving, jarring now and then, the smell of gasoline and something rotted . . . she knew she was in the trunk of a car.

She'd heard the sound of gravel crunching and distant music, an occasional word spoken as if from far away and a man's voice mimicking the words. Then the motion stopped and she could hear a different man's voice say, "Shut up and shut that off!" The music stopped. The distant voice stopped with the music, and she recognized the music now. It was rap. One of them was "rapping." For some reason the idiocy of that made her mad, and her own stupidity for being mad at something so insignificant made her even angrier. "Wannabe rappers" had caught her, and that fact really pissed her off.

The man that had been rapping was now arguing in a heavily accented voice. Jamaican maybe. He sounded nervous. The other man's voice was deep, also with some type of Island accent, and carried well, telling the Jamaican to shut up or he'd tear his head off and shit in his skull. The Jamaican-sounding one shut up.

They were moving again, and she could hear the sound of gravel crunching. She tried to lift her head. Pain shot down her back and neck, so she lay still until the world stopped spinning.

They drove for what seemed like a half hour or less before the car slowed and turned to the left. She heard the deep voice saying something about "the farm." Then she heard the word "Papa" and a chill ran through her. *Papa*. He was the man she had been watching. She had been careful, but not careful enough. She had no way of knowing this would happen. The guy that had given her the information was wrong more than he was right.

The vehicle stopped. The deep-voice guy said something, and then they started rolling again. They didn't go very far before the car halted, and she heard the car doors opening, shutting, and then the trunk opened. Bright light speared her eyes.

She was yanked out of the trunk and sent sprawling on the gravel. A grip like a vise grabbed her wrist and pulled her to her feet, shoving, dragging, and then carrying. She was dizzy and thought she would pass out and then must have. She didn't remember much more until she felt moist breath in her ear and the smell was like rotted meat. Gorge rose in her throat.

She was sitting in a chair. Tied to the chair. Unable to move her arms. The burlap bag was pulled off her head, and she saw a small, skinny young man, with skin so dark it was almost black. He used one hand to untie the ropes. The other hand was on the butt of a black semiautomatic handgun shoved down the front of his pants.

The rope fell free and he pulled the gun, waggling the barrel at her, motioning her to go to a table that sat on one side of the tiny concrete room. When she didn't, couldn't, get up, he held the gun sideways like a gangster and said, "We gon' have some fun." He shook the weapon at her again and grinned, showing a set of ivory teeth.

She recognized the voice. It was the Jamaican guy who helped kidnap her. He was the idiot of the two. She'd gotten lucky.

He must have unbuttoned her blouse while she was out. Her bra was pulled down under her breasts. He must have been pinching her nipples because they were on fire with pain. He took her arm, lifting her out of the chair, and she saw one small chance. She kicked him in the groin. As he went down, she grabbed the gun and shot him in the face. He was still moving, twitching. She shot him in the head and put her back against the wall next to the door. There may be more of them besides the other deep-voiced man.

She saw the door handle twist and the door began opening. Even though there had been two gunshots this one didn't rush in. He wasn't stupid like the Jamaican. Suddenly the door slammed open, smashing her between it and the wall behind her. She had been holding the gun low in a two-handed grip and by reflex she fired down. She heard a scream and the door swung free. She peered around it. A tall, heavily muscled black man was lying on his side in the doorway, with both hands between his legs. Blood gushed down his leg to the floor. Her shot must have ricocheted off the floor, striking him in the crotch.

His dark features were drawn into a mask of pain, but his eyes opened and he glared at her.

"Where am I?" she asked, and leveled the gun at his face.

His lips moved, trying to form words, and she leaned over to hear.

"You gon' die bitch. Papa's gon' . . ." his face scrunched up in pain, and he couldn't finish.

Papa again. "Last chance. Where am I?"

She watched him try to work up some spit. She kicked him in the crotch and heard a sharp intake of breath.

"Papa gon' hurt you. You gon' to the other side."

She recognized the voice. It was the deep-voiced one. She'd shot both of her kidnappers. But who was Papa? Did he have others out there?

"I should let you suffer, but I'm not like you." She fired and the bullet entered under his nose and painted the floor red. She checked him for a weapon and found none. They must have thought she was a helpless woman. Now they knew.

She stepped over the body and moved down the hall to where it intersected with another hallway. The smell hit her first. It smelled like dried urine and something else. Then a soft sobbing sound seemed to come from everywhere. There was someone else, maybe more than one, in here. Maybe they'd been kidnapped too.

"Hello. Where are you?" she said as loud as she dared. No answer except the soft sobbing.

She held the gun two-handed, barrel pointing up, elbows bent into her chest. She bladed herself to see down both hallways. Each had closed doors on both sides. At the end of the one on her right a set of stairs led upward.

"I'll come back for you," she said and raced for the stairs. If she could get out, maybe, just maybe, she could come back with the cavalry.

Photo by George Routt

ABOUT THE AUTHOR

SERGEANT RICK REED (ret.), author of the Jack Murphy thriller series, is a twenty-plus-year veteran police detective. During his career, he successfully investigated numerous high-profile criminal cases, including a serial killer who claimed thirteen victims before strangling and dismembering his fourteenth and last victim. He recounted that story in his acclaimed true-crime book, *Blood Trail*.

Rick spent his last three years on the force as the commander of the police department's Internal Affairs Section. He has two master's degrees. He currently teaches criminal justice at Volunteer State Community College in Tennessee and writes thrillers. He lives near Nashville with his wife and two furry friends, Lexie and Belle.

Please visit him on Facebook, Goodreads, or at his website, www.rickreedbooks.com. If you'd like him to speak online for your event, contact him by going to bookclubreading.com.

A SADISTIC
SEX SLAYER'S
GRISLY DESIRES...

INCLUDES KILLER'S
CONFESSION

Blood Trail

Steven Walker
and
Rick Reed

THE CRUELEST CUT

"As authentic and scary as thrillers get."
– Nelson DeMille

A JACK MURPHY THRILLER

RICK REED

THE
COLDEST
FEAR

"Reed writes as only a cop can ...
impressive and dramatic."
— Nelson DeMille

A JACK MURPHY THRILLER

RICK REED

THE DEEPEST WOUND

"As authentic and scary
as thrillers get."
– Nelson DeMille

A JACK MURPHY THRILLER

RICK REED